Praise for Robert Thorogood

"Very funny and dark with great pace. I love Robert Thorogood's writing."
—Peter James, *New York Times* bestselling author

"This is a gem."
—*Daily Express*

"Deftly entertaining…satisfyingly pushes all the requisite Agatha Christie–style buttons."
—*Independent*

"For fans of Agatha Christie."
—*Mail on Sunday*

"A treat."
—*Radio Times*

"This brilliantly crafted, hugely enjoyable and suitably goose-bump-inducing novel is an utter delight from start to finish."
—*Heat*

T0033391

Also by Robert Thorogood

The Marlow Murder Club
A Meditation on Murder
The Killing of Polly Carter
Death Knocks Twice
Murder in the Caribbean

DEATH
COMES TO
MARLOW

A Novel

ROBERT THOROGOOD

Poisoned Pen
PRESS

Published by Poisoned Pen Press, an imprint of Sourcebooks
P.O. Box 4410, Naperville, Illinois 60567-4410
(630) 961-3900
sourcebooks.com

Originally published as *Death Comes to Marlow* in 2023 in Great Britain by HQ, an imprint of HarperCollinsPublishers Ltd. This edition issued based on the hardcover edition published 2023 in Great Britain by HQ, an imprint of HarperCollinsPublishers Ltd.

Cataloging-in-Publication Data is on file with the Library of Congress.

Printed and bound in Canada.
MBP 10 9 8 7 6 5 4 3 2 1

Chapter 1

AFTER THE EXCITEMENT OF THE previous summer, Mrs. Judith Potts spent the winter returning to the more solitary rhythms of life. She woke late, watched a bit of telly, played clock patience, went for walks when the mood took her—which wasn't in truth all that often—and made sure she set aside time each day to compile her cryptic crosswords for the newspapers.

When the Christmas lights went up in the High Street, she found herself, as she did every year, quietly absenting herself from the festivities. It wasn't that she was opposed to Christmas. Far from it. It was more that she felt it belonged to other people; mostly parents with young children and families hell-bent on enforced jollity.

But if Christmas was a bit of a chore, and the time between Christmas and New Year's Day a baffling week of nonexistence, Judith knew January belonged to her. It was almost her favorite month of the year. No one asked her to do anything in January. Or go anywhere. She could fully recharge her batteries and take stock.

And go wild swimming, of course.

Judith didn't let the fact that it was winter deter her from her near-daily dips in the river Thames. On the coldest days, her swims were of necessity brief, but she never missed the chance to commune with nature, and she loved the zingy feeling her skin had for the rest of the day. She especially loved to swim when she had a problem to work through, which was why she was in the Thames on this particular January morning.

She was trying to solve a mystery.

It had started that morning when she'd picked up that week's copy of the *Marlow Free Press*. Seeing as it was the beginning of the year, the paper was even more bereft of news than usual—the lead story concerned the shock closure of a local postbox—but it was the cryptic crossword that Judith looked forward to the most. It never took her too long to solve, but there was a clarity and simplicity to the clueing she found hugely satisfying. That morning's effort had been no different. However, once she'd finished and looked at the completed grid, she'd had an instinct that something was "off" about her answers. There was something her subconscious was trying to tell her, but she couldn't quite work out what it was. Judith hated loose ends. All puzzles had to be solved, as far as she was concerned, which was why she'd decided to have a good think about it on her morning swim.

And it was because she was thinking about the crossword rather than her surroundings that she mistakenly got into a fight with a swan.

She hadn't meant to, as she'd recount to her two friends Becks and Suzie later that day. It wasn't even her fault as far as she could tell. It was all the fault of a dead duck she'd found floating upside down in the middle of the river, although it hadn't initially looked like a duck at all. She'd thought she was swimming toward a couple of orange-colored twigs that were sticking out of the water. But as Judith got closer, she'd finally seen the white body, neck, and head of the duck submerged underwater, and she'd splashed in a panic over to the side of the river to get away.

In doing so, she inadvertently swam in between a mother swan and her cygnets. As it was January, the cygnets were almost fully grown, but their mother still reared and hissed, her wingspan now wider than Judith was tall. Judith briefly wondered if she could get in between the span of the wings and grab the swan by the neck to take her down. But, like nearly everyone raised in the UK, she knew that a swan "can break your arm," and she also guessed there'd be something unedifying about a completely naked seventy-eight-year-old woman wrestling with a swan.

Because that was the other problem. As was always the case when she went for a swim from the boathouse at the bottom of her garden, Judith wasn't wearing a swimming costume. Of course, she wasn't. They were damp, dank things that clung to your body and ruined the true feeling of freedom swimming gave you.

The swan's head shot forward with a terrifying hiss, and Judith realized she'd have to get out of the water, and fast. At least she knew she was at a bend in the river where few people ever stopped.

Unfortunately, it was precisely because it was such a remote location that it held such happy memories for Ian Barnes. Ian had grown up in Marlow, had moved away some years ago, but had wanted to bring his wife, Mandie, and their two young children back to show them some of the favorite haunts from his childhood. This included the delightful spot on the river where he'd spent so many happy days bird-watching.

It was just as Ian was pointing out the exact tree stump where he'd once seen not one but two kingfishers that a naked seventy-eight-year-old woman climbed out of the river right in front of him and his family, ran a few paces along the bank—her entire body oscillating wondrously—before she threw off a flamboyant salute as she jumped back into the river, her legs tucked up under her so could bomb back into the water with a massive splash.

As she resurfaced, Judith let out a joyous "Ha!" She had of course been mortified to find herself naked so near other people, but she'd decided to style it out by waving at the family and jumping back into the river, so they'd *really* have something to talk about. It was her gift to them.

Judith couldn't stop grinning as she allowed the current to carry her downstream, all thoughts of the *Marlow Free Press* crossword long forgotten. She kept replaying the look on the poor family's face. Their mild-mannered horror would keep her tickled for months.

However, it was because of the incident with the dead duck and the very-much-alive swan that Judith climbed out of the water in the boathouse at the bottom of her garden far sooner than normal. This meant that once she put on her gray woolen cape and swished back to her Arts and Crafts mansion, she arrived just in time to hear the house phone ringing. She grabbed the handset up and a gruff male voice asked her if she was Mrs. Judith Potts.

"Speaking," she said.

"My name's Sir Peter Bailey," the man said in the sort of voice that told men to go over the top in battle. "We've not met before, but I'd like to ask a favor. You see, I'm getting married tomorrow."

"Congratulations," Judith said, noticing that the fire in the grate was still glowing. Her skin was puckered with goose bumps, her feet were cold on the parquet, so she went and sat down in her favorite wingback and let the embers warm her.

"The thing is, I'm having a drinks party this afternoon as a small celebration, and I'd like you to come."

Judith was puzzled. Sir Peter was the head of one of the most preeminent families in Marlow; why the sudden invitation?

"Nothing too formal," he continued. "Lounge suits, dresses, that sort of thing. It's just a few drinks if I'm honest. Two for two-thirty. And wrap up warm. The forecast is for clear skies, but it will still be cold. You know where I live?"

Judith knew where Sir Peter lived. Everyone in Marlow did. But she felt mildly irritated that he presumed she'd drop everything at a moment's notice. She already had plans for that afternoon. She was going to have toasted crumpets in front of the fire with some blackberry jam she'd bought from the Saturday food market. And perhaps a tot or two of homemade sloe gin she kept under the sink in the kitchen for special occasions. In fact, why on earth would she want to give all that up to go to a party?

"That's very kind of you, but why are you inviting me?"

"It's quite simple. I thought the day before my wedding would be a chance to thank some of the key people in Marlow. You know, the Rotary, the parish council, that sort of thing. And I was impressed with how you helped the town last summer."

"Oh, I see. You know about that?"

"Everyone knows how you helped the police solve those horrific murders."

"I hope you don't expect anyone to be murdered," Judith said with a chortle.

"What?" Sir Peter asked. "Of course not. Why would you say that?"

Judith was intrigued. She could tell that her comment had rattled Sir Peter for some reason.

"It was just a joke," she said.

"Well, it was in very bad taste."

"It's only bad taste if someone's killed."

"No one's frightened for their life here. I really don't understand why you'd suggest they were. Do you want to come to the party or not?"

No one's frightened for their life? Judith thought to herself. What an odd thing to say. Why was Sir Peter suddenly so flustered? Judith decided that her crumpets and sloe gin would have to wait for another day.

"I'd be delighted to come to the party," she said.

"Good," Sir Peter said gruffly. "See you this afternoon."

Once she'd finished the call, Judith dialed the number for Becks Starling.

"Judith, hold on," Becks said as she answered. "Colin, stir the roux, would you? How are you?" she said back into the phone. "Sorry, can't chat long, we're out this afternoon." Before Judith could explain why she'd rung, Becks was overtaken by events. "Sam, why do you want a box of matches—there's no reason to want matches, what are you doing? Oh, god," she said back into the phone. "I'm sorry, it's Chloe on call waiting. She spent the night at her boyfriend's house. I need to take this. Anything could have happened."

Becks hung up and Judith realized she'd not spoken, not even once. Judith smiled to herself. Becks was married to the vicar of Marlow, a very nice man called Colin—with all the positive and negative connotations of that word, "nice." Despite having made it her life's work to be the perfect Home Counties housewife and mother, Becks had allowed herself to be pulled into Judith's orbit the year before when there had been a series of murders in Marlow. Since then, they'd become firm friends, even if Becks still worried that Judith was exactly the sort of free spirit her mother had always warned her about. As for Judith, she could see how much energy Becks put into servicing the needs of her family and community, and she just wished her friend spent a tenth of her talents on meeting her own needs. But Becks would never change, Judith knew. It was partly why she enjoyed her company so much.

Judith dialed another number. After a couple of rings, Suzie Harris came on the line.

"Well if it isn't the famous Judith Potts," Suzie said in what Judith felt was a slightly stagey voice.

Suzie was a solidly comfortable fifty-year-old woman and the third member of Judith's gang.

"Apologies for ringing out of the blue," Judith said, "but I think I've just had a very strange conversation."

"Then tell us all about it."

"'What do you mean 'tell us'?"

"You're 'on air,' caller. So you'd better keep it clean," Suzie added with a knowing chuckle.

Judith's blood ran cold.

Following her brush with fame the year before, Suzie had managed to bag herself a midmorning slot presenting on the community radio station, Marlow FM. Suzie would play records, take phone calls to discuss the burning issues of the day, and use every opportunity to promote her dog-walking and dog-sitting business in a way that broke pretty much all broadcasting rules. But then, as Suzie put it, she was a single mother—even though her daughters had long flown the nest—and she'd always hustled to make ends meet. She wasn't going to pass up the chance for free advertising.

"You're broadcasting this?" Judith asked.

"Always happy to take a call from you, Judith." There was a slightly possessive tone to Suzie's words that made Judith pause. Suzie was far too taken with her recently minted celebrity status as far as she was concerned, but that was a matter for another time.

"Really, Suzie, I shouldn't have my calls to you broadcasted to the whole town, but what time does your show finish?"

"I'm handing over to Karen Hird and her Lunchtime Boys at one."

"Good. When you finish, do you want to go to a party?"

Chapter 2

TO THE EAST OF MARLOW, the river Thames bulges around a small island that has a lock on one side and a frothing weir on the other. In the calm water beyond the weir lie some of the town's smartest properties.

Sir Peter Bailey's house, White Lodge, was perhaps the grandest of the lot. It was a three-story Georgian mansion in cream stucco, a grass tennis court on one side, a white-painted glass orangery on the other, and an Elizabethan knot garden of box hedges in between the two. On the riverside, the mown stripes of lawn looked even sharper, even more precise, than anything the neighbors were able to muster. As for Sir Peter's boat moored at the bottom of the garden, it was a sleek motor launch finished in polished wood that he'd imported from Venice.

Everything about the property oozed money, and Suzie didn't quite know where to park her clapped-out dog-walking van when she and Judith arrived. Luckily for them, a fresh-faced teenager in a high-viz jacket indicated that they should park in the field next door to the garden.

"Bloody hell," Suzie said as they climbed out of her van. "Imagine having car parking attendants for your party."

It was one of those January days that was fresh and sunny, with cotton wool clouds in a bright-blue sky, and as Judith and Suzie entered the garden, they could see a hundred or so smartly dressed people chatting and laughing by a gleaming marquee.

"I reckon I could get my house in that marquee two times over," Suzie said. "Are you sure they won't mind you bringing me?"

"Of course not."

"I'm not exactly dressed for a party."

Suzie was an oak of a woman, with ruddy cheeks and a booming voice. She was wearing a bright-red puffa jacket over a faded aquamarine Airtex T-shirt, old jeans with dried mud around the ankles, and an old pair of walking boots.

"I think you look just perfect," Judith said.

"Okay, then I'll just blame you if anyone complains. Now, where are the canapés?"

As Suzie asked the question, a young waiter came over with a tray of champagne. She and Judith each took a glass, although Suzie also took a second glass.

"For my friend," she said to the waiter, indicating an imaginary friend some way away.

"Well, isn't this lovely," Judith said, taking a sip of her champagne and taking in the view.

"Sure is," Suzie said, downing the first of her two glasses. "Bloody hell, the bubbles get up your nose. I don't know why people drink this stuff. So where's this Sir Peter who invited you?"

"I can't see him. But you'll know it when you do. He looks like a major general, all mustache and barking voice."

"Judith?" a delighted voice said, before adding "Suzie?" a touch more carefully.

Becks Starling swished over, and Judith thought she wouldn't see a lovelier sight all day. Becks always looked glossy—with perfect blond hair and manicured nails—but today Judith's friend positively glowed with good health. She was wearing an elegant cream-colored halter-necked dress with a dark-blue cashmere shrug over her shoulders. And Judith's eye was immediately drawn to what looked like a brand-new sapphire ring on her hand. If it was real, it was expensive.

"You look beautiful," Judith said.

"You think so?" Becks said, blushing. "Really?"

"You always look beautiful, but you look particularly pretty today."

Becks was embarrassed in an instant and did what she always did after receiving a compliment—she apologized.

"I'm sorry about our phone call earlier on," she said. "I was so distracted with the kids running around and Colin getting in the way. And I had to get ready for the party. Why were you ringing?"

"Just to invite you to this," Judith said. "So no damage done. You're already here."

"I'm Colin's plus-one. He's marrying the bride and groom tomorrow. He's over there," Becks said, pointing at her husband over by the marquee. As was usual, Colin was wearing a dark suit with a white dog collar, but as was not usual, he was chatting to a woman who was wearing a figure-hugging dress entirely made of gold sequins. Every curve of her body shimmered in the bright sunlight.

They all heard Colin laugh, and even at distance, the three friends could detect a desperate, almost fawning, quality to it.

Becks's brow furrowed.

"Aye, aye," Suzie said. "Prawn tempura at three o'clock."

Suzie had explained to Judith on the way to the party that eating sufficient numbers of canapés at a party was at least a two-person job. You had to have one person facing the party—which she'd deemed Judith's job—while the second member of the team stood almost back-to-back to the first, making sure they clocked every waiter as they arrived from the kitchens. For Sir Peter's party, the caterers had a smaller tent that contained the kitchen and plating-up area, so Suzie had kept herself facing in that direction since arriving.

As a waiter passed on the way to the main marquee, Suzie plucked two large tempura prawns from his platter.

"Ta!" she called after the waiter as he carried on his way.

"I didn't know you knew the Bailey family?" Becks said to her friends.

"I don't," Suzie said while juggling a hot battered prawn in her mouth.

"Nor do I," Judith said before explaining how she was only attending because she'd had such an odd conversation with Sir Peter that morning.

"You can't possibly think someone's going to be murdered?" Becks asked, appalled.

"Of course not. But my mention of murders definitely spooked him. Something's up, you mark my words. By the way, have you seen Sir Peter anywhere?"

"You know it's funny," Becks said. "Now you mention it, I haven't seen him since I got here."

"What if someone's killed him?" Suzie said with an excited spatter of batter, having only seconds before chosen to commit to her second prawn. "Sorry!" she added, which was a mistake, as it meant she spattered even more prawn, this time over Becks's cream dress.

"Suzie!" Becks said, stepping back in horror.

"Sorry!" Suzie said as she used her hand to wipe down Becks's dress, in the process leaving a much larger oily smear on the fabric.

"Oh, god, I've made it worse!" she said.

"Please stop!" Becks said, looking at her friend in frustration. "This dress was expensive."

"I'm so sorry, the prawn tempura's a bit greasy. You'll have to get that seen to," Suzie said, indicating the smear on the dress as though she were offering sage advice.

They all heard the roar of an engine as a battered Triumph sports car with a black fabric roof turned onto the driveway, fumes belching from the exhaust. It parked up by the house, and a man who was wearing tan chinos and a purple floral shirt under a tweed jacket got out of the driver's side and ran his hands through his long dark hair.

Even from a distance, it was possible to see that the man was very handsome.

"Hello, hello," Suzie said. "I like the look of our new guest. Who do you think he is?"

Chapter 3

AS SOON AS THE CAR parked up, a man in his sixties with a bushy gray mustache and slicked-down hair emerged from the house wearing a navy blazer and salmon-pink trousers. He had a glass of champagne in one hand and a cigarette in the other as he marched over to the younger man.

"There he is," Becks said, indicating the man in the blazer. "That's Sir Peter."

They all heard Sir Peter call out, "What the hell are you doing here?"

The younger man laughed as though it was all of no concern and said that it was his home, he could come and go as he damn well pleased.

"Now this is more like a proper wedding," Suzie said, appreciably. "A punch-up."

Over by the main group of guests, a woman peeled off and strode over to join the two men. She was wearing a black coat over a simple black dress, had choppy brown hair and rosy cheeks, and was clearly agitated.

"That's Jenny Page," Becks whispered to her friends. "The bride-to-be. I've only met her a few times, but she's very nice. Very straightforward…"

Becks trailed off as Jenny started remonstrating with the young man, Sir Peter now trying to calm her down, the whole party watching on, agog. Judith guessed that she was perhaps seeing why Sir Peter had been so peculiar during their phone call. There was serious discord within the Bailey family.

"It's my big day tomorrow, how could you do this to me?" they all heard Jenny say to the younger man.

"I'm not doing anything to anyone," he replied, still apparently unfussed.

"Don't you speak to my wife like that!" Sir Peter barked.

"You're not married yet, Dad."

"You have to make everything about you, don't you?" Jenny sobbed. "You can't bear to see anyone else happy."

Jenny burst into tears and dashed inside.

Sir Peter closed the distance between himself and the younger man and started jabbing him in the chest as he continued to castigate him. And then, with a final stab at the young man's chest, he turned on his heels and strode into the house.

Once Sir Peter had left the field of battle, the guests at the party did the only thing trueborn Englishmen and Englishwomen could do. They went back to their small talk as though there hadn't been any kind of disturbance at all. The nearby waiters all raised their trays and began circulating again.

"Are we all just going to pretend that didn't happen?" Suzie asked.

Colin Starling came over and joined the women.

"Hello, everyone," he said. "I take it that's the son, Tristram."

"Sir Peter has a son?" Judith asked.

"And a daughter, Rosanna. She'll be here somewhere. They're from Sir Peter's first marriage. I've had quite a few meetings with Sir Peter and Jenny over the last few weeks, and I believe Tristram doesn't approve of his father remarrying. I don't know why I'm telling you that, it's quite clear father and son don't get on."

"Although I couldn't help noticing you were getting on very well with that lady over there, darling," Becks said with a smile that only Colin didn't realize was deadly.

"Yes, that's Miss Louise. She runs a local dance school."

"*Miss* Louise?"

Once again, Colin didn't realize the danger he was in.

"That's how she introduced herself."

Before Becks could ask any more questions, the young man sauntered over to the group. Up close, he really was very good looking, Judith thought to herself. He was in his late thirties and had a strong jaw and sparkling blue eyes.

"Sorry about the fracas," he said with a rueful grin. "Is there any champagne?" he added with a twinkle to Becks, and Judith felt there was a flirty promise of mischief in the question.

"I'm not sure Sir Peter would be too happy with that," Judith said in her most matronly manner.

"Then how about we just add it to the long list of things he's not happy with?" the man said. "Tristram Bailey. I should have said. And I think I'll go and find that drink. See you at the wedding tomorrow."

Judith and her friends looked at each other, surprised by Tristram's sangfroid after such a public bust-up.

"Well, he seems very sure of himself," Judith said.

In the distance, the bells of All Saints Church rang out across the town to mark 3 p.m. Judith turned and looked in the direction of the church across the river and saw a large motorboat drive past the bottom of the garden. She was just thinking *what a horrible monstrosity* when they all heard an almighty crash from inside the house and the sound of glass smashing.

The whole party stopped to look in the direction of the house, and Jenny appeared at an upstairs balcony, also drawn by the noise.

"What was that?" she asked.

Tristram turned on his heels and headed straight for the house. After a few moments of indecision, Judith took off after him—followed by Suzie, Becks, Colin, and half a dozen other guests.

"Do you know what that was?" Judith called ahead to Tristram.

Tristram didn't reply as he went through a door into the house.

"Sounded…monumental," Judith said to her friends as they entered through the same door and found themselves in a stone-flagged boot room. Tristram had already entered the main hallway, so she carried through to join him, followed by her friends and the other guests.

As they arrived in the hallway, Jenny ran down from upstairs.

"What's going on?" she asked.

"We need to find Father," Tristram said as he started opening doors that led from the main hallway—to the sitting room, a second drawing room, a kitchen—and the other guests also started to spread through the house.

"Isn't he with you?" Jenny asked Tristram.

"I thought he was with you."

"Did you hear where that noise came from?" Judith asked Jenny, wanting to help narrow down the search.

"It came from downstairs somewhere," Jenny said.

"Dad?" Tristram called out, but there was no answer. "Where are you? Dad? Oh god," he said darkly, an idea occurring to him as he walked out of the hallway.

Everyone followed Tristram down a corridor that ended in an ancient wooden door with rusting hinges. He grabbed up the hoop of iron that passed for its handle and turned it, but the door didn't open.

"Dad?" he called through the door. "Are you there?"

There was no reply.

"What's in there?" Judith asked.

"Dad's study."

Tristram turned the handle again and pushed hard at the door with his shoulder.

It didn't budge.

"Someone's locked the door,"

"Is there a key?" Judith asked.

She could see Tristram was beginning to panic as he strode back along the corridor toward the kitchen. As he disappeared, a flustered-looking woman who Judith hadn't seen before ran up to them. She had straight dark hair and was wearing a bright-red military coat that had gold braid on the cuffs and collar.

"What's going on?" she asked.

The woman's manner was brusque, no-nonsense, and, like her coat, a touch military.

"We don't know," Jenny said. "But there was that loud crash and now we can't find Peter."

"Yes, I heard it," the woman said in agreement, which Judith found odd. Of course the woman had heard the noise. They'd all heard it.

"Sorry, who are you?" Judith asked.

"Rosanna," The woman said, surprised by the question. "Rosanna Bailey."

Tristram reappeared from the kitchen holding a fire extinguisher.

"Tristram?" Rosanna said. "What are you doing?"

"Step back," he said.

Everyone gave Tristram space as he stood in front of the door and thumped the heavy fire extinguisher into the wood just above the handle. The door barely moved. Tristram pulled the fire extinguisher back and really smashed it into the door, and this time there was the sound of wood cracking, although the door still didn't budge. He pulled the fire extinguisher back a third time, bashed it into the wood even harder, there was the sound of wood cracking, and the door swung open a few inches.

Tristram pushed into the room followed by the others, and they all saw that a large mahogany cabinet had fallen away from the wall and was lying flat on the floor.

A pair of legs encased in salmon-pink trousers was sticking out from under it.

"Oh, god, Peter!" Jenny called out as she ran to the cabinet. "We need to get this up!"

Everyone rushed to the cabinet, lining up around it, and, with a great heave, they were just able to lift it back up so it was standing vertically again. They could all see the body of Sir Peter lying among shards of glass and various pieces of laboratory equipment that had fallen off the shelves of the cabinet.

There was a slick of blood across his face, his right arm was twisted grotesquely under his body, and his left arm was thrown out to the side, a couple of his fingers bent at a horrifying angle.

He wasn't breathing.

Jenny dropped to her knees at Sir Peter's side and tried to find a pulse in his neck.

"Peter, no! Peter!" she cried.

"Careful of that glass," Colin offered somewhat redundantly, but Jenny wasn't listening as she kept desperately trying to find a pulse in her fiancé's neck and wrist.

"Jenny, you need to get up at once," Becks said, indicating that Colin should go to the woman.

"Everyone, clear the room," Judith called out. "And someone, ring the police!"

At the mention of the police, the group came back to life. Becks and Colin peeled a weeping Jenny away from the body, and the room slowly cleared. Judith stayed behind to have a quick poke around. It seemed like a typical man's study, but what she particularly noted was that there was nowhere a person could have been hiding. Sir Peter had been on his own in the room when the cabinet fell onto him.

She also found herself running her eye over the old metal lock on the door that had ripped through the doorframe. She closed the door to check that the lock did indeed match up with the damage to the frame. It fitted perfectly. The door had been fully locked when Tristram had broken through it—although Judith found herself surprised at how easily the door moved. The wood looked hundreds of years old, the hinges were thick with rust, and since when did an old door close so smoothly? She looked at the hinges and saw that they were glistening.

Someone had recently oiled the hinges.

Judith peered at one of the hinges more closely. There was an odd smell, she thought to herself. Something that wasn't quite right. What was it?

Suzie returned.

"Are you investigating?" she said in a stage whisper that could have started an avalanche in a neighboring valley.

"I don't know," Judith said.

"Becks and Colin have taken Jenny upstairs, and I've made everyone else go outside the front of the house to wait for the police. What's up with the door?"

"It's the hinges. I think they've been oiled. And there's an odd smell."

Susie put her nose to the nearest hinge and sniffed.

"You're right," she said. "I recognize that smell. What is it?"

"So it's not just me?" Judith asked.

"No, I don't think so," Suzie said as she ran her finger down the oily hinge and licked her finger.

"You're right," she said. "It's olive oil."

"That's it!" Judith agreed in realization. "That's exactly what I could smell. Olives. Who'd oil a door hinge with olive oil?"

Chapter 4

EVERYONE AT THE PARTY FROM the catering staff to the guests milled on the driveway at the front of the house, waiting for the police. The only people who weren't present were Jenny, Becks, and Colin. They remained inside White Lodge, upstairs.

"Maybe oiling door hinges with olive oil is what posh people do," Suzie said to Judith. "WD-40 isn't good enough for them."

Judith smiled, but she was looking at the crowd and trying to work out what she felt about Sir Peter's death. She could see Rosanna Bailey standing at the edge of the group, a few friends consoling her. Judith couldn't help observing how easy it was to pick her out of the crowd. Nearly everyone else at the party had chosen muted colors for their outfits, and her pillar-box-red coat stood out like a beacon. Noticing Rosanna made Judith think of Tristram, and she tried to find him in the crowd. She couldn't locate him.

"Can you see Tristram anywhere?" she asked Suzie.

"I can't," she said. "Wonder where he's got to. Did you see the way he looked at Becks?"

"I did."

"Because you're right, she looks great today, doesn't she? And our Mr. Tristram Bailey very definitely noticed her when he came over and talked to us."

"Maybe it was that new sapphire ring she has on her hand. I imagine it cost a pretty penny or two."

"What sapphire ring?"

"Didn't you notice it? You should have a look. It's rather splendid, baguette cut, and set in lovely old gold. I suppose Colin must have bought it for her."

"You reckon he bought her a really nice ring?"

The women shared a glance, both of them knowing how unlikely that sounded.

Two police cars and an ambulance turned into the driveway, lights flashing, and stopped in a crunch of gravel by the house. As they pulled up, Becks came out of the house and headed toward the vehicles.

Judith and Suzie saw a woman get out of the lead car, and they turned to each other and smiled.

"Well, that's a turn up for the books," Suzie said.

"How very gratifying," Judith said. "Shall we?"

"Yeah. I reckon so."

The two women walked toward the police car and caught up with Becks just as she reached Detective Sergeant Tanika Malik.

"We really must stop meeting like this," Judith said.

"What are the three of you doing here?" Tanika asked, surprised.

Tanika was in her early forties, had straight hair tied up in a tight ponytail, and was wearing a charcoal-gray suit. She'd been the acting senior investigating officer of the murders in Marlow the summer before and had only solved the case when she'd co-opted Judith and her friends into helping her.

"It's a complete coincidence," Becks explained, awkwardly. "But when I saw the police arrive, I thought I'd come out and tell you that the man who died, Sir Peter Bailey, was about to marry a woman called Jenny Page. Colin and I have taken her upstairs to her bedroom. She's in a bad way. If you need to speak to her, that's where she is. In fact, I should go back to her—if that's okay?"

"You're with Sir Peter's fiancée?" Tanika asked.

"I am."

"Thanks, that's very good of you. Can you tell her we'll come and talk to her once we've secured the scene? But only when she's ready."

"I will," Becks said, and returned to the house.

Tanika looked at Judith and Suzie and could see the devil in their eyes.

"Are you really saying your presence here is a coincidence?" she asked.

"Well, it's funny you should say that," Judith said. "It's not *entirely* a coincidence. But I'll fill you in once you've processed the body. In the meantime, I think it would be helpful if you treated the death as suspicious."

"What makes you say that?"

Before Judith could answer, an ashen-faced Tristram came over and joined the women.

"You'll want to talk to me," he said to Tanika. "I'm Tristram Bailey. Dad's son. I mean, Sir Peter's son. The man who..."

Tristram petered out, unable to finish the sentence. He looked utterly broken.

"Come on," Tanika said, her professional manner allowing her to be both consoling and practical at the same time. "It's cold out here. Let's get you inside, and you can fill me in on what happened."

Tanika put her hand on Tristram's elbow and steered him toward the house.

Suzie and Judith realized they were at a bit of a loose end, and Tanika had been right when she'd said it was cold. Since the sun had gone down, all the warmth of the day had been replaced by an icy chill.

"It's bloody freezing standing around," Suzie said.

"Then I suggest we go inside," Judith said, looking over at two police officers as they explained to the guests how they were going to be taking their statements.

"We can't interfere. Tanika would kill us."

"'Interfere'?" Judith said in mock outrage. "Interfering is for amateurs." Suzie laughed.

"We investigate."

"Okay," Suzie said. "Then what are we investigating?"

"Sir Peter's kitchen."

"Why? What are we looking for?"

"Isn't it obvious? A bottle of recently used olive oil."

Once inside the study, Tanika took a moment to look at the room where the body of Sir Peter Bailey lay. There was a mess of papers on an old desk and an ashtray and empty wineglass by a faded armchair that was set up by a stone fireplace that was full of ash. Behind the desk there was a couple of old, framed X-ray pictures of human rib cages. She wondered why.

There was a bright flash as one of her officers photographed Sir Peter's body, and Tanika went over to make a visual inspection. Crouching down, she saw that he was lying in a mess of old science equipment and smashed glass flasks, beakers, and jars. There was an old oscilloscope, bent metal stands and Bunsen burner, and valves that were attached to pieces of electrical circuitry. In among the mess there were little yellowed labels in faded ink with words like "Litmus Papers," "Barium Sulphate," and "Aluminum Hydroxide" written on them. There were also smears of various colored powders on the carpet where the contents of the various smashed glasses had tipped.

Tanika guessed that all of the science equipment was perhaps connected to the X-rays on the wall behind the desk.

As for the body, Tanika saw that Sir Peter's hands, neck, and head were cut where the glass lab equipment had crushed into his body when the cabinet fell onto him. There was also dried blood across his face and matted in his dark hair. There'd been significant blunt force trauma. It was no surprise, she thought to herself, as she looked at the wooden cabinet. It was half as tall as her again, at least twenty feet wide, and made from obsidian black mahogany wood. The ornamental carvings along the top of it—and the scrapes and marks on it from many decades of use—made it look like the sort of fixture you'd maybe find in a church or school. She wouldn't be surprised if it weighed a ton.

Considering its significant bulk, she found herself wondering how it had fallen over. The cabinet sat so very squarely on the floor, it was hard to imagine it toppling over under any circumstances. It was a shame the guests had felt the need to lift it back up, she thought. It was understandable of course, but it meant the scene had already been tampered with before she and her team had even arrived.

Tanika went over to look out of the large picture windows. There were thick curtains on either side that smelled of dust and smoke. Outside, below the window, she could see a bed of shrubs in the darkness. As for the windows themselves, they were metal framed, a bit rusty in places, and the locks and catches had been painted over many times. A quick inspection showed Tanika that none of them had been opened for years.

Tanika remembered what Judith had said to her. She knew that Judith could be infuriating sometimes, eccentric always, but she wasn't prone to flights of fancy when it came to the matter of murder. If she said Sir Peter's death was suspicious, then it was worth using that as a starting hypothesis.

She turned to the nearest officer.

"Can you see if you can find the key to the door? I see someone had to smash through it to get to the body."

"I think we've already got it," he said, and held up an evidence bag with an old iron key in it. "It was in the deceased's trouser pocket."

"It was the deceased who locked the door?"

"And by all accounts, he was on his own in here when the rest of the party broke through the door."

"Then can you speak to the family? See if there are any other keys to this room?"

"Sure thing."

Tanika looked from the dead body to the cabinet that had crushed him. What on earth had happened here?

Chapter 5

"OKAY," SUZIE SAID, RUBBING HER hands together as she and Judith entered the house's kitchen, "so we're looking for a bottle of olive oil?"

"Indeed. One that's been used recently," Judith said as she started to open the cupboards and poke around. "But don't touch it if you find it."

"Of course!" Suzie said appreciatively. "In case it has fingerprints on it."

Suzie went over to the windowsill where there was an old-fashioned Roberts Radio. Turning it on, she started to twist the dial to retune it.

"What are you doing?" Judith asked.

"Increasing Marlow FM's reach, one listener at a time."

The radio started playing a song by Bucks Fizz. Suzie announced, "Ah there we are," and then she turned the radio off. "That'll get the family listening the next time they turn this on."

"Do you always retune radios to Marlow FM?"

"Whenever I can."

"Oh," Becks said as she entered the room. "What are you two doing in here?"

"Looking for olive oil," Suzie said as though this explained everything.

"Okay," Becks said, baffled by her friends. "I'm just getting a glass of water for Jenny."

As Becks took a glass from a shelf and filled it with water, she saw that

Judith and Suzie were hunting in cupboards, but she refused to be drawn. It didn't matter what they were up to, she told herself, her duty was to Jenny. Jenny was the one who was grieving. Jenny was the one who needed support. And Becks carried on telling herself that she definitely wasn't going to ask her friends what they were doing as she headed out of the room with the glass of water.

"Okay, you've got to tell me," she said, stopping in the doorway. "Why are you looking for olive oil?"

Judith explained how the hinges on the study door had been lubricated with olive oil.

Becks got the significance immediately.

"That's weird, isn't it?" she said. "You should tell the police."

"I don't think they'd be interested. Not yet anyway. But I've got a theory."

"Bloody hell," Suzie said as she opened the door to a walk-in larder and saw floor-to-ceiling shelves stuffed full of tins of food, pasta, wine, and everything in between. "This is like that scene at the end of *Close Encounters of the Third Kind*," she announced before walking in, wide-eyed with wonder.

"How's Jenny?" Judith asked.

"Really shaky," Becks said. "Not making a whole lot of sense."

"I don't suppose that's surprising after what she's been through. What does she think happened?"

"Why are you asking?" Becks asked.

"I'm not sure her husband's death was entirely accidental."

"You think someone did this to him?"

"Did you see the size of that cabinet? There's no way that fell over on its own. And why didn't Sir Peter just step out of the way when it started to fall over?"

"I see what you mean. But what's this got to do with Jenny?"

"She was in the house at the time. Unlike pretty much everyone else."

"You think she pushed the cabinet onto him?"

"It's a possibility."

"But we all saw her come out onto the balcony upstairs at the same time as we heard the crash."

"I know that's how it looked. But how soon after the cabinet fell over did she appear?"

"Almost instantly."

"Maybe that was long enough."

"Hold on. You think she pushed the cabinet onto her husband-to-be in the study downstairs, ran up the stairs, and then appeared on the balcony a split second later?"

Judith frowned.

"No, it doesn't seem very likely, does it? Not when you put it like that."

"And why would Jenny have wanted to kill Sir Peter the day before she was due to marry him?"

"Now that's a very good question," Judith conceded.

"Oh, my god," Suzie said, as she returned from the walk-in larder. "It's like Narnia in there. But no olive oil, I'm afraid."

"I've not found any either. And that's pretty much all of the cupboards checked as far as I can see."

"But that's impossible," Becks said. "There's no way a family like this would have no olive oil."

"Well, you're wrong there," Suzie said. "We've just checked and they don't."

"In that case, it just means you've been looking in the wrong place."

"How can this be the wrong place? It's the kitchen!"

"I bet you can work out where it is," Judith said slyly to Becks.

"Good idea!" Suzie said, instantly divining her friend's strategy. "If anyone can find the olive oil in this house, it's you. You're the most middle-class person I know."

"Thank you," Becks said, not realizing that Suzie's words weren't entirely complimentary. "But I really don't have the time. I've got to take this water to Jenny."

"I'm sure it won't take you any time at all," Judith said.

"You know these people," Suzie said with a mock sincerity that Becks didn't pick up on. "You *are* these people."

Becks was moved by her friends' support.

"Well, let's see."

Becks took a moment to center herself like a martial arts sensei. She then glanced down at the induction hob and ran her palm over the four cooking areas—and the fifth wok station. It didn't give her anything, so she turned slowly on the spot—again apparently without inspiration—and then she surprised her friends by suddenly crouching down on her haunches, so her eyeline was at the height of the kitchen counter. Judith and Suzie could see a look of puzzlement cross her face as she looked at the white countertop before she snapped back up, strode over to the sink, and peered into its gleaming stainless-steel perfection. Next, she put her index finger to the plughole and pressed down. As she lifted her finger, she looked at what was now on the end of it and smiled.

"You're right," she said.

"Wait, what?" Suzie asked, amazed. "You know where they keep their olive oil?"

"I do."

"How? You haven't even opened a cupboard!"

Becks crossed to the far wall of the kitchen and indicated a little aluminum can with a spout on one side and a plunger on the other. It looked like an old-fashioned mister for spraying flowers, and this impression was made all the more credible by the way it was sitting on a shelf next to an old glass vase that had some sunflowers in it.

"Their olive oil is in this can," she said, reaching for it.

"Don't touch it!" Judith said, moving at speed to join her friend. "We need to check it for fingerprints."

"But how can you know?" Suzie asked. "Seeing as there's no label on it, and you can't see what's inside."

"Oh, don't worry, it contains olive oil," Becks said.

"But it looks like a watering can for those flowers."

"The flowers are dried, they don't need watering."

"But how did you even begin to spot it from the other side of the room?"

"I didn't," Becks conceded. "Not at first at least. But I did spot the Corian worktops to the kitchen counters."

"Come again?" Suzie asked.

"The family have Corian worktops. It's a wonder material, really. They make it in different sections, and then the installers melt and sand the joins together, it's a marvel to watch—and so much cheaper than marble. But the point is," Becks continued, noticing that her audience wasn't quite as interested in the pros and cons of rival kitchen worktop surfaces as she was, "they have one downside. You have to use a chopping board. If you cut things directly onto a Corian surface, you can end up leaving the faintest of knife cuts. And when I looked at the countertop just now, I saw knife marks on the surface that are tinged with green."

Becks returned to the island of cabinets that contained the hob and indicated the countertop to the side. Suzie realized that if she peered closely enough, she could just make out the lightest of scratches where a knife had sliced into the surface. And yes, now she was looking, she could see these shallowest of marks were tinged a light green. Perhaps. It was hard to tell.

"You saw these marks?" Suzie asked.

"It was almost the first thing I saw when I got in here."

"But how do marks on a counter prove a metal can on the other side of the room contains olive oil?"

"Well, that's the easy bit," Becks said, going to the sink and indicating the drying rack where there was a Microplane cheese grater sitting next to a sparkling glass jar with separate metal blades to the side. "The nut grinder attachment to a food mixer has recently been washed up. As has this grater— that you'd only use for the hardest of cheeses, like Parmesan. So I just thought to myself, what would you first chop with a knife that's green and then blitz in the nut grinder of a food mixer with some grated Parmesan? The answer's obvious of course."

The other two women looked at each other, no idea what the answer was.

"It's basil leaves," Becks said. "For fresh pesto."

"Of course!" Judith said, unable to keep the laugh out of her voice. "Fresh pesto. That was my first thought as well."

"And when I found a single pine nut in the drainer of the sink, I knew I was right—which meant there had to be olive oil somewhere, seeing as you use it to make pesto. And it wouldn't be anywhere obvious. You've checked the most likely places. So I looked for the main body of the food processor and saw it was on the far side of the room. And on the little shelf above it are those flowers, but there's also a metal can. Which suggested to me that while the basil was chopped and cheese grated on this side of the room, the pesto was made over where the machine is. It's just a process of deduction. The metal can must contain the olive oil."

Judith and Suzie stared at Becks.

"There's got to be a way we can monetize this skill," Suzie said.

Judith snatched up a pair of yellow rubber gloves that were hanging over the taps on the sink and snapped them on. She then rootled in a drawer until she found a fish slice and, picking up an old table mat from the dining table that depicted Windsor Castle, she approached the metal can.

"What are you doing?" Becks asked.

"Making sure we don't interfere with a possible crime scene."

Judith held the table mat up to the shelf, slid the fish slice under the metal can, and lifted it onto the mat.

"What crime scene?"

"Oh, that's simple enough," Judith said. "I think whoever's fingerprints are on this oil can could very well be the person who murdered Sir Peter Bailey."

Chapter 6

TANIKA WAS LEAVING SIR PETER'S study when she saw Judith approaching with Suzie and Becks. It looked to Tanika as though Judith was wearing yellow marigold gloves and holding a small metal can on a table mat. As Judith reached her, Tanika realized that this was because that was precisely what Judith was doing.

Knowing that Judith had once again involved herself in one of her cases made Tanika feel preemptively weary—not that she didn't think Judith had something to offer. If she'd learned one thing from the year before, it was that Judith and her friends were excellent sleuths, even if they were sometimes chaotic and unreliable. It was more that she'd already spent a whole day at work, knew that she'd missed her daughter's bedtime hours ago, and would no doubt be in the office tomorrow before Shanti and her husband, Shamil, had even woken up.

Tanika pulled herself together. She might be bone tired, but a man had died who'd expected to get married the following day. He deserved her full commitment, and that's what she was going to give.

"Judith," Tanika said. "You've found a metal can."

"I have!" Judith said. "Or rather, Becks found it."

"That you're now bringing to me on a table mat. A table mat, I now see, of Windsor Castle."

"It was Windsor Castle or Balmoral. I thought you'd appreciate the local touch."

"And the rubber gloves?"

"Just protecting the crime scene."

"Perhaps you'd like to tell me what you've done."

Once Judith had explained why she felt the can of oil needed finger-printing, Tanika decided it was time to make a stand.

"You can't go poking around," Tanika said. "You're witnesses."

"If it wasn't for us poking around," Judith said, "you wouldn't know about the oil can."

"Although, do we really need to know about the oil can?"

"I think so. Because whoever's fingerprints are on this can could well be the person who killed Sir Peter Bailey."

If only to stop having to look at Judith in her yellow rubber gloves for a second longer, Tanika called an officer over and asked him to take the oil can away to dust it for fingerprints. He carried the items away with a look on his face that suggested he'd at that moment realized he'd just reached the nadir of his career.

As Judith took off the gloves, Tanika said, "Okay, then, let's do this. Why do you think Sir Peter was killed?"

"A number of things. Firstly, the timing. Who dies of natural causes the day before their wedding?"

"It could happen," Tanika said, although her tone of voice acknowledged that it was a bit of a stretch.

"By a cabinet that coincidentally fell over following an argument?"

"Okay, as it happens, I agree with that one," Tanika said. Her officers had started taking statements from the guests and catering staff, and she'd very quickly learned that Sir Peter had argued with his son Tristram just before he died. "It does seem odd that it fell over at that precise moment. But it's still not impossible."

"But here's the clincher," Judith said in triumph. "Sir Peter warned me he was going to be murdered today!"

"What?" Becks asked, agog.

"Good as said he was going to be murdered," Judith added, a touch more truthfully.

"Hang on," Tanika said. "I don't understand. Did he or didn't he?"

"The point is, I don't know Sir Peter or anyone in his family, but this morning he rang me at home and introduced himself, asking if I'd come to the party this afternoon. Which was surprising, to say the least. But he insisted. He said he wanted to celebrate all of the dignitaries in the town, and that meant inviting me. I didn't point out that if he really wanted me to attend, he could have invited me sooner. But I was at a loss as to why he thought I was a local dignitary. All I've ever done, all we've ever done," Judith turned to include Suzie and Becks, "is help you last year with those awful murders. So I made a quip to Sir Peter that I hoped no one was going to be killed—and then the strangest thing happened. He got all flustered. And he said, 'No one's frightened for their life here.' And then he all but hung up on me. It's why I called Becks and Suzie. It was such an odd phrase. 'No one's frightened for their life here.' Who'd say such a thing?"

"You think he thought someone was going to kill him?"

"I think he believed *someone* feared for their life, and he was worried that something bad was going to happen at his party. Which is why, at the last minute, he decided he wanted me here. As a reliable witness. Or someone who perhaps could stop the killer. Not that I was able to."

"But hold on," Tanika said. "Just because he thought someone's life might be in danger, it doesn't mean he was killed."

"Not again!" Judith said, throwing her hands up in the air.

"What?" Tanika said, surprised by Judith's vehemence.

"It was poor Stefan Dunwoody last year you said couldn't have been killed, and you were wildly off beam on that one, weren't you?"

"Now that's a bit beneath the belt. I was happy to agree it was murder once we'd established the facts of what happened. I just didn't want to leap to conclusions. That's all. And there's a problem if you think Sir Peter was murdered. Tell me—how do you think it happened?"

The women looked at each other, surprised by the question.

"Is this a trick question?" Suzie asked.

"No."

"Okay, let me take this," she said before turning back to Tanika. "Someone pushed a bloody great cabinet onto him."

"Right, sorry, I should have said—I agree, if he was killed, and it's a big if at this stage, then someone pushed that cabinet onto him. But tell me, how was his body discovered?"

"Tristram broke through the door to the study," Judith said, already seeing where Tanika was going with her line of argument.

"You were with him?"

"All three of us, and half a dozen or so other guests as well."

"So why did you have to break through the door?"

"Because it was locked. And I checked the lock myself. The hasp very definitely ripped through the frame of the door."

"That's how it looked to me," Tanika agreed. "And the windows haven't been opened in years. So, tell me, what happened when you got into the room?"

"I'll take this one," Suzie said, happy that once again she knew the answer. "We found Sir Peter under the cabinet. With his legs sticking out like the Wicked Witch of the East."

"Suzie!" Becks yelped. "You can't say that!"

"Oh, come on, you can't pretend you didn't think it as well. The poor man was crushed under that bloody great cabinet, and all we saw poking out were his salmon-pink trousers and brown brogues."

"I honestly didn't think it," Becks said, appalled. "Judith, did you?"

"I have to admit," Judith said, "the thought did float across my mind."

"Look," Tanika said, trying to get the conversation back on track, "the point is, when you broke into the room, who else other than Sir Peter was in there?"

"That's the easiest question yet," Suzie said. "No one."

"Are you sure?"

"Suzie's right," Judith agreed. "There was no one else in there. And nowhere they could have been hiding either. I checked."

"So what we're saying," Tanika said, summing up the situation for them all, "is that Sir Peter's body was found in a room that contained no one else, had only one door into and out of it, and which was locked with a key that was found in Sir Peter's pockets."

"Then there must be a second key," Judith said.

"One of my officers has spoken to Rosanna Bailey, Sir Peter's daughter. She said the only key to the study is an old iron thing, and there's never been a copy made. So, seeing as the room only contained Sir Peter when you broke into it, how did the killer manage to push that enormous cabinet onto him and then get out of the locked study *after* killing him but *before* you all arrived?"

The question flummoxed the three friends, and Suzie and Becks turned to Judith for her response.

"Yes, well, it's going to sound unlikely if you're going to put it like that," she conceded, trying to regain her status in the conversation. "But if the only logical conclusion is that Sir Peter was killed, then how the killer got out of the room is just a mystery that needs solving like the mystery of who killed him, and why he had to die."

"That's quite a lot of mysteries if you ask me."

"That cabinet didn't fall over on its own. Someone pushed it onto Sir Peter. Someone, I admit, who must have been really quite strong."

"Look," Tanika said, holding up her hands to stop the conversation. "I appreciate your help and all you did for me last year, but I really shouldn't have to remind you, you aren't in fact police officers. It's not your job to solve this crime. If indeed there's even been one."

"Boss," a male officer said as he headed over. Judith and her friends could see that it was the same man who'd taken the metal can away for processing.

"I've dusted that oil can," he said like someone who'd just realized that his recent career nadir was increasingly looking like a zenith.

"And?" Tanika said when the man didn't continue.

"Was it a test?" he asked balefully.

"What did you find?"

"I didn't find anything."

"How do you mean?"

"There are no fingerprints on it."

"But there must be," Becks said, disbelieving. "It was used to make basil pesto. And quite recently. Today, I'd imagine."

"That's as well as maybe," the officer said. "But someone's wiped the prints from the can since then."

"Who would do that?" Becks asked.

"Someone who didn't want anyone to know they'd just used it to oil the hinges of the door in the murder room," Judith said.

"We can't be sure it's a murder room!" Tanika said.

"It's just like you said," Suzie said to Judith, ignoring Tanika. "Find out who used the can of olive oil and we find the killer."

"Thank you, Suzie," Judith said as she rootled in her handbag and pulled out a round metal tin. She popped the lid, made a great play of choosing a boiled sweet from among the icing sugar, and put it in her mouth.

"In which case, I think we've got a killer to catch, don't you?" Judith said, before biting down on the sweet with a satisfying crunch.

Chapter 7

A POLICE OFFICER CAME DOWN the corridor and told Tanika that she'd gathered the victim's family in the sitting room. They were ready to talk to her.

"Although," the officer added, "the deceased's fiancée is still upstairs. She's with the vicar and says she's too upset to talk for the moment."

"Oh, god, Jenny!" Becks exclaimed, looking at the glass of water she was still holding in her hand. "Poor woman. She's been through enough today without having to be stuck with Colin."

As Becks hurried off, Tanika turned to Judith.

"Look," she said, "I'll admit it's possible you're right. Let's say this was murder. Somehow. But don't you see? That makes it all the more important you leave well alone."

"Of course," Judith said, as though butter wouldn't melt. "We'll do just that."

"I don't believe you."

"Why on earth would you say that?"

"Because you've never left anything alone. It's not in your nature."

"But I give you my word. Cross my heart and hope to die."

"You promise?"

"I promise."

"Okay, I appreciate that. If you could join the other witnesses outside, one of my officers will take your formal statements. Thank you."

Tanika set off for the main hallway, pleased finally to have dealt with Judith and her friends.

Judith kept pace at her side.

"What are you doing?" Tanika asked.

"Coming with you."

"Where to?"

"The interview."

Tanika stopped dead in her tracks.

"What are you talking about? You just said you'd go outside to talk to one of my officers."

"No, I didn't. That's what you said. I promised I wouldn't interfere."

"You don't think that coming to my interview of the family is interfering?"

"Sadly, I've got no choice," Judith said, a concern both she and Tanika knew was fake. "Sir Peter phoned me this morning. I'm one of the last people he spoke to. You could even say I'm a key witness. It's possible I'll have some special insight. Or perhaps something the family says will remind me of something he said to me. We just don't know at this stage, do we? But I'm sure we can both agree it's critically important I'm there."

Tanika had to concede that what Judith was saying had a logic of sorts. Sir Peter had wanted Judith to be present that day in case something bad happened. Now that something definitely "bad" had indeed happened, it made sense that she should be present as a key witness when she spoke to the family.

"All right," she agreed. "But you have to promise me not to ask any questions yourself."

"Why would I do that?"

"Because you *always* ask questions. You can't help it."

"Well, how about this? I'll really try my best. Although, can you wait here one moment?" Judith added and then slipped back down the corridor to where Suzie was still standing.

Judith stood on tiptoes so she could speak into Suzie's ear and whispered, "Have a hunt around. See what you can dig up."

Suzie gave a pantomime wink—message received.

Judith returned to Tanika with an angelic smile, and the police officer led them both through the house into a sitting room that had egg-yolk silk wallpaper on the walls, oil paintings with little brass lights over them, a grand wooden mantelpiece painted white, and floor-to-ceiling sash windows that overlooked the garden and the river Thames. It was perhaps one of the most elegant rooms Judith had ever seen.

Tristram and Rosanna looked up from where they were sitting, and Judith could see that Tristram's eyes were red rimmed with tears. As for Rosanna, she looked at her with icy disdain.

"What are you doing here?" she asked.

"I'm Judith Potts. Your father rang me this morning. He sounded very worried about what was going to happen this afternoon."

"Does that surprise you?" Tanika asked.

Brother and sister looked nonplussed.

"He was worried about the wedding, I suppose," Rosanna offered. "Who wouldn't be? There were a thousand things to organize."

"No," Judith said, "it wasn't to do with the wedding. It was something else, I think. When I mentioned the word 'murder,' he startled. Yes, that's the word. He startled."

"What?" Tristram asked as though he were only just now noticing that Judith was in the room. "Sorry, what did you say you were doing here?"

"Your father asked me to attend."

"Thank you, Judith," Tanika said, wanting to take control of the conversation. "Can either of you tell me what happened this afternoon?"

Tristram looked at the floor, so Rosanna told the story of the party and how they'd discovered her father in his study. As she talked, Judith noticed a piece of black thread on the coat cuff of Rosanna's right sleeve. Looking at the left cuff of the coat, she saw a gold button in the shape of a sailor's knot, and Judith found herself puzzling over how someone so immaculately turned out hadn't noticed that they were missing a gold button on the right cuff of their coat.

"Thank you," Tanika said when Rosanna finished. "Although can I ask? The guests have told my officers there was an argument between Sir Peter and you, Tristram, just before he went inside?"

Tristram looked up, all pretense at hiding his guilt long gone.

"I'll never forgive myself," he said.

"What happened?"

"I thought it would be funny. But I was also hurting. I wanted to cause a scene. Shake him out of his complacency."

"Complacency?"

"He'd chosen Jenny over me," he said, a note of desperation in his voice.

"Yes, can I ask about that?" Tanika said. "Your father was remarrying?"

"After many years of being a bachelor," Rosanna said.

"What happened to your mother?"

"Mother and Father divorced when we were small."

"How old were you?"

"I was eight, and Tristram six."

"That must have been tough."

"I don't really remember. For as long as I've known, Father's been single."

"Then can I ask, how did he meet Jenny Page, his fiancée?"

Rosanna shared a glance with Tristram. It was obvious that neither of them wanted to explain.

"It's quite simple," Rosanna said, deciding to get the story out of the way as quickly as possible. "She's a nurse. And Father had a major health scare a couple of years ago. All that red wine and fatty food. Anyway, he was diagnosed with type two diabetes, so he got an agency to send him a live-in nurse—who turned out to be Jenny. One thing led to another, they started dating, and here we are, on the eve of their wedding."

"Thank you. That seems straightforward enough. But can I ask, Tristram, what did you mean when you said your father was complacent?"

"What does it matter?" Tristram said, suddenly agitated. "He's dead now, isn't he? Whatever my relationship was with him, it's over, that's how it ended, and I've got to live with myself for the rest of my life knowing I caused his death!"

"That's quite a statement," Tanika said.

"But if I hadn't turned up and goaded him, Jenny wouldn't have got upset, would she? And Father wouldn't have followed her into the house and... Well, I don't know what happened, but he wouldn't have pulled that cabinet on top of him or whatever happened. It's all my fault."

"It's not your fault," Rosanna said dismissively. "It's no one's fault. It's just a horrible accident."

"Can I ask," Tanika said, "what was the argument about?"

"Jenny had banned Tristram from attending the wedding," Rosanna said.

"Why?"

"Because my brother is stupid enough to say out loud what he should keep in his head."

"Which is?" Tanika asked Tristram. Once again, he didn't reply.

"A nurse from nowhere—an orphan, in fact—comes into this house," Rosanna said, "and bags herself a baronet, a country house, and a small fortune in under a year. She didn't hang about."

"You think Jenny was only interested in your father's money?"

"And title. Don't forget that. She was about to become Lady Bailey."

"Although she won't now, will she?" Judith said, working through the logic of the situation. "Not with your father dying before they married."

"No," Rosanna said, as she realized the truth of what Judith was saying. "I suppose not."

"Then can I ask who'll inherit the title?" Tanika asked. "Is that you, Rosanna? As the eldest child?"

Rosanna turned to her brother.

"I think you should answer that question," she said.

Tristram looked somewhat shamefaced as he said, "The baronetcy descends down the male line."

"What's that?" Tanika asked.

"I'll inherit Father's title."

"And all of his money," Rosanna added. "His entire estate."

"But you're not the oldest child," Tanika said, confused.

"I don't make the rules," Tristram said.

"You don't have to accept them, either," Rosanna said waspishly. Judith got the clear impression that sister and brother didn't necessarily get on.

"Can I ask," she said, "when did your family get their baronetcy?"

"At the end of the Civil War," Tristram said.

"Really?" Judith said. "That doesn't seem very likely."

"Why's that a problem?" Tanika asked.

"Well, Cromwell won the Civil War and cut the king's head off. He didn't approve of hereditary titles."

"No, you're right there," Rosanna agreed. "Our family fought for Cromwell during the war, but once the republic fell apart, we switched sides and joined the campaign to restore the monarchy. When that succeeded, Charles the Second gave the family their baronetcy in 1660. You see, the Baileys always bend with the wind. It's one of our most constant features through the generations—our inconstancy. We really can't be bothered with anything so common as principles. We'll change our position six times before lunch if it makes life easier. Except when it comes to inheritance, of course."

"That's enough questions, Judith," Tanika said to Judith.

"Of course," Judith said, folding her hands together. "I'm all done. Carry on."

"Thank you."

"Although, do either of you know who made pesto in the kitchen?"

Tristram looked baffled by the question as he turned to his sister. "Rosanna, was it you?"

"Sure, it was me," Rosanna said, not knowing why the question was so important. "I made us all pasta for lunch. You know, lots of carbs for energy. And to soak up the alcohol. With the party this afternoon."

Knowing that Rosanna had made the pesto, Judith found herself remembering that she'd not seen Rosanna at the party at any time before the cabinet fell over. She'd also arrived later than everyone else at the door to the study.

"Where were you when the cabinet fell over?" Judith asked.

"What's that?"

"Only I didn't see you outside in the garden with the other guests beforehand."

Judith could see that Rosanna was briefly thrown by the question, but she quickly regathered herself.

"Oh, I was there," she said.

"Then I'm sure you'll be able to tell me who came out onto the upstairs balcony when it happened?"

"What's that?"

"It's a simple question. If you were outside in the garden with the rest of us, who came out onto the upstairs balcony when the crash happened?"

"That's easy enough," Rosanna said, looking levelly at Judith. "It was Jenny, wasn't it? It was her on the balcony upstairs."

"You're right, it was," Judith said kindly. "Thank you."

There was a knock on the door, and the uniformed police officer who'd led Judith and Tanika to the sitting room stuck her head in.

"Boss," the woman said. "Sir Peter's lawyer's here. Says he needs to speak to you. As a matter of urgency."

"Then show him in," Tanika said.

"Thank you," a friendly voice said from just beyond the door, and then it opened as a plump man in his fifties strode into the room with ruddy cheeks and a rather weak chin, Judith thought to herself. Everything about him, from his battered Barbour coat to his corduroy trousers exuded the air of a country squire.

"Andrew Husselbee," the man said to Tanika. "I'm Sir Peter's lawyer. I've just heard the tragic news, and I wanted to come as soon as I could."

"Why?" Tanika asked.

Andrew glanced briefly at Tristram and Rosanna, uncomfortable at talking in front of them. But he steeled himself.

"Sir Peter wrote a new will last month, and I think we need to get hold of it as a matter of some urgency."

Chapter 8

ROSANNA ROSE FROM HER SEAT.

"He did it?" she asked, amazed. "He finally wrote a new will?"

"He did," Andrew replied.

Judith could well imagine why Rosanna was so interested. After all, if the previous will had left everything to Tristram, then any changes suggested that Sir Peter had broadened the list of beneficiaries, or changed them entirely—maybe to include Rosanna, his firstborn child. Judith could see that Tristram's brow was furrowed. Yes, the same thought was occurring to him as well. How very interesting.

"I'm sorry," Andrew said, "but it's probably better if I don't say anything more until we have the will in our hands and can read it for ourselves."

"Hold on," Judith said. "Are you really saying Sir Peter wrote a new will last month, and now, a few weeks later, he dies?"

"I know," Andrew said apologetically. "The timing is very unfortunate. Which is why I think we should get it. It's in Sir Peter's safe in his bedroom."

"Now?" Tristram said, but they could see he was trying to stall for time. "Jenny's in there. We can't interrupt her."

Judith caught Tanika's eye, both of them thinking the same thing. Rosanna had only moments before revealed that she and her brother thought Jenny Page was a money-grabber, and now he was suddenly concerned about her well-being?

"Even so," Andrew said, and turned to look at Tanika for her ruling.

"I think I want to see this will," she said. "Mr. Husselbee, why don't you take me to the safe?"

Tanika left the room with the lawyer. However, as she crossed the hall to the main staircase, she once again found Judith walking at her side.

"What are you doing now?" Tanika asked.

"You may need me," Judith said. "To break into the safe."

"*What?*"

"If you can't get into the safe, what with Sir Peter no longer being here to tell us the code, you may need me to break into it. I'm quite the peterman."

"Judith, what on earth is a 'peterman'?"

"A very good crossword synonym, that's what it is. It means someone who can get into a safe without a key or combination. A safecracker."

Tanika decided that she'd had enough of Judith for one evening.

"If you could just stay here?"

"Of course," Judith said.

Once Tanika had gone up the stairs with Andrew, Judith found herself on her own, which suited her just fine. There was a lot to think about.

She went over to an oil painting that hung in the corner of the hallway. It depicted Sir Peter and a woman on a chesterfield sofa with a girl who looked about four years old and a boy who looked about two. Sir Peter's smile made him look effortlessly in charge, his arm around his daughter Rosanna to his side, his other arm around his wife—who had both arms around the young Tristram, who was sitting on her lap. Judith considered the composition, with the father wanting to encompass his whole family and the attention of his wife entirely focused on her son.

Judith found her eyes drawn to the first Lady Bailey. She had long blond hair, and a fresh complexion, and there was life to her that Judith could see was very attractive. Judith wondered why the relationship had broken down. There were no clues in the painting of any tension. And it was interesting that Sir Peter still kept the painting in the hallway, even as he prepared to marry his second wife.

Judith looked at the grandfather clock to the side of the staircase and realized Tanika had been gone a couple of minutes. *Hmm*, she thought to herself, *this is taking longer than she'd expected.*

She heard footsteps on the upstairs landing, and Tanika's face appeared over the balustrade.

"Okay," the police officer said, "can you really break into safes?"

"Of course," Judith said, not entirely truthfully. "Or I wouldn't have said."

"Then would you mind lending a hand?"

"You admit you need me?" she asked with an innocent smile.

"Don't push it."

"Then wait there, I'll come straight up," she said with a smile.

Judith climbed the stairs and followed Tanika into an airy bedroom that was dominated by a large oak bed. Windows on one side of the room overlooked a scraggy bit of garden and a laurel hedge, but Judith's eyes were drawn to the glass doors that opened onto a balcony that overlooked the garden and the rooftops and church spire of Marlow on the other side of the river Thames. At this time of night, the river was silvered with moonlight, and the church spire was lit up like a beacon.

Jenny was sitting on a sofa with Colin to her side, and Becks was on a chair in front of her holding her hands. As for Andrew, he was standing by a little wall safe that had been revealed behind an oil painting that he'd hinged away from the wall.

Judith went straight to Jenny.

"I'm so sorry for your loss," she said.

Jenny nodded in thanks, but without much comprehension.

"You can really get into this safe?" Tanika asked Judith, still not quite believing it could be true.

As it happened, Judith couldn't get into safes, but she'd read the auto-biography of a man who claimed he could, and she was damned if she was going to miss out on the action. Not for the first time, she'd decided that her best strategy was to bluff.

"Not me," Judith said with false modesty. "Richard Feynman."

"Who's he?" Andrew asked.

"A bongo drummer, amateur artist, and physicist who won the Nobel Prize. He had a party trick of breaking into safes when he worked at Los Alamos in the Second World War."

"Seriously?" Tanika asked.

"Oh, yes, very seriously."

"What was his method?"

"Well, let's see about that."

Judith started walking around the room, inspecting all of the pictures and ornaments, picking them up and turning them over, looking for something but not explaining what she was up to.

"Don't mind me," she said. "Won't be long, just talk among yourselves."

The others exchanged confused glances, and Tanika realized she needed to take charge. She picked up her conversation with Andrew.

"What can you tell me about the new will?" Tanika asked.

"Nothing, I'm afraid. Sir Peter wouldn't show it to me. The first I knew about it was when he called me to the house to witness his signature. Along with Chris Shepherd—he's the gardener here. We called him in to be the other witness."

"Sir Peter kept the will's contents a secret from you?"

"It was highly irregular and not like Sir Peter at all."

"Then can you tell me what was in the old will he was replacing?"

"I suppose it doesn't matter. Seeing as it's no longer valid. The old will left his estate in its entirety to Tristram."

"Yes, Rosanna and Tristram said as much. Was Rosanna not mentioned at all?"

"There was a clause saying Tristram would be expected to make a suitable provision for her. An allowance, for example. I never thought it was a satisfactory arrangement. But Sir Peter was adamant. It was all about protecting the baronetcy. His son had to inherit."

"Even though he was secondborn?"

"The Baileys are a very old and noble family; they've never believed in matrilineal primogeniture."

"So maybe the new will made sure Rosanna got her fair share?"

"I very much hope so. She deserves her just rewards, the way she works for the family."

"Especially seeing as father and son weren't getting on."

"Indeed."

"How are you doing with the safe?" Tanika asked Judith.

"I'll be honest, not too well," Judith said breezily. "You see, Feynman's technique was simple, and he claimed it was nearly always successful. But it's not currently working for me. Not yet."

"What was it?"

"Well, when he was helping build the first atomic bomb at Los Alamos, he observed that scientists were so worried about forgetting the codes to their safes that they invariably used a memorable date as their combination. And if you do the math on that, the first two numbers—the month in the American dating system—could only be zero-one through to twelve. And having only twelve options for those two numbers rather than ninety-nine made it a far more manageable process. Especially when the next two numbers were likely to be between one and thirty-one—the days in the month—and the last two were almost certainly a two-digit number from the previous fifty years. Basically, he cut the odds and could crack the code with brute force if he had to. But he rarely had to because he just found that people wrote the combination down on a slip of paper—or in the back of a notebook—somewhere near the safe in question. In a drawer or whatnot."

"Seriously?" Tanika asked.

"That's the problem with magic tricks. If you look at the effect—Richard Feynman breaking into Robert Oppenheimer's safe where the codes for the atomic bomb were kept—you're dumbstruck. But explain your workings and it all becomes so very humdrum. However!" Judith added, heading back toward the group. "Let's follow the logic through. The absence of any kind of aide-mémoire with a six-digit number on it nearby suggests to me that perhaps Sir Peter wasn't comfortable writing the code down. Which, according to Richard Feynman, suggests he'd chosen a memorable date. You've tried Sir Peter's birthday?"

Judith asked this of Jenny, who nodded.

"And the birthdays of his children? And you, Jenny?"

Jenny nodded again, and Judith went over to look at the safe in the wall. The black paint was dull with age, and there was an embossed name on the front, "Marlow Locksmiths & Co." The letters were heavy weighted, sans serif, and looked, to Judith's eyes, remarkably like Futura, the typeface designed by Paul Renner in 1927. So the safe was prewar?

"This was originally installed by Sir Peter's father," Judith said almost to herself. "Does anyone know the birth date of Sir Peter's father?"

"I think I do," Jenny said. "It was in the summer of 1929, I think. Let me see if I can work this out."

Jenny got up from her chair and approached the safe.

"It was August, I think," Andrew said.

"You're right, it was August," Jenny said as she started to twist the dial of the safe from left to right. "Peter told me his father died on the first day of grouse shooting. The 'glorious twelfth,' he called it. So that would make the code 1–2 for the twelfth, 0–8 for August, and 2–9 for 1929."

They all heard a click as the lock disengaged.

"You were right, Judith," Jenny said as she pulled the door open, and everyone approached.

"The will's in a brown envelope, it's not large," Andrew said.

"I don't understand," Jenny said as she stepped to the side.

"What don't you understand?" Tanika asked as she looked in the safe. "Oh, I see what you mean."

The safe was empty.

"But it must be there," Andrew said. "I saw Sir Peter put it in there with my own eyes."

"Maybe he's moved it since then?" Judith asked.

"There's no way he'd have removed it," Andrew said, and Judith and Tanika got the impression that there was something Andrew wasn't saying.

"Why not?" Tanika asked.

"Look, I really can't say," Andrew said uncomfortably.

"I'd like to remind you Sir Peter has just died in very unfortunate circumstances," Tanika said. "If there's anything you can tell me that will help throw light on what happened, it's your duty to say."

"Of course," Andrew said, chastened. "You're right."

"You know what was in the will, don't you?" Judith said.

"No, that's not it. Really, I don't. Although I think Rosanna's correct to presume Sir Peter would have made significant changes in her favor. It's just,

I had a bit of an argument with Sir Peter after he put the will in the safe. I felt he shouldn't have written any kind of will without my advice. He countered by saying it was none of my business and he had to act fast because… Well, there's no easy way to say this, but he said this new will was his insurance policy."

"Insurance policy against what?" Tanika asked.

"He said he was worried his son Tristram was going to kill him."

"What?" Jenny said in horror.

"I know it sounds far fetched," Andrew said. "And that's what I told him. He was talking out of his hat; why would anyone want to kill him, let alone Tristram? But Sir Peter could be incredibly stubborn—and proud for that matter—when he made up his mind. And he was adamant. He was afraid that before he could marry Jenny, Tristram would try and kill him. And he had to come up with a new will as fast as possible as his insurance policy."

Tanika turned to Jenny.

"Did Sir Peter mention this to you?" she asked.

"No," Jenny said, struggling to process what she'd just heard.

"He didn't tell you he feared for his life?"

"No."

"Or that he'd written a new will?"

"No. He kept all this from me."

"But he must have talked to you about Tristram?"

"Of course," Jenny said. "It was all we ever talked about. How Tristram was trying to undermine our relationship. How he was selfish. A 'spoiled child'—that's what Peter always called him. But he blamed himself. Said he'd been too indulgent of Tristram as he grew up. He should have set more boundaries."

"And what do you think?" Judith asked.

"About what?"

"About Tristram."

"I always told Peter it couldn't have been easy for the children having someone like me come into their lives and take their dad away. After all of these years of it being just the three of them. I'm aware they think I'm just after Peter's money, but I was hoping to win them over. In time. I just had to show them how much I loved their dad. That's all I kept saying to Peter. Tristram would come round to us being together. He'd come round to me. It just needed time. But he said nothing to me about being frightened for his life…"

"When did Sir Peter ban Tristram from attending the wedding?" Judith asked.

Jenny looked at Judith, not quite following the question.

"Was it last month, when he wrote the new will? Or more recently?"

"Oh, I see. No, they had their argument at the beginning of December. It ended with Peter throwing Tristram out of the house, and that's when he said he couldn't come to the wedding."

"Tristram used to live here?"

"Until the beginning of December."

"How did Tristram take it?" Tanika asked.

"He was furious, but what could he do? His dad had thrown him out, and Peter didn't want to see him over the Christmas period, either. He said he wouldn't see Tristram until the day after the wedding."

"That's quite a specific date."

"I guess he just meant that when we were married, it would be too late for Tristram to try and get him to change his mind."

"When did you witness the new will, Andrew?" Tanika asked.

"It was the fifteenth of December," Andrew said.

"So," Judith said, summing up for them all. "Sir Peter throws Tristram out of the house after a massive argument at the beginning of December, banning him from attending his wedding, and two weeks later, he writes a brand-new will. His insurance policy—or so he tells Andrew. In case his son tries to kill him before he can remarry. And here we are, the night before the wedding, only a month later, and Sir Peter's suddenly died in mysterious circumstances, and his most recent will, his insurance policy, is now missing."

"Yeah," Tanika said, all thoughts of trying to keep Judith away from the case long forgotten. "That sounds about right."

They all looked at each other, thinking the same thing.

Had Tristram just killed his father?

Chapter 9

THERE WERE ONLY A HANDFUL of guests still outside the house, waiting to give their statements to the two police officers. As they were all cold and keen to get the whole thing over with as soon as possible, they didn't really notice the bright light that bobbed toward them from around the side of the house. It was Suzie, the torch function on her smartphone turned on. She looked around, saw Judith come out of the house, and headed over.

"Judith!" she said.

"You've got something?"

"A cold, I would imagine, and freezing feet, I can tell you that much. But I think I've found something."

"You have?" Judith said as she looked about herself to check no one could hear them.

"I reckon so. Come and see for yourself."

Using her phone's torch to light the way, Suzie led Judith around the side of the house, and Judith realized she was now in the scraggy bit of garden that she'd seen from the side window of Sir Peter's bedroom upstairs.

"I don't think I'd have seen it if the lights weren't turned on," Suzie said as she approached the study window, a sharp trapezoid of light spilling onto the lawn from inside. Looking through the window, Judith could see a police officer helping two paramedics prepare a gurney to the side of Sir Peter's body.

"What have you found?" she asked.

Suzie indicated the shrubs under the window, pulled back the branches of an azalea, and pointed her camera torch at the ground.

There was a footprint in the soft earth.

"A boot print. And it's not the only one. Whoever was here went right up to the window and then went along the side of the house."

Pulling the branches back further, Suzie illuminated more boot prints that led up to the window and then disappeared behind the azaleas altogether.

"Someone was trying to find out what was going on in the study," Suzie said.

"These boot prints must have been left at some point today," Judith said. "It rained all day yesterday and last night, didn't it? These prints have been left since then."

"And it gets better," Suzie said, throwing her torch light onto the nearest print. "There's a cut across the sole of the left foot. All we have to do is find someone who owns a pair of boots with a split in the rubber on the left foot."

Judith could see that Suzie was right. On each left boot print, there was a slash across the sole, where the rubber was split.

"This is brilliant work, Suzie," Judith said.

Suzie beamed.

"We need to tell Tanika at once. Although I don't think she'll take too kindly to being interrupted by me again. I'll go and get Becks. You find Tanika and fill her in."

"What's her problem? We're only trying to help."

"She's got a bee in her bonnet about us interfering with her investigation. So, whatever you do, don't tell her you were looking for clues when you see her. Say you bumped into these boot prints entirely by accident."

"Okay," Suzie said, making sure she'd got the message. "I wasn't looking for clues, I found these prints entirely by accident."

A few minutes later, Suzie returned to the bushes under the study window with Tanika.

"I was looking for clues," Suzie said proudly, having already forgotten what she'd promised Judith. And then she remembered. "No I wasn't!" she corrected. "I was having a cigarette—that's it. I was just around this side of the house totally by coincidence having a ciggie when I saw the prints. I mean, what are the chances?"

Tanika knew that Suzie had told her the truth the first time, but a clue was a clue. As she examined the boot prints, Judith approached with Becks.

"Of course," Tanika said with a sigh. "The other two musketeers."

"I know what you're thinking," Judith called out.

"Believe me, you don't."

"But this is nothing to do with me. Suzie asked me to get Becks."

"I did?" Suzie said, before once again realizing her error and turning back to Tanika. "That's right, I did," she said far more confidently.

"Look, I'm grateful you found the boot print, Suzie, but could you just tell me what's going on?"

"A process of identification," Judith said. "I thought you might like to know what sort of boot left those marks."

"We *are* the police," Tanika said. "We have databases of boot treads to reference. We'll be able to work it out."

"But why wait when we've got access to Becks?"

"I don't understand," Becks said, just as confused as Tanika.

"What can you tell us about that boot print?" Judith asked.

"I'm sure I can't tell you anything," Becks said, surprised to find everyone looking at her. "Although," she added, glancing at the boot print a bit more carefully, "I suppose, if you were to press me, it looks an awfully lot like a ladies' Hunter welly. It's those triangular treads on the heel. You only get that sort of pattern on the ladies' range of Hunter wellies. And if you pushed me, I'd say it was a size seven, from their narrow calf range. Not that I'm any kind of expert of course."

"There you are," Judith said to Tanika. "No need to wait until tomorrow. Those prints were left by a woman with slender calves, size seven feet, and who owns a pair of Hunter-branded wellies."

"With a cut across the sole of the left foot," Suzie added for good measure. "You find the person who owns them, I reckon you've found the killer."

"No," Tanika said, "I'm going to have to stop you there—"

"And I'm going to have to stop you there," Judith said. "Because the three of us have already found you a can of olive oil that's had its fingerprints wiped from it, opened a safe that proves a will is now missing, and now we've found the prints from a pair of wellies in a flower bed outside the murder room."

"That's my point. I still can't categorically say it was murder—"

"I know you have to say that, really I do. You have rules you have to follow."

"Not rules, Judith. Laws. Actual 'don't follow them and you go to prison' laws. And that means I have to follow chains of evidence and due process, making sure that all we do is legal."

"So you do things your way, but we'll do things our way. As soon as you're ready to admit Sir Peter was murdered and you need our help, we'll be here for you. Like we were last time. Come on, ladies," Judith said, and turned and left.

Suzie was quick to follow her friend, but Becks briefly loitered.

"I really don't like interfering," she said apologetically. "But they're my friends."

Tanika gave a reassuring smile.

"Don't worry, Becks. I understand."

With a darting nod of thanks, Becks turned and caught up with Judith and Suzie.

Once they'd gone, Tanika looked down at the footprint. She then walked to the corner of the house from where she could see the lawn sweeping down to the Thames, the immaculate marquee gleaming white in the moonlight. It really wasn't possible to imagine a more idyllic spot, she thought to herself. So how had today ended in such a violent death?

All of her instincts were telling her that Judith was right. Sir Peter had been murdered. But that's what her heart told her. Her head was telling her something different. Because, before she could stand the case up, she knew she'd have to prove in a court of law how someone had managed to commit murder inside a locked room and then somehow magically vanish themselves out of it before it was opened up minutes later. If Sir Peter had been murdered, just how had the killer done it?

Chapter 10

JUDITH AND HER FRIENDS WERE the last of the guests to give their formal statements to the police. Suzie suggested they repair to one of their houses so they could have a quick nightcap and chew over what had happened, but Becks was keen to get back to her children, and Judith also demurred. For all that she'd enjoyed the drama of the day, she still spent most of her time on her own, and being surrounded by dozens of people for so long had been exhausting. She just wanted to get home.

As Judith closed the front door, she felt a sense of calm envelop her. She went over to her side table, poured herself a restorative glass of whisky, and sat in her favorite chair. *What an extraordinary day*, she thought to herself as she considered how it had all started with the odd phone call from Sir Peter and had ended with his murder.

Judith saw her copy of the *Marlow Free Press* sitting on the table to her side. She picked it up, idly wondering if she'd now be able to see what she'd found so puzzling about her crossword answers that morning. It was often the way with crosswords. A question would appear to be impenetrable, and the only way to solve it would be to walk away, forget about it entirely, and then go back and pick it up much later on.

This time, as she'd hoped, the solution to what had been tickling her subconscious arrived in a sudden rush of comprehension. The answers in each of the four corners of the grid, when read one after the other, created a message. In the top left-hand corner, the answer to 1 Across was SIXTEEN; in the bottom left-hand corner, the answer to 27 Across was HUNDRED; the answer in the bottom right-hand corner was SUNDAY; and in the top right-hand corner, the answer to 5 Across was CHEQUERS. Sixteen hundred was clearly a time—4:00 p.m. Sunday was self-explanatory, and Chequers could easily be a reference to a pub on the high street, the Chequers.

Was it a secret message that something was happening—or that there was a meeting—at 4:00 p.m. on Sunday in the Chequers pub? If so, why was the crossword setter communicating like this, and who was he or she trying to send the message to? It seemed so improbable that Judith decided she must be wrong. It was just a coincidence that the answers in the four corners of the grid could be arranged into a message. She put the paper down, resolving to return to the far more important events of the day, but she found her eyes closing. Within moments she was gently snoring.

As for Becks, by the time she and Colin had returned to the vicarage, they were in the middle of a full-blown row.

"You can't tell me what to do," Becks said as she slammed the car keys down on the side table.

"I'm not telling you what to do," Colin said, believing he was being entirely reasonable.

"No, you're not, you're being controlling."

"I'm really not, I'm just trying to tell you that Sir Peter's death is a police matter; you're not to get involved."

"You're jealous, aren't you? That's what this is about. I was the center of attention last summer, and you really don't like it, do you?"

"No, that's not true at all—"

"The vicar of Marlow had to play second fiddle to his wife. Not that you even take an interest in me. I could be solving murders left right and center or, god forbid, up to something much worse, and you wouldn't even know."

"Where's all this anger coming from?"

"How about you go to your study and check your emails like you always do; I'll go and check on the children. As I always do."

Becks kicked off her shoes and thudded up the stairs. With each step, she tapped the band of her new sapphire ring against the balustrade.

Colin stood at the foot of the stairs, agog. The truth was that he hadn't been jealous of Becks when she'd helped solve the murders the year before. He'd been prouder of her than he'd ever been. And there'd been a vitality to Becks since then that he'd not seen for years. But whenever he'd tried to tell her this, he'd get tongue-tied. He didn't know how to tell her how he felt. The irony that he spent most of his professional life communicating with people wasn't lost on him.

The sad truth was that Becks had seemed to be constantly angry with him since then. And the one time he'd asked if she was perimenopausal was the last time he knew he'd get away with asking such a question. But then, Colin's instincts told him that it wasn't his wife's hormones that were messing with her. She still had the same levels of patience and kindness with the children and the parishioners she met; it was only him she seemed to have a problem with. But what could he do about it?

As Colin went to check his emails—after all, he did have to check in on his parishioners at the end of each day—on the other side of town, Suzie was letting herself into her house, and getting a slobberingly joyous welcome from her Doberman dog, Emma. The front of the house was still a jumble of scaffolding poles and planks, the downstairs of the house was still a horror show of scratched linoleum and damaged sofas—an occupational hazard of being a professional dog-sitter, Suzie always said—so she went upstairs to her far tidier private part of the house, opened her tin of tobacco, got out her liquorice papers, and rolled herself a ciggie.

She was buzzing from the excitement of the day and still couldn't quite believe she'd been present at an actual real live murder. She knew there was only going to be one topic of conversation in tomorrow's phone-in on Marlow FM, and the fact that she'd been present at the party where the action had happened would make her interactions with her listeners all the more juicy.

Picking up her phone to find out what social media and other local news outlets were making of Sir Peter's death, she saw she had a message from one of her regular clients. Work was taking him to London the following day, and he wanted to know if Suzie was free to look after his cockapoo dog. There was no way Suzie was missing her radio show, so she texted back to say that sadly she already had her full complement of dogs.

Once she'd done that, she knew exactly who she wanted to talk to about the excitement of the day. It was far too late to chat with her daughter Rachel, but her other daughter Amy lived in Australia. Checking her watch, Suzie guessed that Amy would have just gotten back from the morning school run. With a smile, she picked up her phone and dialed her daughter's number.

The following morning, Judith tried to put Sir Peter's death out of her mind, but she found she couldn't settle. She started to compile a new crossword, but she couldn't quite concentrate, so she went over to her latest jigsaw puzzle to see if that could calm her mind. She'd got it from the Thames Hospice, and the volunteer at the till had been impressed that Judith was choosing to do a thousand-piece jigsaw that was a close-up photo of baked beans. What he'd not known is that there was no way Judith would do a jigsaw that contained only baked beans—she found the thought of them en masse revolting. No, her new idea, just to stretch her a bit, was to turn the puzzle over so that there was no picture for her to follow at all, just a flat gray color to every piece. But it required all of her focus to place the pieces, and her mind kept drifting back to Sir Peter.

Judith realized that drastic times called for drastic measures, so she decided to have a tidy-up, although she didn't get any further than picking up the day before's copy of the *Marlow Free Press*. After looking at the answers she'd written into the four corners, she once again found herself wondering whether they'd meant to spell out a message or whether it was a coincidence. She turned to the front page, found the phone number for the main desk of the paper, and dialed it. When the call was answered, Judith asked to be put through to the crossword editor.

"I don't think we've got one," the woman on the end of the line said.

"Then can you tell me who looks after your crossword setters?"

"That's easy. That's me."

"You know who sets your crosswords?"

"Yes. Although there's only one person. I'm in touch with him every week. Or rather, he's in touch with me when he sends them in. And you know what? He never needs to be chased; you could set your clock by him. He emails his puzzle every Monday morning at nine a.m."

"That's wonderful to hear."

Judith went on to explain that she was also a crossword setter. When pressed, she even admitted that she set crosswords for the national newspapers.

"That's amazing," the woman said. "All of them?"

"But the point is," Judith said, wanting to keep to the matter at hand, "I admire your crossword setter very much, and I wanted to get in touch with him."

"I'm sorry, but that won't be possible."

"I understand you can't give out his details, but if I give you mine, would you pass them on?"

"That's the problem. He does the crosswords on the condition we never contact him."

"What?"

"I know it sounds odd, but he's been doing it this way for years. He doesn't charge, doesn't miss a single Monday, and I really don't know who he is. Between you and me," the woman added confidentially, "I don't even know his name or that he's even a 'he' for that matter. He—or she—signs off their emails 'Higginson.'"

"Yes, I see that's what he calls himself in the paper."

It was customary in the world of crosswords for a setter to hide their anonymity behind a jokey nom de plume. All of Judith's crosswords were published under the name "Pepper," a word play on her surname, Potts. As for the *Marlow Free Press* setter's name, "Higginson" was perfect, as it was a good name anyway, and Higginson Park was the biggest communal space in the town.

"You're really sure you can't make contact with him?"

"Funnily enough, a couple of years ago, I wanted to send him some flowers on behalf of all of us here. He'd been doing the crossword for ten years. I remember his email back to me. It was polite, almost old-fashioned, but he said that if anyone ever uncovered his identity, he'd stop sending his crosswords in. And free content is free content, so we left it at that."

"Surely someone knows who he is?"

"Possibly one of the old hands. But they've left over the years. No one's currently at the paper who's been here even close to as long as ten years. And I'm not sure I should even be telling you this. I don't want to lose him."

"No, of course. But how strange."

"When you say it out loud like that, it does seem rather strange, doesn't it? But I'm afraid there's really no way for me to tell you who he is."

Judith thanked the woman for her time and hung up.

She found herself drifting over to her bay window to mull what she'd just learned. It was one of those winter mornings where the sun was a smudge of light behind the clouds. The grass in her garden, which she thought, not for the first time, she really should cut more often—in fact, at all—lay on its side in heavy clumps of frosted white. On the Thames just beyond, a cold fog hung just above the water that sent a chill through Judith's bones.

Had it only been yesterday that she'd spoken to Sir Peter on the phone? The more she thought about it, the more she decided he'd been almost pleading for her to go to the party. In fact, his call was a cry for help, wasn't it? And who would be so heartless as to refuse assisting someone who had then been murdered only a few hours later?

Judith went over to her handbag and pulled out the ball of red wool with knitting needles in that she kept in there from one year to the next in the optimistic hope that she'd one day take up knitting again.

She pulled the needles out and looked at the remaining ball of red wool.

Yes, this would do perfectly.

It was time to get to work.

Chapter 11

IN MAIDENHEAD POLICE STATION, DETECTIVE Sergeant Tanika Malik was also trying to make sense of Sir Peter Bailey's death.

The postmortem report concluded that Sir Peter had died from blunt force trauma to the head caused by a heavy object—for example, the cabinet that fell onto him. All of his other injuries, bruises, and broken bones were also consistent with him being crushed to death. What was more, the report said that his death had been almost instantaneous. He had no drugs or toxins in his system apart from a small amount of alcohol and no unexplained pre- or postmortem injuries.

As for digital forensics, they'd failed to throw up anything of note from their initial hunt through Sir Peter's computer and phone. His emails were mostly concerned with meeting friends for dinner or organizing shooting trips. It looked as if he lead a life of complete leisure. And although he often referred to Jenny as "She Who Must Be Obeyed," it was clear from his correspondence how much he loved his fiancée. He deferred to her in every choice for the wedding, and he readily professed that she was the "love of his life."

As for Jenny's many messages to Sir Peter, she came across as a practical-minded woman who brooked no disagreement. A typical nurse type, Tanika thought to herself. And while there seemed to be no correspondence between Sir Peter and his son Tristram, Rosanna was constantly in touch informing her father of decisions she was making—to do with how their farms were performing, grants from the government, employment issues, and all of the myriad concerns of a large estate. Sir Peter didn't always immediately reply, which frustrated Rosanna as she chased her father with follow-up emails, but he generally agreed with what his daughter suggested in the end—just as he tended to agree with all of Jenny's suggestions, Tanika realized.

Sir Peter wasn't quite the dominating force in the family that she'd at first presumed.

The only active lead that digital forensics had so far developed came from one of Sir Peter's messaging apps. They'd found four messages that had arrived the week before Christmas, but the original messages had all been deleted by Sir Peter, along with his replies. It was still possible to see the date and time that the messages and replies had been sent, but Tanika found the secrecy out of keeping with Sir Peter's other interactions, in which he was always open—sometimes gushingly so—and quite happy to be indiscreet and at times downright bitchy. What was so sensitive about this particular exchange that meant it had to be deleted? Tanika knew it would be nigh-on impossible to get the messaging company to reveal the content of the messages, so she'd tasked one of her team with identifying the owner of the phone number that had contacted Sir Peter those four times. Maybe knowing who had sent those messages would help her work out their contents.

As Tanika worked, she couldn't shake the feeling that Judith was right. Sir Peter's death wasn't accidental. Because of this, she'd asked for background checks to be run on Jenny Page and the rest of the family, with a particular focus on Sir Peter's son, Tristram. After all, Sir Peter believed that his son had wanted to kill him—enough to throw him out of his home, ban him from his wedding, and write a new will "for insurance," whatever that meant. Although, she had to admit, they only had the lawyer Andrew Husselbee's word that Sir Peter feared that his son wanted to kill him. They'd not found any evidence in Sir Peter's possessions—either physical or digital—that corroborated this assertion. But then, why would Andrew lie about something so important?

As for how the killer could have done it, there were two options as far as Tanika could see. The first was that the perpetrator had pushed the cabinet onto Sir Peter, locked the door on the inside, put the key into Sir Peter's pocket, and then hid in the room until the guests broke the door down and came in. This hardly seemed credible as they now had a number of witness statements who all said the room had only contained Sir Peter's body when they broke into it. Was it really possible that all of the witnesses had failed to see someone hiding in the room? But then, the other option was just as implausible because it involved the killer pushing the cabinet onto Sir Peter, leaving the room, locking the door from the outside, and then somehow getting the key through the locked door and into Sir Peter's pocket.

This made Tanika wonder if there was perhaps a third option. Had someone made a copy of the key? It was hard to imagine who would have had the skill to copy an iron key like the one to Sir Peter's study door. She imagined it was too old-fashioned for a high street key-cutting shop. Nonetheless, Tanika had instructed an officer to make inquiries at all of the key-cutting shops and ironmongers in a fifty-mile radius of Marlow. Had they ever made a copy of the key? She had also asked a specialist forensic locksmith to take apart the lock from the study door and get all of the dust, rust, and loose flakes of metal inside it analyzed. Any copy of the original key would have been made out of modern metal, and there was every chance that some of that metal would have flaked off when it was used in the old lock. Certainly, if there were any flakes of modern metal in the lock mechanism, it would be hard to explain considering that the family was saying that there was only one very old key that would fit.

Tanika's phone rang. The caller display said "Dad," and her hand hovered over the answer icon. Ever since her mum had died following a stroke seven years before, her dad had come to lean more and more on his only daughter, even though he had two sons who could also help out. But her dad took the view that it was a daughter's job to look after her ailing parents. And there was no doubt her father was ailing. His memory had been on the slide for years, but it was when Tanika had recently visited and found the flat covered in Post-it Notes with messages written to himself that she realized she had to act before it was too late. She'd suggested that her dad sell his house and move into assisted living, but he'd said no. She'd suggested an occupational therapist advise him on how to future-proof his home, but he'd said no to that as well. She'd found a carer to come in for an hour every morning. No, again. In fact, anything that changed his life even one iota was unacceptable as far as he was concerned. And that had increasingly included even talking about whether or not he was suffering at all from memory loss. Tanika had of course offered to take him to the hospital for testing—it had been the first thing she'd suggested—but her dad had said no.

In the meantime, he had taken to calling Tanika each day to help him sort out the minor inconveniences of his life—and often many times throughout the day as he didn't always remember having spoken to her earlier on.

Tanika wasn't in the mood to answer the call, and she very definitely didn't have the time to answer the call.

She answered the call.

"Dad," she said.

"What am I having for dinner?"

"I'm at work."

"The fridge is empty."

"Oh, okay, then how about you go out and get something?"

"You know I can't cook."

"It doesn't have to be fancy. Just a nice ready meal from the supermarket."

"They're too small. I'm still hungry when I've eaten them. And they taste of plastic."

Tanika decided that she might as well offer up the inevitable end point to the conversation. It would at least truncate the call.

"How about I pick something up for you on the way home?"

"Would you do that for me?"

"I'm more than happy to."

"A nice piece of fish. I need to keep up my omega-three. That's what you're always telling me."

"Then I'll do you some fish."

After negotiating with her father over what fish would be acceptable, and agreeing she'd check the color of the fish's eyes to make sure it was fresh, Tanika finally hung up.

She found herself staring at nothing for a few moments.

Tanika startled from her reverie as the door banged open and a man in his late fifties walked confidently into the room, wearing a smart gray suit. He was broad in the beam, had a rugby player's broken nose, and a buzz cut of gray hair. It took Tanika a while to register who it was.

"Sir?" she said, rising from her chair.

The man in front of her was Detective Inspector Gareth Hoskins. It was only because he'd been signed off sick the year before that Tanika had been able to lead the murder cases the previous summer. Since then, he'd remained "off sick," and she'd remained acting senior investigating officer.

"Detective Sergeant," Gareth said in a friendly manner that nonetheless reminded Tanika of their relative ranks.

"What are you doing here?"

"This is my office."

It was true. Tanika had been using DI Hoskins's office since she'd taken over.

"And I'll be needing it back. The super has assigned the Bailey case to me. I'll be SIO from now on. But don't worry, you'll still be a very important member of the team. I'd like you to work as my document handler. Can you be out of here in half an hour?"

Tanika looked at the crayon-and-pen drawings taped to the window that her daughter Shanti had made for her and the framed pictures of her, her husband, and daughter on the desk. This had been her home from home for a year.

"Of course, sir."

"Great stuff," DI Hoskins said, heading back to the door, before turning back to look at her.

"It's good to be back," he said with a smile.

The smile didn't reach his eyes.

Chapter 12

THE NEXT MORNING, JUDITH LED Suzie and Becks into her sitting room, where she'd laid out a pot of tea and three cups and saucers. Becks had brought a lemon drizzle cake that was still warm from her oven, and, as she put it down on Judith's card table, her eyes were drawn, as they always were, to the one pane of glass that was noticeably more see-through and flatly clear—the glass that had been replaced after being shot out by a bullet the year before.

"The cake's nothing special," she said as she handed out portions to Suzie and Judith.

"If you made it, I'm sure it's delicious," Judith said.

"Aren't you having any?" Suzie asked Becks.

"Just watching my weight," Becks said with a tight smile.

Suzie looked at her friend and realized that she did indeed look even more trim than normal.

"I don't know anyone else who could lose weight over Christmas," Suzie said, and then she remembered what Judith had said at the party. "In fact, Judith was saying how great you're looking, and I agree with her."

"You really think so?" Becks said.

"And look at that nice new ring Colin got for you."

"What ring?"

"The sapphire ring," Suzie said, indicating Becks's ring. "It is real, is it?"

"Oh yes, it's real," Becks said, and hid her hand in her lap. "It's nothing."

Suzie and Judith shared a glance. Why was Becks suddenly being so coy?

"Colin did buy it for you?" Suzie asked.

"Of course he did; who else would buy me expensive jewelry?" Becks said, but it was clear to Judith and Suzie that she was lying. "Anyway," she said, turning to Judith and trying to move the conversation on, "why did you want to meet up?"

"Good question," Judith said, also deciding to protect Becks's privacy. "I just wanted to know if you'd both help me."

"With what?" Suzie asked.

"With the Sir Peter Bailey case."

"Of course! Sorry, that was a bit dense of me. Sure. I'm in."

"Becks?"

Becks paused for barely a second.

"Definitely," she said. "When I can, though. I've still got responsibilities in the parish. And the kids need me. And on Tuesdays, my friend Zoë wants me to help run a protest choir—"

"But you'll help?" Judith said, wanting to foreclose on what she knew would otherwise be a never-ending list of Becks's responsibilities.

"Oh yes," Becks said.

"Bravo!" Judith said, delighted.

"Although, I bet you've worked up a few theories already," Suzie said with a chuckle. "Haven't you?"

"You know what? I think I've done a bit better than that," Judith said, taking hold of the little key she wore on a chain around her neck.

Suzie's and Becks's eyes darted to the door in the corner of the room that was locked by a thick padlock. They'd discovered the year before that Judith had somewhat overreacted after her husband died in suspicious circumstances—*very* suspicious circumstances as it happened—by starting to collect all of the local newspapers. Before too long she'd become a hoarder of all of the printed materials she could lay her hands on, from parish newsletters to national broadsheets.

Over the autumn, Becks had worked on Judith, saying she should get rid of her dusty library of bone-dry papers, not least because they were a fire hazard. Then, in the week between Christmas and new Year, Judith announced that she was ready to have a bit of a cleanup. There were two rooms to her secret archives, and while Judith wouldn't countenance touching the further room—it was where all of the oldest documents from the time of her husband's death in the 1970s were stored—she knew that the nearer room was mostly full of terrible tat from the last decade or so. This room wasn't her "holy of holies" at all; it was more the by-product of a personality trait she'd allowed to get out of hand. And it was this nearer room, this altogether "safer" room, that Judith had agreed to let Becks help her clear.

Becks had pounced, ordering containers, builder's masks, a job lot of hoover bags, and whole shopping trolleys of cleaning equipment. But the task hadn't gone quite as well as Becks had hoped. Judith had allowed them to start pulling down the towers of newspapers that reached almost to the ceiling, and she'd also agreed to empty the floor-to-ceiling shelves that were just as stuffed with yellowing papers, but, during the process, Judith had become increasingly withdrawn. By the end of the first day, they'd cleared most of the papers from one end of the first room, but Judith announced that she'd had enough and she didn't want them finishing the job. In fact, she wanted Becks to leave. At once, as it happened. Becks had tried to push back, but Judith wouldn't budge. She wanted Becks to leave, and she didn't want anyone touching the room anymore.

She hadn't let either of her friends into the locked rooms since.

But now, as Suzie and Becks followed Judith to the padlocked door, they shared a glance, both wondering the same thing. Had Judith started hoarding again?

Judith unlocked the padlock and pushed the door open. Going in, Becks was relieved to see that the half of the room that she'd cleared with Judith was still as clear as she remembered—although that wasn't quite true, she realized, as she could see bits of paper and what looked like bright-red string attached to the empty bookshelves.

"Oh, my god, it's just like the movies!" Suzie said as she saw what Judith had done.

"Is that wool?" Becks asked, amazed.

There was a large map of Marlow stuck to the wall, with photos and printouts of Sir Peter and his family pinned to the side, and a spiderweb of red wool running from each pinned family photo to pins that marked locations on the map.

Judith had created a homemade police incident board.

"Where did you get the photos?" Becks asked.

"It's amazing what you can find on the internet," Judith said proudly.

"And you've got the clues as well," Suzie said, indicating an A4 sheet with "Leads" written on it, underneath which there was a photo of an olive oil can, another of a wellington boot's tread, and some clip art of a last will and testament.

"This is like a parlor game," Becks said excitedly. "What story can you make from an olive oil can with no fingerprints on it, a split welly boot, and a missing will?"

"A story that ends in murder," Suzie said darkly as she inspected the faces of the family. "So what do you reckon?"

"Well," Judith said, "I think we can all agree Tristram's our—oh, what's the word?"

"I don't know," Suzie said.

"Helen Mirren played her on the television."

"The Queen?" Becks asked, confused.

"No, of course, not the Queen—prime suspect, that's it! Tristram's our prime suspect."

"Damned right he is," Suzie agreed. "He argued with his dad beforehand."

"And let's not forget, his father already thought he was trying to kill him."

"Which is why he wrote a new will."

"A will that's now gone missing," Judith said. "Meaning the old will is still valid, the one where Tristram inherits everything. So, that's plenty of motive right there."

"But we were all with Tristram outside when the cabinet fell over," Becks said. "He can't be our killer."

"Then who can it have been?" Suzie asked. "Everyone was out in the garden with us."

"They weren't, you know," Judith said. "Jenny was also inside the house at the time. Although I take Becks's point that I don't quite see how she could have been pushing a cabinet onto her betrothed downstairs at the same time as she was upstairs."

"And I'll tell you what else," Suzie said. "There's no way a bride would kill her groom the night before her wedding. Not when that marriage was about to make her rich."

"And not just rich," Becks added. "Also a Lady. As soon as she married Sir Peter's, she'd have become Lady Bailey."

"I agree," Judith said. "All of which suggests to me that there must have been a third person in the house when Sir Peter died. Someone we don't know about. Who was in the study with Sir Peter."

"And who pushed the cabinet onto him," Suzie said.

"Before then getting out of the locked room," Becks added.

"Yes, that part of the story is the hardest to explain," Judith conceded. "But the alternative is that the cabinet fell over by its own accord, and I find that just as hard to believe. So I'm suggesting we find out who could have done it and see if we can't work out the how of it as we go along. And I know exactly where we should start if we're saying someone else was in the study with him. His firstborn, Rosanna. She says she was at the party with the rest of us when Sir Peter was killed. But she was wearing a bright-red coat, and I don't remember seeing it anywhere beforehand. Did either of you?"

Becks and Suzie both agreed they didn't recall seeing anyone wearing a red coat at the party.

"And there's something else," Judith continued. "When I asked Rosanna to name who appeared at the upstairs window just after the crash, she eventually named Jenny, but there was something not quite right about her answer. She's hiding something, if you ask me."

"Like the fact that she was actually in Sir Peter's study pushing the cabinet onto him?" Suzie asked.

"Exactly!" Judith said. "Because I keep thinking about Sir Peter's phone call to me. He was ringing because he thought his life was in danger. I'm sure of it. Which means, as far as I'm concerned, he was asking me to investigate if he suddenly died in suspicious circumstances. And I think we should accept the case. Even though our client's dead. Don't you?"

Chapter 13

"I DON'T UNDERSTAND," JENNY SAID, as she led Judith, Becks, and Suzie through to the kitchen of White Lodge. "Peter rang you yesterday morning?"

Judith looked at the younger woman and saw that she seemed even more absent than she had been the night before. It was like she'd completely withdrawn or was processing information much more slowly than everyone else.

"Sir Peter wanted me at the party for a reason, and I think it's like your lawyer Andrew was saying last night. He feared for his life."

"That's not possible."

"And yet, I'm sorry to say, here we are."

"You really think someone did this to him?"

"I think it's a strong possibility. And I should warn you, the police are going to think you're involved."

Jenny's mouth opened in surprise.

"How can they think that? I loved him, I was going to marry him, he was…" Jenny subsided into a kitchen chair.

"I know," Becks said in full "vicar's wife" mode, "how about I make us all a nice cup of tea?"

Becks went over to the cupboards, effortlessly divining where all the cups were and which of the very many doors opened onto a fridge so she could get the milk.

Judith sat down next to Jenny.

"I'm sorry to ask," Judith said, "but do you know of anyone who might have wished Sir Peter harm?"

"No, of course not."

"What about Rosanna?" Suzie asked.

Jenny shook her head. "No. She comes across as a bit cold at times, but that's just because Peter was so much larger than life—and Tristram so emotional—she plays her cards close to her chest. But she's been a rock to Peter. And me. I don't know what I would have done without her."

"How do you mean?"

"She runs the family estate. She's brilliant at it. But she also helps out with running the house. She's wonderful, really."

"Like making a pesto and pasta lunch for everyone yesterday?" Judith asked.

"That's typical of her," Jenny said with a sad smile. "She's so smart. Always one step ahead. I hadn't thought to eat anything, I was just running around, so stressed. So full of myself. So self-absorbed."

"You were the bride," Becks said kindly. "It's your job to be self-absorbed."

"But can you tell me," Judith asked, "how did Rosanna get on with Sir Peter?"

"There were the odd tensions of course, but nothing serious."

"What sort of tensions?"

"It was always business, never personal. It never affected their relationship. But Peter wasn't great at forward planning, he just liked spending his cash on having a good time. Or on his friends. It's why I loved him. He was impetuous."

"That was a problem?"

"Rosanna's so careful, always counting the pennies. And I don't want you to get the wrong idea. Peter did nothing to endanger the family business. He just wanted to spend his income on having fun, and Rosanna wanted him to invest. He said we had more money than we could spend in a lifetime, what was the point?"

Becks came over with a steaming mug of tea that she handed to Jenny.

"I've put in a couple of teaspoons of sugar."

"Thank you."

"Can I ask?" Judith said. "You were originally hired as Sir Peter's nurse?"

Jenny smiled at the memory.

"That's right. Although we actually first met in Florence, in Italy."

"You did? Were you on holiday?"

"Hardly. Back in the day, I'd trained as a nurse. But the NHS was too tough. It was crazy. In my late twenties, I left the world of hospitals and waiting lists and joined an agency who match nurses with wealthy clients who needed live-in help. So, the year before last, I was working for a client who had houses in London, Paris, and Florence. She was in her eighties, lived on her own, and was really quite frail. I was her live-in nurse, although it wasn't just about the blood pressure checks and making sure she was taking her pills. It never is, really. I was also her friend. Someone she could talk to."

"And play cards with, I'd imagine," Judith said with a smile, remembering how she'd similarly looked after her great-aunt Betty for many years.

"That's it. She was a demon at gin rummy. So that's what I was doing in Florence—having a great time, if I'm honest. But when I had any time off, I was always on my own. And getting attention from men. Not because they were attracted to me, I don't think; they just wanted to talk to me. Or ask me if I was lost. You know what it's like."

The women shared a moment. They all knew what it was like.

"So when this older guy started talking to me in a bar, I just thought he was another pest. A man who thought he had a right to talk to me because I was on my own."

"What was he doing in Florence?"

"Peter told me he was there to find his son. Tristram's an actor, you see, and he'd been doing a play in Florence. But he'd started having an affair with one of the cast members and was refusing to go back to the UK. So Peter had come out to Florence to track him down before he burned through any more of his money. That's what Peter told me. Then, when I mentioned I was a nurse, that was all he wanted to talk about. He said he'd just been diagnosed with type two diabetes and he needed to turn his life around, healthwise. I tried explaining to him that it needn't be such a limiting disease, but he wasn't having any of it. He said that once he'd found Tristram and got him back home, he'd need a professional to take him in hand and train him." Jenny paused in her story as she remembered the encounter. "As I say, I didn't think much of him at the time, but I gave him the details of my agency in case he wanted to hire a nurse. I was just being polite, really."

"A couple of weeks later, he rang the agency and asked me to be assigned to him. I don't know why. I hadn't been particularly friendly to him when we'd met. Far from it, in fact. But he told the agency he wouldn't take no for an answer, and the thing is, the woman I was working for had realized she needed more help than I could offer. She'd decided to go into a nursing home. So I was coming up to the end of my contract with her. In the end, it was easy for me to say yes. Work is work."

"When was this?" Judith asked.

"The year before last. And then I started working for Peter last February. If I'm honest, I didn't warm to him. Not at first. He was exactly how I thought he'd be. Port and cheese after every meal, calling women 'fillies'— never happier than when he was shooting pheasants with the other land-owners in the area. All male, of course. And everything was a joke to him, nothing was serious. He was a nightmare, actually. Wouldn't take his meds, wouldn't look after his health. Just like he said he'd be."

"What changed?"

"I don't know, but, when you're a live-in nurse, you can't be around someone that much without them revealing their true selves to you. And I realized that all of Peter's bluster was just that—bluster. Underneath all that confidence was someone who… It's hard to explain, but I don't think he was actually that confident at all."

"Why was that do you think?"

"I think it's something to do with growing up with a fortune to inherit and nothing to aim for. Life's not worth living if there isn't a bit of a struggle, don't you think? And the thing is, there was a far more loving side to him I got to see. He adores his children."

"Even Tristram?" Judith asked.

"Even Tristram."

"That's not how it's appeared to us."

"They're too similar, that's the problem with them both. Passionate, too prone to fly off the handle. But I could see how much it upset Peter. He knew his relationship with Tristram was broken, but he didn't know how to fix it."

"According to Andrew Husselbee, it was more than broken. Did Sir Peter really not mention to you that he thought Tristram wanted him dead?"

"He didn't, and I'm trying not to feel betrayed, if I'm honest. If only he'd told me what was going on, perhaps I could have helped mend things. It wasn't like Peter to keep secrets from anyone, let alone me. Why didn't he tell me?"

They all heard a noise from the direction of the door. Judith held up her finger for them all to be quiet, but there was no further noise, so she indicated to Suzie to keep talking and started tiptoeing toward the door.

"You're right," Suzie said, trying to keep the conversation going. "It makes no sense he didn't tell you."

Judith yanked the door open, and a startled Tristram fell a few steps into the room.

When he straightened up, he looked both embarrassed and furious at the same time—and a touch confused, Judith saw. She realized that maybe he wasn't quite as bright as all that.

"Do you make a habit of listening at doors?" she asked.

"When they belong to me," Tristram said, having recovered some of his poise, "I think I can listen at whatever door I want. I only came to find Jenny to ask her when she's leaving."

Jenny didn't seem to understand the question.

"This is my house now," Tristram said. "So when are you going?"

The women were outraged.

"Her fiancée died yesterday," Becks said.

"Yeah. I know. He was my dad. But it means the house is mine, and I want her gone."

"You've made a fast recovery," Suzie said.

"What's that?"

"Last night you were all cut up. You seemed to have got over your dad's death quick enough."

"You don't have the first idea what I'm going through," Tristram said dismissively.

"It's not your house," Judith said, interrupting. "You've not inherited anything until your father's estate clears probate, which will take months. And anyway, what makes you think you've inherited his house?"

"The oldest male always inherits in the Bailey family. Always has done. Since the seventeenth century."

"Until your father wrote a new will last month."

"Yeah well, that's what the lawyer's saying. Doesn't mean it's true."

As Tristram spoke, Judith reached into her handbag and pulled out her tin of travel sweets.

"Then can I ask you a question?" she asked, picking out a dusty lemon sweet. "Why exactly did your father throw you out of the house at the beginning of December?"

Judith popped the sweet into her mouth, knowing her casual manner was irritating the hell out of Tristram.

"Isn't it obvious?" he said, his right hand clenching into a fist. "We had an argument."

"What was it about?"

"I don't have to tell you."

"You don't have to, but it's a reasonable question."

"There's nothing reasonable about any of this."

"What did you and your father argue about?"

"It's none of your business, okay?" Tristram said, anger flashing. "What I did with Dad was between him and me—what are you even doing here?"

"We're here as Jenny's guests," Suzie said, stepping up to Judith's side to create a further barrier between Tristram and Jenny.

"That's right," Becks said, stepping up to join the barricade, although it was obvious from the way she hovered just behind Judith's shoulder that she was far less comfortable confronting Tristram than her two friends.

"And Jenny's asking you to leave," Judith said, putting her tin of sweets back into her handbag as though she was now finished with the conversation. "So you'd better go."

"You can't tell me what to do."

"I'd say you have two options. You can leave peacefully, or we'll phone the police and they'll make sure you leave whether you want to or not."

"Jesus!" Tristram said, but the women could see that he was buying himself time while he worked out what to do.

He turned on his heels and stormed off.

No one said anything for a few seconds, and Judith found herself remembering the boot prints Suzie had found outside the study window. They'd almost certainly been left by someone who'd been trying to spy on what was going on in the study, and here was an example of Tristram spying on them in the kitchen. Did he make a habit of eavesdropping?

"Becks," Judith said, "are you sure those boot prints outside the study were left by a woman's wellington boot?"

Becks was surprised by the question, but she gave it her full attention.

"Oh yes," she said. "The women's range of Hunter wellies have really a quite different pattern on the sole to the men's range."

"So it was definitely a woman outside the study?"

"Unless Tristram was wearing a pair of women's wellies," Suzie offered, realizing where Judith's mind had taken her.

"Is that even possible?" Judith asked.

"I suppose it depends on how small his feet are," Becks said.

"What are you talking about?" Jenny asked.

Looking at Jenny, Judith was reminded that Sir Peter's bedroom had a window directly above the study window and the shrubbery where they'd found the footprints—and that Jenny had been in the room just before the cabinet was pushed onto Sir Peter.

"You know when you went upstairs after you argued with Tristram?" Judith asked. "Did you see anyone in the garden to the side of the house?"

"No," Jenny said. "I didn't look out of that window."

"Are you sure?" Judith pressed. "It's possible there was someone hiding in the bushes right below your bedroom window."

"I didn't see anyone," Jenny said, but the women could see that there was something she wasn't saying.

Judith and her friends exchanged glances. What was this?

"Look," Jenny said, "I shouldn't be embarrassed about this, but the thing is, I didn't look out of any of the windows in the bedroom because I'd gone there to have a cigarette. I know I shouldn't smoke, and I don't really—it's

Peter, he got me back into it—but every now and then I crumble. Like yesterday. After Tristram had humiliated me in front of everyone, I knew Peter had left a packet of cigarettes on the mantelpiece in our bedroom. So that's why I went upstairs. I was having a secret ciggie."

"It's not your fault what happened to him," Becks said.

"I'm his nurse, I'm supposed to keep him safe."

"But you can't be expected to be with him twenty-four hours a day."

"And you can't change the past," Judith said with a world-weary sigh. "You just can't. However," she said, geeing herself up, "you *can* change the future, and you should know you've nothing to worry about from Tristram. He can't throw you out of the house. It still belongs to Sir Peter until probate is cleared. Which means you can stay here."

"I reckon we have to find the new will," Suzie said. "I mean, what if he left the house to you? Or a good chunk of cash? Have you really no idea where it is?"

"I didn't even know he'd made a new will," Jenny said. "He never told me."

"Then we need to start looking for it," Judith said breezily. "After all, there's a moral issue here. The will represents Sir Peter's last wishes. You could argue that the best way of honoring his life is that we do everything in our power to try and find it."

Jenny went over to the sink and turned the tap on. She got herself a glass, filled it with water, took a sip, turned back to the others, and looked at them.

"You're right," she said carefully. "I think we should try and find his will."

Judith smiled.

"Then I suggest we pull the house apart until we find it."

Chapter 14

JUDITH, BECKS, SUZIE, AND JENNY started their search for the missing will in Sir Peter's study. The window frames and ironwork on the door had graphite smudges from where the police had dusted for fingerprints. It was the same with the wooden cabinet that had fallen onto Sir Peter and killed him. In front of it, the rug was still covered in laboratory equipment and smashed glass from the various jars and flasks that had broken when the cabinet had fallen over.

"Are you okay doing this?" Becks asked Jenny.

"Not really," Jenny said, but then the women saw her stiffen her resolve. "Peter's will wasn't in his safe; it's got to be in the house somewhere."

"Let us know if it gets too much," Becks said.

"So where do you recommend we start?" Suzie asked.

"Maybe with his desk. He kept a whole load of papers there."

As Jenny, Becks, and Suzie started to look through the desk, Judith went and looked at the wooden cabinet. Now it was standing up again, there was a gap between it and the wall, where it hadn't quite been returned to its original position. Judith slipped into the narrow space. The back was covered in dust and old cobwebs, and there was an old metal hasp attached near the top. Turning around, she saw that a corresponding iron hook was buried deep in the wall. It only stuck out a couple of inches, but it looked like a serious piece of ironmongery, and Judith could see that it was aligned to hook into the hasp on the back of the cabinet. It made sense that such a massive piece of furniture had an extra piece of security to make sure it didn't topple over.

The fact that the hook hadn't been ripped out of the wall, or the hasp pulled from the back of the cabinet, suggested to Judith that before the murder, someone—or some people, considering the cabinet's weight—had lifted it up just enough to get it off its restraining hook.

Judith put her palms against the cabinet's dusty back, pushed, and was surprised when she felt it tip forward a tiny bit. Looking up, she realized that with the heavy wooden carvings across the top of it, the cabinet was top heavy. It would still have taken quite a bit of strength, almost certainly more than she possessed, but she no longer doubted it would have been possible for someone to push it onto Sir Peter.

Judith stepped out from behind the cabinet.

"There's a hook that the cabinet's supposed to be attached to," she said.

"It's been removed?" Suzie asked.

"No, but someone detached it. Maybe years ago. Maybe only recently. Jenny, is the cabinet normally secured to the wall?"

"I've no idea," Jenny said. "I've never looked. It's just lived against that wall. Sorry."

"I suppose it doesn't matter. But seeing as the cabinet was unhooked, I'm sure someone strong would have been able to push the whole thing over. Although, can I ask? Why does Sir Peter even have a cabinet of science equipment? I thought he was a country squire."

"It's something to do with Peter's father," Jenny said. "He set up a medical company after the Second World War. He invented an X-ray machine or something."

"Which explains the X-ray images behind the desk," Judith said.

"That's right. I think they're of Sir Peter's father and his business partner. They were the first X-ray images their machines took."

While Judith and Jenny were talking, Becks drifted over to the smashed lab equipment on the floor in front of the cabinet.

"Is magnesium safe?" she asked. "Or magnesium tape, I should say."

Becks indicated a tall glass jar on the rug that had a handwritten label on it that said "Magnesium Tape."

"Magnesium's entirely stable," Judith said. "As long as you don't set it on fire. Then it burns like a firework."

"I don't understand," Suzie said, going over to her friend. "The jar's empty. What does it matter what the label on it says?"

"I was worried it might have left a residue behind," Becks said. "Or poisonous...something. I wanted to be careful."

"Why's it of interest?" Jenny asked, coming over to join the other women.

"The jar hasn't smashed."

"So?" Suzie said.

"Well, it's just that every other glass object in the cabinet smashed when it fell to the floor. But not this one jar. It just struck me as odd, that's all."

"You're right," Judith said as she took in the smashed glass and lab equipment that was spread out on the carpet. The mess covered a rectangular area that matched the shape of the cabinet, and Becks's jar was the only piece of glassware that had survived the fall.

"Hold on," Judith said and looked about herself for something long and thin she could use to pick the jar up. Going to the mantelpiece, she saw a little stand made from brass that looked like it might have once held an ornament of some sort. She saw that there was an inscription on a brass plaque to "Judge Sir George Bailey, Q.C.," and a date, 1906. Seeing as the man was a judge, Judith guessed that the stand had once held a gavel.

"Is there normally a gavel here?" she asked.

Jenny came over, puzzled.

"Yes," she said. "There is. I think it belonged to one of Peter's relatives."

"Any idea where it might be?"

"No. Sorry. I don't come in here very often. This was Peter's refuge."

Judith was frustrated and went over to Sir Peter's desk. The gavel wasn't there either—it would have been ideal for what she was looking for—but there was quite a long screwdriver in a desk tidy that contained some pens and old coins.

She picked up the screwdriver and returned to the glass jar at Becks's feet. She inserted it into the jar's neck, scooped it up, and carried it over to Sir Peter's desk. She very carefully lowered the screwdriver so the jar was standing upright again.

The morning sun was streaming in through the windows, and the glass sparkled in the sunlight. In fact, Judith realized, it sparkled like it had recently been cleaned.

"Hold on," she said, as she reached into her handbag and pulled out her tin of travel sweets. Then, with the precision of a scientist working in a high-risk facility, she oh-so-carefully unscrewed the lid. Putting the lid to one side, she held the tin up to the jar and blew across the top of it—icing sugar puffing up into the sunbeam and drifting down onto the jar.

"What are you doing?" Suzie asked.

"Dusting for fingerprints," Judith said.

"With icing sugar?" Becks said.

"The glass surface is hard enough, I'm sure it will be fine. Now, isn't that interesting?" she added before moving around the table to the other side of the jar.

Judith blew dust into the sunbeam again and watched it settle on the glass.

"If I'm not mistaken, and I don't think I am, there are no fingerprints on this jar."

Judith looked over at all of the smashed glass and lab equipment on the floor.

"There are no fingerprints?" Jenny asked, nonplussed.

"Fingerprints last a long time on glass," Judith said. "For years."

"You know that?"

"Old episodes of *Murder, She Wrote*," Judith said apologetically.

"Maybe it's just been cleaned really well?" Suzie said.

"I don't know," Jenny said. "That doesn't sound right. I never come in here to clean, and I'm not sure Patricia does, either. She's our cleaner. Peter didn't like people interfering with his things. But it doesn't make sense it would have no fingerprints on it, does it? Even if you cleaned the jar, it would still have your prints on from when you put it back on the shelf, wouldn't it?"

"That's my thinking as well," Judith agreed.

"Can I see?" Suzie said as she approached, but she bumped into the corner of the desk, the bottle lurched and fell off the table, smashing into dozens of pieces on the floor.

"Oh god, I'm so sorry!" Suzie said, horrified by her clumsiness.

"That was evidence, Suzie," Becks said like a parent telling off a child. "You can't go galumphing around crime scenes."

"Galumphing?"

"You know what I mean."

The women looked at the smashed glass on the floor.

"You know what?" Suzie said, deciding she'd try and save the situation. "I might have done us all a favor."

"How?" Becks asked.

"I've just proved what you were saying. That glass jar should have smashed when it fell from the cabinet."

"You're right," Judith said. "The glass was just as weak as it looked. It couldn't wait to smash, could it?"

Judith looked back at the cabinet and the shards of smashed glass on the floor. Why had this one jar survived when the others hadn't?

"I think we need to tell the police about this," Judith said.

"You mean that I broke it?" Suzie asked, worried.

"No, don't worry about that. But we need to tell Tanika that there was a glass jar that's been wiped clean of fingerprints that didn't smash when it fell from the cabinet. It could be important."

While Becks, Suzie, and Jenny carried on the search for the will elsewhere in the house, Judith pulled out her phone and called Tanika. Once she'd explained about the glass jar, Tanika wasn't sure she'd heard correctly.

"You're saying there's an important bit of evidence, but you smashed it?"

"There's really no need to focus on the negatives. And it doesn't much matter. Whatever fingerprints were on the jar—or weren't—will still be there. It's just in a few pieces, that's all. And while you're about it, I think you should dust all of the equipment and glass that fell from the cabinet. I think there's a pattern here. Remember how the olive oil can also didn't have any fingerprints on it? Our killer is very careful to make sure they don't leave their fingerprints behind at the scene."

"What are you even doing in Sir Peter's study?"

"Jenny's asked us to help her find the missing will. And I know you'll say we shouldn't interfere, but we're not interfering. We're helping a friend."

"Don't worry, we need that will found, I don't mind who finds it. And thanks for the tip-off about the fingerprints. I'll get an officer sent down to collect the evidence."

Judith wasn't sure she'd heard correctly.

"You *don't* mind us investigating?"

"But you're not investigating, are you? It's like you said. You're just helping your friend. As long as you call in any clues you stumble across, you're just helping us with our inquiries."

Judith thanked Tanika and hung up the call, feeling slightly uneasy. Since when did Tanika not mind them investigating one of her cases? It was very strange indeed.

Putting the thought to one side, Judith crossed the hallway and found Becks, Suzie, and Jenny in the house's boot room. There was a row of rain-coats on pegs running down one side, with various types of walking and welly boots underneath, and two porcelain butler sinks on the other side.

"So what have you got?" she asked as she entered.

"Jealousy," Becks said from the end of the row of boots.

"I'm with Becks," Suzie agreed. "To have this sort of space. A whole room just for your coats and boots."

"I know," Jenny said, looking about herself in appreciation. "I had nothing when I was growing up. Less than nothing. I told myself I didn't need anything. And I don't, really I don't. But it's been so nice not to worry. To feel secure for once."

A wave of grief hit Jenny.

"Do you want to take a break?" Becks asked.

"Yeah, I think I do. I need to get away. Take a drive. Clear my head."

"Do you want one of us to come with you?"

"No, that's okay. You stay here and keep looking for the will."

"Is there anywhere you think we should be looking in particular?" Judith asked.

"No, search everywhere you can think of. Nothing's off-limits. Pull the house apart. I want Peter's will found."

Once Jenny had left, Becks updated Judith on where they had gotten to in their search.

"There's no will in this room," she said. "We've looked in all the cupboards and coat pockets."

"And in the boots," Suzie added.

"I suppose there isn't a size seven wellington boot with a cut across the left sole?" Judith asked.

"There aren't any women's Hunter wellies here," Becks said. "Which is hardly a surprise."

"Why?" Suzie asked.

"Hunters stopped being fashionable for women at least ten years ago."

"Wait," Suzie said, wanting to check. "Are you saying there's a fashion in wellington boots?"

"Of course."

"Are you serious?"

"I don't know why it should be such a surprise. There's a fashion in everything."

"So what's the current fashion boot?"

"That's easy. 'Le Chameau Vierzonord.'"

"Sorry, what?"

"It's what the Duchess of Cambridge wears."

Suzie took a moment to take this on board.

"I've got so many questions," she said. "But I don't reckon I want to hear any of the answers. But to answer your question, Judith, none of these wellingtons have a cut across the left sole."

After a few more minutes of searching, the women decided they should look elsewhere and moved on to the kitchen. After nearly half an hour of looking, they once again concluded there was no will stuffed behind the tins of plum tomatoes or in the glass jars of pasta. It was the same in the sitting room. They found no secret envelope under the cushions or behind the oil paintings on the wall.

"Anyone get the impression we're wasting our time?" Suzie said.

"Rubbish," Judith said. "Every time we finish a room, we're learning something new."

"Yeah. The will's still missing."

"Let's try upstairs," Judith said. "I suggest we start with Tristram's room."

It was easy for the women to work out which bedroom had belonged to Tristram before he'd been thrown out of the house. The walls were covered in posters for theatre shows, and there were shelves of books on acting and published plays.

As the women started their search, Judith found herself looking at the theatre posters. She found one for a show called *Savonarola* that had Tristram's face front and center, and then the faces of four other actors slightly behind. The text below the image explained that the play was to be performed at the British Council in Florence. So this was the theatre show that Tristram had been doing when he bunked off with one of his cast and refused to come home?

Judith looked at the faces on the poster, all of them men. Had Tristram's affair been with one of the men in the cast, or was there a woman connected with the production who wasn't on the poster? Judith looked at the other names listed and saw that the director and producer of the show were also men. She decided to file the information away for another time.

"There's no will here, either," Suzie said, exasperated.

"Then let's move on," Judith said. "We can't give up now."

"We can, you know. We could give up and go for a nice cup of tea somewhere. And a slice of cake."

"But we promised Jenny we'd look everywhere," Becks said. "We can't let her down. Come on," she said as she went to the door. "I think we should look in Sir Peter and Jenny's bedroom next."

But it was just the same in that room as well. They looked under the bed and mattress, in the en suite bathroom, and Suzie even looked up the chimney of the little fireplace in the corner of the room.

"If there's a will hidden up the chimney," Becks said, "it will have burned ages ago."

"Not if no one's lit a fire since Sir Peter died," Suzie said, impressed with her deductive skills.

"Well, is the will up there?"

"As it happens, no," Suzie admitted after the briefest of glances up the flue.

As Becks and Suzie bickered, Judith remembered that Jenny had said she'd come to the room to have a cigarette. She went over to the mantelpiece and saw an old packet of cigarettes with a cheap lighter sitting on top of it.

"You could actually try looking," Suzie said to Judith testily.

"No, of course," Judith said. "Just thinking about what happened."

Judith looked about herself and decided to search a nearby wardrobe.

"The sooner we get to finish in this room, the sooner we get to go home," Suzie said.

"We still have to be thorough," Becks said. "Because if we prove there's no will in the house, then that's useful information. Isn't it?"

"You reckon?"

"And even if we don't uncover the will," Judith said as she looked inside the wardrobe, "who knows what else we'll find of interest."

Her tone caught her friends' attention.

"You've got something?" Becks asked.

Judith bent down and picked something up from the wooden floor at the back of the wardrobe.

"What is it?" Suzie asked.

"It's funny because I thought it was odd at the time."

"What was?"

"The cuff to Rosanna's coat."

"What about it?"

"It's just that she was so well turned out. Not a hair out of place. A brand-new coat. And yet, she was missing one of the buttons from her cuff."

"So?" Suzie asked, having lost the thread of the conversation some time ago.

"The buttons on the rest of the coat were gold and in the shape of a rope knot. So, in answer to your question, seeing as she lost a coat button that day, what I'd like to know is, how come I've just found it on the floor of the wardrobe in Sir Peter and Jenny's bedroom?"

Judith opened her hand, and they could all see a gold button in the center of her palm.

Chapter 15

THE BAILEY ESTATE OFFICE WAS in one of the offices of the Old Barrel Store, a redbrick former brewery just off Marlow High Street. Rosanna was surprised to see Judith and her friends at the door but showed them through to a dark office that had a couple of leather armchairs by a fireplace, oil paintings and old maps of the family's holdings on the walls, and a large desk that was laden with piles of paperwork. In many respects, it reminded Judith of a tidier version of Sir Peter's study.

"I'm sorry I can only give you a few minutes," Rosanna said, returning to her desk. "I'm due in Hambleden in half an hour. I'm meeting a planning officer about some building work."

"Don't worry," Judith said, "we won't take up any more of your time than we have to. We just want to know how the button from your red coat ended up in your father's wardrobe in his bedroom."

As she said this, Judith dropped the gold button onto the desk.

Rosanna barely reacted.

"What's this?" Rosanna said, picking it up.

"A button from the coat you were wearing at the party."

"You're saying you found it in Father's wardrobe?"

"We did."

"You're right. It looks like the button I lost at the party. I've no idea how it ended up in the wardrobe. Are we done?"

Rosanna got up, but Suzie wasn't having any of it.

"We most certainly aren't done here," she said, taking a step toward Rosanna that could only be construed as threatening. "You were hiding in the wardrobe, weren't you? That's how it got there."

"Suzie's right," Judith added. "It's why you looked so guilty that first time we talked and I asked you who came out onto the balcony when Sir Peter died. You didn't see her from the garden, did you? You were actually in the same room as Jenny."

Having been put under pressure by Judith and Suzie in turn, Rosanna looked at Becks to see what she was going to say, and Becks shook her head apologetically, suggesting that she was as uncomfortable with the whole conversation as Rosanna was.

"There are any number of explanations for how it got there," Rosanna said carefully.

"But only one that's true," Judith said. "And you're better off telling us because if you don't, it'll be the police who'll be asking you next."

Rosanna was almost impressed.

"Are you *blackmailing* me?" Rosanna asked.

"Hardly," Judith said, fishing out her tin of travel sweets and popping the lid. "Just pointing out that we don't have to make a formal record of our conversation. Unlike the police. Seeing as I'm sure there's a perfectly innocent explanation for why you were hiding in your father and Jenny's wardrobe on the day he was killed. Travel sweet?"

Judith offered the tin to Rosanna.

"Very well," Rosanna said, ignoring the tin. "Because you're right. There's a perfectly innocent explanation. First thing you should know, I didn't mean to hide."

Judith put the lid back onto the tin.

"Of course," she agreed.

"It all stems from Father's bloody will."

"What about it?"

"I found out he'd written a new one just before Christmas."

"But I saw how you reacted when Andrew Husselbee told us about it. You acted surprised."

"Tristram's not the only actor in the family."

"How did you find out?"

"Chris told me. The gardener. He'd just cut some hedges and had started a bonfire. This was a couple of weeks before Christmas. Well, you know how a fire draws you toward it. We got chatting, and he asked me if I knew what was in Father's new will. I was shocked. It's like I told you. Father had always said he had no choice over his will. The baronetcy and the estate had descended down the male line for hundreds of years. It all had to go to Tristram. But I also knew there'd been the bust-up between Father and Tristram, so if Father had now changed his will, there was only one conclusion I could draw. He must have left some of his estate to me. Or all of it. I mean, obviously Jenny would have got her share as soon as she married Father. But this wasn't about the next few years. It was about making sure that when he and Jenny died, the will reflected the fact that I'm the only member of the family who does any bloody work around here. I deserve my share."

"Yes, Jenny said how very good you are at your job," Judith said.

"She did, did she?" Rosanna said, surprised. "I wasn't sure she'd even noticed. She was so wrapped up in Father. The point being, once I knew there was a new will out there, I couldn't stop thinking about it. And you know what it's like when you keep turning something over and over, you start going a bit mad. Before too long, I was trying to get into Father's safe whenever I visited. I knew that's where he'd have put it. Worse than that, I actually started going to White Lodge just so I could try and get into the safe.

"I tried every combination I could think of. Father's birthday, Jenny's, Tristram's, mine. Nothing worked. And it's Jenny and Father's bedroom; they were in and out of it the whole time as they prepared for the wedding. But then the day of the drinks party came along, and I knew I had another chance. I could see Father and Jenny were chatting away to friends outside, so I came into the house and headed upstairs. I'd got a list of new numbers to try on my phone, but none of them opened the safe."

"Is that so?" Judith asked pointedly.

"I didn't get into the safe that day any more than I'd done on the days before. Anyway, almost as soon as I'd started, I heard raised voices outside.

Before I knew it, I heard someone come up the stairs. I didn't dare get caught breaking into the safe—how would that have looked?—and I didn't have any time to think, so I hid in the wardrobe. And I was just in time, if you ask me. It was Jenny. I saw her as I closed the door."

"Did she see you?" Judith asked.

"No. She went straight to the fireplace. She was upset."

"Then what happened?"

"I don't know. I couldn't see. But I could hear her. I think she lit a cigarette."

"Yes, that's what she told us."

"We've known for ages she sometimes has a secret cigarette with Father."

"I don't get it," Becks said. "She was his nurse."

"I know. And she was when she first arrived. She had him keeping food diaries, cutting out the booze, and drinking these foul smoothies that seemed only to be made from kale. And it worked. He lost a load of weight, his diabetes was brought under control, it was a miracle, if you ask me. She was a force for good. But it takes a rod of iron to keep Father in check. It always does. And he's always been good at corrupting people. Getting them to have an extra glass of wine or a second helping of food. Life is for living, he'd announce to anyone who'd listen. And I don't know how it happened, but he started to slip back into his old ways, and this time Jenny seemed to let him."

"Were they dating by then?" Becks asked.

"I don't know. Looking back, I think they must have been. Once Jenny stopped being Father's nurse and became his girlfriend, she had less control over him. And he had more over her."

"So you're in the wardrobe?" Suzie said, wanting Rosanna to get back on track.

"And I'd decided I'd just step out and admit to what I'd been up to. I'm a grown woman, I shouldn't be hiding in wardrobes, but that's when I heard this almighty crash from downstairs. I dared open the door of the wardrobe a tiny crack and saw Jenny go out onto the balcony. For a split second, I considered making a run for it, but I bottled it and closed the door—and I was lucky to. As soon as I did, Jenny came back in from the balcony and ran downstairs. I had so much adrenaline going, I took a minute or two to recover. And I could hear a commotion going on elsewhere in the house. I didn't know what was going on. In the end, I left the wardrobe, came downstairs, and that's when I found out what had happened. But I suppose that's how that button ended up in the wardrobe. I must have caught it on something when I was hiding in there."

Rosanna looked at the women as though what she'd just described was all rather commonplace and boring. Judith wondered what it would take to shake Rosanna's composure. She was clearly a woman who put great store in always being in control.

But Judith couldn't help also noticing that Rosanna had just admitted that when she'd first met Judith, and acted surprised at the news that there was a new will, her reaction had been just that—an act—and it had been totally convincing, Judith knew. So why should Judith believe anything Rosanna said now?

"You really think someone did this to Father, don't you?" Rosanna asked.

"We do," Judith said.

"Does that surprise you?" Becks asked.

"Of course. Father was an old buffer. A figure of fun. Who'd want to kill him?"

"You know your dad was worried Tristram was going to kill him?" Suzie asked.

Rosanna laughed, not entirely kindly.

"That's not possible," she said. "Seriously. Tristram's always been spoiled. Flies off the handle if he doesn't get his own way, but he couldn't do that to his own father."

"How do you and your brother get on?" Becks asked.

"It's complicated," she admitted. "I love him, but he drives me to distraction. He's impatient, that's his problem. He's a pretty good actor, but he won't take the small jobs he gets offered. In small theatres around the country. Or spear carrying for bigger shows in London. He says he's better than that. And then he complains when he doesn't work."

"Does he often not work?" Becks asked.

"I don't think he's had a job in over a year."

"What does he do for money?"

"He has a small allowance from Father. And living in White Lodge always cost him nothing."

"Where's he living now?"

"With Mother. She lives in that row of terraces opposite the old Waitrose. But to answer your question, I bet Tristram would say to his cronies how he wished his father would die so he could inherit, but he wouldn't mean it. Not really. Crazy though it is to say, despite all his complaining, he loved Father."

"Jenny said they were too similar."

"Yes, we used to talk about how they were like chalk and chalk, those two. So full of themselves and yet so thin-skinned in their own way. It was a pretty toxic combination."

"Then how can you be so sure he wasn't behind your father's death?"

"Tristram doesn't have the guts."

Rosanna's answer sizzled with such anger that it gave Judith an idea.

"Is it possible he had an accomplice?" she asked. "Someone with more pluck than him, if he couldn't have done it himself?"

Rosanna look startled—guilty, almost.

"What's that?" she said, but only to stall giving an actual answer.

"There *is* someone else, isn't there?" Suzie asked, eagerly.

Rosanna wasn't sure what to say, and then the women saw her look over to the wall where there was a framed family tree written out in faded calligraphy. The names and lines of connection within the Bailey family went back hundreds of years.

Rosanna looked back at the women.

"No, there isn't," she said.

"That's not true," Suzie said, "there's someone."

"There really isn't," Rosanna said, closing her laptop and unplugging it. "Now I really have to get to this appointment. And If you're going to persist with saying Father was killed, then all I can say is that I'm sure it wasn't Tristram—or any kind of accomplice—and it very definitely wasn't me. As you've inadvertently just proven with that button, I suppose. I was in a wardrobe upstairs when that cabinet fell onto him. I suppose I should be grateful it came off," Rosanna added, picking the button up from her desk and putting it in her pocket. "It's my alibi."

Rosanna left the office, and a deeply frustrated Judith followed her out with her friends.

"The family tree won't protect you," Judith said as Rosanna started unlocking a bicycle. "All that history, and it all belongs to the men. Just as your future belongs to your brother now."

"I don't know what you're talking about," Rosanna said.

"You're the firstborn. You do all the work. But Tristram's about to become your boss. Because he's going to inherit. And he's going to want to laud it over you, isn't he? Because we both know he will. In fact, I bet he can't wait to tell you how you've been running the estate wrong all of these years. How he's going to do it all better. And this is the twist!" Judith added, surprised by a sudden insight. "He's going to mess it all up, isn't he? Because he's not like you. He's not bright. He's not hardworking. But he believes he's superior to you—a typical man."

Rosanna hesitated—once again the women could see that she was considering saying something. Privately, Judith was delighted to see that she'd finally managed to shake Rosanna out of some of her complacency.

But then the shutters came down.

"You're wrong," Rosanna said. "We're a good team, Tristram and me. We've always been a good team. We'll do a brilliant job running the estate together. Now, I've got to get to Hambleden."

And with that, Rosanna got on her bike and started to cycle away.

"Why's she protecting him?" Suzie asked.

"It makes no sense to me," Judith agreed. "There's no way he'd protect her."

Becks startled as she heard her phone trill. She got her phone out, surreptitiously checked it, flushed bright red, and slipped it back into her handbag.

"Everything okay?" Judith asked.

"Actually, there's somewhere I've got to be."

"There is?" Suzie said, picking up on her friend's embarrassment.

"It's nothing of interest. Just church business. Really quite boring, actually. But I'd better go. At once."

"Do you need any help?" Judith offered.

"No!" Becks said in a panic, before she regathered her poise. "That's very kind, but it's nothing. Although I do have to go right now. See you later."

Before she implicated herself any further, Becks headed down the high street in the direction of the vicarage.

"What was that about?" Suzie asked.

The women saw Becks carry on past the vicarage.

"Okay, so she's not going to the vicarage," Suzie said. "I suppose she'll be going into the church. Seeing as it's church business. It would make sense."

Just before Becks reached the church, she ducked down one of the little alleys that crisscrossed the town and vanished from view.

"Hold on," Suzie said and looked at Judith, knowing they were both thinking the same thing. "Where's she going?"

"I think that's a very fair question."

"We should follow her."

"What?"

"Come on, I know you want to know what's going on as much as me. Because you're right, Becks is looking different, isn't she? And she got all spooked when we asked her about her new sapphire ring. So why's she now getting mystery phone calls she can't tell us about?"

Judith bit her lip for a few seconds.

"You're right, I do, come on," she said, and headed off in pursuit, Suzie quick to follow.

When the two women reached the entrance to the alley, they skidded to a halt, took a moment to gather themselves, and then stuck their heads around the wall just in time to see Becks leave the other end and turn right. The women raced off down the alleyway as fast as they could, stopping in a thunderous halt as they reached the end. Looking around the corner once again, they saw Becks turn up a little street down the side of the Two Brewers pub.

Trying to look as invisible as possible, which, in truth, was really not very invisible at all, Judith and Suzie crossed the road and turned into the street just in time to see Becks hurry up to a terraced house. They saw her straighten her hair, steady herself, and then press the doorbell.

Soon after, the door opened, and a dark-haired man in his forties stepped out and hugged Becks, before ushering her inside. Moments later, Becks appeared at the upstairs window and closed the curtains.

Judith and Suzie looked at each other, utterly speechless.

"That's why she couldn't tell us about her new ring," Suzie eventually managed.

"I don't believe it," Judith said, but it was clear she agreed with her friend. "Not Becks."

"You mean a woman who's married to one of the most boring men in the world? Let's be honest, there's only one reason why a married woman would secretly visit a man in his home in daylight hours, go straight upstairs with him, and close the curtains so no one can look in."

Judith looked at her friend and knew she agreed.

Becks was having an affair, wasn't she?

Chapter 16

TANIKA SAT AT HER DESK in the Major Incident Room and struggled to contain her frustration. It wasn't so much that DI Hoskins had taken back his old job, although the timing was suspicious as hell as far as she was concerned. It was because she could already tell that he was losing interest in the Bailey case. Once he'd reviewed the evidence, he'd rubbed his chin in a play of weighing up the facts and then proclaimed to his team that he just didn't see how anyone could have pushed the cabinet over and then got out of a room that was locked by a key they'd found in the deceased's pocket. All Tanika's protestations that the death was still suspicious were listened to carefully—that had always been DI Hoskins's management style, listening carefully to others' opinions—and then he'd said he wasn't going to change his mind. That had also always been his management style.

It didn't help that Tanika had found no evidence that showed how the killer could have gotten out of the locked room after pushing the cabinet onto Sir Peter. All of the locksmiths her team had contacted had all said they'd not made a copy of the key to the study—and most of them said they didn't have the ability to do so anyway. It was such an old key. Even more frustratingly, when Forensics had taken the lock apart, they'd not been able to find any metal filings from a recently made key inside. All they'd found was dust, rust, and ancient iron flakes from the old key's use over the decades.

As for her new role within the team, it was hard for Tanika not to take her demotion to document handler as a personal slight. Not that it wasn't an important job—making sure all the evidence was correctly logged and linked was critically important—but the job was something of a step down for the person who'd been an acting senior investigating officer only days before.

Tanika returned to her task of tagging scans of the last six months of Sir Peter's bank statements. She knew that her personal feelings were no excuse for sloppy work, so, before she uploaded each bank statement, she ran her eye down the entries. After all, it seemed common sense to make sure they'd been correctly digitized. Sadly, apart from the fact that he banked with the Queen's banker, Coutts, Sir Peter's personal account wasn't very interesting. The balance was just over twenty thousand pounds. Sir Peter didn't spend any money on utilities or household bills—Tanika imagined there was another bank account out there that covered that—this account was just a long list of restaurant, pub, and taxi bills, Wine Society orders, and a number of payments to the Royal Automobile Club in London. No single bill was all that outrageous—until Tanika's eye was drawn to four cash withdrawals just before Christmas Day. They were each for five thousand pounds, and they'd been taken out on the 17th, 19th, 22nd, and 23rd of December.

Scrolling back through the account, Tanika saw that the balance had been just over forty thousand pounds at the beginning of December. She checked the November statement and saw that the balance had also been around the forty-thousand mark. It was the same with his October statement. In fact, Tanika was able to check the statements for the whole year, and Sir Peter's balance never dipped far below forty thousand pounds. He also never took out cash for any amount larger than a few hundred pounds.

The four trips to the bank to remove twenty thousand pounds just before Christmas were very definitely anomalous. So what had he been up to? Was it money for presents? It felt far too much, and if he'd known he'd need twenty thousand pounds in cash, why not take it out in one chunk rather in smaller withdrawals spread over a number of days?

But it was more than that, Tanika realized. There was something about the payments—or the timing of them—that resonated with her. What was it? Tanika was nothing if not methodical, so she got out her notebook and wrote down the four dates that Sir Peter had taken out the money. What was it about them that had tickled her subconscious? It was strange, she found herself thinking idly, that the first and second dates had a day in between, and then, after a gap of a couple of days, the remaining ten thousand pounds was taken out on consecutive days.

It was as she considered the consecutive dates that she realized what was troubling her, and luckily Tanika was perfectly placed to check whether she was right.

She got up the records of Sir Peter's messaging apps and opened the screenshots of the text exchange that he'd subsequently deleted. It was just as she remembered. The text of the exchanges had been deleted, but the date stamps and caller ID for the messages remained. Each message was dated the day before the days he took out each five thousand pound tranche of cash. The deleted messages had come in on the 16th, 18th, 21st, and 22nd of December, and the cash had been taken out on the 17th, 19th, 22nd, and 23rd.

It was obvious to Tanika. Someone had sent a message to Sir Peter demanding five thousand pounds—in cash—on four occasions, and Sir Peter had gone to his bank the next day, taken out the money, and then handed it over. He'd also made sure to delete the message that had asked for the money, and his reply.

Tanika remembered that when she'd been in charge of the case, she'd tasked one of her team to identify the phone number that had sent the text messages to Sir Peter's phone. When she checked the relevant record on her computer, she was pleased to see that the screengrab of the exchange now had a hypertext link embedded in it. She clicked the link and learned that the messages had been sent to Sir Peter's phone from a virtual number that was registered to a company based in Vanuatu in the South Pacific.

There was no doubt in her mind now. Whatever was going on between Sir Peter and his mystery texter was underhand at best and illegal at worst. Tanika started heading out of the Incident Room before she'd even consciously decided what she should do with this information. When she found herself arriving at DI Hoskins's office, she knocked once and entered without waiting to be called.

"Chief," she said, and then stopped as she saw that DI Hoskins was already in a meeting with their Superintendent. "Sorry for interrupting," she added.

"No, come in, Detective Sergeant," DI Hoskins said, and Tanika was reminded how welcoming her boss could be when he was in front of his superiors.

"I hope you don't mind your reassignment," the Superintendent said—a man who, to Tanika's eyes, was almost entirely defined by how tired he always looked. "I was just telling DI Hoskins how well you've kept his seat warm during his absence. I take it you'll be intending to take your inspector qualification now?"

Tanika was still trying to orient herself within the conversation.

"What's that, sir?"

"Seeing as you've been working as a DI for the last year, I hope you'll be taking the formal exam."

As it happened, Tanika hadn't given it much consideration over the last year. She'd been too busy keeping her head above water—doing as well at work as she could, helping look after her daughter, and dealing with her dad—that she'd just had a vague hope that DI Hoskins would stay "off sick" for as long as possible.

"A sentiment I'd echo," DI Hoskins said while also wanting to move the conversation on. "So, what's worth interrupting my meeting?"

Tanika explained how Sir Peter had received four text messages from what looked like a burner phone registered in Vanuatu and how Sir Peter deleted each message and his reply before then taking out five thousand pounds in cash the day afterward.

"That's not the behavior of an innocent man," she concluded.

Tanika could see the Superintendent was watching DI Hoskins for his reaction.

"I'd agree with you," DI Hoskins said, and Tanika felt a thrill of excitement. Finally, they were going to treat the case with the seriousness it deserved!

"However," he continued, "everyone's got secrets. Things they wouldn't want the wider world to know. I know I do. And even if Sir Peter was up to his neck in dodgy dealings of some kind or another, the postmortem made it clear he died when the cabinet fell onto him. There were no other toxins or substances in his body. Nothing other than some alcohol, which I don't need to remind you would have impaired his judgment. And he was found on his own in a room that was locked, the only key to that lock being found in his pocket. So, irrespective of what was going on in Sir Peter's life, how can we plausibly say he was murdered?"

"It's a suspicious death, sir."

"And that's where I have to disagree with you again. There's not much that's suspicious. A bloody great piece of furniture fell on him."

"But how did it fall over? And why at that precise moment? He was getting married the day after. And his will's still missing."

"Wills go missing all the time. And if you're so sure it was murder, how do you think the killer got out of the room afterward?"

As he spoke, DI Hoskins gave the Superintendent a conspiratorial wink that he didn't try to hide from Tanika.

Instead of losing her temper at the two men who were her immediate bosses, Tanika found herself, as she always did, hiding her fury in apparent acquiescence.

"I don't know, sir."

"The reason you don't know is because it's impossible. As you've just admitted. Now, we're stretched enough without trying to solve murders where no murder's taken place. I suggest you finish logging the necessary evidence, and then I'll find you a nice new murder case to help with."

"Yes sir," she said, and with a tight smile turned and left the room.

By the time she'd returned to her desk, Tanika knew that DI Hoskins's intransigence left only one option open for her. Because if he wasn't going to take the case seriously, then she knew three people who already did. As she contemplated what she was about to do, she couldn't stop herself from smiling. It was time for her—perfect, head girl Tanika Malik, dutiful daughter, wife, and mother—to go rogue.

Chapter 17

FOLLOWING BECKS'S CLANDESTINE ENCOUNTER WITH the middle-aged man the day before, Judith and Suzie agreed to a crash meeting at Hurley Lock. It was convenient for both of them, as Judith could walk there from her house, and Suzie could take some of her dogs for a run-around.

As Emma and a rather magnificent fawn-colored saluki dog called Princess raced around the field in wide loops, Judith and Suzie sat on a bench just upstream from a row of parked canal boats.

"We can never tell Becks we followed her," Judith said as her opening gambit. "She'd never forgive us. I don't think I forgive us."

"No, of course," Suzie said, "but we've got to say something."

"We don't. We can't interfere."

"No—right—I agree. What Becks does with her life is none of our business."

"Exactly."

The women sat in companionable silence.

"Although we could just ask her," Suzie said.

"We absolutely can't," Judith said firmly.

"No, of course," Suzie agreed instantly. "You're right."

The women once again fell into silence, although Judith could tell that Suzie was gearing up for another go at changing her mind.

"She must be going through hell if this is what she's doing," Judith said, trying to move the conversation on.

"You're not wrong there," Suzie agreed. "She's always so perfect. There's no way she'd have done this if she was happy. So, just going back a bit, if we *were* to say something to her, what do you reckon we'd say?"

"We'd say nothing—we just agreed we wouldn't say a thing."

"I know, and we won't, I promise. But if we did—that's all I'm saying—*if* we did, what would we'd say?"

Judith sighed. Suzie wasn't going to give up, was she?

"I think we'd say that we're here for her. That whatever she's going through, we're on her side and she can talk to us any time she wants."

"Brilliant. And then we'd ask her who she's boffing?"

"No, we wouldn't!"

"Why not?"

"It's none of our business! Suzie, look at me. You have to promise. We're not going to overstep the mark. We're Becks's friends."

"All right," Suzie said, although she wasn't happy with the ruling. "Don't worry about me, my lips are sealed, you won't hear a dickie bird."

Judith looked at her friend. There was almost no one she knew who was less capable of keeping her promises. Apart from herself of course. It was why she enjoyed Suzie's company so much.

"But bloody hell," Suzie said in wonder, "Becks unfaithful? Who'd have thought it?"

"I know, it's incredible," Judith agreed. "You know what? I think my bum's gone completely numb."

Suzie laughed.

"I know what you mean," she said. "It's too bloody cold to be sitting out in the middle of winter. Anyway, I need to get on. I've got to get to a dog-sitter."

"What?"

"I've got to do the radio show later on, and I'm able to take Emma into the studio with me—she just sits in the corner silently, looking at me. But there's no way I can broadcast with Princess in there as well."

"Hold on," Judith said, still confused. "But your job is being a dog-sitter."

"I know."

"So why do you need a dog-sitter?"

"Well, sometimes a dog-sitter needs a dog-sitter," Suzie said, a touch irked by the question as she got up from the bench.

"Hold on, am I getting this right? You're being paid to look after Princess, and you're passing that money on to a second dog-sitter to do the job for you?"

"The alternative is I don't look after her at all—and I've turned down enough work as it is to do the radio show. Mind you, the dog-sitter I'm using charges more than I do. Which sticks in the craw, I can tell you. Dog-sitters are so bloody expensive in Marlow."

Suzie called the two dogs in, and while she clipped a lead to Emma's collar, Judith saw that the saluki wasn't wearing a collar at all. It was still attached to the lead that Suzie held in her hand.

"Should you really have been letting her off the lead without her collar?" she asked.

"Not really," Suzie said as she reattached the collar around Princess's neck. "But her owner never lets her have a proper run. She's a show dog, you see, and he's obsessed with her breaking a leg and not being able to win any more prizes."

"But what's that got to do with the collar?"

Now that she'd reattached the saluki's collar, Suzie indicated a gray plastic pebble that was attached to the collar by the brass identity tags.

"This is a tracker. There's an app that allows you to see where the dog is in real time. It's for tracking Princess if she's ever stolen by thieves. Or gets lost in the wood. But also, as I found out after the first time I let her go for a run off the lead, it's for her owner to spy on me and make sure that when I say I'll never let her go running off the lead, I never let her go running off the lead."

"That's very clever of you," Judith said. "But what sort of dog owner won't let their dog off the lead?"

"I'm convinced the only reason why Princess wins any prizes at all is because I take her collar off and let her run around. It keeps her healthy."

"I'm sure it does. Come on."

The two friends started to head back to Hurley. After they passed the nearest canal boat, they heard a woman's voice behind them say, "I thought it was you."

They turned to see Rosanna standing on the deck of the canal boat.

"Oh, hello," Judith said.

"What are you doing here?" Suzie asked.

"I live here," Rosanna said, indicating the canal boat as she got her bike off a rack and hefted it onto the grass.

"It's beautiful," Judith said. Through the windows, she could see a woman moving around inside. She was wearing a thick jumper, floral pajama bottoms, and had straight blond hair with the ends tipped with bright-blue dye.

"I've been thinking about what you said," Rosanna said. "Yesterday."

Suzie was about to reply, but Judith dug her elbow into her friend's side to remain quiet.

"And you're right," Rosanna said. "Tristram's going to screw it all up." There was a vulnerability—a brittleness, even—to Rosanna that Judith realized she'd not seen before. "And if he's innocent, then it really doesn't matter what I tell you. Does it? But can I ask, are you really sure Father thought Tristram wanted to…this is crazy, but that he wanted to kill him?"

"That's what Andrew Husselbee told us."

At the mention of the lawyer's name, Rosanna looked at the woman inside the canal boat.

"If that's what Andrew says, then it must be true," she said, almost to herself. "And I'm not sure it means anything anyway, but I think Tristram's got a girlfriend on the side. Has done for years. Someone he won't tell us about."

"Have you asked him about it?"

"A few times, but his private life is his private life. That's how it is with Tristram."

"What can you tell us about her?"

"Next to nothing. Although, last summer, when I was at White Lodge, I walked in on Tristram whispering sweet nothings into his phone, and when I teased him about it, he blushed bright red. Like I'd caught him out."

"What sort of sweet nothings?" Suzie asked.

"About how they just had to be patient, their time would come, they just had to be there for each other, that sort of thing."

"And you really have no idea who he was speaking to?" Suzie asked.

"None at all. But he was definitely really weird about it. When I asked him about it later on, he denied he'd even been on the phone to anyone."

"Now why would he do that?" Judith asked.

"I've no idea. But that's what I was going to tell you yesterday."

"Thank you," Judith said.

Rosanna smiled sadly, got onto her bike, and cycled off.

"Now that's a turn-up for the books," Suzie said.

"It is, isn't it?" Judith agreed. "Although, if Rosanna's remembered the conversation correctly, that didn't sound to me like he was talking to a girl-friend. That sounded like he was talking to an accomplice."

"I'd agree with you there."

Judith's phone rang, so she got it out of her handbag to see who was calling.

"It's Tanika," she said. "I wonder what she wants?"

Chapter 18

JUDITH, BECKS, AND SUZIE STOOD in Higginson Park watching dozens of tiny children scream and shout as they played on the swings and slides. Judith loved watching children play. The chaos and noise of them. She often found herself wondering how society turned these free spirits into drab grown-ups. But on this occasion, she was also keeping half an eye on Becks. The realization that her friend was having an affair had unsettled Judith more than she'd have liked to admit. Suzie was right—the whole point about Becks was that she did "the right thing." What on earth had happened to her that had made her transgress?

"I love the swings and slides," Suzie said, and Judith smiled in agreement.

"I remember taking my two to the local park," Becks said. "This was when we lived in Greenwich. Sam climbed on top of this strange wooden house, it was huge, I don't know how he got there, it was so dangerous."

"But I bet he got down okay, didn't he? They do, don't they?"

"He fell off and broke his arm. It was about the worst day of my life."

"Oh," Suzie said, trying not to laugh, and Judith found herself smiling as well. Affair or not, Becks couldn't really change, could she?

"It's not funny. Why would you laugh at that?"

"No, of course not, I'm sorry, it's just that, only you would think playgrounds are death traps."

"They are when they're not properly supervised."

A middle-aged woman in a shoulder-to-knee gray puffer jacket saw Suzie and came over.

"Are you Suzie Harris?" she asked. "From Marlow FM?"

Suzie seemed to grow an inch taller.

"I am," she said.

"I listen to you every day, I think you're amazing, can I have your autograph?"

"Me?" Suzie said with impressive modesty while also reaching into her pocket and pulling out a business card and pen. "Really, I'm nobody," she said as she signed the back of the card with a flourish and handed it over. "It's about the listeners. You're the real stars of the station."

"Thank you so much," the woman said before turning to Judith and Becks.

"Your friend's famous," she said, as though that were the beginning and end of the matter, and then she turned and walked away.

Once she was gone, Judith could see how much the interaction with the woman had meant to Suzie. She was all puffed up, like a mother hen.

"Does that happen often?" Becks asked.

"No," Suzie said, proud as punch. "That was the first time."

Judith wasn't sure that the adulation of people you didn't know was the healthiest source of self-esteem, but then she found herself remembering that the very first time she'd seen Suzie, she'd been talking to a local news TV crew that Tanika had specifically told her she wasn't allowed to talk to. She'd always had her head turned by being in the public eye, hadn't she?

"Hello everyone," a voice to their side said, and the women saw that Tanika had joined them. "Thanks for agreeing to meet like this."

"Always happy to help," Judith said. "But why the cloak and dagger?"

"I've been taken off the case."

"What?" the three women said as one.

"Well, not quite. But I've been demoted."

The women were outraged.

"But you're brilliant at your job," Becks said.

"That's very kind of you."

"Kind?" Judith said. "It's nothing less than the truth."

"I've only been acting up, though. All of this time."

"Acting up?"

"It means that when DI Hoskins wanted to return from sick leave, he could."

"And now there's been another murder, he suddenly comes back? He couldn't handle you taking all the credit once again?"

"The timing is...unfortunate," Tanika said, not wanting to speak ill of one of her superiors. "But more worryingly, he doesn't think Sir Peter was murdered."

"Pshaw!"

The women looked at Judith, confused. What had she just said?

"But you do?" Becks asked Tanika.

"I'll be honest, I've thought he was murdered pretty much from the off."

"You could have said something," Judith said to Tanika.

"I really couldn't. Not while I was SIO. But now I'm not, it doesn't matter what I think. The case will stay open, DI Hoskins is too smart to close it down immediately, but no one will be actively investigating."

"We have to catch the killer!" Suzie said, and a nearby four-year-old girl stopped running, burst into tears, and ran back across the play area to the arms of her mum.

"Oops," Suzie said. "Sorry."

"The thing is," Tanika said, "I can't go against my boss's orders."

Understanding finally came to Judith.

"I see," she said in appreciation. "Which is why you told me on the phone that you didn't mind us looking for the will at White Lodge. And why you now want to meet us secretly."

"I can't formally ask you to do anything. I'm not here in an official capacity. But perhaps you could carry on poking about a bit? See what you can dig up on Sir Peter and his family, because I don't think we've come even close to finding out what was really going on."

Judith didn't immediately reply, but Tanika could tell that her silence was critical. After all, if Judith and her friends had been so helpful last time, why should they be downgraded to amateur sleuths this time?

"What did you find out about the olive oil in the door hinge to Sir Peter's study?" Judith asked.

Tanika nodded, understanding that Judith was asking her to prove her bona fides.

"We had it checked out, and the olive oil on the door's hinges matches the olive oil you found in the metal can in the kitchen."

"The metal can that had been wiped of prints."

"And you should know, all of the science equipment that fell off the cabinet had been wiped of prints as well. But when I told DI Hoskins, he just said they must have had a good cleaner."

"But it's like Jenny said at the time," Becks said. "Even a good cleaner would leave fingerprints behind when they put whatever they'd cleaned back on the shelf."

"Which is my thinking as well," Tanika said. "Someone wiped all of the fingerprints from the scientific equipment on purpose. Just as they wiped their prints from the olive oil can. But there's something I want you to look into in particular. Sir Peter took five thousand pounds out in cash on four separate occasions just before Christmas. Each time he did, it was right after getting a message from an untraceable phone number registered in Vanuatu—a message he then deleted. He also deleted all of his replies."

"That sounds dodgy as hell," Suzie said.

"What were the dates?" Judith asked.

Tanika looked about herself to check no one was looking, and handed over a slip of paper with the dates written on. Judith put the note into her handbag and pulled out her little tin of sweets. Popping the lid, she offered the tin to Tanika.

"Travel sweet?" she asked, and both of them knew that Judith was in fact offering far more than a simple boiled sweet.

Tanika was aware of the deal she was about to agree to.

"Thank you," Tanika said, "that would be lovely."

She took a sweet and popped it into her mouth.

"Have you run checks on the family?" Judith asked.

"We've run background checks on all the key players, and I'm sorry to say they've all got a clean bill of health. Jenny Page's nursing agency said she was efficient, reliable, entirely trustworthy, and had been working for them for nearly fifteen years. In all that time, they'd not had one complaint."

"Then what about Rosanna Bailey?"

"I spoke to some of the people who work for her, and they all said she was capable, but she doesn't suffer fools, and one person said she could be ruthless. The sort of employer who'd sack a permanent worker on a Friday and hire a temp to cover their job on a Monday if it'll save a few pounds."

"Typical boss," Suzie said. "Then what about Tristram?"

"Tristram I got mixed messages about. Some people said he was arrogant, full of himself, a typical rich boy who'd never had to do a proper day's work in his life. But I spoke to his old head teacher who said she thought all of his arrogance was a front, he was deeply insecure, and he'd do anything to gain approval."

"Any sign of a girlfriend?" Judith asked.

"No," Tanika said. "Has he got one?"

"Rosanna said she overheard him on his phone whispering what she called 'sweet nothings' to someone last summer."

"Well, if it was last summer, maybe it's fizzled out?"

"It's possible. But Rosanna said he told this person that they had to bide their time. Have you made any progress on working out how the killer got out of the murder room afterward?"

"I'm sorry, that remains a mystery. What about you?"

"No, we're still just as in the dark. It's so infuriating. Sir Peter was murdered, I've no doubt about it—"

"I'm not so sure," Becks said, interrupting.

"Not now, Becks," Judith said, talking over her friend.

"I'll tell you what," Tanika said, "if anyone can work it out, it's you three. Now I need to get back to the office before I'm missed. Anything you find out, you have my phone number. Ring whenever, day or night."

Tanika turned and walked away. The three friends watched her head toward the gates of the park.

"You've got to stop saying he wasn't murdered," Suzie said.

"I know," Becks said. "Sorry."

"I can't believe Tanika's been demoted," Judith said. "It's just about the most disgraceful thing I've ever heard."

"Then we *have* to catch Sir Peter's murderer," Suzie said. "To get her back her job."

"Agreed. And I think we should start with this secret girlfriend. Because it occurs to me there is someone who might be able to identify her."

"Who?"

"The person who took Tristram in when he got thrown out of White Lodge, and the rest of his family turned their back on him. His mother. Rosanna said she lived in one of the terraced houses opposite the old Waitrose. I suggest we go and find which one she lived in and talk to her. Don't you?"

Chapter 19

WHEN IT CAME TO IDENTIFYING where Lady Bailey lived, Becks's impeccable knowledge of the middle classes once again came to the rescue. Despite there being a row of over a dozen terraced houses where Lady Bailey might have lived, Becks walked confidently up to the seventh door along and knocked on it.

"What on earth makes you think this is her house?" Judith asked.

Becks was perplexed by her friend's surprise.

"All of the other front doors and windows are black, or white, or natural wood," she said. "This door's been painted in Farrow and Ball."

"What's that?" Suzie asked.

"I think it's Elephant's Breath."

Suzie didn't know what to say to that.

"Bless you?" she eventually offered.

"What?"

"Sounded like you sneezed."

"Elephant's Breath is a color in the Farrow and Ball range," Becks said, surprised that she had to explain. "It's sort of in between Mouse's Back and Dead Salmon," she added, believing that this cleared up the situation. When she saw that it didn't, she went again: "It was just about the most fashionable color about ten years ago."

"Are you saying that colors can be fashionable?" Judith asked with a smile. "Like wellington boots?"

"Of course!"

"It's like a different world," Suzie said in wonder.

The door was opened by a woman in her sixties, cigarette in hand, wearing a fake leopard skin fur coat, light-gray tracksuit trousers, and fluffy white slippers.

Suzie smirked, knowing that for all Becks's fine words, she'd chosen the wrong door.

"Lady Bailey?" Judith asked, knowing that Becks had in fact hit the bull's-eye.

"Yes?" the woman drawled in a posh voice.

Suzie was stunned. It was all she could do to stop her mouth from falling open.

"We're friends of the family," Judith said. "Our condolences for your loss."

Lady Bailey flicked some ash into the street.

"That's very kind of you," she said.

"We're also helping the police try and find out what happened. Would it be all right if we came in for a quick chat?"

Lady Bailey looked at the three women and decided she'd got nothing better to do with her time.

"Come on in, then," she said, and headed into her house, leaving the front door open.

Judith led her friends through the hallway into a snug sitting room, all dark oak beams and oil paintings hanging crookedly on the wall. There was a vase of silk poppies in the window, blocking the sight of traffic whizzing past, a small TV balanced on a side table with silver-framed family photos, and a large ashtray full of cigarette butts on the other.

The whole room smelled of stale cigarette smoke.

"Now, who'd like a drink?" Lady Bailey asked.

"That would be lovely," Becks said.

"Gin or vodka?"

"Just a cup of tea, thank you," Becks said with a firm glance at Judith and Suzie, the message clear that they weren't to start drinking gin with Lady Bailey.

"One moment, then. Won't be long," Lady Bailey said as she disappeared into a little kitchen just off the sitting room.

As soon as they were on their own, Judith went over to look at the framed photos. Three of them showed Lady Bailey with Tristram, and there was only one of Rosanna. She was on her own in the photo.

Judith also saw an envelope with a bank's logo on the outside. She picked it up, nodded to Suzie to keep lookout—who immediately understood and slipped over to the door—and Judith pulled out the statement from inside the envelope. Becks mouthed in horror, "What are you doing?"

Judith scanned the statement and quickly got the impression of a simple life led modestly. Small, almost daily purchases from Sainsbury's and no extravagances or travel or restaurants. As for income, there was a state pension of three hundred pounds and a standing order for one thousand pounds that arrived every month.

Suzie coughed loudly, and Judith just managed to jam the statement behind her back as Lady Bailey entered the room, holding a tray of tea things.

"Do you mind if I have sugar?" Judith said, hoping it would send Lady Bailey back into the kitchen.

"I've got some here."

"Is it brown?"

"A little ramekin of brown and a ramekin of white."

Judith's smile became slightly desperate. How could she get Lady Bailey's bank statement back into the envelope without being seen?

"Sorry to bother you," Becks said, "but do you have any oat milk?"

"Of course," Lady Bailey said with the sort of smile that made it clear that she saw Becks's question as a challenge, and headed back to the kitchen.

The moment she was gone, Judith stuffed the statement back into its envelope and slapped it back onto the table, wiping it down to try and smooth it out—turning around with a big smile just as Lady Bailey returned to the room with a carton of oat milk.

"That's very kind of you," Becks said.

"You have lovely children," Judith said, indicating the photos on the side table.

"Thank you," Lady Bailey said, happy to be distracted. "They're very special to me."

"Yes, I can see that. Tell me about them."

"It's my favorite subject. What do you want to know?"

"Did they get on with their father?"

Lady Bailey took a sip of her tea before she answered.

"Of course they did."

Judith raised an eyebrow.

"I know what you're suggesting, but Tristram and Peter were always going to have a fiery relationship. If you ask me, Peter was jealous of him."

"Really?"

"He was a vain man. Don't let anyone tell you different. And I think he was jealous of Tristram's youth and looks. He hated being reminded of how old he was. And because of that, he belittled everything Tristram did. Which was so hard on him when he struggles with his confidence anyway.

"We've heard Tristram argued with Sir Peter last month. Quite badly. Which is how he ended up living with you. And we were at the party where… well, Sir Peter died. He and Tristram had a blazing row just beforehand. I didn't see a lack of confidence there."

"He did? Stupid boy. He can't help himself. It's a defense mechanism. If he feels painted into a corner, he comes out fighting. But it's all bluster, really. The more you get to know him, the more you realize he's soppy—like a Labrador puppy. And loyal like a Lab, too."

Judith was intrigued. Lady Bailey was backing up Rosanna's view—also offered by his old teacher—that Tristram was actually far more fragile and impressionable than he at first appeared.

"You know how they say you should judge a person by his friends?" Lady Bailey continued. "Well, Tristram passes that test with flying colors."

"Who are his friends?"

"Why, me, of course. But he has others. From school mostly."

"Any girlfriends?" Judith asked as though the matter was of no real consequence.

"I think he always has someone on the go," Lady Bailey said, almost with pride. "Not that he tells me what he's up to. But I think he rather bounces from one girlfriend to another."

"He's had more than one?"

"Of course."

"We'd heard that there was one in particular who was perhaps special to him. One he maybe makes secret phone calls to."

"That's interesting," Lady Bailey said, taking a sip of tea as she considered what to say. "Since he's started staying with me, I sometimes come into the room and hear him on the phone—which is when he ends the call or slips out for a bit of privacy. It's understandable. This place is barely more than a two-up two-down. But I like the idea of him settling down. I do hope you're right."

"Have you ever heard him mention the woman's name?" Judith asked—although she found herself remembering that, according to Jenny, Tristram had absconded with a cast member when he'd been performing his play in Florence. "Or his?"

"I don't think he's ever been interested in men," Lady Bailey said. "He's not had reason to, of course. Women find him so very attractive. But there's no point in me trying to find out. When Tristram doesn't want you to know what he's doing, you don't find out what he's doing. He can be very secretive that way."

Judith glanced at Becks and Suzie, and knew that they, like her, had latched on to the word "secretive." Was this proof once again that Tristram hadn't in fact been overheard by Lady Bailey and Rosanna talking to a girl-friend, but to an accomplice instead?

"What about Rosanna?" Judith asked, trying to make their interest in Tristram seem less obvious. "How did she get on with Sir Peter?"

"I'll be honest, Rosanna's loyal and hardworking, but she's never appreciated Peter. She just thinks he's a misogynist. Which he isn't, I hasten to add. He's never hated women. Dear god, he doesn't hate women. But he is pro-man, that much is true. He's very much a chauvinist."

"I heard they argued over business matters."

"You can say that again. Rosanna and her father would go at like hammer and tongs; I wondered sometimes if it wouldn't end in violence—not that I'm suggesting she'd ever harm him," Lady Bailey added hurriedly. "But there is an anger there. I sometimes think it's what makes her work so hard. She's trying to prove to her father that she's as good as any man. Do you mind if I smoke?"

"Of course," Judith said. "It's your home, you can do what you like."

Lady Bailey reached for an all-white packet of cigarettes with the Cartier logo on the front and pulled out a long white cigarette. She then used a gold lighter to light it.

"What brand are you smoking?" Suzie asked, intrigued.

"Cartier."

"The jewelry company?"

"That's right."

"They make cigarettes?"

"I have to import them now. It's my one peccadillo. Do you smoke?"

"I do," Suzie said. "But not those," she added, eyeing the bevel-edged packaging suspiciously.

"Would you like one?" Lady Bailey asked, and Suzie found herself conflicted. She wanted a cigarette now that Lady Bailey was smoking, but she felt too embarrassed to get out her tatty rolling kit, and she definitely knew she didn't have the confidence to smoke an imported cigarette made by a French jewelry firm.

"No, I'm good, thanks," she said.

"Do you mind me asking what happened between you and your husband?" Judith asked.

Lady Bailey took a drag on her cigarette before answering.

"I try to focus on the present," she said. "We've always stayed in touch. We still make decisions together."

"That's the best way for the children," Becks said with the wisdom of a vicar's wife.

"What we're basically asking," Suzie said, "is who left who and why?"

Lady Bailey looked shocked, believing herself to be too well bred to answer such a blunt question. But she also knew what the truth was.

"It was me," she said. "I left him."

Judith and her friends waited, and Lady Bailey continued.

"There was no irreconcilable difference. No cruelty. If there was one thing Peter never was, it was cruel."

"So what was it?" Becks asked.

"His affairs. He couldn't meet a woman without trying to bed her, and not all of them managed to resist his overtures. When I challenged him, he didn't even try to hide it. He always implied he had appetites that needed meeting, as if that excused his behavior. And that none of the women meant anything to him; it was just a bit of fun. When I asked whether I meant anything to him, he'd just laugh. As far as he was concerned, my job was to provide him with children, put up with his affairs, and then, in time, we'd grow old together. It's how it was in the Bailey family. How his father had been, and how he was."

"He was unrepentant?"

"Totally. Peter never did guilt. It's what first attracted me to him. He was so much fun—he called the world how he saw it and the devil take the hindmost. But I expected him to change when we married."

"Men don't change," Suzie said sadly.

"Some do," Becks said, but just as sadly.

Becks and Suzie shared a sympathetic smile.

"So why was he remarrying?" Judith asked.

"I've no idea," Lady Bailey said. "But we're none of us getting any younger, and Peter always was a hypochondriac. Since I'd provided him with children, maybe what he now wanted was a nurse."

It was obvious to Judith that Sir Peter's remarriage upset Lady Bailey far more than she was letting on. In fact, looking at Lady Bailey, Judith was reminded of the oil painting she'd seen in the hallway in White Lodge. It depicted Sir Peter with his arms around his wife and daughter, whereas Lady Bailey had her arms around Tristram. But what really struck Judith, as she looked at Lady Bailey all these years later, was how the effervescence and life that was so obvious in the painting had been replaced by a dullness—a weariness, Judith thought to herself as she watched Lady Bailey stub her cigarette out.

Judith could tell that Lady Bailey was getting bored with them.

"Can I ask?" Judith said. "There's evidence that Sir Peter had recently paid someone twenty thousand pounds in cash. Just before Christmas. I don't suppose he gave that money to you?"

"Ha!" Lady Bailey said. "That man gives me nothing. Nothing! Because he may be rich, and everyone's friend, but that's when you're in his gang. If you leave—or get booted out—you're dead to him. He gives me a pittance. Do you see the house I live in? All I've got left is the title."

Judith felt a jolt of electricity.

"You're right," she said. "That's all you've got."

"What do you mean by that?"

"You don't have money," Judith said as she worked through her theory out loud. "Or a grand home. But you do have the title. Lady Bailey. And you'd have lost that the moment Sir Peter married Jenny Page, wouldn't you?"

"I won't have that woman's name mentioned in here, thank you very much."

"She was about to become Lady Bailey—and you, what would you have become? Mrs. Bailey. That's quite the climbdown, isn't it?"

"I take it you're not suggesting I killed my ex so I could keep my title?" Lady Bailey said, appalled. "I know I look cheap, but I'm not that cheap."

"Can I ask?" Becks said, wanting to act as peacemaker. "If not you, do you know who Sir Peter might have given that money to?"

Lady Bailey looked at Becks, and her English Rose presence seemed to calm her.

"I've no idea," she admitted. "Twenty thousand pounds is a lot of money, even for Sir Peter."

"Then have you any idea who might have wished him harm?" Judith asked.

That got Lady Bailey's attention.

"You don't think his death was an accident?" Lady Bailey asked.

"Someone killed him," Suzie said, before Becks could point out her more skeptical position.

"How horrible," Lady Bailey said with a shudder.

"So if you had to settle on someone who might have wanted him dead, who would you choose?"

Lady Bailey didn't immediately reply, but her silence spoke volumes.

"There *is* someone, isn't there?" Judith said, pouncing.

There was the sound of a key in the lock of the front door. Lady Bailey rose from her chair in anticipation.

Tristram entered the room and saw the women.

"What are you all doing here?" he asked.

"I was just showing them out," Lady Bailey said, her loyalties instantly with her son.

"Good," Tristram said and clumped up the staircase.

"Yes, I really must ask you to leave," Lady Bailey said, going to the little hallway.

Judith exchanged glances with her friends, all of them noting how suddenly Lady Bailey had become timid in the presence of her son.

They allowed themselves to be ushered to the front door.

"But there is someone, isn't there?" Judith said. "Someone who had reason to wish your ex-husband ill."

"Possibly," Lady Bailey said. "His name's Chris Shepherd."

It took Judith a moment to place the name.

"You mean the family gardener?"

"If you're asking who might have wanted Peter dead, he's the only person I can think of."

"Why?"

"He'll tell you the story. He'll tell anyone who asks the story."

"Can you give us a clue, though? Just so we know what to ask him?"

"Sir Peter's father betrayed Chris's grandfather. There's been a blood feud between the two families ever since."

"Do you know where we might be able to find him?"

"At this time of day, he'll be in the Two Brewers, finishing a liquid lunch. Now I have to go, Tristram will be wanting something to eat. And I really must ask that you don't come back. I've told you too much as it is."

With that, Judith and her friends found themselves ushered onto the pavement, the front door firmly closed behind them. Next, they heard the sound of a lock being turned.

"Well, that didn't go how I expected," Suzie said, summing up the feelings of all three women.

"Let's take a walk," Judith offered.

Becks checked her watch.

"I've got to be back at the vicarage for two. There's a parish council meeting."

"I'm sure we'll be done by then."

"Why?" Suzie asked. "Where are we going?"

"Isn't it obvious? The Two Brewers. We need to talk to Chris Shepherd."

Chapter 20

ON THE WAY TO THE Two Brewers, the women discussed their encounter with Lady Bailey in depth. Judith's main take-home was that, once again, while Tristram's overheard phone calls might have been to a girlfriend, they could just as easily have been to an accomplice—male or female—as they plotted to kill Sir Peter together. Suzie's main observation, and she really struggled to move on from this fact, was that Lady Bailey might have talked like Margaret Thatcher, but she dressed like Bet Lynch. As for Becks, she said so little on the way to the Two Brewers that even Suzie noticed.

"Are you okay?" Suzie asked as they arrived at the pub.

"I don't think I should go in," Becks said, looking through the window.

"A pub's too down market for you?"

"No, of course not. It's not that."

"So what is it?"

"I just…don't want to go in," Becks offered somewhat lamely.

"You are allowed to be seen in a pub at lunchtime," Judith said. "Even as the vicar's wife."

"It's not that…" Becks trailed off. "Oh, look, it's fine. Come on, then. Let's go in. See if Chris Shepherd's here."

Becks led the way, Judith and Suzie sharing a quizzical look before following. However, as soon as they entered the main saloon area, they understood why Becks had been so hesitant. There were two men sitting at the bar. One was wearing an old gray fleece, gardening trousers with padding on the knees, and was reading a copy of the *Marlow Free Press*. The other was the man who they'd seen giving Becks a hug just before she'd gone into his house and closed the curtains to be alone with him. He was sitting on his own eating a ploughman's lunch, but there was an intensity to the way he was focusing on his food that suggested he'd noticed Becks and was trying to not look in her direction.

As for Becks, Suzie and Judith saw her color, pretending that everything was normal.

"Is that Chris there?" she asked, indicating the man who was reading the paper.

"Let's go and find out," Judith said, deciding to take charge of the situation.

She led across to the bar and smiled.

"Sorry to interrupt, but are you Chris Shepherd?"

Now they were closer, the women could see that the man was in his fifties, had curly black hair, and had a tanned and lined face—rather like a walnut, Judith thought to herself.

"What of it?" he said in a gruff voice.

"Sir Peter Bailey's gardener?"

Chris lowered his newspaper and looked evenly at the women.

"We're friends of Jenny," Judith continued. "And she's trying to get to the bottom of what happened to Sir Peter."

Chris's silence maybe meant that Judith should continue talking, or that he wasn't interested at all in talking to the women. They couldn't tell.

"Why weren't you at the party?" Suzie asked.

"Didn't want to go, did I?" Chris said.

"You were invited?" Judith asked.

"The wedding was enough for me. Didn't need to go to the party the day before as well."

Seeing how reluctant Chris was to talk to them, Judith decided that honesty was the best policy.

"We don't think Sir Peter's death was entirely accidental." Chris's interest sharpened. "And we've just been talking to Lady Bailey, who said Sir Peter's father wronged your grandfather."

"She said that, did she?"

"She said there was a blood feud between the two families."

"I've been working for Sir Peter for fifteen years, does that sound like a blood feud?"

"No, I suppose when you put it like that, perhaps it doesn't."

"It's Lady Bailey who's got the blood feud. Against her ex, if you ask me. Because if you're looking for someone who doesn't forgive or forget, and someone who I reckon's capable of killing *anyone* to get her own way, it's her."

"You don't like her?" Becks asked, before realizing that Chris had perhaps already answered her question.

"So what is the blood feud she mentioned?" Judith asked.

"Do I have to explain?" Chris asked.

"She said you'd be happy to."

"There's not much about life that that woman gets right."

"What happened?"

"Okay, since you're asking. But let's do this quickly, because it's all in the past. It all started when Sir Peter's dad left the Ministry of War after the Second World War. He'd been an administrator in charge of the department that developed X-rays or something. Anyway, his star scientist was my grandad, and they were best mates. They both came from Marlow, so that's what they had to start off with. When the war finished, Sir Peter's dad convinced my grandad to go into business with him. They were going to make X-ray machines together."

"Is your grandad the other X-ray in Sir Peter's study?" Judith asked, remembering how Jenny had told her that the X-rays in the study belonged to Sir Peter's father and his business partner.

"That's what I've always been told."

"Bit weird having the insides of a relative in someone else's house," Suzie offered, and Chris smiled for the first time.

"I know what you mean," he said. "Anyway, this X-ray company was basically a side hustle for Sir Peter's dad to his main business of owning all the land around here. He had no interest or knowledge of science; he was just the finance. But for my grandad, it was his life's work."

"Hold on," Judith said, an idea forming. "Who did that cabinet of science equipment in Sir Peter's study originally belong to?"

"That was my grandfather's originally."

"But it's now in the Bailey family home? How did that happen?"

"My grandad built a prototype of an X-ray machine for Sir Peter's dad, but they couldn't get any hospitals to order it. And weren't able to get anyone to manufacture it. It was a busted flush. So they wound up the company. As a thank-you for all of his work, Sir Peter's dad bought out my grandad's share of the company. That's when he got hold of his cabinet of science equipment. But guess what? Not long after, Sir Peter's dad found a factory who wanted to make the X-ray machines after all. And hospitals who wanted to place orders. And, because he'd bought my grandad out, Sir Peter's dad owned the whole company. He made all the money."

"He stiffed him," Suzie said, appalled.

"He stiffed him," Chris agreed.

"That's wicked," Judith said.

"You're not wrong. But it was seventy years ago. More than seventy now. And the bit Lady Bailey forgets is that my grandad got over it. He didn't care. The machines were named after him. No one pretended he wasn't the guy who'd designed them. Not least Sir Peter's dad. He always credited my grandad as the guy who'd come up with the machines."

"So what happened to your grandad?"

"He became a science teacher at Borlase's, and he always said he got far more pleasure out of teaching than any money would have brought him."

"There's no way I'd forgive the Bailey family," Suzie said.

"You and Lady Bailey both. But I just wished she'd drop it. Not everyone's as bitter as her. I grew up really proud of my grandad. There isn't an X-ray machine in the country that doesn't exist because of what he achieved. Isn't that enough?"

Chris downed the remainder of his pint, and Judith realized they wouldn't have much longer with him.

"How did you end up as Sir Peter's gardener?" she asked.

"He offered me the job. When things were tough for me. I'd had a tricky divorce. My business had gone under. I was down on my uppers. And we bumped into each other in town. Got talking, and then went for a drink—in here, as it happens. One drink turned into a few more, and by the end of the night, I was Sir Peter's new gardener. I've been with him ever since."

"It was that easy?" Suzie asked.

"It was his dad who ripped my grandad off. Nothing to do with Sir Peter. Or me, for that matter. And Sir Peter said he'd always look after me. Right the wrongs of the past. Which he did."

"How did he right the wrongs?" Judith asked.

There was the briefest of hesitations before Chris answered.

"I told you," he said easily. "He employed me when no one else would. But if you're looking for someone who had a problem with Sir Peter, it's Tristram you should be looking at."

"Yes, this is what everyone's telling us. Their relationship was tricky."

"They were always at each other's throats, those two."

"Although there was a particularly bad bust-up at the end of November, wasn't there?"

Chris eyed Judith carefully.

"You know about that?"

"Sir Peter thought Tristram was going to kill him. Or at least that's what Andrew Husselbee, the family lawyer, said."

"I wouldn't believe anything that man says. You can spot when he's lying, his mouth's moving."

"He's not trustworthy?"

"He's a lawyer," Chris said as though this was all the answer he needed to give. "But he's not wrong on this occasion. I was in the garden and Sir Peter and Tristram were in the study with the window open when it all kicked off. Mind you, I didn't take it too seriously."

"What did you hear?"

"It was crazy. Sir Peter was shouting about poison—saying he wasn't going to put temptation in Tristram's way again, he was going to keep his study locked from now on. Until the wedding. And then it would be too late for Tristram."

"He thought Tristram was trying to poison him?"

"I wouldn't take it too seriously. Sir Peter was always flying off the handle and making outlandish claims. He loved the drama of it all. He had so little to do with his life, he had to blow everything up."

"But he said was going to keep the study locked to put temptation out of Tristram's way?"

"Something like that. But it's not relevant, is it? No one poisoned anyone. Grandad's cabinet fell on Sir Peter, that's what I heard. And I don't care how much Tristram hated his dad, there's no way that could have done it. He's got no backbone that one. Don't let all his posturing fool you. He's spineless. The kind of guy who'd join a cult, you know? Doesn't know who he is, if you ask me."

"But I imagine he'd be the sort of person who might use poison?" Judith asked.

"That's exactly how he'd kill you, you're not wrong there. He'd do it a distance. Like a coward. Not wanting to get his hands dirty. Thinking about it, that boy's never got his hands dirty, has he? Never done a stroke of work. I reckon pushing a cabinet over's too much like hard work for him."

"Have you told the police Tristram and Sir Peter argued over this poison?" Judith asked.

"What's the point? It was months ago. And nothing happened from it, did it?" Chris said and turned to the barman. "All right to put my drink on the tab?"

"Sure," the man replied.

"'Cos I think we're done here," he said to the women.

Chris got up from his stool and headed to the front door.

"Just one last question," Judith said to his departing back. "What was in Sir Peter's most recent will?"

Chris stopped at the doorway.

"Why are you asking?" he asked.

"Andrew Husselbee said you were one of the witnesses."

"Then why don't you ask him what was in it?"

"He says he doesn't know. Sir Peter wouldn't show the will to him."

"He didn't show it to me, either. But it's proof Sir Peter and I got on, isn't it? When you think about it. He trusted me enough to witness his will. And I liked him enough to do it."

And with that, Chris turned on his heels and left the pub.

Before the women could say anything, the barman came over and picked up Chris's pint and his newspaper.

"Is that today's *Marlow Free Press*?" Judith asked him.

"Sure," the man said.

"Could I have it a second?"

The barman handed it to Judith. She turned to the puzzles page and tore out that week's crossword puzzle. Folding it in half, she slipped it into her handbag.

"Thank you. I don't need the rest of it."

"Okey-dokey," the barman said as he picked up the paper and left again.

"This week's crossword," Judith said by way of explanation to her friends. "So what do we think of Mr. Shepherd?"

"I don't believe him," Suzie said. "No one can be that laid back about someone stealing their family's money."

"I'm inclined to agree with you," Judith agreed.

"Although he's a gardener, isn't he?" Becks said. "Someone who goes into gardening isn't driven by money in the same way as other people, are they? And he was right about one thing. Sir Peter must have trusted him if he was getting him to witness his will."

"That's maybe true," Suzie conceded. "Then what about that story of Sir Peter thinking Tristram was trying to poison him?"

"That just sounded far fetched, if you ask me," Becks said, and her friends saw her throw a nervous glance at the man they'd seen her with the day before.

"You okay there, Becks?" Suzie asked.

"What's that?"

"Only, you keep looking at that man over there," Suzie said, ignoring the warning glance from Judith.

Becks blushed.

"I don't know what you're talking about," she said.

"Nor do I," Judith said to her friend, and was relieved when they all heard a phone start to ring. Judith fished around in her handbag and pulled out her phone. She didn't recognize the number on the screen.

"Hello?" she said as she answered the call.

"It's Jenny, Mrs. Potts," a distressed-sounding Jenny Page said on the other end of the line.

"How can I help you?"

"It's Tristram. He's here at White Lodge, and he's shouting and threatening me. Please, you've got to come at once, I'm not safe!"

Chapter 21

SUZIE'S VAN SCREECHED TO A halt outside White Lodge, the three friends piling out of it and heading to the house where they could hear raised voices coming from inside. The front door was locked, so they went round to the back and came in through the boot room.

"Call those bloody women off!" they heard Tristram shouting from inside.

"Please, I'm begging you, can you leave!" Jenny said.

"Quick," Judith said and bustled into the main hallway.

"Nothing happened to Dad, why are you telling everyone he was killed!"

"I'm not, I'm not, but something happened to him. We have to find out what."

The voices were coming from the sitting room, so Judith, Becks, and Suzie barreled in and saw that Jenny was cowering in an armchair while Tristram stood over her, pointing aggressively in her face.

"Jesus Christ!" he said, "and here they are again! Why do you keep turning up?"

"Step away from Jenny at once," Judith said in a tone that brooked no disagreement.

Tristram looked at Judith, fury in his eyes.

"I said, 'at once,'" Judith repeated.

Tristram threw his hands up in the air and took a step away from Jenny.

"And leave this house," Judith added.

The women could see that Tristram wanted to defy Judith, but he then shrugged as if to say it was no bother to him.

"Don't you have anything better to do?" he said to them.

"Don't you?" Suzie threw back at him.

"This is my home."

"Not yet, it isn't."

"And may never be," Judith added. "Depending on what is in your father's will."

"Ha!" Tristram said and started to leave the room. "There's no new will."

"You think he got his lawyer and Chris Shepherd to witness something that wasn't his will?" Judith asked.

"That's what I'm thinking. It wasn't in his safe when you all opened it up. And I've spoken to Andrew, and he's confirmed the only will he's got leaves everything to me. So it's just a question of time," he said, and then, flashing a filthy look at Jenny, he left the room.

Judith set her shoulders and followed him out.

"We've talked to Chris Shepherd," she said, and Tristram stopped in the hallway, his back to her. "You didn't know he was in the garden by your father's study when you and he had your big set-to last year, did you? He was able to tell us exactly why your father threw you out of this house and why he banned you from his wedding and changed his will. Chris heard the whole thing. Every word."

Becks and Suzie had come out during Judith's speech and flashed a puzzled look at her—their faces saying "'no, he didn't'"—but Judith put her fingers to her lips: they were to stay silent.

Tristram turned and started to approach.

Judith held her ground.

"We'll tell the police your father said he was going to have to keep his study locked from that moment on. How he couldn't put the temptation of poison in your way again," Judith said as though it was merely the next thing on her list to say, rather than the second of only two things they'd gleaned from Chris. "Unless you have a different version of events and want to set the record straight?" Judith added, as though she was already bored by what Tristram might be about to say.

"I was just looking at Grandfather's old chemicals in his cabinet," Tristram said, his pride pricked. "I couldn't believe they'd sat there for the last however-many decades. And I thought I knew everything that was on those shelves, but this time I saw a little glass jar on the top shelf that had 'cyanide' written on it. So I got it down. I was looking at it when Father came in, saw me with the bottle, and he just lost it. He was deranged. Did he really think I wanted to do him in, and if I did, was I really going to let him find me holding a jar of cyanide in his study?"

"But that's not all, is it? Chris told us more," Judith lied, hoping to finesse even more information out of Tristram, but she could see that he was confused.

"That's everything. He refused to believe I was telling the truth, that's what it was like being me with him. Especially after that cow got her claws into him."

"You mean Jenny?"

"She thinks she's been so clever. Wheedling her way into this house, getting Father to fall in love with her—which isn't hard. Give him a supply of decent claret and three meals a day, and he'd fall in love with anyone. But the last laugh's on her, isn't it? Because her money grabbing got her nowhere. He died before she could marry him."

As Tristram spoke, they all noticed that Jenny was standing in the doorway by the kitchen, listening to every word.

Tristram was distracted by the chime of his mobile phone. He pulled it out, saw that he'd received a message, and then shot a panicked look at Jenny before returning the phone to his pocket, where it continued ringing.

"Aren't you going to answer that?" Judith asked.

"No," he said, but then he seemed to change his mind and turned around and left through the front door at speed.

The four women went over to the window and saw Tristram take out his phone and start talking into it as he strode to his old sports car. He appeared to be remonstrating with the person on the end of the line—losing his temper, in fact.

"What do we think?" Judith asked. "Is this one of Tristram's clandestine calls?"

"What's that?" Jenny asked.

"Lady Bailey told us Tristram's been making secret phone calls since he moved in with her," Becks said.

"And Rosanna said the same thing as well," Suzie said.

"Really?" Jenny said. "Who are the calls to?"

"We don't know," Judith said. "Lady Bailey and Rosanna said they thought it could be Tristram's girlfriend. But we're thinking it could also be his accomplice. Someone who was inside Sir Peter's study pushing the cabinet onto him while Tristram was outside all sweetness and light establishing his alibi."

"You really think so?" Jenny asked.

"We know Tristram's in the clear. He was in the garden with us. But *someone* was in the study pushing the cabinet onto Sir Peter. And seeing as Tristram benefits the most from his father's death, what if that person was his accomplice?"

"The person he's talking to on the phone," Suzie added.

The women watched Tristram get into his car—still talking into his phone—and then he drove off with a spurt of gravel.

"Then we have to find out who he's been speaking to," Jenny said, suddenly animated. "They could be the person who killed Peter!"

"I agree," Judith said.

"We should follow him."

"It's a bit late for that," Becks said. "We won't catch up with him now. ."

"You reckon?" Suzie said, an idea occurring to her. "I think I know *exactly* how we can follow him."

Chapter 22

"WE INTERRUPT THIS PROGRAM FOR an emergency broadcast," Suzie said into the microphone in the studio of Marlow FM. The early afternoon presenter, a retired geography teacher called Trevor, was standing in the corner of the room, terrified of the three women who'd stormed in only seconds before and grabbed the microphone from him.

"It's Suzie Harris," Suzie continued. "And longtime listeners will know I run a dog-sitting business. Well, the most terrible thing has happened. My lovely Doberman pinscher has just been dognapped. Just this second! In Marlow! I didn't see who took him, but I think it was a man who was driving a dark-green sports car. You know the sort, an old Triumph or Spitfire—or whatever it's called—but it's a green two-seater with a black fabric hood. If you could look out of your windows right now and see if you can see a green car driving past, call in. You know the number. I want to get my lovely Emma back. Call if you see a green sports car in Marlow." Suzie looked at the computer screen to see what music had been queued up. She then turned back to the microphone and said in mellifluous tones, "And now, some Neil Diamond."

Suzie clicked an icon on the screen with the mouse and pulled the fader down on the microphone.

"Thanks, Trevor," she said.

Trevor nodded but didn't say anything. This was mainly because Marlow FM's studio was very small—it was built into an old store room at the back of Sea Cadets Hall—so he felt really very near to the three women indeed. A green light lit up on the mixing desk and Suzie pounced, expertly fading down the music at the same time as she faded up her microphone.

"You're on air, caller."

"Hello Suzie," a reedy voice said over the speaker.

"Maggie, how are you?" Suzie said and immediately grimaced at her tactical mistake. As everyone at the station knew, you *never* asked Maggie how she was.

"I could be better," Maggie said mournfully. "If I'm honest, my sciatica's playing up—"

"Got to jump in there, Maggie; have you seen the green sports car?"

"Oh yes, I have."

Suzie waited a beat and then turned on her upbeat radio personality again.

"That's great. Where have you seen it?"

"It just went past my window."

"And what road are you on?"

"Station Road."

Another green light lit up on the board next to the first.

"Thanks so much for calling. Okay everyone, so it looks like the green sports car is heading up Station Road. Got to go to another caller now." Suzie clicked a switch on the board. "You're through to Marlow FM, you're live on air."

"I just saw a green car turn onto Dedmere Road!" an old man boomed.

"Thanks for calling, Brian. So if it was on Station Road and is now on Dedmere Road, it's heading east toward the commercial estate. Any listeners in the east of Marlow, go to your windows and see if you can see a green sports car outside. There's a dog's life at stake!"

Suzie faded the music back up while they waited for the next call.

"You're amazing," Becks said.

"I have a certain connection with my listeners," Suzie admitted.

A green light on the board flashed.

"You're through to Marlow FM," Suzie said, fading the music out.

"Oo sorry, I'm out of breath," an elderly woman's voice said.

"That's all right. Take your time."

"I've just chased a green sports car down the street. On my mobility scooter."

The women shared an amazed glance as they pictured an old woman chasing Tristram's car down the street.

"But I lost it. Your poor dog!"

"What dog?" Suzie asked, before remembering. "Oh, of course, my dog, sorry, I'm just too upset. Do you remember where you lost the car?"

"At the junction of Dedmere Road and Alison Road. It took me a bit of time to get on the mobility scooter. But when I got to the junction, the green car had vanished."

"Then thank you, caller. Anyone else seen a green car on Alison Road in the last few minutes? Call me if you have."

Suzie pushed the fader on the music back up again and turned to look at her friends, her cheeks flushed.

"How do you know what buttons to push?" Judith asked.

Trevor took half a step forward.

"Actually—" he said.

"It's just buttons," Suzie said, talking over Trevor. "If you can drive a car, you can drive a radio desk."

Trevor frowned, unhappy at having his hard-won skills dismissed so breezily, but he didn't dare contradict Suzie.

"Come on," Suzie said to the mixing desk, looking at the lights that would indicate someone was ringing in. They remained dark.

As the seconds stretched to minutes, and Suzie followed the Neil Diamond track with Barbara Dickson's "Caravan," the friends began to realize that no more listeners had seen Tristram's sports car. Suzie would interrupt the music every thirty seconds or so to ask for their listener's help, but no one rang in.

After ten minutes of waiting, they accepted the trail had gone cold, and the women started to leave the studio.

"But what about your dog?" Trevor asked plaintively.

"Oh of course!" Suzie said, and leaned back to the studio microphone. She pushed a fader up and said, "Okay everyone, don't worry, Emma's been found. She's safe and sound. But thanks to all our loyal listeners who rang in—she was only found because of you. And remember, if you're wanting someone who'll go the extra mile for your pets, think Suzie Harris. These are the lengths I'd go to for my pet. I'd do the same for yours."

Pulling the fader back down and flashing a smile for the benefit of a now-deeply confused Trevor, she left the studio with her friends.

"We lost him," Suzie said, disappointed.

Judith looked at her friend and realized how comfortable she looked behind the desk. She could well understand why she'd been giving up dog-walking shifts to pursue her radio career, even though the work was unpaid.

"Not necessarily," she said. "It's possible your listeners lost sight of him on Alison Road because that's where his destination was. If he pulled into a driveway or into a garage, maybe his car wouldn't be seen?"

"But how are we going to find out where he stopped?" Becks asked.

"Or if he stopped at all?" Suzie added.

"I'm not sure we'll be able to," Judith said. "But I know someone who will."

Chapter 23

AS SOON AS JUDITH GOT home, she rang Tanika and explained how Tristram had raced off in his car during a heated phone call and that they'd lost him at the junction where Dedmere Road met Alison Road.

"How on earth did you even manage to follow him that far?" Tanika asked.

"You don't want to know. But if you identify the number of the person who rang Tristram this afternoon—just before 2 p.m.—you'll very possibly reveal the identity of the person who was in the study killing Sir Peter while Tristram was outside establishing his alibi."

"That's a great idea. Unfortunately, I don't think I'll be able to do it."

"Whyever not?"

"I'm not the senior investigating officer; I can't raise warrants to seize phone records."

"Then ask the senior investigating officer to do it."

"He won't. I'm so sorry. But whenever I've asked him to do anything to progress the case, he's not interested. Remember, he didn't think that Sir Peter taking out twenty thousand pounds in cash following text messages from a burner phone registered in the South Pacific was relevant. As far as he's concerned, there's been no murder. And Tristram receiving a phone call won't change his mind."

Judith pursed her lips.

"Tell me about this senior investigating officer of yours."

"He's a good copper," Tanika said, not wanting to betray a fellow officer. "He's good at his job."

"Balderdash!" Judith said. "If he's ignoring you, he sounds like a chauvinist. What if you go over his head to his boss?"

"The Superintendent is likely to take DI Hoskins's side in this."

"Another man?"

"Another man."

"I don't know how you put up with it," Judith said, not that she expected Tanika to reply. The reality of life lived in a world where the men carved out the power, status. and money was hardly a new revelation to either woman.

"Any chance you could poison him?"

"I don't think it's that bad," Tanika said, laughing. "Not yet anyway."

"I only mention poison because we found something else of interest," Judith said, and told Tanika how they'd spoken to Lady Bailey, who in turn had told them that Chris Shepherd's family had had a potential fortune stolen from them by Sir Peter's father and that Chris had overheard the argument at the end of November that had ended with Tristram being thrown out of his home by Sir Peter.

"Seriously?" Tanika asked. "Sir Peter thought that Tristram was trying to poison him?"

"We confronted Tristram just before he did his runner, and he didn't deny it. He just said it was all an innocent mistake. He'd been looking at a bottle of cyanide in the cabinet of chemicals in the study when his father walked in. It was all a terrible misunderstanding. I should add, the various family members we've been able to speak to have all painted a picture of Sir Peter being melodramatic and somewhat quick to anger. I think it's definitely a possibility he could have got the wrong end of the stick."

"And I can't help noticing that Sir Peter wasn't in fact killed with poison. So what are we saying? All of Sir Peter's attempts to write a new will, and him telling his lawyer that Tristram was trying to kill him, was just him overreacting?"

"I don't know. It's possible he put Tristram off using cyanide, which is why he came up with the plan to crush his father with the cabinet."

"I'll tell you what I can do. Let me speak to the team who documented the contents of the study and let me see if there's a bottle of cyanide listed. If there is, then that suggests that maybe what Chris Shepherd said was true."

"And if there isn't any cyanide, it could just mean that what Chris said was still true, it's just that someone's since removed it."

"That's a possibility, I suppose. We'll keep working this end. See what we can dig up. And thanks for all of your work. I'm so sorry you're not able to get any kind of formal clearance to do this."

"Don't worry, we both know who to blame for that, and it's not you."

Once they'd said their goodbyes, Judith knew she had a lot of thinking to do, so she decided to go for an afternoon swim. The water in the Thames was ice cold, but it sharpened her thinking, just as the warming cup of hot chocolate in front of the fire afterward loosened them. But on this occasion, Judith found that she couldn't concentrate properly. Whenever she tried to think about the case in any kind of detail, she just kept coming back to the fact that if they'd identified where Tristram had driven off to, they'd perhaps have identified the person who'd killed Sir Peter for him.

Assuming Tristram was behind his father's death, of course.

Picking up her iPad, Judith searched for Lady Bailey's landline number, called it, and, when Lady Bailey answered, asked if she or Tristram knew anyone who lived on or near Alison Road.

"Alison Road?" Lady Bailey said, as though it were a foreign country, and Judith realized that she was drunk. "What on earth would he have been doing there?" Lady Bailey slurred.

"I don't know," Judith said, and decided to see if she could take advantage of Lady Bailey's inebriation. "But I suppose he's been so secretive of late, hasn't he? Like you said."

"Ha!" Lady Bailey said. "You're talking about his fancy lady, aren't you?"

"I'm so glad we agree," Judith said. "How long has it been going on for?"

"Years. I asked him about it, and he denied it, of course. He's always secretive; you're right that's exactly the right word for him. But a mother knows. When I do his laundry, I can smell a woman's perfume on his shirts. And he doesn't always come home at night," Lady Bailey added, but Judith could hear that she wasn't sure if she'd revealed too much.

"I'm so pleased for him," Judith said, trying to keep Lady Bailey on her side.

"Are you? I'm so glad. Yes, I'm pleased for him as well."

Thanking Lady Bailey for her time and hanging up, Judith decided to call Jenny to see if she could add to what she'd just found out.

"You've been speaking to Lady Bailey?" Jenny asked, once Judith explained why she'd phoned.

"Only about Tristram, and only to try to find out who might have wished Sir Peter ill. Historically of course. But she said she thought Tristram has been seeing someone for the last year. Or maybe longer."

"That's very interesting," Jenny said, "because I've been thinking things over at this end, and I'm sure I've not heard anyone mention Tristram having a girlfriend. Peter certainly didn't."

"Then do you know if Tristram knows anyone who lives on Alison Road?"

"Why Alison Road?"

Judith explained how they'd tracked Tristram's car but had lost him after he turned onto Alison Road.

"I'm sorry," Jenny said. "Nothing springs to mind. Rosanna lives in a canal boat just beyond Hurley Lock, so he wasn't visiting her."

"Yes, Suzie and I bumped into Rosanna by her boat. She lives with someone, doesn't she?"

"That's right. Her girlfriend, Katie Husselbee."

"Husselbee? Is she a relation to your lawyer?"

"She's his daughter. Everyone calls her Kat. She's also a lawyer, works for the same company as her father, but she's very passionate about the environment. Does work for lots of protest groups for free. She's a very impressive woman."

Judith wasn't making the progress she'd hoped for.

"Then what about Chris Shepherd? Does he live near Alison Road?"

"What makes you ask about him?"

"Lady Bailey thinks Chris held a grudge against Sir Peter."

"I'm not sure that's true," Jenny said, thoughtfully. "Chris can be a bit gruff, but I don't think he's got a bad bone in his body. He loves nature, and being outdoors, and he has plenty to get his teeth into here. Not that it matters. He doesn't even live in Marlow. He comes in every day from Reading in an old truck. When it works," Jenny added with a smile in her voice. "It's always breaking down."

Judith knew that Reading was some distance southwest of Marlow, and Tristram's car had last been seen driving east out of the town.

There was a pause on the line, and Judith got the impression that Jenny was building up to saying something.

Judith waited.

"You don't believe him, do you?" Jenny asked.

"Believe whom?"

"Tristram. What he said today. About me being a gold digger."

"Of course not."

"But the thing is, I can't deny it," Jenny said. "I've always tried to say it was about love, and it was, don't get me wrong. Or at least affection and attraction. Peter was such enjoyable company, so full of life…" Jenny gathered herself before making herself continue. "But Tristram's not wrong, either. I wanted the security that he'd bring as well. I can't help it. I'm not getting any younger, and nursing has kept me off the dating market. I'd sort of thought I'd have to work for the rest of my life. The idea of finally being financially secure was a big part of Peter's appeal."

Judith could hear the relief in Jenny's voice as she confessed.

"It's only natural," Judith said. "Tristram said you were an orphan."

"I went from foster home to foster home when I grew up. Some of them nicer than others, some of them with foster siblings who were great, but most of them weren't. If I'm honest, I've been fighting my whole life. To get an education, to get qualified, to make a success of my work. The idea of putting all of that behind me…?"

Jenny paused, and Judith once again intuited there was still more the younger woman wanted to say.

"I suppose what I'm trying to say is, my motives for wanting to marry Peter weren't perfect."

"No one's motives are ever pure. Not when you get down to it."

"But that's why I want his will found. I want to know what money he's left me."

And there it was, Judith knew—the shameful confession that Jenny had been building up to.

"That's entirely natural."

"That makes me a bad person. A money-grabber."

"When there's as much money at stake as there is with Sir Peter's estate, I know I'd be the same."

Judith finished the call, poured herself a small tot of "thinking scotch," and went into the next-door room to look at her makeshift incident board.

She found herself drawn to the picture she'd printed of Tristram. It was a black-and-white photo that Judith recognized as a "10 x 8" that actors used to show to prospective directors. He really was a very handsome young man, but she found it interesting that he wasn't smiling in the photo. The image he was going for was very "Heathcliff"—dark, handsome, and dangerous. But then, Judith remembered how Rosanna, Lady Bailey, and Chris Shepherd had all been at pains to say that Tristram was all bark and no bite. So which was it? Was he a dangerous man capable of killing—as his father believed—or was he just a weak person with anger management issues?

Judith thought it would be efficacious to have another small top-up of her whisky, but rather than take her glass back to the decanter in the sitting room, she decided to go and get the decanter and bring it over to the glass. Once she returned, she poured the smallest of splashes of golden liquid into her glass and took a ruminative sip.

So what had they learned?

Everything still suggested that even if Tristram hadn't pushed the cabinet onto his father, he was still very possibly involved. He certainly benefited the most from his father's death. Unless—impossible though it seemed—was there some way he'd managed to kill his father while never stepping foot in the study?

Looking at the other photos on the wall, Judith was reminded of how Rosanna had lied about her whereabouts from the start. The poor woman, though, Judith thought. She was the only member of the immediate family who managed to hold down a job. And yet, despite being Sir Peter and Lady Bailey's firstborn child, she wasn't due to get any of the house or money when her father died—which, as she'd mentioned to her, was reason enough for her to want her father to stay alive. Once Tristram inherited, he'd have control of everything. So, she might have been hiding in a wardrobe for somewhat dubious reasons when Sir Peter died, but it didn't make sense that she'd want her father dead.

It all kept coming back to the will, didn't it? Because if, as seemed possible, Sir Peter had changed it to include Rosanna, or had actually left his entire estate to her, then that very possibly changed everything. It was all so frustrating, and Judith recognized the feeling she reached when she got stuck compiling a crossword. All of the possible options felt like they were swirling around in her head, and she knew she'd not be able to make any more progress for the time being.

Thinking about crosswords reminded her of the page of the *Marlow Free Press* she'd torn out of Chris Shepherd's newspaper. Topping up her glass with the merest splash of whisky, she went back to the sitting room, sat down in her armchair, and started rooting in her handbag for the piece of paper. She smoothed it out on her lap.

Ignoring most of the clues, she looked at the Across questions that put answers into the four corners of the crossword grid.

The first was: *1. Small fish Ida swallowed once a week (6)*

There were two halves to every cryptic question—the half that was the literal synonym for the answer, and the other half that was the "cryptic clue." Judith smiled to herself because she instantly saw that this particular clue was as elegant as it was simple. The cryptic part of the clue was "Small fish swallowed Ida" because "small fish" often meant the setter was looking for the word FRY, as in "small fry." "Ida swallowed" simply meant that FRY had "swallowed" IDA, which would give the answer of FRIDAY—as the other half of the clue confirmed: FRIDAY was indeed something that happened "once a week."

Judith looked at the next clue, 26 Across: *Alternative to LSD causes medical emergency (7)*

Judith once again found herself smiling. As a crossword setter, she'd used LSD herself as it was such an elegant misdirection—particularly when it was put in a medical setting, as was the case with this clue. "LSD" wasn't a reference to an illegal drug; it was actually the old-fashioned abbreviation for the British currency of pounds, shillings, and pence. As for the cryptic part of the clue, a word like "emergency" would often be an indicator that an anagram was being looked for. In this case "medical emergency" meant that the answer was an anagram of "medical," for example, DECIMAL—which was the correct answer, as "decimal" was indeed an alternative to pounds, shillings and pence.

28. Slide inside and risk a tendon snapping (5)

As for 28 Across, Judith didn't immediately have an instinct as to what she was looking for. "Snapping" could suggest that she was looking for an anagram, but TENDON was a six-letter word, so that didn't seem right. Next she looked at the word "inside." As a matter of course, Judith checked to see if she could create a five-letter word from any five-letter sequence of letters "inside" the clue itself. As soon as she looked at the question in this way, she realized that the letters S, K, A, T, and E appeared consecutively "inside" the phrase, AND RI<u>SK A TE</u>NDON SNAPPING. So the second half of the question was the cryptic clue that gave the answer SKATE—as did the more literal first half, as the word "skate" meant to "slide."

Three down, one to go. The final clue was: *3. Pull up a playing field (4)*

Judith guessed, from its brevity—and from the fact that she was only looking for a four-letter word—that this was a simple clue where there was no particular trickery, each half of the clue offering up different synonyms for the same four-letter word. A playing field could be a park, she knew, and she was pleased to realize that she'd stumbled across the answer at her first attempt. After all, if you "pull up" in a car, you PARK, which is, of course, also a word that means "playing field."

Judith looked at the four answers she'd written into the four corners of the grid. If she read them in a counterclockwise order from the first clue, just as she'd done with the previous week's puzzle, she got the answers FRIDAY, DECIMAL, SKATE, and PARK. Decimal meant a system of arithmetic based on the number ten, so was this a reference to ten o'clock? It seemed a bit tenuous to Judith, but if that's what it meant, then the rest of the message was another instruction to meet up—wasn't it?—on Friday at 10 a.m. in the Marlow skate park. But had she got that right? And if so, who'd left the message? And why?

All Judith knew for sure was that the following day was Friday and she knew exactly where she'd be at ten o'clock.

Chapter 24

THE FOLLOWING MORNING, JUDITH RANG Becks and asked to meet her at the skate park at 10 a.m. Judith didn't phone Suzie, as she decided instead to drop in on her and ask in person. This was because, following her visit to Marlow FM, she wanted to talk to Suzie about her radio career. As far as Judith was concerned, anyone who was that good at their job deserved to be doing it full-time—even if it ended up making Suzie more famous, which Judith still believed could prove too heady a brew for her friend.

When she arrived on her bike, Judith was shocked to discover that the front of Suzie's house was still mostly a building site of scaffolding and ripped tarpaulin. She hadn't visited her friend since the summer before, but she'd presumed that her friend had finished her building work.

"What are you doing here?" Suzie asked as she opened her front door.

"Just thought I'd pop round. Can I come in?"

Suzie went back inside, leaving the door open. Judith followed her friend into a linoleum-floored hallway and was met with slobbering joy by Emma.

"Who's a good girl!" Judith said, rubbing Emma's ears affectionately.

Once they'd agreed that Emma was looking particularly well, and Judith had turned down the offer of a cup of tea, she decided to get down to business.

"Now, first I need your help with a bit of a mystery. It's got me flummoxed. Are you free to come to the skate park with me for ten a.m.?"

"Sure. As long as whatever we're doing is finished in time for my show."

"Don't worry, it should be. But talking about your show, it's why I wanted to see you."

"Why?"

"Because I saw yesterday how brilliant you are. The way you pushed and pulled all those buttons and levers while talking to people—it's not something I'd ever be able to do. You have a real rapport with your audience. And I know how important the station is to the local community. The way you chatted to the people who rang in made that as clear as day."

"You really think so?" Suzie said, bursting with pride.

"But I also know you're turning down dog-sitting work to do it."

"I'm not."

"You are."

"I'm not."

"You literally told me you were."

"I did?"

"When we were up by Hurley Lock."

"Oh that's right, I did. Bit of a giveaway. But it's not a biggie, it's only in the mornings I can't look after any dogs. I have to prepare for the show."

"Of course. But I was wondering, is there any way you could get paid for your radio work to make up for the dog-sitting work you're turning down?"

"That's not possible. We're all volunteers."

"Then how about you get work at another station? One that pays."

"Why would I want to work at a different station? Marlow FM's where I want to be."

"But what are you doing for money?"

"You think I'm short of money?" Suzie said, offended.

"Suzie, the front of your house is still missing."

As it happened, since she'd cut back on her dog-walking business, Suzie's bank accounts had all slipped into the red. And her credit card spending had also started to spiral out of control. Christmas was an expensive time of the year anyway. In truth, her lack of income was worrying her sick, but she coped by trying not to think about it.

"That's got nothing to do with money," she said. "The builder's coming back. He'll finish the job."

"Is that the same builder who didn't finish the job last year?"

Suzie didn't immediately reply.

"Maybe," she eventually offered.

"You need to hire someone new."

"I can't," Suzie said, frustration tightening her voice. "I've paid the other guy to do it."

"He's not coming back."

"He could."

"When did you last have contacted him?"

"Do you mean, which year? Look, don't you worry about me," she said, summoning a brightness to her voice she didn't actually feel. "Something will turn up. It always does. But the key point is, you think I'm good on air?"

Judith couldn't help herself from smiling at her friend's vanity.

"I don't just think you're good. I think you're the best. You've got to carry on doing your show, but you've also got to keep earning money."

"Thanks, that means a lot. And you're right, I've got to make the radio work square with the paid work. I'll put my thinking cap on. Now come on, let's get to the skate park. You can tell me why we have to be there on the way."

Judith allowed her friend to put her bike into the back of her van and drive her over to Higginson Park. Once they arrived, they crossed the cricket pitch to the skate park just beyond, where they found Becks already waiting. She was wearing fluffy boots and fluffy gloves that she was banging together to keep warm.

"So what's this mystery you want solving?" Becks asked as they arrived.

Judith explained how the *Marlow Free Press* crossword setter had been sending out secret messages.

"To meet in the skate park?" Becks asked, surprised.

"That should be easy enough to explain," Suzie said. "It'll be a drugs drop of some sort."

"I don't think crossword setters normally deal drugs," Judith said.

"They don't normally solve murders, either."

"Touché," Judith said with a smile.

The three women looked at the half a dozen kids clattering up and down the ramps on their skateboards and scooters. None of them were over the age of about ten. Many of them were with their parents.

"I don't think it's drugs," Becks said.

The clock in All Saints Church started to strike ten, and the three women looked about themselves. Apart from the children already skating, there was an old woman heading to a nearby bench where she sat down next to a similarly aged man who was wearing thick gloves and a tweed hat. But then they saw a male jogger running toward them just as a female jogger was approaching from the direction of the Thames Path. The younger man checked his watch, and Judith and her friends shared excited glances. Was this the ten o'clock meeting?

Having checked the time, the male jogger veered off and started running around the boundary of the cricket pitch, while the female jogger touched the nearest structure of the skate park, turned around, and ran back the way she'd come.

The two joggers never even got within twenty yards of each other.

As the clock struck for the tenth time, the women realized they'd witnessed no secret meeting.

"How about we give it five more minutes?" Judith said.

After five more minutes of standing in the cold, the kids were still whizzing up and down the ramps, their parents watching on, and the old couple was still sitting on the bench. That was it.

"Well, that was a waste of time," Suzie said.

Judith tended to agree. In fact, was she wrong about there being secret messages in the *Marlow Free Press* cryptic crossword?

"I'm not sure I'd agree it's a waste of time," Becks said, indicating a woman who was walking across Higginson Park toward the river. "Look over there. It's Lady Bailey."

"Sure," Suzie said, unimpressed. "She has to be somewhere."

"But we need to stop her before she gets away," Becks said, striding off at speed, and Suzie and Judith shared surprised glances before following.

"Good morning, Lady Bailey," Becks said as she caught up with the older woman.

"Good morning," Lady Bailey said as she stopped.

"Those are a lovely pair of wellies."

"Now why would you say that?" Lady Bailey said as Judith and Suzie arrived, and they finally realized what was going on.

Lady Bailey was wearing wellington boots that were bubblegum pink and very slender ankled.

Becks went in for the kill, a smiling assassin.

"That color of pink is unique to Hunter wellies, isn't it?"

"It's just a bit of fun."

"And I see you take their slender calf range."

"I'm lucky enough to have good genes, but I don't really see what this has to do with anything."

Judith saw an area of wet mud by the path side.

"Would you mind standing in that mud for a second?" she said.

"Don't be ridiculous," Lady Bailey said, her patience snapping.

"It would be a great help to us," Judith said.

"Seriously?"

"It will only take a moment. And then we'll be on our way. Promise."

Lady Bailey realized that the quickest way to get rid of the three women would be to do as they asked, so she took a couple of steps and stood in the mud.

"Happy now?" she said.

"Nearly," Judith said. "Could you come back?"

"Very well," Lady Bailey said, and returned to the women. "Now can I go?"

"No," Judith said, looking at the footprints.

"I beg your pardon?"

"You're not going anywhere."

Lady Bailey had left two clear footprints in the mud. Across the left sole, there was a split in the rubber sole.

"It was you, wasn't it?" Suzie said, amazed. "Who was in the flower bed outside Sir Peter's study when he was killed!"

"I don't know what you're talking about," Lady Bailey said, but the women could see she was flustered.

"When Sir Peter died," Judith said, "we found boot prints in the mud outside the window to his study. And Becks here worked out the footprints came from a pair of size seven Hunter wellies."

"From their slender calf range," Suzie added.

"But most importantly, there was a distinctive cut across the left sole. A cut that perfectly matches your boot. You were there when he was killed, weren't you?"

All of Lady Bailey's self-confidence crumbled.

"Oh god," she said. "You have to believe me, I had nothing to do with his death."

"Then how about we join you on your walk, and you explain everything that happened that afternoon?"

Lady Bailey looked at the women and then nodded like someone who'd just realized that they were for the gallows.

"You're right. It's been eating me up, if I'm honest, I'd be glad to get it off my chest. And this time, I promise, I'll tell you the truth, the whole truth, and nothing but the truth."

Chapter 25

"SO ARE YOU GOING TO admit it?" Judith asked as they walked along the Thames Path together. "Were you outside your husband's study window when he was killed?"

"You make it sound so bad."

"He was murdered, and you were there. I think it's very much as bad as it sounds."

"I just wanted to see."

"Who?"

"Her." Lady Bailey could see that the other women didn't understand. "That woman."

"You mean Jenny?" Becks said, understanding finally dawning.

"I knew I shouldn't, but I couldn't help myself. It was like an itch. I'd not ever seen her. Why should I? I'm never at White Lodge. But she was marrying Peter, I had to know what she looked like. Prepare myself for all the photos I'd see of her afterward as the bride. It'd be in the local papers, wouldn't it? Or Rosanna would show me; she's never wasted a chance to stick the knife in. She can be ruthless that one. I had to see what she looked like."

The women's hearts went out to Lady Bailey.

"Tell us what happened," Judith said in a far kinder tone.

"There's a public footpath that goes down the side of the garden. Linking the Thames Path to the access road that leads to the house. Not many people know about it. Peter's allowed the laurel hedges down that side of the garden to cover up the path almost completely. But I know it's still there. And I'd heard from friends that the drinks party was happening—quite a few of them couldn't wait to tell me—so when it was in full swing, I walked across Marlow Bridge, headed along the Thames Path to the edge of the garden, and then I pushed past the first laurel bush and sort of scraped along the old path between the bushes and the fence of the property next door.

"About halfway along, there's quite a large bed of shrubs in the garden right by the laurel hedge, so I was able to push through the laurels and hide in among the buddleias. I was so pleased with myself. From my position, I could see down the garden at the whole party and the marquee by the river."

"You didn't think what you were doing was a bit foolish?" Becks asked.

"Of course! But you know what it's like when you get overtaken by an idea? All that mattered to me was to see the bride. But I couldn't work out who she was from the bushes. I was too far away. There were too many people. But I saw that if I crossed the lawn to the house, I could get a better view and still be hidden by the corner of the house. So I decided to have a closer look."

"You didn't mind if people saw you?" Judith said, impressed.

"Oh no, I cared deeply. But there was no reason for anyone to be on that side of the house; it's really not overlooked at all. There's just Peter's study on the ground floor and the window to his bedroom above it. And the thing is, the curtains were closed to the study."

"They were?" Judith asked sharply.

"Yes. I'm not sure I'd have been so brazen if they hadn't been."

Judith and her friends shared a glance. After all, as they'd all seen soon afterward, when they'd broken into Sir Peter's study, the curtains had been open.

"Anyway," Lady Bailey continued, "I was just about to step out onto the lawn to cross to the house when I saw Tristram come out of the front door of the house."

"You did?" Judith said. "Are you sure?"

"He's my son, of course I'm sure. I was so lucky, really. If I'd stepped out of the bushes a second earlier, he'd have seen me. But instead, I watched him walk up the driveway and then disappear onto the road. Once the coast was clear, I scooted across the garden toward the study window."

"A quick question," Judith said, interrupting. "Your son, how did he look?"

"I don't know. What do you mean?"

"Did he look troubled? Or was he in a rush at all?"

"No, he was just walking toward the road. It's not very significant."

"Was anyone else with him?"

"No. I can't see how it matters. Peter and his guests were on the lawn down by the river, Tristram had gone, the coast was once again clear. And you know what? I decided I wouldn't skulk, I'd walk tall. If I was seen, I'd come up with some kind of excuse to explain what I was doing. Not that I had anything prepared. But it was my new plan. It had once been my house after all."

"So you walked across the lawn and hid in the shrubs under the study window?" Becks said.

"No, certainly not. I had no plan to hide in any more shrubs. I just wanted to see the new woman. But after I'd crossed the lawn and was just starting to peer around the side of the house, that's when I heard a car arrive on the gravel. I was surprised, I can tell you. It was Tristram in his sports car. He'd only just left and now he was back? Anyway, that's when things started to happen very fast. I saw Peter coming over to confront Tristram, and *that's* when I hid in the shrubbery. And I'm glad I did, because Tristram and Peter were soon going for it hammer and tongs only a few feet away—which was when I finally saw his woman. I don't see what he sees in her. Not at all. I mean, she's thin—but then she's young, of course she's thin—but she's got an angular face, she's all elbows and knees. That's what I thought. And that hair! You'd have thought you'd get a proper hairdo before your wedding day."

"You overheard what they were saying?" Judith asked, wanting to keep Lady Bailey on track.

"I did, and it was shocking. Tristram was being quite insolent, I have to admit. Saying he didn't care what offense he caused, it was his home, and he'd come and go as he pleased. His prospective stepmother was in tears.

She really doesn't have the fiber to marry a man like Peter. And she said she was going to her bedroom; she couldn't take any more of the pair of them arguing. Once she'd left, that's when it really kicked off between Peter and Tristram, and I've never seen Peter in such a fury. He was telling Tristram he knew what his plan was, how he'd known for some time, and that's why he'd banned him from the wedding."

"Sir Peter said he knew what Tristram's plan was?" Judith asked.

Lady Bailey realized she'd inadvertently implicated her son.

"It was just a figure of speech. He was angry, that's all. And then Peter went into the house. But the point is, I could still see Tristram even after Peter had left. And he looked terrible. Of course he did. He never likes arguing with anyone, it's just he's got a bit of a temper, and Peter always made him lose it. As soon as Tristram returned to the party, I didn't hang around. I got out of the bushes and dusted myself down before crossing back to the edge of the garden and the safety of the bushes there. If you must know, I felt really quite stupid by this stage. I'd so nearly been seen, and I now knew I really didn't know what I'd have said if I had. In fact, I'm not ashamed to admit I was shaking. I pushed through into the laurel hedge, but I took one last look at the house, and that's when I saw him for the last time."

"Who?" Becks asked.

"Peter. He was inside his study."

"You said the curtains were drawn."

"Sorry, I should have said. When I looked back from the hedge, I saw him open the curtains."

"Was there anyone else with him in the study?"

"Not that I saw, but I wasn't really looking. I was more interested in checking that Tristram was okay. He was talking to some women at the party as far as I could see."

"That was us," Becks said.

"Good. Then I don't need to tell you Tristram had nothing to do with Peter's death."

"But were you able to see what was going on in the study when the cabinet went over?" Judith asked.

"I was too far away, and the sun had just come out; it was shining on the windows to the study. I couldn't see inside. Not really."

"That seems a bit convenient," Suzie said.

"I can't help that. There was a glare of sunlight on the windows when I heard this almighty crash from the direction of the house. Although, at the time, I just presumed a waiter had dropped a tray with bottles of wine on it. Or something. I had no idea I'd heard the moment Peter had died. Awful really, when you think about it. I just turned around and left as quickly as I could."

"Did you see all of us head for the house?"

"No, I was heading down the gap beyond the laurel hedge by then. But since you're asking, that's how my boot prints ended up under the window of Peter's study."

Lady Bailey looked at the women as though she now expected the matter to be closed.

"I've asked you this before," Judith said, "but are you sure it wasn't you who asked Sir Peter for twenty thousand pounds?"

"Absolutely not, I've got my pride, you know."

"I'll be honest," Suzie said. "I don't think someone who hides in bushes at her ex-husband's house has much pride."

"And if we're being logical," Judith said, "we only have your word that you were in the bushes when the cabinet fell over, don't we?"

"What on earth are you suggesting?"

"You've admitted you went up to the study window, but only because Becks was able to recognize your brand of Hunter wellies from fifty yards." Becks blushed in delight at the compliment. "All that story about Peter opening the curtains and you not being able to see inside because of sunshine on the windows? You can't prove any of it."

"Of course not. I was on my own."

"Then let me suggest a different story. You went to the study window when you saw Sir Peter inside. And because he was on his own, you went round the front of the house, entered through the front door, and went to the study where you killed your ex-husband by pushing the cabinet on top of him, before slipping out of the house again before anyone saw you. And then, as the guests ran into the house to see what had happened, you saw that the coast was clear and slipped back into the laurel bushes and made good your escape."

"That's not what happened, how dare you!" Lady Bailey said, instantly furious. "I'm the wronged party here; it was my husband who betrayed me, who made me leave him. And now I live in that hovel, surviving on his handouts, and I don't have anything!"

Judith looked at Lady Bailey and saw such bitterness in her—such sharp disappointment and rage—that she had no doubt she'd have been capable of pushing a heavy cabinet to the ground.

"You're right," Judith said. "You've got nothing more than a title at present. A title you'd lose when Sir Peter remarried. But you and Tristram have always been as thick as thieves. Even in the oil painting in the hallway of White Lodge, it's clear how close you two are. And with Sir Peter dead, Tristram would be in charge of the family fortune, wouldn't he? He wouldn't want his mother living in poverty in a two-up two-down. I bet if you played your cards right, you'd be allowed to move back into White Lodge. In fact, when you get down to it, you had motive many times over to want your husband dead. And you were in the vicinity—as you've just admitted to us—so you had the opportunity as well. In fact, now I'm thinking about it, it would make sense if you were the accomplice we've been looking for all of this time. The person your son's been ringing and telling that they need to be patient and wait."

"What are you babbling on about?"

"When we asked you whether Tristram had been making clandestine phone calls, you admitted that he had, but he'd been calling a secret girlfriend. So what I'm wondering is, what if you were saying that to put us off the scent? In reality, the phone calls Rosanna heard him making were to you. Because you've been your son's accomplice all along. It was you in the study killing Sir Peter while Tristram established his alibi outside."

"This is madness!" Lady Bailey said. "I admit I'm close to Tristram, and I agree he's been hard done by, but I was on the other side of the garden, already heading away from the house when I heard that crash."

"But you can't prove it, can you?"

"Wait!" Lady Bailey said as a thought occurred to her. "I think I can.

When I came out of the bushes by the river, I was seen. I can't believe I blanked it, but almost as soon as I stepped onto the Thames Path, I saw Major Tom Lewis driving past on his boat. He shouted a hello to me. I called something or other back—I don't remember. But he saw me. Only seconds after the crash."

Judith remembered that just before Sir Peter died, she'd seen a large boat driving past the garden on the river Thames.

"Oh right," Suzie said, skeptically, "and now you're saying you have an alibi after all? How very convenient."

"There's no need to take that tone with me. If you're going to accuse me of murder, you ask Major Lewis if he saw me, and he'll be able to confirm my story. Now I think you've humiliated me enough for one day, don't you?"

Lady Bailey looked at the women, her chin held high, and then she turned on her heels and headed back in the direction of the high street, and the friends watched her go in companionable silence for a few moments.

"I think we've just found our killer," Suzie said.

"I know what you mean," Becks agreed. "That was so clever of you, Judith, to realize that Tristram's secret phone calls could have been to his mother all along."

"Tell you what I want to know," Suzie said. "Why was Tristram in the house beforehand? He must have arrived on foot if Lady Bailey said he then arrived in his car a few minutes later."

"Assuming she can be believed," Becks said.

"Of course," Judith agreed. "We need to speak to Major Lewis, don't we?"

"I can do that," Becks said. "He sings in the choir and we've got even-song tonight. I'll ask him when I see him."

"Good idea. And in the meantime, I think we should try and find this path down the side of Sir Peter's garden. See if Lady Bailey's story could be even remotely true. And then, I think we need to find out why Tristram was in White Lodge beforehand. Although I've got a theory as to why he might have been there, and it could be just what we're looking for."

"Why?" Suzie asked keenly. "What do you think he was up to?"

"One thing at a time I think. Hedge first, and then Tristram."

Chapter 26

AS THE WOMEN APPROACHED MARLOW Bridge, they could see that there was a disturbance of some sort. Cars were backed up and angrily honking their horns, and there were people with flags on the bridge blocking traffic.

"What's going on?" Becks asked an onlooker.

"It's a climate protest," the man said.

"But we've got to get across," Becks said.

"They're only stopping cars. They're letting pedestrians through."

"Come on, then," Judith said, and led her friends onto the bridge past the backed-up cars.

There were about twenty people with flags, banners, and various rattles and whistles making a racket, and a couple of police officers trying to move them on.

As the protestors chanted "There is no planet B! There is no planet B!" Judith saw that Rosanna was sitting cross-legged at the front of the group holding a handmade sign that proclaimed "You can ignore me, but you'll regret it."

Judith approached, her friends at her side, although she could see that Becks was looking edgy.

"I'm not sure I should be here," Becks said.

"This is all rather wonderful," Judith called over to Rosanna as they passed.

Rosanna was surprised to see Judith and her friends and stood up.

"What are you doing here?" she asked.

"Like the three billy goats gruff, we're trying to get to the other side," Judith said. "But I'm very happy to see you youngsters making a stand. Nothing gets changed in society without direct action. Just ask the suffragettes. Although, I didn't have you pinned down as a climate protestor."

"It's not what I'd normally do," Rosanna admitted uncomfortably. "I'm not a natural protestor, but sometimes you have no choice. Events mean you have to take action."

"Yes, you're right," Judith said, looking at Rosanna levelly. "Sometimes you just have to take action."

The woman with blue-tipped blond hair—who Judith and Suzie had last seen in Rosanna's canal boat, and who they'd since learned was Andrew Husselbee's daughter, Kat—came over.

"Are you being hassled?" Kat asked Rosanna before turning to face Judith. "We have a right to public protest. It's protected by the European Convention on Human Rights."

Now that Judith was looking at Kat more closely, she could see that her eyes shone with a fervor that was somewhat startling.

"You're Kat, Andrew Husselbee's daughter, aren't you?" Judith asked.

"What's that to you? Come on, Rosanna, we've a job to do."

Kat led Rosanna away, but as soon as they'd rejoined the main group, she had a change of heart and strode back to Judith and her friends.

"Dad approves of what I do, you know that, don't you?" she said.

"I'm sure he does," Judith said, and, before Kat knew quite what was happening, she'd whipped her tin of sweets out of her handbag and popped the lid.

"Travel sweet?"

Kat couldn't quite work out what Judith was doing, and looked about herself—at the shouting protestors, at the police—and then back at the woman who was holding a tin of sweets out to her.

"No thanks," she said.

"Suit yourself," Judith said before popping a sweet and surveying the boisterous scene. "It's not exactly Paris '68. But nothing's really been like Paris '68, either before or since," she added wistfully.

"You were in the Paris riots in 1968?"

"You know about it?"

"Everyone who believes in protest knows about it. What was it like?"

Judith's eyes sparkled at the memory.

"I'd just come down from Oxford and was at something of a loose end. So went to Paris that summer. It was *wonderful*—in reflection, of course. At the time, it was all rather hot and bothersome. But can I ask? We're trying to help the police get to the bottom of what happened to Rosanna's father. Would you mind telling me what you think of the Bailey family?"

"That's easy enough," Kat said. "The Baileys are everything that's wrong with this country. Getting rich on the backs of others' hard work. And then staying rich, generation after generation—even when they don't even do anything to earn that money. They're vampires."

"Sit on the fence, why don't you," Suzie said with a smile.

"You like them?" Kat asked, angrily.

"We hardly know them," Becks said.

"At least Rosanna's dad saw sense in the end."

"How do you mean?" Judith asked.

"He cut Tristram out of his will, didn't he? And he was right to. There's no way he deserved to inherit. Not the way he behaves."

"How do you know he cut him out of his will?"

"He told me. It was Christmas Day. Jenny had put on a real feast—even doing vegan dishes for me, which is a first for that family, I can tell you. Later on I found Peter in his study with a glass of wine. He was looking at those spooky X-rays behind his desk. He seemed really old. Kind of weak, you know? And he never looks weak. So I asked him if he was okay, and he said he was worried he'd done a bad thing to Tristram. I asked him what he was talking about, and that's when he said he'd written a new will and he'd cut Tristram out of it. He wanted to know whether he'd done a bad thing. I said it was his money, he could do what he liked with it."

"Did he say who he'd left his money to?"

"You mean, like Rosanna? I didn't ask. It was Christmas Day."

"But Rosanna thinks she'll now inherit?"

"She has no idea. Not for sure. If I'm honest, I've been worried about her. She's become so fixated with this bloody will, it's all she wants to talk about. I think it's been driving her a bit mad. It's just another example of how money corrupts, if you ask me. And buckets of the stuff corrupt even more. Not that it matters. The new will can't be found, can it?"

"And that doesn't bother you?"

"I'm a lawyer, and I've seen too many families torn apart by wills. If it turns up, then it turns up. If it doesn't, then it doesn't. There are more important things in the world to worry about," Kat added, indicating her fellow protestors.

"We don't want to keep you any longer," Judith said, "but can I ask, why weren't you at the party?" she asked.

"What's that?"

"You're Rosanna's girlfriend. I didn't see you at Sir Peter's party the day before the wedding. Why was that?"

"God, I didn't want to hang around a bunch of stiffs all afternoon."

There was something slightly "off" about Kat's answer, and she could see that Judith didn't quite believe her.

"Oh, all right, if you must know, I was getting my hair done. For the big day. Okay?"

Judith smiled to herself. She could well imagine how an eco-warrior like Kat didn't want to admit that she was prettifying herself for a society wedding.

"Where was this?" she asked.

"Divas and Dudes."

"I know it," Becks said. It was where she'd taken her children to get their hair cut when they were small. "Don't they just do children's hair?"

"The owner's an old friend. She does my hair. So if you're trying to suggest I was somehow involved, I was at the hairdressers."

A pink-cheeked young man came over in a flustered rush.

"The police are saying they can move us on."

"Bloody hell!" Kat said, and went with her friend over to the police officers and started remonstrating with them.

"That's the first proof, isn't it?" Suzie said. "That Sir Peter cut Tristram out of his new will?"

"Assuming Kat's telling the truth, of course," Judith said.

"Why would she lie?"

"Sorry," Becks said, looking at some photographers who were snapping the protestors, "is it all right if we move on? Right now?"

"Of course," Judith said with a laugh, and the three women crossed to the other side of the bridge and turned along the river past the Compleat Angler hotel. They joined the Thames Path in the direction of Bourne End.

"I think we need to check Kat's alibi," Judith said.

"You don't believe her?" Becks asked.

"I don't believe anyone—not until we've proved they must be telling the truth."

"Damned right," Suzie said. "Although, it would be kind of weird, don't you think, if she was in the study killing Sir Peter while her girlfriend was upstairs hiding in a wardrobe."

"I know what you mean. That does sound a bit strange when you put it like that."

"Are we really sure there was anyone in the study killing Sir Peter?" Becks asked.

"Yes," Judith and Suzie said at the same time.

"Sorry. Just checking we were still sure."

"Yes, we're sure," Suzie said.

As the women walked in between the grand houses and the sometimes-nearly-as-grand boats at their moorings, they debated which multimillion-pound house they most wanted to own. For Suzie, size was everything, and she was particularly drawn to a three-story gin palace that was parked by a modern house that was mostly a wall of glass that overlooked Marlow lock. Becks recoiled at the thought.

"Imagine keeping all that glass clean," she said.

"I reckon if I can afford a house that size," Suzie said, "I can afford to pay someone else to clean the glass."

Judith enjoyed listening in to the conversation but didn't join in. After all, she already lived in a house on the Thames that she felt was perfect in every way.

The path stopped at a locked gate, which all three women had previously thought was where the Thames Path ended, but they could now see that the thick laurel hedge marked the edge of the Baileys' garden. If Lady Bailey was to be believed, the Thames Path had once cut inland, but the hedge was now blocking it.

"Shall we?" Judith asked.

Becks and Suzie weren't sure.

"Don't worry, I'll lead," Judith said.

As Judith pushed into the thick foliage, her mind was swept back to the summer before when she'd pushed through similar bushes and found the dead body of her neighbor floating in the river just beyond. She doubled down on her resolve.

Keeping the thick laurel hedge to her left, a high wooden fence immediately to her right, Judith pushed onward and was pleased to see that there was indeed a path of sorts she could follow, although she had to keep pushing the thick laurel branches back to keep going. She was like a car being squeezed by the tall rollers in a car wash, she thought to herself.

After about a minute of fighting along the path, she saw the faintest gap in the hedge and stopped. Pulling the branches back, she saw a bed of shrubs on the other side, and White Lodge was standing a little way away across the lawn. She could see the azalea bushes under Sir Peter's study window and the smaller window of his bedroom above.

Judith saw a white cigarette butt in the mud. As her friends joined her, she bent down and picked it up. The word Cartier was written around the filter in gold.

"It's like she said," Judith said. "Lady Bailey was here."

"Spying on her ex-husband," Suzie said, almost appreciatively. "So what's the plan now?" Suzie asked. "We go and talk to Tristram?"

"No," Judith said. "Now—finally—I think it's time we found Sir Peter's missing will."

Chapter 27

INSIDE WHITE LODGE, JENNY WAS standing in the study, taking it all in. She could still see the thinnest slithers of glass sparkling on the carpet. If it weren't for them—and the smashed door frame where the lock had ripped through—there'd be no obvious signs that a tragedy had ever happened.

"Jenny?" she heard Judith call from the body of the house.

"In the study," she called back.

Judith, Becks, and Suzie arrived in the doorway.

"You okay?" Becks asked.

"I was just trying to work out what happened in here. How someone could have done this to him. How Tristram could have done this to him," she added by way of clarification.

"Oh?" Judith asked.

"I'm trying to be logical. He's the only person who benefits from his dad's death. And I know you're saying he might have been working with someone, but what if it's just a lot simpler than that? Tristram killed his father on his own."

"Even though he was outside in the garden at the time?" Becks said.

"But that's what I've been thinking. What if Peter really was in here on his own and pulled the cabinet over by mistake?"

"But why would he do that?" Suzie asked.

"I've no idea. Maybe he was trying to reach something he'd put on top of it. I once caught him storing some chocolate oranges out of view up there. Which was him all over. Who even eats chocolate oranges anymore? But he was furious after his argument with Tristram, so what if he came in here, locked the door so he had some privacy, and then tried to reach up onto the top of the cabinet and ended up pulling it over onto himself? Meaning it was a horrible, horrible accident. We then all break through the door just after, but this is what I was wondering, what if I made a mistake when I checked his pulse? What if he was still alive?"

"Is that likely?" Judith asked.

"I don't know. It's my job to know how to take a pulse, but I wasn't thinking straight. It was all so shocking. What if I got it wrong? I was whisked out of here before I could take a second reading. It's possible—maybe—he was still alive."

"Oh, I get it!" Judith said, remembering that when she and Suzie had waited outside the house with the rest of the guests after the murder, she'd not been able to see Tristram in the crowd. "You're saying that after we all left the house to wait for the police, Tristram crept back in here?"

"It's a possibility. And the thing is, some of the lab equipment that fell off the cabinet was quite heavy."

"So Tristram picked up something big and heavy and delivered the coup de grâce. Meaning Sir Peter died long after we all thought he did?"

"I don't know," Jenny said. "It sounds so far fetched when you put it like that."

"But it's a very definite possibility, you're right. I think it makes it all the more important we find the missing will."

"Yes," Jenny said, "and I've been wondering about that as well. Because the four of us have gone through this house like a dose of salts and haven't been able to find it. So, what if the reason we can't find it is because it's not here?"

"That makes sense," Becks agreed. "So where is it?"

"I don't know. But again—trying to keep things simple—if it's not inside, perhaps that's because it's outside?"

"My thinking exactly!" Judith said. "In fact, we've just found out that

Lady Bailey saw Tristram leave the house on foot a few minutes before he arrived in his car."

"He did?" Jenny asked, surprised.

"So, if he were here beforehand because he was getting the will, the question is: What did he do with it?"

"That's easy," Suzie said. "He'll have burnt it. In a fireplace. And there are three to choose from, aren't there?" Suzie said, getting into her stride. "There are fireplaces in the study, the sitting room, and in your bedroom upstairs."

"I don't think he burnt it," Judith said.

"How can you be sure?"

"I can't be. But what if someone walked in on him burning a document a few minutes before his father was found dead? How would he have explained that? And you know what paper's like in a fire. There are always little bits of it that don't burn. I think it would have been too risky. So I'm tending to agree with Jenny. What if he hid the document outside? Somewhere he was able to dump it between the front door and the street. Who'd ever think to look there?"

With Judith leading the way, the four women left the house and walked up the gravel drive. The tennis court was on their left-hand side behind a low privet hedge.

"You wouldn't stuff a will in a hedge, would you?" Jenny said.

"I don't think so," Suzie agreed. "Anyone could see it."

"I suggest we try beyond the beech," Judith said, indicating a beech hedge that was covered in dry brown leaves that ran along the other side of the drive. It didn't take long to see that no paper had been stuffed into it anywhere. However, there was a brick archway that led through to a knot garden and the orangery that was full of exotic flowers.

The women stepped through the arch to have a quick look, but there didn't seem anywhere obvious to hide a will there, either.

Suzie went up to the door to the orangery and tried it. It was locked.

"Is this normally locked?" she asked.

"The key's in the house, but yes," Jenny said. "It's to stop theft."

Jenny paused, her brow furrowing.

"What is it?" Judith asked.

"Someone's been digging in the compost," Jenny said, indicating a large metal cage to the side of the orangery that was full of mulchy compost. The surface was entirely level and light brown, but there was a small mound of darker-colored mulch near the edge. "The last time I was here, this was completely level."

The other women joined Jenny and looked down at the little pile of darker compost. They were all thinking the same thing.

"I'm not putting my hand in that," Becks said.

"I'm not sure I want to, either," Judith agreed.

"It's only dead leaves," Suzie said, taking off her coat and handing it to Jenny.

Rolling up her sleeve, she shoved her hand into the wet mulch and then screwed up her face as she concentrated on feeling around in the compost with her fingers.

"I hope you never become a vet," Becks said.

"Aye, aye, what's this?" Suzie said.

She pulled her arm out of the mulch, and there was a small piece of ripped paper in her hand. It was wet through, but it had a smear of blue ink on it.

Suzie lay it on the mulch, and although the ink had bled in the wet of the compost, it was just possible to see that it was a handwritten letter of some sort.

This is the I
    Being of so

"That's Peter's handwriting!" Jenny said.

Suzie went back to the hole she'd created and thrust her hand back into it. After a few moments of feeling around, she pulled out another piece of paper.

"What does it say?" Jenny asked eagerly.

"Well, let's see," Suzie said and placed it next to the first. They could see that it contained the signature and name of Chris Shepherd.

Suzie went back to the hole for a third time and started pulling lumps of compost away in her hands until she reached the depth where the bits of paper were. Picking out the remaining pieces, she handed them to Judith, who put them next to the first two pieces in an attempt to re-create the original document. By the time Suzie was done, the original document was mostly re-created and they could all read it.

10th December 2022

This is the last will and testament
of Sir Peter Bailey.
    Being of sound mind and body, I leave my
entire estate to Jenny Page. If I die in
suspicious circumstances, please investigate my
son, Tristram Bailey. He'd stop at nothing to
make sure I don't marry the love of my life.

Underneath the text, there was Sir Peter's swirling signature and the signatures and names and addresses of Andrew Husselbee and Chris Shepherd.

"He left everything to me," Jenny said, trying to process what she was reading.

Judith, Becks, and Suzie didn't know what to say.

"But does it count, now we've found it?"

"I'm sorry," Judith said, "I don't see how it can."

"But you can see for yourself! He left everything to me!"

"In a will that's been torn up."

"It's what Peter wanted!"

The friends could see that Jenny was beginning to get hysterical—understandably so as far as they could see. Suzie and Judith glanced at Becks, wanting her to intervene, so Becks put her arm around Jenny's waist.

"Why don't we go back to the house?" she said. "We can leave the others to call the police."

As Becks ushered a distraught Jenny away, Suzie looked at Judith for confirmation of what they'd just discovered.

Judith nodded in agreement.

"It's not legal," she said. "Although I can't help noticing the envelope is missing."

"How do you mean?"

"We've got the will, but where's the envelope it was in?"

"Forget the envelope!" Suzie said. "All that matters is the will. Tristram got it from the house just before he killed Sir Peter—just like Jenny said. He got the will, tore it up, hid it in the compost, and then went out into the road where he got into his sports car so he could make a big and splashy entrance only seconds later. And now Jenny won't get anything, will she? She's lost the house, and all of Sir Peter's money."

Both women took a moment to realize how awful this was for Jenny.

"And Sir Peter knew it was coming, didn't he?" Judith said, a swell of anger growing within her. "That's why he wanted me at the party. Why he wanted to write a new will that left everything to Jenny—even before they'd married. Because he feared Tristram was going to kill him."

"Which he did, didn't he? Even though we can't prove it. And now he's going to inherit everything. The title, the house, the fortune. He's just got away with murder, hasn't he?"

"But how did he do it?" Judith asked, at her wit's end. "How did he manage to kill his father considering he was outside talking to us when he died?"

Chapter 28

WHEN DETECTIVE INSPECTOR GARETH HOSKINS arrived with two police officers, Judith showed them over to the compost heap.

"What on earth made you think of looking in a compost heap?" he asked.

"Tristram Bailey was seen leaving the house just before the murder."

"Murder?" DI Hoskins asked, amused.

"I'm not going through this again. Sir Peter's will is on top of the compost, someone tore it up and hid it, although I think you should at least note that the envelope it came in seems to be missing."

"You're worried about a missing envelope?"

"No, but I hope that you'll be," she said before turning to leave.

"One moment," DI Hoskins said, not happy that Judith had ended the conversation. "Even if Tristram Bailey left the house just before Sir Peter died, what made you look in this compost heap?"

"As I'm sure you know, before Sir Peter threw Tristram out of his house at the beginning of last month, he accused his son of trying to kill him—with poison—and then wrote a new will. It was just a process of deduction that led us to the compost heap."

"How on earth do you know all this?"

"How on earth do you not?"

DI Hoskins didn't immediately reply.

"I'll need you to make a formal statement," he said.

"Of course. What you do with the information is very much up to you."

With a smile that said she really was done with the conversation this time, Judith headed back to the house. She could see that a dark-blue Jaguar car was now parked outside White Lodge, and she wondered who'd arrived while she was talking to the police.

Inside, she found Jenny and Suzie in the kitchen with Andrew Husselbee.

"Hello Mrs. Potts," Andrew said warmly.

"Please, it's Judith. What are you doing here?"

"Jenny rang with the news."

"He's saying the will isn't legal," Jenny said.

"It's regrettable," he said sadly, "but it's the law."

"It's what Peter wanted!" Jenny sobbed.

"We don't know that."

"We do! He signed the document. He dated it! It's in his handwriting. He left everything to me. I should get his money, I want his money!"

"But there's an alternative explanation that's just as valid. He wrote the will, just as you say, but he then changed his mind and tore the whole thing up."

"And hid it in the compost heap?" Suzie asked.

"It's a fair point," Judith said. "Why didn't he just put it in the bin?"

"Sadly, we'll never know," Andrew said. "But in law, a will that's been torn up isn't valid. It just isn't. It would be wrong for me to give any other impression. I'm sorry. But can I ask, this torn-up will that you found? Did it leave any legacies to anyone other than Jenny?"

"He left it all to me!" Jenny said, and it was clear she no longer cared how grasping she looked.

"How do you mean?" Judith asked.

"I wanted to know if he'd left any kind of gift to Chris Shepherd."

"Why on earth would he have done that?"

"When we were witnessing the will, Chris asked Peter if he'd made good on his promise. Sir Peter reassured him that he had—and said it in such a way that implied that Sir Peter had left a bequest to Chris in his will. But the thing is, as I explained to Sir Peter afterward, the will wouldn't have been valid if there had been any kind of gift or legacy to Chris."

"How so?"

"If you're left a bequest in a will, you're not allowed to be a witness to that will."

"That makes sense," Suzie said.

"But Peter assured me he'd told Chris what he called 'a little white lie' so that he'd still witness the will. There wasn't in fact any kind of bequest to him. Sir Peter was rather dismissive, in fact. He said something like, 'why would I leave money to my gardener?' It was a less than attractive side to Sir Peter. He could be rather snobby when the mood took him. I suppose I'm just being nosy in trying to find out what the truth of the situation was."

"Wait," Judith said, her mind racing. "Chris was expecting to receive something in the new will?"

"Only because that's what Sir Peter told him."

"So, if he'd ever found it," Suzie said, "he'd have realized Sir Peter had lied to him, and he could have torn it up and hidden it in the compost heap—of course he'd have chosen the compost heap, he's the gardener here—and then might have gone to the study on the day before Sir Peter's marriage and murdered him!"

Andrew's brow furrowed.

"What is it?" Becks asked.

"It's possible. But Chris has known for weeks he wasn't being left anything in the new will. I told him that afternoon. After we'd witnessed the will. I was leaving White Lodge, and Chris was going back to work in the garden. I went over and had a word with him. It was the right thing to do, and, as a lawyer, you always have to do the right thing. Even if it makes you feel uncomfortable. It's always better in the long run. But I made it clear to him that, despite what Sir Peter had suggested, he wouldn't be getting any kind of legacy from the will. I'm sorry to say it exercised Chris quite a lot."

"Is that lawyer talk for something?" Suzie said.

"He got angry," Andrew said. "I had to stop him from going back into the house and confronting Peter there and then."

The women exchanged looks. Why hadn't Chris mentioned any of this to them when they'd talked to him in the Two Brewers pub?

"What does it matter what he did or didn't know?" Jenny said. "He wasn't left anything—and I was, that's all that matters. It should all come to me!"

"And yet, that won't happen," Andrew said sadly. "I have Sir Peter's only intact will, from many years ago. It leaves his entire estate to Tristram. I'm sorry."

"But he can't get everything?"

"I'm afraid he does."

"This house? His money?"

Andrew didn't say anything, which was all the answer Jenny needed. She turned and walked out of the room.

"What a terrible outcome," Andrew said sadly. "I think Jenny will need her friends to rally around for a while."

"When will Tristram get his inheritance?" Judith asked.

"You're given a year after the day of death for probate. I'll make sure we don't submit to HMRC until the three hundred and sixty-fifth day."

With another sad smile, Andrew left.

"This is terrible," Becks said. "Jenny should have got everything. It's what Sir Peter wanted."

"But why did he lie to Chris Shepherd?" Suzie asked. "Why not just get someone else to witness the document?"

"Because there's a type of Englishman, isn't there?" Judith said. "Who's wealthy, overeducated, won't take anything too seriously because nothing ever hurts them. Their wealth keeps them insulated from their mistakes."

"They never grow up," Suzie said.

"Exactly. So they just say whatever it is the person they're talking to wants to hear. You and I would call it lying, but they just think they're keeping everyone happy. They're basically children. For all practical purposes, Sir Peter was a liar. He lied to his wife when he cheated on her. And he lied to his gardener by promising to leave him money when he had in fact left him nothing. Although, I'll tell you what I want to know. Why didn't he leave anything in the new will to Rosanna?"

"You're right," Becks said. "That is strange. Not that it matters, though. Because Rosanna never managed to get into the safe in her father's bedroom. She never found the new will, did she? Or she wouldn't have had a reason to be in a wardrobe upstairs while he was being killed downstairs."

"But why not leave her any kind of a legacy?" Judith asked again.

"I don't know," Suzie said. "He was mad? Or maybe he'd just had one of his bust-ups with her that Jenny told us about—and Lady Bailey confirmed. Remember, she said she sometimes thought their arguments might end in violence."

"Although, Jenny said their arguments were never personal," Becks said. "It was always about business."

"All arguments are personal," Suzie said. "And everyone's told us how melodramatic Sir Peter was. Everything about this new will is melodramatic, I reckon. Leaving his whole estate to his girlfriend. Naming his son as his killer. Look," Suzie said, suddenly animated. "Sir Peter names his son as his killer, why don't we just admit it, he's the killer! What's so hard about that to understand?"

"But he can't be," Becks said. "He was standing in front of us when his father died."

"Unless it's like Jenny said," Suzie said, "and Sir Peter wasn't quite dead when we found his body. Which allowed Tristram to slip back into the room afterward and finish him off with a heavy bit of laboratory kit."

"I don't know," Judith said. "That would mean he'd have laid on the floor, injured, for a number of minutes, wouldn't it? I can't help thinking the pathologist would have picked up on that in the postmortem—that it took him a long time to die. If you ask me, my money's still on Tristram having a mystery accomplice who killed Sir Peter on his behalf. It's all too neat, him talking to us outside at the time otherwise."

"But how can we track her down?" Becks said.

"Or him," Suzie added.

"That's *exactly* the right question!" Judith as an idea occurred to her. "We should track this person down. After all, we're pretty sure Tristram went straight to them after the argument on the phone the other day. That or we just lost him on Alison Road entirely by coincidence."

"But how can we track down the person he was talking to?" Becks asked.

"Suzie," Judith said as she turned to her friend with a smile, "when are you next looking after that lovely saluki dog of yours?"

Chapter 29

AS IT HAPPENED, SUZIE HAD recently told Princess's owner that she wouldn't be able to dog-sit for her any longer. Judith found it hard not to wince when she once again learned how her friend was turning down paid work, but she realized her plan could work just as well without Princess. All they had to do was get one of those tracking pebbles Princess wore around her neck. And then, instead of using it on a dog, they could use it to track Tristram's car.

A quick trip to a high-end pet shop on Marlow high street resulted in Suzie purchasing the same brand of tracking pebble. This was then followed by the three women taking a very long and fractious afternoon trying to set up an online account that synced with Suzie's phone. Once the two devices were able to communicate with each other, they then found Tristram's sports car parked near his mother's house, and, with Suzie and Becks checking to make sure no one was looking, Judith unclipped a couple of the poppers that attached the fabric hood to the back of the car, and wedged the tracking pebble in between the leather seats. A couple of pops on the fastenings, and the hood was back in place, and Judith moved away, soon to be joined by her friends.

"Now all we have to do is wait for him to drive onto Alison Road, and this time we can see exactly where he goes," Judith said.

Over the next couple of days, Tristram didn't drive his car anywhere, and then, on the third day, he drove to the supermarket and back again. The following day he went to London and returned in the evening. It was very frustrating for the women. He didn't go anywhere near Alison Road.

Then, late on the afternoon of the fifth day, Suzie was at home with Emma when her smartphone trilled an alert. It was a notification from the tracking app that the pebble was on the move. There was no reason to believe that Tristram was going anywhere of interest, but Suzie's excitement started to mount as she saw the blue dot on her phone turn onto Station Road. This was the route Tristram had taken when they'd lost him last time.

When the dot turned onto Dedmere Road, and then stopped halfway down Alison Road, she knew that they'd struck gold. This was the location of Tristram's girlfriend—or accomplice—wasn't it?

After Suzie phoned Becks and Judith and picked them up in her van, she drove them all—including Emma—to Alison Road, where they parked up in a little turning a few houses along from where the blue dot was marked on the map.

Once Suzie had turned the engine off, she insisted they go into the back of the van so they could look through the windscreen without anyone in the street seeing them. For this purpose, she'd brought three camping chairs and some supplies that she'd grabbed from her kitchen in case they got hungry.

"Brilliant work," Judith said, once they were set up, Emma lying on an old blanket at her feet.

They'd had one stroke of good fortune. Although a thick hedge hid Tristram's sports car from the street, they could see that it was parked next to a small van with the words "Marlow Mocha" painted in a swirling golden script along the side. Even better than that, they could see into the sitting room of the raised ground floor as the curtains weren't drawn. And they could see that Tristram was inside having a blazing row with a woman.

It was hard to see the woman clearly, but she looked as though she was about forty years old, had straight dark hair down to her shoulders, and was wearing a little yellow floral dress over a pair of jeans.

"Does he argue with everyone he knows?" Suzie asked.

"Looks like it," Becks agreed.

"But is that what's going on?" Judith asked. "I'd say from his body language, he's trying to convince her of something. Or apologizing. But he's remonstrating with her I'd say rather than arguing."

"And she's not budging, is she?" Suzie said with a dark chuckle. "He's not getting through to her."

"So who is she?" Judith asked. "Have either of you seen her before?"

"I don't think so," Becks said.

"Nor me," Suzie said. "Although I recognize that van. It serves coffee down by the train station."

"You're right," Becks said. "It does."

"So what do we think?" Judith asked. "Are we looking at Tristram's girlfriend? Or his accomplice?"

As she spoke, they saw the woman go up to Tristram and wrap him in her arms. It seemed to calm him down. She then kissed him. He started to kiss her back, enthusiastically.

"This feels so very wrong," Becks said, as Tristram and the woman carried on kissing. Mercifully, the woman then took Tristram by the hand and led him from the room.

"This answer's at least one of the questions," Judith said. "Whether or not she's Tristram's accomplice, she's very definitely the girlfriend we've been looking for all of this time. The one he's been keeping secret from everyone. I wonder why."

"So what's the plan?" Becks asked.

"Well," Suzie said with an air of satisfaction. "I've got two packs of party rings, a family bag of Wotsits, and a three-liter bottle of Value lemonade. I reckon we settle in."

Suzie ripped open the family bag of crisps and got out a packet.

"Wotsits anyone?"

"Wotsits?" Judith said, accessing her inner Lady Bracknell.

"Your loss," Suzie said and popped a cheesy crisp into her mouth. "Our first stakeout," she said with her mouth full as she opened the bottle of lemonade with a satisfying hiss. "Sorry, I've only got the one mug."

Suzie fished an old mug out of the pocket of her coat and filled it up.

"Donuts! I should have got donuts," she said before taking a glug of lemonade. "If this is going to be like the movies."

Suzie popped another Wotsit.

"So have there been any more crazy crossword codes?" she asked Judith by way of making conversation.

"You mean in the *Marlow Free Press*?" Judith replied. "I don't know. The paper comes out tomorrow."

"So what do you reckon? There'll be another one?"

"I've no idea. But it's a possibility."

"My money's still on it being a way of buying and selling drugs."

"But if you want to buy or sell drugs, don't you just pick up the phone? Or send a text."

"Like Sir Peter did when he took out that money," Becks said.

"Exactly! I've been thinking about that a lot. And I don't think we should say we knew what happened on the day he died until we've found out for sure who he gave all that cash to, and why."

"It must have been someone who was savvy with technology," Suzie said. "Seeing as they used a fake phone number."

"It sounds like the sort of thing my Sam would do," Becks said. "You know, set up a fake phone number and then buy something terrible from the dark web—like nitroglycerin—just to see if he could do it."

"Are you serious?" Judith asked.

"He's a seventeen-year-old boy, and they can be quite stupid when it comes to things like that. How are your children, Suzie?"

"My two? They're fantastic. Rachel is coming down with her partner next weekend, and I'm planning to fly to Australia to see Amy in the spring."

They all heard a phone ring. Becks pulled her mobile out of her handbag, saw who was calling, and busied the call.

Suzie and Judith exchanged glances—Becks was blushing bright red.

"Who was that?" Suzie asked.

"Oh, no one," Becks said.

Her phone started ringing again. Becks was now in a panic and took the call in a fluster.

"I can't talk right now," she whispered into it. "No, not now, you'll have to wait."

She hung up the call and jammed her phone back into her handbag.

"Okay," Suzie said, "what was that about?"

"What was what about?" Becks asked.

"That phone call."

"Oh…it was nothing."

"Didn't sound like nothing to me. Judith," Suzie said to her friend. "We need to talk about the elephant in the room."

"What elephant in the room?" Becks asked.

"You're right," Judith said to Suzie. "But let me handle this," she added, knowing they'd need to be delicate.

"We saw you with that man," Suzie blurted.

Oh, never mind, Judith thought to herself.

"What man?" Becks asked in a fluster.

"After that time the three of us talked to Rosanna at her estate office. Remember? You got a phone call, and you said you had to go and deal with some church business. But you didn't go to the church. Or the vicarage."

"You were spying on me?"

"I'm sorry to say that we were," Judith said. "But only because we were worried about you. And it wasn't really spying. We were just checking you were okay."

"And what was it you found?" Becks asked in a small voice, although it was clear she already suspected what it was that they'd found.

"You visited a man in his house. And were—well, there's no easy way to say this—you were intimate with him. And then we saw you go upstairs and close the curtains."

"You saw all that?"

"Not just that, because the same man was in the Two Brewers when we talked to Chris Shepherd, wasn't he? Which was why you didn't want to go into the pub. You'd seen him sitting at the bar. And then when we were all inside, you and he pretended you didn't know each other while we were talking to Chris."

"Which is how we know whatever you're both up to isn't on the level,"

Suzie said. "I mean, what two people who know each other pretend they're strangers in public?"

Becks looked at her friends and knew she couldn't keep up the pretense any longer.

"Oh god," she said. "I'm in such a mess. You've got to help me."

Chapter 30

"WHATEVER YOU SAY TO US," Judith said. "You know it doesn't matter, don't you?"

"Damned right," Suzie agreed.

Becks nodded, not that her friends' words were making it any easier. She didn't know how to start.

"Why don't we help?" Judith said. "You're having an affair."

"What?" Becks said, startled. "No!"

"You don't have to pretend to us," Suzie said. "We can all see how boring Colin is. Who'd marry a vicar?"

"I would," Becks said, hurt by Suzie's words. "I mean, I didn't. I married a banker, we had all that money and trips to the theatre and restaurants, it was amazing—but he became a vicar, and I've always supported him."

"But you have needs as well," Judith said.

"I really don't. And I know he could be more exciting, but he's given me two wonderful children and is a good man. That means a lot. And he loves me. I know he does. I'd never betray him or the children."

"Wait," Suzie said, her mind spinning. "You're *not* having an affair?"

"No."

"Why not?"

"But the clothes you were wearing at Sir Peter's party," Judith said, wanting to move the conversation on from Suzie's opinion of Becks's marriage. "And the brand-new sapphire ring you've got. What's going on?"

"I'm too embarrassed to say."

"How bad can it be if it's not an affair?" Suzie asked.

"Tell you what," Judith said. "How about you tell us who that man was?"

"Who?"

"The chap you visit in daylight hours behind closed the curtains."

"His name's Viv. Viv Rodericks."

"Why did you pretend not to know him when we were in the pub?"

"I made him promise. No one can know about us."

"So you *are* having an affair!" Suzie said, glad the conversation was back on track.

"No, he's not my lover. It's worse than that."

Suzie was now all at sea.

"What can be worse than that?"

"He's…"

Becks took all of her courage in her hands to make her confession.

"He's my financial adviser."

Judith and Suzie didn't quite know what to say to that.

"The reason he closed the curtains is because the sun was shining on his computer monitor."

"And the way he hugged you?"

"Look, I can explain. After all the excitement the three of us had last year, I felt I could do anything. Colin was so impressed, and I have to admit I liked the attention from the parishioners, too. I felt seen. But the months passed, and Colin sort of went back to being Colin. Kind, of course, but not attentive. And the kids completely forgot that their mum had helped solve a string of murders. I was just the taxi driver who was late to pick them up or the caterer who refused to put chocolate bars in their packed lunch. But I'd changed, I knew I had, and I decided to rebel. And do something I'd always wanted to do, but never had the nerve to."

"Wait," Suzie said. "You don't let your kids have chocolate bars?"

"Now's not the time," Judith said. "What did you decide to do?"

"I took some of my savings. Not much. Just five hundred pounds, and invested it. Financial markets are something I'd always been interested in. From when Colin was a banker, but I'd not had the courage to put my money where my mouth was."

"Oh, I get it!" Suzie said. "You lost it all. And then took out more money to cover the loss—because that's what I'd do as well. And when that went, you realized the only way to get your money back was to risk even more. And before you knew it, you'd got into a spiral of debt. I can understand. Been there. Done that. Bought the T-shirt. Well, not bought the T-shirt, got it on credit and then had the debt wiped out in a county court judgment."

Suzie realized she'd slightly misjudged the mood of the van.

"Sorry," she said. "You were saying?"

"If you're in debt," Judith said, "there are all sorts of organizations that can help. The Citizens Advice Bureau, for a start."

"No, it's worse than that."

"Worse than being in debt?"

"I invested it in cryptocurrency—Sam had been banging on about it for months—and within six months I'd turned that five hundred pounds into just over a hundred thousand pounds."

Judith and Suzie were speechless.

"And that's *bad* news?" Suzie eventually managed to splutter.

"It's terrible! It was only after I'd starting making all that money that I started doing research and discovered how immoral crypto is. All those computers data mining twenty-four hours a day use up more power than Norway—and I'm getting rich from it!"

Suzie tried to orient herself within this new reality.

"Hang on," Suzie said, "you're seriously saying you're rich and that's a problem?"

"In an attempt to mend the mess of all that money I'd made, I got in touch with Viv. I know him through the church. He's an ethical broker. He helped me research companies that aren't destroying the planet. Together, we moved my money out of crypto and into a UK-based company that was researching clean energy for the electric car market."

"But that's good," Judith said. "You're using your money to make the world a better place."

"That's what I thought. The day after I invested, the company ditched their clean energy division so they could focus on their core business—which, I should have said, was exhaust pipes for petrol cars—and the shares went through the roof. I'd made an extra fifteen percent in twenty-four hours."

"So that's why he was hugging you!" Judith said, delighted. "He was offering his commiserations!"

"I know! It's been a disaster! Everything I touch turns to gold and it feels so wrong. There's so much poverty in Marlow. In our parishioners."

"Then give it to a good cause," Judith said, inadvertently catching Suzie's eye as she spoke—and each woman knew, as though through telepathy, that they were both thinking the same thing. Suzie was short of money and needed to pay a builder to finish the extension on her house, and Becks was trying to find a worthy cause to give her money to. She was perfectly placed to solve some of Suzie's financial woes. Suzie's jaw tightened—she was, if nothing else, proud—and Judith felt embarrassed, even though she hadn't said anything.

Becks, however, was still in her own world of financial woe.

"I want to give my money away," she said. "I know it's the right thing to do. But the thing is, I made this money, it's something I did on my own. Not as Colin's wife, or the kids' mother. As me. And giving it up makes me feel like… I don't know, I can't exist. You know, do things for myself."

Suzie was still scowling, and Becks's words settled around the women like a cold fog.

"Don't say it," Suzie said to Judith.

"Say what?" Becks asked.

"If it's worrying you," Judith said to Becks, trying to keep the conversation away from Suzie, "have you thought of telling Colin?"

"He'll disapprove and be all weird about it," Becks said.

"But will he? Because you're right. He's a good man. And I think he'll be happy that you're happy."

"Look, it's cold as brass monkeys back here," Suzie said, rubbing her hands together for warmth. "We're not going to be seeing Tristram and his floozy for a while, are we? And we know she'll be serving coffee at the train station tomorrow. I reckon we could go and talk to her then. How about we pack up for the day?"

"Actually, that suits me as well," Becks said, and Judith knew that Becks's motive for ending the stakeout was so very similar to Suzie's. They were both embarrassed that the conversation was getting too close to the bone.

Suzie clanged open the back door of the van and got out. Judith was quick to follow, and, as they crossed the road, she tried to speak to her friend.

"Suzie—" she started, but Suzie just called back to her, "Check no one's looking," and slipped past the Marlow Mocha van so she could approach Tristram's parked sports car.

Judith checked the road while Suzie popped the fasteners on the fabric hood, pulled out the tracking pebble from in between the seat, and clicked the hood back into place. By the time Suzie returned to the road, Judith realized that the moment for talking to her friend—or even trying to explain that she didn't think she was a charity case who Becks should give her money to—had passed.

They crossed the road back to the van. When they got there, they discovered that Becks had gone.

Chapter 31

THE FOLLOWING MORNING, THE THREE women met in the Marlow Railway Station, a tiny wooden hut on the edge of the town's commercial estate. The only train that ever arrived or left was one carriage long and was known affectionately by locals as "The Marlow Donkey."

"You left in a hurry last night," Suzie said to Becks as she sat down on the bench next to her friend.

"Sorry," Becks said, although it was clear she wasn't really very sorry at all. "I had to get away."

"You could have said goodbye."

Judith was used to Suzie and Becks bickering, but there was an edge to their exchange this morning that worried her. Becks was clearly feeling brittle after her confession, and Judith could also tell that Suzie was worried that her need for money would come out.

"Now come on, the pair of you," she said, trying to jolly them along. "We're here to look at the person who maybe killed Sir Peter Bailey."

Judith nodded her head at the Marlow Mocha van, and the friends could see that the woman they'd seen with Tristram the day before was serving a short queue of customers. Rather disappointingly from their point of view, she seemed friendly, and capable, and she always seemed to have a kind word or joke to share with everyone she served.

"She looks lovely," Becks said, summing up for them all.

"She does, doesn't she?" Judith agreed.

After a few more minutes, the three friends saw that the queue had cleared, and they watched the woman come out to wipe down the little table she'd placed to the side of the van that had the milk and sugar on it.

"I think it's time to put our best foot forward," Judith said, standing up.

"What's the plan?" Becks asked.

"I was thinking of asking for a coffee and taking it from there."

Judith led her friends over to the coffee van. As they arrived, the woman said, "Good morning, ladies," in a cut-glass accent as she refilled a little box with fresh paper tubes of sugar. "What can I get you?"

Now they were up close, Judith could see that the woman's dark hair was held in place with a black Alice band, she had a string of pearls around her neck, and she was wearing a fitted shirt in bright pink under a navy-blue down vest. She looked like a typical horsey type—like a young member of the royal family, Judith found herself thinking.

"Just a black coffee for me," Judith said. "What are you having?" she asked her friends.

"A white coffee for me," Suzie said. "Full-fat milk."

"Do you do herbal teas?" Becks asked.

"We've got everything. What would you like?"

"Do you have turmeric?"

"One turmeric tea coming up, and two Americanos, one with milk as it should be."

As the woman turned to her machine, the three friends looked at each other, all similarly nonplussed. There was no way someone as open and friendly as this could be involved in murder.

"Do you mind me asking," Judith said. "What's your name?"

"It's Sarah," the woman called back over her shoulder as steam poured out of the machine into a cup. "Sarah Fitzherbert."

"You've got a good spot here, Sarah."

"Thank you. I had to convince the council it was worth having a coffee stall here at all."

"They didn't approve?"

"It was a no-brainer to me. I came down here and spent two weeks counting the people who got off and on the train during rush hour. I worked out that if even one in twenty people bought a drink from me, I'd be able to make a profit."

"That's very enterprising of you."

"Yes, well, there's nothing you can't achieve if you set your mind to it," Sarah said as she turned back to the women and put the drinks down on the counter. "Now, would you like any biscuits or cake? I make all the baked goods myself."

"It looks lovely, but I'm sure we're fine," Judith said at the same time as Suzie said, "I'd like a brownie, please."

"Of course," Sarah said with a smile. "And good choice. It's gooey as anything."

Sarah put a slice of brownie onto a paper napkin.

"Is that everything?" she asked.

"I think so," Judith said, reaching into her handbag and pulling out her wallet. As she tapped her bank card onto the card reader, she decided to make her play.

"You know, I've been trying to place you while we've been talking," she said. "And I think I've seen you before. You're Tristram's friend, aren't you? I think I've seen you with him. Or perhaps he mentioned a Sarah Fitzherbert to me?"

"He did?" Sarah asked.

"I can't remember. At my age, you forget almost everything."

"But you know him?"

Judith noticed a touch of desperation in the question.

"If I'm honest," Judith said, "we've only got to know Tristram since his father died. That was such a sad business, wasn't it? I don't suppose you knew Sir Peter at all?"

"Oh yes. My family have been friends with the Bailey family for years. Tristram and I basically grew up together."

"Which is why you're such good friends."

"Such *close* friends," Suzie added with a slow wink.

Sarah looked at Suzie, puzzled.

"I'm sorry," Judith said. "Perhaps we should have said right from the start. You see, we're trying to get to the bottom of what happened to Sir Peter. We were there when it happened. It was so very shocking. And the police don't seem to know what they're doing at all."

"You don't think so?"

"I don't," Judith said, and decided that it was time to start probing. "For starters, they think Tristram could be involved in his father's death. We don't, I hasten to add."

"We don't?" Suzie asked.

"We used to," Becks said, who'd been quicker to guess at Judith's strategy. "But now we're not so sure."

"If you say so," Suzie shrugged, still apparently none the wiser.

"You see," Judith said, wanting to get the focus back onto Sarah, "Tristram benefits so greatly from his father's death, doesn't he? And there's all this circumstantial evidence that suggests he wanted his father to die. The way the pair of them argued, the fact that Sir Peter threw him out of his house last year. Actually, when you think about it, it's no wonder the police think Tristram was perhaps behind his death."

"It's really upsetting him," Sarah said. "How everyone's treating him like he's a suspect. Just because he inherits."

"It goes without saying, we know he can't possibly be involved. He was talking to the three of us in the garden when his father died."

"Ah, got it!" Suzie said, understanding finally coming to her. "Sorry," she said to the others. "As you were."

"So," Judith continued, "we were wondering if there was anything you could tell us about Tristram that would help the police understand him better?"

"You're really interested?"

"Absolutely."

"Because no one understands Tristram like me. We've been dating since we were about fourteen."

"You've been an item all that time?" Judith asked, surprised. After all, Lady Bailey had told them that her son had had a number of girlfriends over the years.

"It's been on and off," Sarah admitted, her smile tightening. "Sometimes far more off than on, if I'm honest, but we always get back together in the end."

"Oh, I get it," Suzie said. "He strays."

"The point is, he always comes back, that's what matters. Not that he goes away but that he comes back."

Sarah's answer was surprisingly upbeat as far as Judith was concerned. It was like Sarah was a 1950s housewife who was desperately trying to keep up appearances.

"So are you together at the moment?" Suzie asked.

"Of course," Sarah said.

"Even after your row yesterday?" Suzie asked.

Sarah's eyes widened. "You know about that?"

"It's possible," Judith said, trying to recover their position following Suzie's overplaying of their hand, "that we were walking past your house yesterday and saw you and Tristram in your sitting room."

"But that's not the point," Becks said, accessing her most sympathetic vicar's wife manner. "All we're trying to do is understand Tristram better."

There was such kindness in Becks's question—although it was also perhaps the fact that, like Sarah, Becks was wearing a quilted down vest over a fitted shirt—that Sarah realized she could open up.

"Tristram's like a kid, really," she said indulgently. "He has impulses, and he acts on them. That's all. It's what makes him so wonderful. He's so spontaneous, there's so much energy. And it helps that he's gorgeous as well, of course."

"And when you say he has impulses, are you referring to more than his affairs?" Judith asked.

"He doesn't have affairs, he strays," Sarah corrected, once again smiling with bright-eyed devotion as she made her point. "But yes, he's impulsive in everything. I mean, after his father died, he told me it was over between us. Can you imagine?"

"What reason did he give?" Suzie asked.

"That's the thing, he didn't! He just said 'it had to be.'"

"'It had to be'?"

"That's what he kept on saying, as though that explained anything."

"After all this time?" Judith asked as a prompt.

"Exactly! After I'd waited all this time! Tolerating his slips, always being the forgiving one. And now his father was dead, he was dumping me? I was… Well, there aren't words for how that made me feel."

"Which is why you rang him the other afternoon," Judith said. "And tore a strip off him."

Sarah was now so involved in her story that she didn't notice that Judith had revealed a part of the story she couldn't plausibly have known.

"I told him that if he didn't come round at once, I'd do something he'd regret. He said I was being crazy—that's the word he keeps calling me, crazy!—when the only person who's been crazy is him if he thinks it's over between us. But I had to get through to him, he had to understand what was at stake."

"And then when he got to you…?"

"I was the one who was upset, but it was him who burst into tears the moment he saw me. Just like that. He said he'd done a terrible thing and he was sorry, so very sorry. I forgave him. But that's the thing. I always have that effect on him. I'm his safe space. I calm him. He stayed the night, and the next morning I knew we'd be together again. Forever. I made him promise."

"And he did?"

"Of course. But then, we've always been together. Even when he thought we'd been apart. We'll die together. That's what we promised when we were teenagers. We'd be together forever. Like those old couples you read about in the papers."

"And when you marry him, you'll become Lady Bailey," Judith said, wanting to gauge Sarah's response. "A millionaire many times over, and chatelaine of White Lodge, one of the finest houses in Marlow."

"I know, right?" Sarah said, unable to hide her excitement at the idea, although she quickly realized she'd perhaps revealed too much, picked up a cloth, and turned around to start cleaning the pipes on the coffee machine.

Judith and her friends exchanged glances, all of them thinking the same thing. Sarah desperately wanted to be Lady Bailey, didn't she?

"I don't suppose you're engaged?" Judith asked.

"We've always been engaged," Sarah said, her back to the women. "Tristram asked me to marry him when we were seventeen."

"And now you'll marry?"

"Oh yes. Now we'll marry. Tristram doesn't have to worry about his father any longer."

"He didn't marry you because of his father?" Suzie asked, puzzled.

Sarah turned back to the women.

"Sir Peter always liked me—that's not what I meant at all. It's more that Tristram was always in his father's shadow. I've always felt he couldn't get on with his life while his father was alive. So now…?"

Sarah made no attempt to hide the anticipation she felt at considering a future without Sir Peter in it.

"Where were you at three p.m. on the Friday that Sir Peter died?" Judith asked.

"I'm sorry?"

"The police will want to know where you were. Now they know you and Tristram are an item. And I suppose it's also a bit odd that you weren't at the party."

"That's easy to explain. I was invited, of course I was. But I refused to go."

"Why?" Suzie asked.

"Because of how Sir Peter treats Tristram."

"Oh, of course!" Judith said. "He wasn't invited, so you wouldn't go, either."

"Do you know he never saw Tristram in a play? Not once. He said what Tristram did wasn't a real job. This coming from a man who's never worked in his life. But all that's going to change now. I'm going to mend that family, that's what I'm going to do. That's all I've ever wanted to do."

"But to answer, the question?" Suzie asked.

"Where was I when he died? That's easy enough to explain, I was on a walk."

"On your own?"

"Yes, on my own."

"Did anyone see you?"

"Let me see. I worked at the coffee cart until about one p.m., went home for some lunch, and then I headed out toward Bourne End at about two p.m. I'm sure there are people who remember seeing me. Oh, yes, I know! I popped into the pub there—the Bounty—to use their loo before I came back. I spoke to one of the barmen. This would have been sometime around three p.m."

"You spoke to a member of staff at the Bounty at three p.m.?" Suzie asked. "The precise time that Sir Peter was dying back in Marlow?"

"Oh," Sarah said, the idea apparently only at that moment occurring to her, "If you put it like that, I suppose I did."

The next train had arrived while the women were talking, and a number of customers were heading for the van.

"I've got to serve my customers now," Sarah said. "Would you mind taking your drinks and moving away?"

"Sure," Suzie said as she picked up their cups and started to head off, Judith and Becks following.

"If she was a compilation album," Suzie said in a stage whisper to her friends as they caught up with her, "you know what it would be called? *Now That's What I Call Mad.*"

"She was a bit startling, wasn't she?" Judith agreed. "It's the title, isn't it? It corrupts everyone who comes into contact with the family. They all want to be Lady Bailey. Except Jenny, perhaps," she added thoughtfully. "I've never got the impression she was interested in the status of the title. She just wanted the financial security. Understandably so."

"So what are we saying?" Becks asked. "We've finally worked out how it was done? Tristram was outside at the party looking all innocent, while Sarah was inside killing Sir Peter? All so she could marry him and become Lady Bailey."

"It's a possibility," Judith said. "We need to find out if Sarah really was at the Bounty pub at three p.m. like she said."

"Tell you what," Suzie said. "After I've done my radio show, I'll go up to the Bounty and see if anyone can remember seeing Sarah that afternoon."

"Good idea. Which reminds me—Becks, did you by any chance speak to Major Tom Lewis last night?"

"Oh, I'm so sorry, I forgot to say. I did. And it's bad news. He's got one of those really big gin palaces with a driving position on the top deck. And he said he was driving past White Lodge in his boat when he heard the bells of All Saints Church strike three. Seconds later, he heard the sound of glass smashing—and a massive crash—coming from inside White Lodge. And then, at about the same time as everyone started to head into the house, he saw Lady Bailey step onto the Thames Path right in front of him out of a laurel bush."

"'At about the same time'?" Suzie asked.

"I made a point of trying to pin him down on how much time elapsed between the crash and her appearance on the path, and he said it could only have been a matter of seconds. He was sure of it."

"There's no way you could push the cabinet onto Sir Peter in the study, get out of the house, cross the garden, and down the pathway to the river in only a matter of seconds," Suzie said.

"But it gets even worse than that. He also said that from his driving position on his boat, he could see the whole garden. And after the crash, he only saw people head into the house. No one left the house and crossed the lawn to the hedge. Least of all Lady Bailey. And he said he'd definitely have seen if anyone had tried to leave the house."

"I see," Judith said, disappointed.

"But that's okay," Suzie said, trying not to be downhearted. "It just means Lady Bailey can't be our killer. Which is fine by me, because my money's on Sarah Fitzherbert. I bet I can't find anyone up at the Bounty who saw her at three p.m. that afternoon."

"You're right," Becks said. "If we've just ruled out Lady Bailey, and we've always known Jenny and Rosanna were upstairs in the bedroom—and Tristram was out in the garden—then who else, other than Sarah, could be the killer?"

"Although we still perhaps need to check out Kat Husselbee's alibi for the time of the murder," Judith said. "For completeness's sake. I'll pop into Divas and Dudes on the way home…"

Judith tailed off as she saw a vehicle approaching.

"Judith?" Becks asked.

"That's a very nice truck," Judith said, indicating a gleaming utility truck with alloy wheels that had a pile of gardening equipment and a lawn mower in the back.

"It is," Suzie said. "But we were trying to work out who killed Sir Peter Bailey."

"As am I," Judith said, her eyes still on the truck as it approached. "Look who's driving that—it's Chris Shepherd."

Becks and Suzie looked at the truck a bit more closely and saw that it was indeed being driven by Chris Shepherd.

"So?" Suzie asked.

"Ladies, I think we've just found what we've been looking for all of this time."

"We have?"

"But I think we're going to have to channel our inner Kat Husselbee," Judith said as she stepped out into the road and held up her hands to stop the truck.

Chapter 32

CHRIS SHEPHERD WAS DRIVING ALONG the road when a woman stepped out in front of him. He slammed on the brakes just in time to stop himself from running her over. The woman he now saw looking at him over his bonnet was Judith Potts.

"Good morning!" she said as though stepping out in front of the traffic was an everyday occurrence to her—which it probably was, Chris grumped to himself.

Chris pressed a button to lower his window.

"What are you doing?" he called out.

Judith came round to the driver's side, and Chris could now see that the woman's two friends were standing on the side of the road. The taller of the two stepped out into the road to continue to block his car.

"Now that looks like a lovely truck," Judith said at the driver's window.

"Can you get out of the road?"

"Just one question. When did you get it?"

"What sort of a question is that?"

"When we asked Jenny Page about you, she said you drove an old truck that kept breaking down. But I can't help noticing that what you're driving doesn't look anything like an old banger. So I'm thinking you maybe bought it as a Christmas present for yourself."

"Can you tell your friend to get out of the way?"

"Absolutely. Just as soon as you tell me when you bought that car."

"I don't have to tell you anything."

"Suzie, take down the number plate, would you? I'm sure we can look it up online."

"What is this?" Chris said, looking in his rearview mirror. A car had stopped behind him and was waiting for him to move off again.

"When did you buy your truck?" Judith asked again. "It's an easy question."

A second car pulled up behind Chris's truck. The first car honked its horn.

"Those cars are getting very impatient."

"All right—if it makes you happy, I bought it just after Christmas."

"You did, did you? How very interesting."

"Now, I'm off to White Lodge. Some of us have jobs to get to."

Chris revved the accelerator of his truck; Judith waved at Suzie to get out of the way—Suzie got the message sharpish and stepped back onto the pavement as Chris drove off, leaving Judith on the road.

There was another beep on a horn, and with a start, Judith realized she was still blocking the traffic.

"Sorry!" she called out and scurried back to her friends on the roadside. As the cars passed, Judith gave them a regal wave, reveling in having caused a bit of havoc.

"What on earth was that about?" Becks asked.

"Sorry, I didn't have time to explain. But don't you find it odd that a gardener would have such a smart truck?"

"Sure," Suzie said. "But he can spend his money on what he likes."

"Oh, I quite agree with that. In fact, I'm grateful he has such expensive tastes. Come on."

Judith led off down Station Road, her friends hurrying to catch up with her.

"Where are we going?" Becks asked, having not really followed what had happened.

"To the library, of course," Judith said, as though it were the most obvious answer in the world.

Marlow Library was a converted early twentieth-century villa that had been extended at the back. As Judith and her friends passed through the white gloss doorway, they smiled a hello at the librarian and went past the children's books to the periodicals.

"What are we looking for?" Becks whispered.

"All of the recent local newspapers," Judith said. "In particular, their cars for sale sections since the twenty-third of December."

"That's quite a specific date."

"I've got quite a specific theory. Remember, we're still looking for the twenty thousand pounds of cash that Sir Peter took out of his bank account just before Christmas."

The penny dropped for Suzie first.

"You think he gave that money to Chris?"

"I've no idea, but as far as I can see, there's only one person close to the family who's suddenly spent a large amount of money since Christmas. I suggest we start looking."

The women started going through the archive of local newspapers, and after a few minutes, Suzie let out a delighted "ha!"

"You've found the truck?" Judith asked.

Suzie looked at her friends as though she was surprised to see them.

"No," she said, and then tore a page out of the paper. She then folded the paper over and stuffed it into a pocket of her coat. She put her fingers to her lips, indicating that she didn't want the others to talk to her about it, and they all went back to looking for any advertisements for a truck for sale—although it took Becks and Judith a bit of time to get back into the task. What had Suzie just torn out of the paper?

As it happened, it didn't take them long to find what they were looking for. Most of the local papers only had a motoring section once a week, so there were only a few editions to go through since Christmas. They found the advert in the January 10th edition of the *Maidenhead Advertiser*. A second-hand Ford Ranger truck that was for sale from a private dealer for £19,000. There was a number listed to ring, so Judith asked to borrow Becks's phone and dialed the number.

"Hello," a man's voice said on the end of the line.

"This is the Maidenhead Police Station."

Becks and Suzie looked at Judith, scandalized, but she just shrugged as if to ask what else could she do.

"Why are you ringing?" the man said on the other end of the line.

"We're tracking a sum of money that we believe was procured through fraudulent means."

"I've done nothing wrong."

"There's no suggestion you have. But can you confirm two small details? You sold your Ford Ranger truck car a few weeks ago to a man called Chris Shepherd. Is that right?"

"I did," the man said, eager to please.

"And he paid in cash, didn't he?"

"I've got the paperwork, it's all above board."

"Can you please answer the question? He paid in cash, didn't he?"

"He did."

"Do you still have any of that cash with you?"

"Mostly. I've not had time to take it to the bank yet," the man added.

"Oh that's just terrific," Judith said enthusiastically before resetting her manner. "Please don't touch the money. One of my officers will be around to collect it. We'll be in contact to arrange a time."

Judith hung up and Suzie gave a big thumbs-up.

"You know it's illegal to impersonate a police officer," Becks said.

"I didn't impersonate a police officer," Judith said, pretending to be offended.

"I just heard you! And you used my phone. If the police trace that call, they'll think it was me!"

"You worry too much," Judith said.

"In this instance, I don't think I'm worrying enough. We both heard you. You impersonated a police officer."

"I didn't. If you recall, I said, 'Hello, this is Maidenhead Police Station.' I was impersonating a building, and I can't imagine there's any law that says a person can't impersonate a building. Now don't worry, Tanika will be able to sort it out when we tell her. But in the meantime, I suggest we go and have a chat with our surprisingly wealthy gardener, don't you?"

Suzie drove her friends over to White Lodge, where they found Chris raking up leaves by the tennis court.

"Hello again!" Judith said cheerily. Chris looked up as the women approached but didn't answer. He just kept on raking. "The question I want to know is, how did you get the money out of Sir Peter? What leverage were you able to use?"

Chris bent down, got up two bits of cardboard, and carried a handful of leaves over to his wheelbarrow.

"I'll tell you what I want to know," Judith said. "How did you even begin to set up a dodgy phone number registered to—where was it?"

"Vanteetee," Suzie said confidently. "No, that's not right. Vantutu?"

"Vanuatu, that's it! Thank you, Suzie," Judith said before turning back to face Chris. "I suppose it doesn't matter how you did it. But, using that phone to hide your identity, you asked for cash from Sir Peter on four separate occasions, for a total of twenty thousand pounds. As for why, well, that's obvious, isn't it? You were angry. Understandably so. After all these years of Sir Peter telling you he'd look after you, you discovered he'd betrayed you. Just like his father had betrayed your grandfather."

"I don't know what you're talking about," Chris said, although it was clear to the women that he was listening to every word.

"Now there you go lying again. It really won't do. We spoke to Andrew Husselbee, and he told us how angry you were when he told you that in witnessing Sir Peter's will you were de facto guaranteeing that you couldn't get any kind of legacy from him. Even though, the very same afternoon, Sir Peter had said that he'd left you money."

"You don't give up, do you?"

"Thank you, that's very kind. We don't. As I was saying, I can well understand why you'd want to get money out of Sir Peter. Although you made a bit of a boo-boo when you paid for your new truck with the cash that Sir Peter gave you. We've spoken to the chap who sold you the truck, and he's still got plenty of the money you gave him—which will be covered in Sir Peter's fingerprints, I'm sure. And yours, now I'm thinking about it. Which will be really quite incriminating. But that just brings me back to my original question. How did you get Sir Peter to give you all that money?"

Chris looked at Judith and decided he'd pretend he wasn't that bothered.

"All right," he said. "Since you're asking, you're right. Sir Peter gave me the money to buy my truck. But there was nothing underhand about it. It was a trade, fair and square."

"Thank you. How was it a trade?"

"Just before Christmas, I sent Sir Peter a message saying I was a great-nephew of his father's lawyer."

"An anonymous message from a fake phone number."

"I'm allowed to protect my identity. It's a basic right. Anyway, I said I'd been going through some of my great-uncle's old papers and found proof that Sir Peter's dad had done over his business partner back in the day. I said it was some company that made X-rays, and the man he'd screwed over was called Mike Shepherd."

"I suppose that's the name of your grandfather?"

"Mike Shepherd, my grandfather," Chris agreed. "But in the message to Sir Peter, I said I was prepared to sell Sir Peter the relevant documents that incriminated his dad for five thousand pounds."

"That's blackmail!" Becks said.

"I don't reckon so. I had something I wanted to sell. He had the money to buy it. So I sold it to him."

"I'm not going to press the point," Judith said, "but Becks is right—this was blackmail, pure and simple. You have no such documents, do you? Or you'd have revealed them years ago and got a big payout from the Bailey family. And you most certainly wouldn't have needed to do it anonymously by hiding behind a fake phone number."

Chris shrugged, making it clear how little he cared.

"Sir Peter fell for it, though, didn't he?" Judith said.

"It was only five thousand pounds. Nothing to him."

"How did it work?"

"It was simple. He had to post the money to a PO box I'd set up. Once I'd got the money, I'd send him the documents."

"But that's not what happened, is it? Because five thousand pounds wasn't enough. So you asked for another round of cash. And then another, and another."

"It wasn't my fault I'd underestimated the price he was willing to pay. But after he'd paid twenty grand, his last text to me was pretty explicit. He wasn't prepared to pay anymore. Which suited me just fine. Twenty grand was more than I'd expected to get. So much more than I'd hoped he'd leave me in his will. It had always been my dream to own a proper truck, and twenty grand was plenty enough for that. More than plenty."

Chris couldn't stop himself from smirking.

"What you did was illegal," Becks said.

"Was it though? I gave him the documents, didn't I?"

"Is that the line you're going to take?" Judith asked.

"Of course I handed them over. And if they now can't be found, that's not my problem, is it? In fact, I reckon he destroyed them as soon as I gave them to him. I mean, seeing as they proved his dad was a thief."

"We both know you're lying about any such documents existing," Judith said, drawing herself up to her full height, which wasn't very tall at all. "It was a con, pure and simple."

Chris looked down at Judith, a sneer on his lips.

"Prove it," he said.

"No, I'm not having this," Judith said, fury bursting from her. "Because I don't think twenty thousand pounds was enough for you, was it? You hoped it would be. You even bought yourself a nice new truck to make yourself feel better. But it didn't. Which is why you came up with a new plan. And you know what I'm reminded of? The character of Leonard in *Howards End*. He's killed at the end of the story when a bookcase falls onto him. It's a rather apt metaphor—just as Sir Peter being killed by your grandfather's cabinet of laboratory equipment is just as apt. It's almost poetic, really. Sir Peter's father stole your grandfather's future when he took his cabinet from him. And now the cabinet was the instrument of vengeance, killing the son of the man who'd wronged your family."

"It's a nice story, but it's just that—a story."

"Where were you at three p.m. on the day Sir Peter died?"

"It's none of your business."

"Were you in his study, pushing the cabinet onto him?"

"Jesus Christ, woman," Chris spat. "If you must know, I was at Platts, okay?"

Platts was the name of the garage in Marlow.

"What were you doing there?" she said.

"The bloody truck was belching smoke, wasn't it?" he said bitterly. "The mechanic there was able to tell me I'd been sold a lemon. After all this time, I finally get the kind of compensation my family has always deserved, and I bloody buy a truck that hardly works. You can laugh now."

"I don't think it's something to laugh about."

"Good. Because neither do I."

"Although there's an irony here, isn't there? Your old truck kept on breaking down, and so does your new truck. Have you thought of maybe not having a truck?"

Judith looked at Chris and saw a mixture of emotions play across his face. There was passion there, and anger, of course—but she was interested to see there was also what looked like self-loathing as well. She almost felt sorry for him. Almost.

"You want to know the truth?" he said bitterly. "That man's lied to me for years. Worse than that, he's been laughing at me. Stringing me along, telling he'd do right by me when he had no intention of doing anything of the sort. Even getting me to witness his will; how sick is that? So yeah, taking that money from him was the least I was owed—the least my family was owed—and I'm glad he's dead. Is that what you wanted me to say? I'll admit it. The world's a better place without him in it. Happy now?"

As Chris picked up the handles of his wheelbarrow and trudged off, Judith realized that Lady Bailey had been right all along. There really had been a blood feud between Chris Shepherd and Sir Peter Bailey. And there was no doubting that Chris was a strong man. He would have found it easy to push the cabinet over onto Sir Peter. What was more, he'd now been forced into admitting that he'd extorted money out of Sir Peter in December. Who was to say he wasn't the person who'd then killed him in January?

Chapter 33

JUDITH TRIED TO MEET UP with Tanika that afternoon, but she explained she was tied up with another case and couldn't get away from the station. It wasn't until the following morning that Judith and her friends finally met up with her, this time at Marlow lock. They updated Tanika on what they'd learned from Sarah Fitzherbert and how they'd finally found out that it had been Chris Shepherd who'd extorted twenty thousand pounds out of Sir Peter.

"I don't know how you do it," Tanika said in admiration, once the women had finished.

"It helps that we're working on the presumption Sir Peter was murdered," Judith said.

Tanika sighed. "I know. DI Hoskins is still insisting our resources are better spent elsewhere."

"But surely he changed his tune when he found Sir Peter's will torn up and buried in a load of compost?"

"That's the thing. He's a very stubborn man. As far as he's concerned, until someone can explain how Sir Peter was killed inside a locked room, it couldn't have been murder. By the way, have you made any progress on that?"

"No, none at all," Judith said. "Although Jenny had an idea. She was wondering if, in all the commotion, Sir Peter was actually still alive after they pulled the cabinet off him, and she failed to find a pulse. It would have allowed Tristram to come in after we'd cleared the study of people and then kill him—long after we all thought he'd died. It would explain how Sir Peter was found inside a locked room. It was Sir Peter who locked it and put the key in his pocket."

"It's a great theory," Tanika said. "Sadly, it won't wash."

"I thought you might say that."

"How long did it take you to break into the room?"

"A few minutes, I reckon," Suzie said. "Four or five, I'd imagine."

"Well, I can tell you, the postmortem said Sir Peter died from his wounds in a matter of seconds. There's no way he could have clung on to life for the four or five minutes it took you to break through the door. If Sir Peter's heart had been beating through all that, no matter how faintly, the distribution of blood within his body—and external bruising—would have looked completely different. The pathologist would have been able to tell that Sir Peter's heart had continued to beat for all those extra minutes."

"It wasn't just those four or five minutes, either," Judith admitted. "It then took us a good minute or so longer to clear the room. And I then loitered a few minutes more having a look around and a chat with Suzie."

"Then that's that," Tanika said. "There's no way Tristram could have killed Sir Peter after you all left the room. I'm sorry, but there's only one explanation that fits the postmortem. Sir Peter looked dead on the carpet when you broke into the study because he really was dead."

"But that means the killer managed to vanish from a locked room!" Becks said. "Which is impossible," she added, and even she seemed to realize that this was hardly a point that needed making.

"Although there is another explanation, isn't there?" Tanika said. "Unpalatable though it is."

"Don't say it," Judith said, a warning tone to her voice.

"Look, I agree Sir Peter's life was…complicated. As you've found out, there's a gardener blackmailing him for crimes committed by his father, an ex-wife about to lose her fancy title who was stalking him in the bushes, and a firstborn daughter who got nothing in the will and was hiding in a wardrobe upstairs. Added to all that, we've got Sir Peter's fiancée, who was about to become seriously rich—so she's lost everything—and, of course, a secondborn son who, every time we uncover new evidence, seems to appear even more guilty."

"Please don't say it," Judith repeated. "Did you manage to get any fingerprints from the torn-up will we found in the compost?" she asked, wanting to distract Tanika from her main point.

Tanika sighed.

"DI Hoskins didn't want the pieces of paper tested, but I convinced him it would look bad if he didn't. He had the last laugh. We were able to lift partial fingerprints from the paper, but they matched the fingerprints of Sir Peter, Andrew Husselbee, and Chris Shepherd—and no one else. The only three people who'd been involved in creating the will were the only three people whose fingerprints were on it. As you'd expect. Which once again proved that Sir Peter hadn't been murdered as far as DI Hoskins was concerned. But the thing is, what if he's right?"

"You said it!" Judith groaned.

"I know it feels wrong after all of this time. Or seems unlikely. But how can it be any more unlikely than any of the other scenarios?"

"How could his death be an accident?" Judith asked indignantly.

"Jenny said Sir Peter kept things on top of the cabinet," Becks said.

"That's really not very helpful," Judith said.

"I'm sorry, but she did," Becks continued. "She said he'd once kept chocolate oranges up there. I only mention it because I've been thinking about that a lot. How he kept things hidden on top of his cabinet. Because we know Sir Peter's will wasn't in his safe when you opened it up. You said yourself the safe was empty. So what if his will wasn't there because he'd hidden it on top of the cabinet? And he was trying to get it down after his argument when he pulled the cabinet onto himself?"

"That's actually quite a good theory," Suzie said.

"No it isn't," Judith said, exasperated. "If he'd been reaching for his will when he died, why didn't we see it near his body?"

"Seriously?" Suzie said, not that bothered. "In all the drama of finding his body, would we have even noticed it?"

"We might not have done," Becks said, testing the idea and finding she liked it, "but Tristram would have. Wouldn't he? And maybe he quietly pocketed it before later shredding it on his way out and hiding it in the compost heap."

"That's a plausible story," Tanika said. "Above all, it explains how Sir Peter was found behind a locked door, the only key to the room in his pocket."

"Look," Judith said, but her friends could see that she was extemporizing, "we shouldn't get too fixated on this locked door. What if there was more than one key? That could explain how the killer locked the door from the outside with his copy of the key while he left the original key in Sir Peter's pocket."

"Sadly," Tanika said, "that's just not possible. Before I was taken off the case, I got the lock in the door taken apart. There were no shavings or filings from any modern metal found inside the lock anywhere. There really was only one key to that room, and it was found in Sir Peter's pocket."

Judith pursed her lips. Much as she wanted to disagree with what Tanika was suggesting, she had to admit that the police officer's version of events had a certain logic to it.

"No, I'm not having it," she said, realizing with a start that she'd briefly allowed herself to be seduced by the easy option. "Right from the start, Sir Peter's been my client. He hired me because he knew his life was in danger. Did you ever find out what poison was in the cabinet?" she asked, realizing there was still another lead that might yet prove how Sir Peter was murdered.

"That's also a dead end," Tanika said. "Officers logged everything that fell from the cabinet, and there was no cyanide in a bottle, or a label, or anything resembling any kind of poison on the carpet."

"So somebody took it out of the room before Sir Peter died," Judith said, reenergized. "And you have to ask, why would someone want to take a bottle of poison out of a room if they weren't up to no good?"

"Judith," Tanika said tolerantly, "maybe there was no poison in the study because Sir Peter disposed of it after his argument with Tristram last year."

"Or maybe Chris Shepherd wasn't telling the truth," Suzie offered. "After all, we know he blackmailed Sir Peter out of twenty grand. Why should we believe him when says Sir Peter and Tristram's argument was about a load of cyanide? The whole thing could be made up."

Judith didn't immediately have an answer to that.

"I know this is so very disappointing," Tanika said. "But I think we're going to have to start imagining that Sir Peter's death wasn't murder."

"I refuse to believe it," Judith said. "I simply refuse."

"I understand. It's hard sometimes. You've spent so long presuming Sir Peter must have been murdered, and done so brilliantly at uncovering all the goings-on at White Lodge, but what if his death really was just an accident?"

Tanika's phone rang, she pulled it out and answered.

"DS Malik," she said, before turning away from Judith and her friends as she listened to what the person on the other end of the call had to say to her. "Say that again?" she said. It was obvious to the others that Tanika was hearing bad news. "Okay, I can be there in five minutes," she said in a rush. "Send the team, I'll hold the fort until the detective inspector arrives."

Tanika hung up and turned back toward her friends. She looked as if she'd just seen a ghost.

"What is it?" Judith asked.

"It's Sarah Fitzherbert. She's just been found by a neighbor in her house. She's dead. Excuse me, I need to get to Alison Road at once."

Tanika tried to put all thoughts of murder to one side as she approached Sarah's house, a uniformed officer already outside it erecting "Police Do Not Cross" tape. Once she'd shown her warrant card, the officer explained that a female neighbor had seen Sarah slumped on her sofa through the window. When she knocked and Sarah didn't wake up, she got her spare key, let herself into the house, and that's when she found the body.

"Cause of death?" Tanika asked.

"Looks like she died in her sleep."

"Could she have done this to herself?"

"She's not left any kind of note behind."

"Okay, then I'm going in to secure the scene until DI Hoskins gets here."

"Yes, Sarge."

Tanika went into the house and pushed open the door to the sitting room. She found Sarah sitting on the sofa in her pajamas, but lying sprawled over the side of the armrest. Tanika could tell from the pallor of her skin that she'd been dead for some time.

On the carpet in front of her, there was a glass tumbler on its side. Most of its contents had spilled out and been absorbed by the carpet, but she could see that there was still a residue of clear liquid on the inside. Tanika felt a shiver run through her as she recalled the conversation she'd had with Judith only minutes before. But, looking at the body, Tanika could see there was no obvious reason to believe that Sarah had been poisoned. Maybe there was a spilled glass on the floor for the simple reason that she'd knocked it over when she'd died?

And yet, Tanika knew, there was the bottle of cyanide that, according to Chris Shepherd, had once been in Sir Peter's study, and which couldn't now be found. Tanika knew there was a simple postmortem test for cyanide poisoning, although it was far more fallible than the movies suggested. In about one in three cases, it's possible to smell the scent of almonds from the deceased's mouth, although the rest of the time, there's no smell at all. Tanika put her head as close to Sarah's as she dared and inhaled air in through her nose.

She could smell the faintest scent of almonds.

She should have been surprised, but something about the realization just made her feel terribly sad. She knew in her heart that she'd been expecting Sarah's death to be murder from the minute she'd heard about it. How many fit and healthy young women died of natural causes in their home? And she didn't believe it was suicide, either. Not if there was no suicide note.

There was only one logical conclusion. The killer had struck again.

Tanika was quietly furious. Not just with the killer, but also with DI Hoskins. She knew in her core that if only he'd treated Sir Peter's death as a murder from the start, this second death might have been avoided. At that moment, Tanika vowed that she'd do everything in her power to make sure that she now saw the case through to the prosecution of the murderer. Even if it meant destroying her own career in the process.

In the distance, Tanika heard the wail of an approaching siren.

Chapter 34

FROM THE MOMENT DI HOSKINS and his team arrived at Sarah's house, things moved fast—although Tanika came to hear most of what happened secondhand later that afternoon. This was because, on arrival, DI Hoskins thanked Tanika for being the first detective on the scene, and then sent her back to Maidenhead Station to start logging the evidence as it came in.

It was after 1 a.m. when Tanika was finally allowed to leave. She knew that her husband and daughter would be warm in their beds, fast asleep—she couldn't wait to get home to them—and yet she sat at her desk, almost too tired to get out of her chair. But it was so much more than that. She felt ashamed. She knew that if they'd made different decisions, there was a good chance Sarah would still be alive.

Tanika said good night to the officers who were going to be working through the night and headed down the staircase to the main exit. But as she reached the ground floor, instead of going through to the reception area, she clanked the fire exit open and went out the back of the building.

It was freezing outside, but Tanika was buoyed by the clear sky and sparkling stars—and the memory that she'd made a very important phone call to Judith Potts from the exact same spot the year before.

She knew what she had to do. She got out her phone and dialed a number.

The person on the end of the line didn't pick up. Just as Tanika was thinking about ringing off, a man's voice croaked, "Hello?"

Tanika felt a smile warm her face.

"Judith, it's me. Tanika."

"Good grief, hold on," the voice said, and then there was a pause while Tanika imagined that Judith was drinking a sip of water to clear the frog from her throat. She was half-right, as Judith was certainly taking a sip to loosen her voice, but it wasn't water that was in the glass on her bedside table.

"That's better," Judith said, her voice now far clearer. "Are you all right?"

"I'm fine."

"Becks and Suzie?"

"Don't worry, everyone's well. I just wanted to update you on the Sarah Fitzherbert case."

"I'm all ears," Judith said without missing a beat.

"You'll be pleased to hear that following her death, DI Hoskins has brought Tristram Bailey in for questioning. He's being held in the cells, pending charge."

"You think he killed her?"

"Sarah Fitzherbert was killed by cyanide poisoning, and we found residues of cyanide in the glass she drank from before she died."

"It's the missing poison!"

"That's what I told DI Hoskins. To his credit, he's listening."

"He thinks both deaths are linked?"

"Finally."

"Then what about the bottle the cyanide came from? Have you been able to find it?"

"Not yet, but we've an officer searching Lady Bailey's house, and Tristram's car as well."

"Lady Bailey won't like that."

"I believe she's made her feelings known."

"Then what about Tristram? Has he confessed?"

"Not yet. He's denying he had anything to do with her death."

"How's he acting?"

"I've not been in the interview room with him, but I watched the video feed. If I'm honest, he's acting like someone who's just discovered that his girlfriend has died. He's shocked. Unable to string together any coherent thoughts. He's a mess."

"Unless the whole thing's an act, of course. He is an actor after all."

"However he's acting, the physical evidence is pretty incriminating. His fingerprints are all over the glass Sarah drank from before she died. As well as Sarah's fingerprints, of course."

"That's fantastic news. So what do you think happened?"

"If you ask DI Hoskins, Sarah's murder makes no sense. Especially now we know she was Tristram's girlfriend."

"But that's not your take on it."

"No. I think it's possible to imagine that Sarah was involved in the murder of Sir Peter."

"Yes, that's what we've been thinking. She was desperate to marry Tristram, she made that very clear to us when we spoke to her. She would have done anything for him."

"Even commit murder?"

"Very possibly. There was enough at stake. All it would have taken was Tristram spinning her a tale that they'd get married the moment his dad was out of the way. And I remember Lady Bailey told us the curtains were drawn on the study window just before Sir Peter died. So what if they were drawn because Sarah was already in there hiding, and she didn't want to be seen by anyone outside? Then, while her boyfriend was outside the house establishing a very public alibi, she waits until Sir Peter comes in and pushes the cabinet onto him."

"How did she get Sir Peter to go into the study?"

"Maybe she just called him in? The only other people in the house were Jenny and Rosanna, and they were both upstairs. They wouldn't have heard."

"So what are you saying? Sarah got Sir Peter to stand in front of the cabinet?"

"That wouldn't have been too hard. 'Oh, Sir Peter, I'm trying to get this object off a high shelf. Can you help me?' And then, as he's standing there, she pushes the cabinet onto him. Assuming she had the strength to get it to fall over."

"I'll tell you what I can't make sense of," Tanika said. "If we're linking this back to Sir Peter's death—".

"His murder," Judith corrected.

"Of course, sorry. His murder. It's all connected to his wedding, isn't it? It can't be a coincidence that he died the day before he was due to marry."

"Agreed. Unless it was done as a massive misdirection. of course. After all, correlation isn't causation. Maybe the killer killed him the day before his wedding because he knew the timing would make us think Sir Peter's death was related to his marriage when it wasn't at all."

"It's possible," Tanika said, although she didn't sound very enthusiastic. "Nonetheless, considering the timing, it's far simpler to presume the murder was connected to the wedding. And this is what I don't get. Why make it so elaborate?"

"Go on," Judith said.

"If you wanted to kill Sir Peter, you could just put a pillow over his head in his sleep."

"Maybe. But you'd have had to get past Jenny."

"Okay. Then how about you wait until Jenny's out one day and shoot him, making it look like a burglary gone wrong? Why go to all of the effort of killing him inside a locked room at a party the day before his wedding?"

"So, let's think about this. Jenny's in the clear because she was upstairs when Sir Peter was killed. We all saw her. And Rosanna was in the same bedroom as well, so she also can't be the killer. Even if she was hiding in the wardrobe. Then, if we're to consider other people who might have benefited from Sir Peter's death, Tristram was outside in front of all of us and didn't go back into the house until we all did. As for Lady Bailey, you should know that Becks has now spoken to Major Tom Lewis, who was passing on his boat at the time. He swears that Lady Bailey appeared on the Thames Path mere seconds after the crash and that he would have seen anyone leave the house and cross the garden at the side of the house. She's in the clear as well."

"Then what about Chris Shepherd?"

"After you went to Sarah's house this afternoon, I went on a little bike ride into Marlow. My first stop was Platts garage, where I spoke to a nice mechanic who confirmed that he'd spent all that Friday afternoon with Chris fixing his truck. He also said that the truck was a terrible purchase, which was at least partially gratifying, but there are dozens of people at the company who'll swear Chris never left that afternoon at any time. He can't be the killer any more than any of the others can be. I also popped in to see the lovely woman who runs Divas and Dudes hairdressers."

"Why?"

"To check up on Kat Husselbee's alibi as well. Just in case, for some reason, she'd been in the study killing Sir Peter—either for Rosanna or for some other reason yet to be established. But the owner of the salon said that on the afternoon that Sir Peter died, between the hours of two and five p.m., she was cutting and coloring Kat's hair. Which is all a way of saying that *everyone* who might have wanted Sir Peter dead has a proven alibi for the time of the murder. They're all in the clear. All except Sarah Fitzherbert."

"You told me she was at the Bounty at the time."

"That's what she told us, but I don't think she was. Suzie took her dogs up to the Bounty this afternoon. She couldn't find any members of staff who remembered seeing Sarah at three p.m. on the day that Sir Peter was killed."

"She was lying to you?"

"It's how it's looking. There's one more person who was working that day—who wasn't there for Suzie to talk to today—but assuming they also didn't see her, then that's no one in the whole pub who can confirm that Sarah was at the Bounty when Sir Peter was killed. And that's surprising, isn't it? You'd have thought someone would have remembered seeing her."

"But they don't because she was in the study committing murder," Tanika said, testing the idea. "You're amazing, Judith. Because it all makes sense now, doesn't it? Sarah killed Sir Peter so she could marry her boyfriend Tristram and inherit the title, the house, and all the money. But Tristram was just using her. And once she'd done his bidding, he killed her to make sure she could never reveal his role in his father's death."

"Actually, this fits with what Chris Shepherd told us. He said that Tristram wouldn't have the gumption to push a cabinet over—whereas I can well imagine a self-starter like Sarah doing exactly that. And then, as Chris said, Tristram was very happy to take the coward's option and use cyanide to kill Sarah."

"I'll get an officer to go to the Bounty pub tomorrow to interview that last member of staff. Make sure he or she didn't see Sarah Fitzherbert."

"Good idea," Judith said.

Judith thanked Tanika for the update, and after she hung up, she tried to feel happy that Tristram might soon be behind bars. But it didn't quite feel right to her. There was still plenty about the case that remained unsolved—not least, if Sarah were the killer, how she then managed to get out of the locked room afterward.

Judith knew there was no way she'd be able to sleep now, so she threw back the covers on her bed, reached for her dressing gown, and went downstairs to the room where her makeshift incident board was. Looking at it, she knew it would need updating, and all of the new facts would need cross-referencing with what they already knew.

It was going to be a long night.

Chapter 35

BY MORNING, JUDITH HAD UPDATED all of her index cards and deployed even more connecting wool and pins on her incident board, but she hadn't got any closer to proving with any certainty who had killed Sir Peter, or how Sarah's subsequent murder fitted into it all. It was so tempting to presume that Sarah had been the first killer and Tristram the second, but Judith couldn't see why Tristram would have been so stupid as to leave his fingerprints on the glass Sarah drank from. Unless it was a mistake? Or perhaps someone was trying to set him up.

Judith heard the clatter of the letterbox.

Putting all thoughts of the case to one side, she scurried back through her sitting room to the front door and saw a copy of that morning's *Marlow Free Press* sitting on the parquet. Scooping it up, she went back to her card table and opened the paper at the puzzles page before she'd even sat down. Taking up one of her pencils, she attacked the clues that gave her the answers in each of the four corners of the grid.

1 Across: *A kiss plus three more could be unlucky (8)*

The first clue seemed briefly impenetrable to Judith, although "a kiss" would often be the letter X, as people signed letters with an "x" when they wanted to leave a kiss. However, X "plus three more" made her wonder if the X was in fact the roman numeral for ten—which was when she found the solution. After all, X—or ten—"plus three more" equaled THIRTEEN, which was indeed an "unlucky" number.

Buoyed by her first answer, she looked at 3 Across and knew from the punctuation at the end of the clue that it was an amusing clue: *Just like that soldier who makes barrels?! (5,6)*

The convention was that when a setter broke any of the crossword conventions—normally in the pursuit of a good joke—they ended the clue with a question or exclamation mark. Or both, as was the case here.

Judith knew that any crossword setter worth their salt would know that the correct term for someone who makes barrels is a "Cooper," and a British soldier's nickname, since the First World War, has been "Tommy"—which brought a smile to her lips as she realized that the answer was TOMMY COOPER. He was a comedian whose catchphrase, when he did magic tricks, was that he did them "just like that."

On to the third clue—Judith knew the answer as soon as she'd read it, even though she didn't immediately know how the clue worked. *17. Scarlet follows bully without love to one of Stoke, Desborough or Burnham (7)*

Any crossword setter—or indeed anyone from Marlow, perhaps—would have known that Stoke, Desborough, and Burnham were the constituents of the ancient administrative region known as the Chiltern Hundreds. So the phrase "one of" them suggested that the answer was HUNDRED. Looking at the other half of the clue to see if she was right, Judith quickly realized that SCARLET wasn't a girl's name, it was the color RED, and that it "followed"—i.e., came after—"bully without love." Well, Judith thought to herself, if you bully someone, you hound them. So, "hound without love" meant she was to take the letter O—as "love" in the tennis scoring system represented zero—out of the word HOUND so that she was left with HUND. And HUND when followed by RED gave HUNDRED. She was delighted with her answer. Now on to the final clue!

23. Leader of the oligarchs desires a yacht before tomorrow (5)

"Leader of" could be a simple instruction to take the first letters of the words that followed, and she quickly saw that if she took the "leader of" the phrase "The Oligarchs Desires a Yacht," she got the letters T, O, D, A, and Y, and TODAY was indeed "before tomorrow."

So, now she had her four answers, did they spell out a secret message?

As before, Judith read the four answers in order, starting from the top left-hand corner. She got "Thirteen Hundred Today Tommy Cooper." "Thirteen Hundred Today" was easy enough to understand—it was suggesting a meeting at 1 p.m. today, the day the paper was published. But "Tommy Cooper"? But then, thinking about it logically, Judith noted that it had always been the word in the corner of the grid that was part of the message, which would suggest that she could ignore "Tommy" and it was only "Cooper" that meant anything. There was a coffee shop on the industrial estate called Coopers, wasn't there?

With a thrill, Judith realized that the mystery crossword setter would be at Coopers coffee shop at one o'clock that day. And this time, she wouldn't fluff it. She was going to find out what on earth was going on.

But first, she still had a double killer to catch—or double killers—and she'd already decided how she was going to do it.

"I've brought a carrot cake," Becks said as she entered Judith's incident room. "And a separate pot of the icing. There's never enough icing."

"That's lovely, thank you," Judith said as she showed Becks to a little occasional table she'd set up where Suzie was already waiting with a pot of tea, some cups, and saucers and side plates.

"I knew you'd bring something," Judith said. "I've already got out the plates."

"I've not got long," Suzie said. "I need to get to the radio station in a bit."

"And the Rotary are holding a soup-and-bread lunch at the Elgin Halls at midday," Becks said. "I'm helping out."

"Of course," Judith said. "As it happens, there's somewhere I need to be at one as well, but until then I thought it would be instructive if we went through everything we've learned."

"*Everything?*" Suzie said, checking her watch.

"As much as we've got time for. Because now we've got a second murder, we need to go back over the facts we know and check to see if they're still true."

"But we know who the killers are. Sarah killed Peter, and then Tristram killed Sarah."

"I don't know," Judith said. "I still find it interesting that no one mentioned Sarah's name before we uncovered her existence. Not Sir Peter when he rang me, and not anyone else afterward."

"They didn't think she was involved," Suzie said, unbothered. "Why should they mention her?"

"Because we kept banging on about how Tristram must be the killer, and even Sir Peter's will named Tristram as his killer. So why was it, when Tristram was shown to have a perfect alibi, no one asked whether he'd inveigled his girlfriend into committing murder on his behalf?"

"Oh, I see what you mean," Becks said, and she took her side plate of carrot cake to the board where she indicated the photo of an olive oil can that Judith had downloaded from the internet. "There's something else I thought of as well. Someone who works in catering—like Sarah—might have thought of using olive oil on squeaky hinges to keep them quiet."

"Good point," Suzie agreed.

"Look," Judith said, "why don't we take each suspect one by one, and try and make a case for how they could be the killer."

Suzie and Becks were happy to agree to their friend's plan, but each time they considered one of the names on the board, they quickly had to agree that the person had an unbreakable alibi—and at no time did the women even begin to work out how any of their potential killers could have vanished from the locked room afterward.

The bottom line was, the only suspect who could have been in the study when Sir Peter died was Sarah Fitzherbert, seeing as no one at the Bounty pub could remember seeing her at the time that Sir Peter was killed.

"Although, we're still waiting to hear from the last member of staff," Judith said, as she picked up her phone and dialed a number. "Ah, Tanika!" Judith said as the call connected. "Just wanting to find out if you've proven Sarah Fitzherbert's alibi yet."

Judith listened to what Tanika had to say.

"Oh," she said. "I see. Well, thank you for letting me know. Yes, we'll be in touch."

"What did she say?" Suzie asked eagerly as Judith hung up.

"Tanika got her boss to send a police officer to the Bounty this morning. He was able to speak to the last remaining member of staff. And this staff member's given a statement saying that at the precise moment Sir Peter was being killed, he was speaking to Sarah Fitzherbert in the pub."

"What?" Suzie said, appalled.

"It's just like Sarah told us. She was miles away, asking if she could use the loo."

"Was this member of staff sure of the time?" Becks asked.

"Apparently so. He was a few years below Sarah at Great Marlow School. He recognized her but couldn't remember her name, so he did a bit of googling once he'd spoken to her until he'd worked out who she'd been. He was able to show his browser history to the officer. He started his searches at 3:03 p.m. And there's no way Sarah could have been in the Bounty at three minutes after three, having killed Sir Peter in his study a couple of minutes beforehand."

"But that's no good!" Suzie said. "That means *everyone's* got alibis! Jenny was upstairs in her bedroom when Sir Peter was killed. And so was Rosanna, even if she was hiding in the wardrobe. Lady Bailey was coming out of a bush in front of Major Lewis on the Thames Path. Chris Shepherd was at Platts getting his car fixed. Kat Husselbee was getting her hair cut at Divas and Dudes. And Sarah bloody Fitzherbert was about two miles away, using the loo. All of them might have had motives for wanting Sir Peter dead, but none of them could have been in the study pushing the cabinet onto Sir Peter."

"One of them was," Judith said. "We just have to work out who. Unless, of course, there's someone else out there who might have been in the study committing murder."

"Like who?"

"I really can't imagine who else benefited from Sir Peter's death."

The women looked at each other, all three of them knowing the case was slipping away from them. After all, how could Sir Peter be killed by someone who wasn't even in the room at the time of the murder?

"Let's go through the physical evidence," Judith said. "Maybe that'll help us work out who the killer is, or how they did it?"

But this new approach was no better. Whether they discussed the olive oil can, or the boot prints in the flower bed—or the will that was missing until it was found torn up in the compost heap—the women didn't feel they were gaining any new insights or moving the case on in any way at all.

Just to be thorough, Becks reminded them of the glass jar they'd found intact on the floor of the study.

"Good point," Judith said. "There was maybe something fishy about that, wasn't there?"

"Considering how I was able to prove how fragile it was," Suzie said proudly.

"Which you did by knocking it onto the floor," Becks said.

"As I say, it was me who proved how fragile it was. But I'll tell you what I want to know," Suzie said, wanting to move the conversation on. "What made you want to look for fingerprints on it, Judith?"

"I don't know," Judith said. "It just seemed the right thing to do—to check for fingerprints on a piece of potential evidence. And I'm sure I wouldn't have bothered if there hadn't been such a strong sunbeam coming in through the window. It really lit up the glass. I could see pretty quickly that there weren't any smears on it at all. It sparkled in the sunlight. Good grief!" Judith said, plucking down a photo she'd printed out of a laboratory glass jar. "We checked that jar for fingerprints in the morning, didn't we?"

"Yes?" Suzie said.

"What time?" Judith asked, excitement burning in her eyes.

"It was about half ten, I'd say," Becks said. "Or a bit before."

"It couldn't have been much later," Suzie agreed. "I was at Marlow FM by eleven."

Judith was stunned. "But that's impossible." she said.

"What is?" Suzie asked.

An alarm on Suzie's phone started to chime, and she picked it up and silenced it.

"Talking of which," she said, "I've got to run. I need to get to the radio station."

"No, of course," Judith said. "Don't let me keep you."

"But you've just made a breakthrough!"

"I don't know that I have," Judith said, not entirely truthfully. She knew she'd just made a stunning discovery; it was just that she didn't have the first idea what it meant.

When Becks said she also needed to get away, Judith realized that she should do what she always did when she was stuck with a problem.

"A good swim will help sort out my thoughts," she told her friends as they left. "Although can you both meet me at White Lodge this afternoon just before three p.m.?"

"Why three p.m.?" Becks asked.

"Not three p.m., just before. Maybe five-to. That should do it. Because, if I've got this right, I think this afternoon, we might be able to identify the killer."

Chapter 36

JUDITH'S DIP IN THE RIVER reinvigorated her, and while she wasn't yet able to prove who the killer was, she knew there was now a critical aspect of the case that she saw with perfect clarity—assuming the results of her experiment at three p.m. were as expected. Until then, she had the perfect opportunity to go to Coopers café and finally get to the bottom of the secret messages she'd been decoding in the *Marlow Free Press*. And while she was there, she could continue to work on the case. It really was turning into a red-letter day, she thought to herself.

Coopers served the commercial estate near Suzie's house and was built into a redbrick unit in a drab sequence of commercial units. Inside it had been transformed into a funky bar, with comfortable sofas up by the door, the rest of the space filled with metal-framed tables and chairs, and low-wattage industrial lights hung from the ceiling. As was typical, the owner's dog, a black Labrador, was asleep on one of the sofas, and the rest of the place was full of a mixture of workers, students, walkers, and young parents all looking for somewhere to get their caffeine fix.

Judith saw a table in the corner and took a seat. When the waiter came and took her order, she asked for a peppermint tea. But seeing as the coffee at Coopers was the best in Marlow, it seemed a waste not to have one, so she changed her order to a lovely latte with full-fat milk, and maybe she could have one of their sausage sandwiches? It's not that Judith was hungry, but she needed to place a big enough order to wait until 1 p.m., she knew. And a slice of the millionaire's shortcake she'd seen on the counter as she walked in would help sell her cover story even further.

Judith was struggling to concentrate on the people in the café as her mind continued to bounce around the case like a ball in a pinball machine, but she kept telling herself that she wouldn't know if she were right until 3 p.m. She had to be patient. And, most importantly, she didn't want to miss "Higginson" by being distracted.

She made herself look around the room, and as the clock ticked ever closer to 1 p.m., she could feel her excitement mounting. Was there a secret drug dealer in the crowd? Or someone shifting secret contraband of some sort. Or—and this was where her money was—having an affair.

In particular, Judith scanned the faces of the three people who were sitting at tables on their own. There was a student wearing headphones who was typing at her laptop, a male dog walker in his fifties eating lunch with his golden retriever at his feet, and a woman in her sixties who was dressed for a winter walk but was also reading an old book, a cup of coffee on the table getting cold in front of her.

Judith had an instinct that the woman reading the book was the person who'd set the clues. There was an air of waiting about her.

That's when the old man Judith had last seen on the bench at the skate park shuffled in, his tweed hat on his head, his thick scarf wrapped around his neck, his hands hidden inside calfskin gloves.

Judith was stunned. The old man's appearance couldn't be a coincidence, but was this really "Higginson," the person behind the secret messages?

Judith watched the man go up to the counter and order a cup of tea. He then took it to a table in a quiet corner. Judith knew it was time to act, but first she just wanted to finish her shortcake, so she wolfed the last piece and munched it as she crossed the café to finally meet her nemesis.

"Mr. Higginson, I presume," she said, as she reached the table and sat down.

The man looked startled.

Now she was up close, Judith could see that he was in his late eighties, had wispy white hair, and the most startling blue eyes. He'd have been a looker back in the day, Judith knew.

"Who are you?" the man stuttered.

"You've led me a merry dance," Judith said.

"I'm sorry, I really don't know what you're talking about."

"You're not getting rid of me that easily. You're Higginson, the crossword setter for the *Marlow Free Press*, aren't you? I saw you at the skate park last week. At the exact time the answers to the four corners of the puzzle said someone would be there. I then saw you meet a woman on the park bench. And if I'm not much mistaken, you're meeting the same woman today. Or perhaps a different one. I wouldn't want to presume."

As Judith was speaking, she saw the woman who the man had met at the skate park enter the café, go to the counter, and talk to the waiter.

"No, I was right the first time. The same woman. Now I don't want to judge, I'll be the first to admit it's none of my business, but you can't leave a trail of bread crumbs like this and not expect me to follow it. And if you're not going to say anything, that leaves me presuming that the woman who's about to walk over here—as both you and I know she will—is someone you're romantically entangled with. Which, and I really can't state this enough, is none of my business, but it's why you have to meet secretly, isn't it? I imagine you can't let your wife know."

As the woman started to come over with her cup and saucer of tea, the man finally found some confidence.

"You're right about one thing," he said. "I'm romantically entangled with her. But my wife doesn't mind."

"Ha! That's what all men say."

"Really, she doesn't."

The woman slowed as she saw Judith already at the table. Now she was up close, Judith could see that the woman was also in her eighties, had a smart haircut, and there was an air of intelligence about her—like one of the female dons who used to teach her at Oxford, Judith thought.

"Hello," the woman said, and Judith noticed that she didn't seem at all bothered by her presence.

"Hello," Judith said.

"I'm afraid we've been rumbled," the man said to the woman.

"Oh well," the woman said, "I suppose that's always been the risk. Mind if I join you?"

"Of course," Judith said, now feeling out of her depth. What on earth was going on?

The woman put her tea down on the table, got a chair from a nearby table, brought it over, and sat down.

"Hello, dear," she said to the man with a smile.

"Hello, dear," he said back, and then they both looked at Judith.

"Why is it that you're organizing secret meetings, but I'm the one who feels in the wrong?" Judith asked.

"I suppose I should be flattered," the man said. "At least you do the crossword each week."

"Of course I do. I'm 'Pepper.'"

"I'm sorry."

"I also set crosswords. My nom de plume is 'Pepper.'"

The man was delighted.

"You're Pepper?"

"It's a pun on my surname—I'm Judith Potts. 'Pepper Pot.'"

"Your clueing is wonderful."

"It's very kind of you to say, and I very much enjoy your work."

"You really worked it out?" the woman asked.

"It wasn't hard. But please put me out of my misery, what is it that I've worked out? Why all the cloak and dagger?"

The man turned to the woman and took her hand in his.

"She thinks we're having an affair," he said to her.

"How wonderful!"

"You aren't?" Judith asked.

"Oh, no," the man said.

"But I don't understand. You said you were romantically entangled."

"We are," the woman said. "We're married."

This was just about the last thing Judith had expected to hear.

"You are? Then why the sneaking around?"

"Because it's exciting," the man said, a gleam in his eye.

"And something to look forward to," the woman said. "I go to Pilates every Thursday morning, and then I sit down with that week's *Marlow Free Press* and do the crossword. Once I've finished it, I see the secret message that only I know to look for. And then we meet up as though we were having an affair. It adds a spark to the week."

There was a sudden crash as one of the waiters stumbled and his tray of glasses smashed to the floor. The whole café was shocked into silence, the waiter apologized profusely to the nearby tables, and slowly the customers returned to their conversation, although there was a sense of unease in the air that took a short while to dispel.

Judith returned her attention to the couple in front of her.

"You pretend you don't know each other?" she asked.

"Not entirely, but we met in our teens, and our courtship was very exciting. Staying away from our parents and the teachers at school. It's a way of capturing that excitement. Even though we're so ancient."

"What if a friend works it out? Or comes to the wrong conclusion, like I did?"

"Oh that's all part of the fun," the woman said. "The danger. Not that it's real danger, of course. We're just having fun."

Judith was delighted to hear the happy couple's story, but she realized there was something about the conversation, or the setting in Coopers, that was striking a chord with her. It was something to do with the murder of Sir Peter, or perhaps Sarah, she wasn't sure which, but she had a sense that the tectonic plates of the case had just shifted.

"I think that's the most delightful story I've ever heard," she said with a broad smile.

"Thank you," the woman said.

"And I really wouldn't want to impinge on such a romantic occasion. I promise I won't gate-crash any more of your dates. But know that I'll be doing your crossword every week, and whenever I see where your trysts are going to be, I'll be smiling."

"I think we'll probably stop now," the man said. "Now we've been caught red-handed."

"Yes, I think that's right," the woman said. "It was only fun when it was a secret."

"Then I can only apologize for being the party pooper," Judith said, although she could see that the couple didn't seem too bothered.

"Oh, don't worry," the woman said, putting her hand over her husband's. "We'll find something else to do to pass the time. Don't you worry."

"I don't doubt it."

Judith thanked the couple once again and left the café. But all she could think was, what on earth was the connection she'd just made?

Chapter 37

BY THE TIME JUDITH ARRIVED at White Lodge just before 3 p.m., she was feeling frustrated. She kept playing the conversation at Coopers over in her mind and also trying to recall every detail of being there, but she couldn't unlock her subconscious. Whatever it was that she'd half thought remained just out of reach, and it was driving her crazy.

She barely noticed Suzie and Becks arriving in Suzie's van.

"You all right there, Judith?" Suzie asked as they approached.

"Oh, of course," Judith said, refocusing on her friends with a smile. "Just thinking about the case."

"Or cases plural," Suzie said.

"Indeed."

"I spoke to Jenny," Becks said. "She's got a doctor's appointment this afternoon, but she left the house keys under a flowerpot in case we need to get into the house."

"That's good to know," Judith said. "Come on, let's see what we can find."

Judith led off to the garden at the side of the house where Sir Peter's study was. The other two women shared a glance and followed.

"What are we looking for?" Becks asked as she caught up.

"We'll see it when we see it," Judith said. "Or, to put it another way, we won't see it when we don't see it. Assuming I'm right—which, I have to say, I think I am."

"You're not making much sense," Suzie said.

"Sorry, I'm excited. We've got to be there for three p.m. sharp."

Judith didn't go to the study window but instead crossed the lawn to the shrubbery by the laurel hedge where Lady Bailey had said she'd been standing at the time of the murder.

"What are we doing?" Becks asked, but it was too late; Judith was already striding into the shrubbery.

Becks looked at Suzie and realized they'd have to follow.

Stepping through the bushes, they found Judith checking her watch.

"Okay, as we all know, Sir Peter was killed just after the church clock struck three, which should be about now."

"Why do we need to stand where Lady Bailey was standing?" Becks said.

"Where she said she was standing," Judith corrected.

They all heard the bell of All Saints Church strike, followed soon after by two further strikes on the bell.

"The cabinet went over about now, crash!" Judith said. "And all of us in the garden started to stream toward the house."

"But we know Lady Bailey can't be our killer," Becks said. "I spoke to Major Lewis. He wouldn't lie to me."

"Now that's *very* interesting," Judith said, her eyes fixed on the house. "I was right. But what does it mean?"

"What does what mean?" Suzie asked.

"What Lady Bailey told us wasn't true," Judith said, but it was obvious to her friends that she was saying the words out loud to try them out.

"What did she tell us?" Suzie asked.

"Shh!" Becks said. "Don't interrupt."

"What she told us *can't* be true. Not when you consider the glass jar that you found in the study, Becks. Good grief, the glass jar, it was empty, wasn't it? Is that what Lady Bailey saw? Hold on, but that can't be right, because that would mean…"

A shiver ran up Judith's spine as she realized, in one glorious moment of revelation, what had been relevant about her trip to Coopers café, and the whole case fell into place.

"It can't be," she said, but—again—it was clear to her friends that she was trying out the idea and was discovering that it very much could be. "Oh, that is *very* clever!"

"You know who the killer is?" Suzie asked, unable to keep quiet any longer.

"Do you know what?" Judith said, still reeling from her breakthrough. "I think I do."

"And how they killed Sir Peter?"

"Oh yes, very much so. I know that now."

"And how they got out of the locked room afterward?" Becks asked.

"And why he had to die, and then—of course!—why Sarah had to die afterward."

"No, wait," Suzie said. "You got all that from standing here and looking at the house."

"Not just looking at the house," Judith said. "Looking at the house at three p.m."

"Can I guess?" Becks asked. "Because I've got a theory."

"You do?" Judith said, delighted.

"Maybe."

"Then why didn't you say anything," Suzie asked, exasperated.

"Because I've never really believed he was killed in the study. It just always seemed so impossible. But are you now saying that that's really where he was killed?" Becks asked Judith.

"He was killed in the study," Judith agreed.

"Then I think it was Rosanna who did it."

"How interesting," Judith said, encouraging her friend. "Go on."

"Because this case has always been about alibis, hasn't it? Every time we find someone who could have wanted Sir Peter dead, it turns out they've got an unbreakable alibi. But if one of them's the killer, then their alibi can't be quite as watertight as we think. And I'm not sure Rosanna's alibi holds up. She said she was in the wardrobe, but was she?"

"She was able to tell us it was Jenny who came into the bedroom and went out onto the balcony," Suzie said.

"*Everyone* at the party saw Jenny go onto the balcony," Becks said. "Anyone could have told her later on that Jenny was upstairs at the time."

"Then what about the coat button Judith found at the back of the wardrobe?"

"But that's what I was thinking—what if she put it there on purpose knowing we—or the police—would find it later on? That would allow her to pretend to be embarrassed at being caught out, and then pretend she was reluctantly being forced into admitting that she was in the wardrobe at the time of the murder. When she wasn't. She was downstairs in the study, killing Sir Peter."

Becks looked at Judith in triumph.

"That's a wonderful story," Judith said. "But I'm sorry to say it's just that, a story. Rosanna's not our killer. Because, whether or not she was in the wardrobe, and I'm inclined to believe that she was in fact there, how did she manage to kill her father inside a locked room and then somehow manage to be outside of it when we opened it up afterward? Can you explain that?"

Becks frowned.

"No," she said. "I don't suppose I can."

"But you can?" Suzie asked Judith.

"I think we need to go inside White Lodge before I can prove it for sure," Judith said. "There's something we need to check. Did you say Jenny left the keys out for us?"

The women found the keys that Jenny had left for them and let themselves into White Lodge. Once there, Judith headed straight for Sir Peter's study.

"Okay, so if it's not Rosanna, are you going to tell us who the killer is?" Suzie asked.

"Just as soon as I've checked behind the cabinet," Judith said as she approached the cabinet that was still standing upright a foot or so away from the wall. She slipped behind it.

"Why do you need to check behind the cabinet?"

Judith stepped back out into the room, but her friends could see that she must have wiped her right hand along the back of the wood as it now had dust and cobwebs on it.

She rubbed her fingers together.

"What are you looking for?" Becks asked.

Judith went over to the fireplace.

"Dust," she said. "Or rather, ash actually. The missing gavel!" she exclaimed, indicating the little stand on the mantelpiece.

"What missing gavel?" Suzie asked, now knowing that she'd either lost the thread of the conversation or was going mad.

"This is a gift that was given to an ancestor," Judith said, indicating the bronze stand on the mantelpiece. "It's supposed to hold a judge's gavel, but it's no longer here."

"And that's important?" Becks asked.

"I think it's critically important. And if I were a betting woman, and I must confess, I very much am, I think we'll find it in the ash in the fireplace."

"Seriously?" Becks said. "You see a gavel that's missing from a stand and predict it's going to be hidden in that pile of ash?"

"Well, there's one way to find out," Judith said.

Judith picked up a fire poker and started to prod it into the ashes of the fireplace, seemingly at random. After a few scrapes around, the end of the poker hit something. Judith used the poker's tip to push the object out of the ash.

It was a gavel fashioned out of bronze.

"You're kidding!" Becks said.

"Well, that's very gratifying," Judith said. "I think that proves my theory."

"Okay, you've *got* to tell us what's going on."

Judith's phone rang, but she didn't seem to hear.

"Judith," Becks said, "that's your phone."

"Oh, of course," Judith said, fishing her phone out of her handbag. "Tanika," she said as she answered the call. She listened for a few seconds and then became agitated. "No, that's no good. He can't." After a few more words from Tanika, Judith cut into the conversation. "Hold on, I'm going to need to think about this, let me call you back in five minutes."

"What is it?" Suzie asked as Judith hung up.

"It's that stupid Detective Inspector Hoskins. He's released Tristram on bail."

"Is that very stupid?" Becks asked.

"I think so," Judith said, and then the women saw her thoughts crystallize. "Oh my word, this is no good, no good at all." Judith turned to Becks and Suzie. "I think there's going to be a third murder!"

"He's the killer after all?!" Suzie asked as Judith started dialing a number on her phone at speed.

Judith held up a finger as she waited for the call to connect.

"Jenny, thank god you answered. You've got to come home at once, you haven't a moment to lose, Tristram's just been released by the police, and your life's in danger."

Chapter 38

WHEN JENNY GOT TO WHITE Lodge, Judith explained how she thought that Tristram would try and kill her. The younger woman was horrified.

"He's the killer? We have to tell the police!"

"Inspector Hoskins has never believed Sir Peter was murdered. There's no way we'll be able to convince him that Tristram is going to try and kill you."

"Are you serious?"

"We're dealing with a ruthless killer, and that's why we've got to keep you safe."

"What about that female police officer who's been here? Would she believe you?"

"Tanika? She's no longer in charge."

"Then what can we do?"

"Our only hope, I'm sorry to say, is to wait until he shows himself, and then we call the police."

"But why not call them now?"

"They won't come. The man in charge is an idiot. And we won't have the proof until Tristram shows himself. But you won't be on your own. There's Becks, me, and Suzie who'll wait with you. We'll be your eyes and ears. And I promise you, the moment Tristram appears, as I'm sure he will, we'll be with you. There's no way he'd dare risk harming you in front of three witnesses."

"Although he's got quite a rage on him."

"He'll still realize he can't harm you."

Jenny frowned, deeply worried, and Judith could see her desperately trying to process what she'd just been told.

"He needs to show himself," Judith said, wanting to make it as simple for Jenny as possible. "And *then* we can go to the police."

"Okay," Jenny said, although it was clear that she really wasn't very happy about it all.

Seeing as it was now dark, Judith and her friends helped Jenny close the curtains to the house.

"This feels so dangerous," she said.

"Don't worry," Judith told her. "You stay downstairs. Becks, Suzie, and I will be upstairs, and we'll keep the lights off. We'll be able to look out of the windows through gaps in the curtains."

Leaving Jenny in the kitchen, Judith went upstairs with Suzie and Becks.

"She's right," Becks said. "I don't think this is a good idea."

"We've got no choice," Judith said. "Seriously. We'll only know I'm right when Tristram shows himself. Now get to your positions. I'll take Jenny and Sir Peter's bedroom. Becks, you stay on the landing—keep your eyes on the driveway. Suzie, you're looking out over the tennis court side of the house."

The women split up, and Judith went into Jenny and Sir Peter's bedroom. She'd chosen it because it had a view of the side garden and laurel hedge that Lady Bailey had used to creep up to the house. It was Judith's belief that if Lady Bailey knew about the secret path that led to the house, Tristram would as well. And he almost certainly didn't know that his mother had revealed its existence to Judith. It was how he was going to approach the house, Judith was sure of it. It's how she would have approached if she'd wanted to arrive unseen by anyone to commit murder.

As she waited and watched, she let her mind wander over the details of the case. It was so improbable that she and her friends would be staking out the garden of White Lodge late at night like this, but what she'd not revealed to anyone was that she still couldn't quite believe the conclusion she'd come to. And yet, she knew from her years of setting crosswords, sometimes the solution—improbable though it at first appeared—was nonetheless correct. It was like the time she first learned that the phrase *Eleven Plus Two* was also an anagram of *Twelve Plus One*. It didn't matter how much every instinct in her body said these facts couldn't be true; they were nonetheless true.

For the moment, though, there was still a scintilla of doubt in her mind. A doubt she knew she'd be able to dispel if Tristram revealed himself.

There was a flash of silvered moonlight on the laurel hedge down by the river. Had the leaves just moved? Judith tried to imagine how long it would take a person to push along the path beyond the hedge, and yes, wasn't that another rustle of leaves in the moonlight?

Judith's heart quickened, but before she could work out if she was correct, a dark figure burst out of the hedge and ran for the house. She was so shocked—by the person's sudden appearance, at the speed of their movement—that she stood rooted to the spot for a few seconds before she could will herself to move.

She turned and ran from the room as fast as she could.

As she reached the top landing, she called out to the others, "He's here!" and Suzie and Becks appeared from their rooms. Before they could communicate any further, they heard a door bang open downstairs and a man's roar of fury.

They clattered down the stairs as they heard Jenny scream, and burst into the kitchen to a terrifying sight.

It was Tristram, just as Judith had predicted, and he had Jenny on the floor, his body on top of her pinning her to the ground, his hands around her throat—her face bright purple as the breath was choked out of her, her eyes bulging.

Judith and Suzie ran to Jenny's aid and started clawing at Tristram's back to pull him off—screaming at him to leave Jenny alone—but he couldn't hear them, his fury had driven him to superhuman strength, his hands gripping ever tighter around Jenny's throat—and then a firm pair of hands reached into the melee and pulled one of his hands from Jenny's throat.

It was Tanika.

The moment Tristram lost the grip of one hand, Becks, Suzie, and

Judith were able to pull Tristram's other hand off Jenny, and he let out a roar of frustration as Tanika threw herself onto his back and handcuffed his hands tightly together.

"Tristram Bailey, you're under arrest for attempted murder," she wheezed as she rolled off his body, Tristram struggling on the floor with his hands tight behind him, the metal cutting into his wrists.

There was a retching sound, and the women saw Jenny pull herself to all fours as she tried to get air into her body again. She took deep gulps of air, but her breath was a terrifying rasp, and her neck was already a livid red of torn and bruised skin.

Tanika was the first of them to get to her feet.

"Bloody hell, Judith," she said.

"One moment," Judith said, trying to recover her breath.

"What the hell were you thinking?" Suzie blurted.

"What?"

"You said she'd be safe! You said there'd be no danger!"

"I didn't think he'd actually go through with it," Judith said.

"He's deranged, of course he was going to go through with it."

"Judith, that was too much," Becks said.

"I said I was sorry," Judith said, but they could all hear the irritation in her voice. "We had no choice."

"There's always a choice," Suzie said. "And we should have chosen the police."

"She's got a point," Becks said. "You misjudged, Judith. You misjudged badly."

"It wasn't my fault."

"What if he'd killed Jenny?"

"He didn't."

"It was bloody close," Suzie said.

"You can't blame me."

"Then who do you want us to blame?" Suzie said, her adrenaline driving her into a sudden fury. "You always think you know best, don't you? Sticking your nose into other people's lives, judging them for not having enough money, or telling them they've got to finish the building work at their house—and what bloody business is it of yours what choices I make, or how I lead my life! How *any* of us lead our lives!"

"Suzie—" Judith said, trying to reach out to her friend.

"No, I'm out of here, I've had enough," Suzie said and strode over to the door to the kitchen. "You'll want my statement, Tanika. You can get it from me tomorrow. You coming, Becks?"

Everyone could see that Becks was in a quandary—being asked to choose between Suzie and Judith.

She made her choice.

"I'm sorry, Judith, Suzie's right. You've always gone too far, but this time it's too much. You used Jenny as bait, and I can't forgive that. I need to get home. Right now. To Colin. To safety."

Becks crossed the kitchen, Suzie—with one final baleful glare at Judith—opened the door for her friend and the pair of them walked out.

Tanika helped Jenny to a chair and asked her if she was all right. She nodded weakly. As for Tristram, he was lying on the floor, his eyes closed in a grimace as he wept great wracking sobs of fury and remorse.

Through the kitchen window, they saw Suzie and Becks get into Suzie's van and drive off. As the van turned onto the main road, a police car turned into the driveway, lights flashing and siren blazing. It drove up to the house and parked next to the squad car that Tanika had arrived in. DI Hoskins got out with two uniformed officers, and the three men ran for the house. A few seconds later, the door to the kitchen burst open and they entered, taking in Jenny sitting at her kitchen table, Tanika at her side, Judith standing somewhat forlornly by the window, and a handcuffed Tristram on the floor.

"Detective Sergeant, what the hell is going on?" DI Hoskins barked.

"Mr. Bailey just tried to kill Jenny here," Tanika said. "I was able to apprehend him."

"But what were you doing here?"

"As soon as I heard you'd released Mr. Bailey, I started staking the house out."

"Why?"

"It was obvious what Tristram would do next. To anyone with half a brain at least."

"I beg your pardon?"

"But then, I've always known this was a murder case. Unlike you, sir."

"You're not senior investigating officer, you have no right to be acting independently on the case."

"Although it was lucky I did," Tanika said, indicating Tristram. "If we'd left this to you, there'd have been a third murder."

The uniformed officers were shocked by Tanika's insolence, but DI Hoskins went extremely still.

"Say that again."

Tanika remembered the vow she'd made to Sarah Fitzherbert after her death.

She lifted her chin and looked directly at her boss.

"If we'd left this to you, sir, Jenny Page would be dead."

"Get out," DI Hoskins said. "Now. You're suspended for subordination with immediate effect."

Tanika looked at DI Hoskins a long moment, and then she headed for the door. The uniformed officers stepped to one side so they didn't get in her way.

"Please take Mr. Bailey into custody," DI Hoskins ordered his two officers. "And check that Ms. Page is all right."

As one of the men went to check on Jenny, and the other roughly pulled Tristram to his feet, they all saw Tanika get into her squad car outside the windows and drive off.

Afterward, Judith wasn't sure if what followed took a few minutes, or much longer, but once Tristram had been removed, an ambulance arrived and a paramedic checked Jenny over. Fortunately, the paramedic announced that there wasn't likely to be any long-term damage, and the best thing Jenny could do was take some painkillers and get as much sleep as possible.

There was no question of taking her statement after her ordeal, and DI Hoskins arranged to return in the morning.

"The important thing to remember," he said to Jenny, "is that we have Tristram behind bars now. He's never getting out again. It's over."

Jenny smiled weakly, although it was obvious that she was still struggling to process what had happened to her.

"I'll stay with you for a while," Judith offered.

"I'll be okay," Jenny said.

"It's the least I can do," Judith said, and it was obvious how much she was feeling responsible for Jenny's brush with death. "I can help you lock up. Make sure you're safe."

DI Hoskins thanked Judith for her help and left with his officers, Tristram pushed roughly ahead of them.

As soon as the police left, Jenny burst into tears. Judith pulled up a chair and hugged her, offering her support.

"I'm sorry, I'm so sorry," Jenny kept saying over and over.

"Can I get you a drink?" Judith offered. "A nice herbal tea? Something stronger?"

"I didn't believe he'd come here. Even though you said he would. I thought you were overreacting."

"I'm afraid that the gavel I found in the fireplace proved to me that I wasn't even close to overreacting."

"What gavel?"

"Actually, why don't you come with me to the study and I'll be able to explain to you how Sir Peter was killed."

"You know? Because that's one thing I don't get. How did Tristram do it? How did he kill Peter? He was outside in the garden…?"

"It was all rather clever," Judith said as she led Jenny through the house. "And it's funny," she added as they entered the study, "how the solution was always in this room. Not so much hidden in plain sight, as hidden in a pile of ash. Because this case has always revolved around the how of it. How did the killer push a heavy cabinet onto Sir Peter and then escape through a locked door? But when you think about it, the mystery of this murder goes deeper even than that. As Tanika said to me a while back, why go to all of this effort? Maneuvering Sir Peter into his study the afternoon before his wedding, pushing a cabinet onto him, and then doing a fancy trick with the lock on the door. It's why I kept coming back to the idea that Tristram was the killer. After all, one of the reasons why you'd want to make the death of someone look accidental is if you'd be prime suspect if the police thought it was murder. But *the day before the wedding*, that's what kept niggling me. As a date, it seemed so willfully chosen, didn't it? To inflict maximum pain to the family. To you, in fact."

Jenny nodded, understanding the point well.

"Which was so very clever of you."

"I'm sorry?"

"Seeing as it was you who killed Sir Peter. Just as it was also you who went on to kill poor Sarah Fitzherbert."

Jenny didn't seem to understand what Judith had just said.

"You're the killer, Jenny. Not Tristram. As that gavel in the fireplace proves."

Chapter 39

"WHAT?" JENNY SAID, BUT JUDITH was gratified to see a watchfulness in her eyes. "You saw what Tristram just tried to do to me!"

"I know, and I almost feel sorry for him. But I'd only just worked out that you were the killer when Tanika called to say that Tristram had been released on bail. If I'm honest, I was still disbelieving of the conclusion I'd drawn, but I knew that if I was right, Tristram would attack you. Which made my use of you as a tethered goat somewhat immoral, of course. But then, let's not get too bogged down in morals. You're a double murderer. Not that I can prove it. I mean, not so it would stand up in a court of law."

"This is a sick joke."

"Do you mind if I sit down?" Judith said, and went to the armchair by the fireplace. "If I'm honest, I feel really quite tired and somewhat nervous. I didn't get much sleep last night. And I'm putting myself at your mercy. Although I'd add, the police saw that I stayed with you when they left. And that you were the only other person in the house. If anything bad happened to me, I don't see how you'd be able to say anyone else was behind it."

"I want you to stop this madness right now. I loved Peter."

"You didn't. You were just after his money. Of course you were. He was rich."

"And I don't have it! I don't get a penny!"

"I know, it was so very smart of you, wasn't it? After all, as Becks remarked that first day, why would a bride kill her rich husband-to-be *the day before her wedding*? If you'd just waited twenty-four hours before offing him, you'd be a millionaire, the owner of this Georgian mansion, and styled Lady Bailey for the rest of your life. Instead, because you weren't in fact married, you got nothing. But here's what this also means: if you *had* waited twenty-four hours, you'd have been the prime suspect. Not Tristram. As Rosanna said, a woman appears from nowhere, ensnares a vain and self-absorbed man, and on the very first day that she'd be due to inherit his entire estate, he dies in a tragic accident? The police would immediately throw their spotlight onto you. In fact, if Peter were to die any time after you'd married him, suspicion would always fall on you."

"But Peter had already left everything to me. Hadn't he? In his will. The one he wrote in December."

"Yes, it must have been a terrible shock to you when Andrew Husselbee arrived saying there was a new will. After all, your whole plan was based on it appearing as though you didn't benefit in any way from Sir Peter's death. And here was a document that might say you inherited everything—the one thing you'd gone to such enormous efforts to make sure would never happen.

"But you were able to improvise quite brilliantly. I remember that night well. Andrew said he'd seen Sir Peter put the new will into the bedroom safe with his own eyes. It's hardly a stretch to imagine that if he put it in there a month ago, it was still there on the day he died. Your heart must have been racing as I tried to guess the code to open the door. Your plan would be fatally undermined if the will inside it left any kind of legacy to you.

"It's funny how you didn't offer to help with the code until I suggested we try the birth date of Sir Peter's father. Even then, I think you'd have pretended to get the numbers wrong if it hadn't been for the fact that Andrew also knew the date. So suddenly you're babbling about Peter telling you all about "glorious twelfth," but—and here's the key point—it was only now, when you knew the safe would be opened whether you liked it or not, that you offered to do it yourself. You knew your only hope was to try and block our view of what was inside as you opened it—which allowed you to slip any envelope you found in there up your sleeve. Or down your décolletage. Or wherever it was you hid it. But you spirited the envelope out of the safe as you stepped away and we all crowded around it. I imagine you then made a better job of hiding it while we weren't looking. Under a pillow on the bed, or wherever.

"And let's be honest, who'd be looking too closely at you? We'd bought into the lie that you were the grieving fiancée. Why would you have ever wanted to keep Sir Peter's will a secret? Especially when you could have benefited financially from it. But, as I say, your whole plan was based on you *not* benefiting financially from Sir Peter's death. I can't imagine how shocked you must have been when you later opened the envelope and had your worst fears confirmed. Sir Peter—foolish, lovestruck Sir Peter—had indeed left everything to you."

"This is all just crazy."

"It isn't, as both you and I know."

"Then how on earth do you think I managed to push over a cabinet on the ground floor inside a room that was locked while I was on a different floor at the time?"

"I'd be delighted to explain. But first I should tell you that I know you weren't working alone. You've had an accomplice all this time. I don't think it would have occurred to me if I hadn't bumped into a lovely couple in Coopers café. They're married, but they sometimes pretend in public that they don't know each other. It set me thinking—of people in this case who might have pretended they didn't know each other when in fact they were secretly involved with each other. Your accomplice was Tristram."

"Okay, now that's insane."

"No, it's far from insane, but then, you and Tristram have worked so hard to make it look like you hated each other ever since you came into the family. When in reality, yours and Tristram's was a deep, and very definitely warped, but also terrifyingly intense, love."

"The man just tried to kill me."

"And that's how I was finally able to prove that he was indeed your accomplice. Your plans had begun to spin out of control by then. But I'll come to that. First, let's go to Florence. At the beginning of last year. When you first met Sir Peter in a bar. You told us he chatted you up, but let me tell you a slightly different story. You see, Tristram's got the poster for the theatre show he was doing in Florence on the wall of his bedroom. It had only four people in it, all of them men. And the other names on the poster were also men. It struck me as puzzling at the time. There was no reason why Tristram shouldn't have had his affair with a man, but no one else mentioned that he was interested in men. So I found myself wondering, where was the woman in the production who'd turned his head? But then, I thought, what if in reality he'd fallen in love with someone else? Someone who we know was in Florence at that time—looking after an elderly spinster as it happened. That person being you."

Judith could see that Jenny was hanging on her every word. *Good*, she thought to herself. She should.

"Although I wonder if 'falling in love' is quite the right phrase. Tristram's mother said that Tristram's like a loyal Labrador, and Chris Shepherd said he was fundamentally weak, the sort of person who'd join a cult. I think that when you met Tristram in Florence, you saw him for what he was—a rather dim posh-boy who came from a superrich family. So you set about grooming him. At first, I'm sure it was just about getting access to his credit card. But I'm just as sure that, during pillow talk, Tristram would have told you all about how wealthy he was going to be, how his wife would become Lady Bailey, and how she'd get to live in a mansion in Marlow. You knew you could keep Tristram slavishly in love with you, but it occurred to you, why should you have to wait until Sir Peter died before Tristram inherited his fortune? Maybe there was a way of accelerating his father toward death?

"I don't know exactly when you hatched your diabolical plan. But I imagine it was when you learned that Sir Peter had come to Florence to fetch Tristram back to the UK. And Tristram—poor, craven, impressionable Tristram—allowed himself to be persuaded by you. And although it would involve you seducing his father, let's not forget that Tristram was prepared to be party to the murder of his father, a man who he'd felt crushed by his whole life. No pun intended, seeing as we both know how he died. But I wonder if using his son's girlfriend to seduce the father just added to the deliciousness of the plan. I'm sure that's how you characterized it to Tristram.

"Tristram of course told you that Sir Peter had recently been diagnosed with diabetes, so you made sure you bumped into him in a bar and revealed that you were a nurse for hire—just as you told us. What else happened that night, we can't possibly know for sure as Sir Peter's no longer here to tell us. But I'm guessing you seduced him. Made him fall in love with you. Or in lust, at least. And then, after Sir Peter returned to England with his errant son in tow, not realizing the mortal danger he was putting himself in, he hired you to be his live-in nurse. Poor man. He thought he was having his wicked ways with a younger woman; little did he know he'd let a black widow spider into his home.

"And when you and Tristram met up again, you pretended that you didn't know each other. And that you hated each other. I don't think that was too hard for you, seeing as I don't believe you love anyone very much. Ironically, it helped that Rosanna was also on to you from the first, believing that you were only after her father's money. If only she'd known the half of it.

"When no one was around, you and Tristram plotted how best to kill Sir Peter. As you know, Tristram wasn't quite as discreet as he should have been, meaning he was spotted making secretive phone calls—by both his mother and Rosanna. The presumption they made was that he had a girlfriend on the side. When we then uncovered the existence of Sarah Fitzherbert, I have to admit I made a terrible mistake. Because I'd been looking for a secret girlfriend—and here was a secret girlfriend—I presumed that the two were one and the same person. But Tristram had more than one secret girlfriend, didn't he?

"But let's not get ahead of ourselves. Because here—finally!—was the genius of your plan. You would get Sir Peter to propose to you, and then dispatch him *the day before the wedding*. Who'd then suspect you of being the murderer? You'd quite literally be the last person who'd have wanted him dead. Or so it would appear. But then if, after some time, you and Tristram started dating, people would of course gossip, but you wouldn't have been committing any kind of crime. And lord knows, stranger things have happened than a girlfriend falling in love with her dead lover's son. It was such an elegant plan, really.

"All you had to do was come up with a way of killing Sir Peter as near as possible to the wedding day. And here you hit a bit of a snag. As DS Malik and I agreed the other day, it's not easy killing someone. Or let me rephrase that. It's easy to kill someone you have absolutely no connection with, but you knew the police would investigate you the moment Sir Peter died in suspicious circumstances. So what's a murderous girl to do?

"Tristram briefly thought of using poison. But Sir Peter caught him trying to remove it from his study, which didn't make your job any easier. But it did help you come to a realization. Sir Peter's death had to look like an accident. In fact, you decided that the best kind of accident he could suffer would be when it would simply be impossible to see how he could have been murdered. Which is why he ended up dying inside a locked room that had only one key—which was found in his pocket.

"And, of course, you knew Tristram would be a lightning rod for any police investigation, so your plan had to make sure that he had a truly unbreakable alibi. Which is why, I now realize, it was almost certainly Tristram who invited me to the party.

"It was quite a clever flourish, really. After all, I didn't really know how Sir Peter spoke. It was quite easy for an actor like Tristram to impersonate his own father. I mean, imagine pulling off your coup de théâtre of the murder and having no one who the police trusted nearby to witness it. Having a police officer at the party would be too risky, but what about that old dear who solved those murders last year? I can well imagine how the pair of you thought I'd be the perfect person to confirm to the police that Tristram had indeed been outside at the party when Sir Peter died. It's why Tristram came over and talked to me and my friends while you were committing murder. In a funny sort of way, I'm flattered. You considered me a reliable witness."

"You do you realize this is all conjecture," Jenny said.

"Oh, I quite agree, although there'll be elements that can now be proven. That you and Tristram became an item in Florence? Bank statements and witness testimonies will be able to prove that. And, as you know, there'll be all sorts of evidence in this room of how you did it. Come on, it was so clever, there must be a bit of you that wants to hear me confirm how brilliant you were. In fact, you only made one mistake. You planned a winter wedding rather than a summer one."

"That was a mistake?"

"Oh yes," Judith said, glad finally that she was managing to draw Jenny into the conversation. "It's how I managed to work out that you were the killer, and how you did it."

"Now this I'd like to hear."

"Very well. Let me tell you how you killed Sir Peter Bailey."

Chapter 40

"I'D LIKE TO POINT OUT," Judith said, "now that we're talking, that there were a number of other clues—anomalies, really—that also presented themselves. Like the missing gavel from the mantelpiece. And the 'curious incident,' as Holmes would say, of the glass jar that didn't break. What else? Well, let's see, Rosanna's testimony that you had a cigarette when you went to your bedroom after the argument at the party, Lady Bailey's observation that Tristram left the house just before he arrived in his car—and a hook on the wall that had once been used to hold the cabinet against the wall. All of these little details aren't necessarily all that interesting when taken in isolation, but if you line them up in the right order, they tell the most incredible story."

"What if I admit you're right?" Jenny said, suddenly interrupting.

A thrill ran through Judith. She'd hoped that, as she'd tightened the noose, Jenny would offer some sort of deal.

"Admit to what?"

"That I fell in love with Tristram. In Florence. And that we made a plan for me to seduce his father."

"And…?"

"Very well—that we planned to kill him."

"Thank you," Judith said. "I really can't tell you how gratifying it is to hear you say that."

"But before you get too pleased with yourself," Jenny said, "I'll just remind you you're entirely on your own in the house. The police are no longer here."

"I know, but believe me, I'm no threat to you. All that matters to me is that I hear the truth."

"Then I can tell you the only truth you need to know. Your friendly detective sergeant was sent away with a flea in her ear, wasn't she? And as for your friends? They couldn't wait to ditch you."

"I'm aware of the danger I'm in," Judith said calmly. "But this could be my only chance to talk to you properly. Not that I think you should be unduly worried. As we both know, I don't see how anything we say to each other in this room could be admissible in a court of law. But the thing is, I set crosswords for a living. I just can't bear to leave a puzzle unsolved. And nothing has been more of a puzzle than Sir Peter's murder. My only hope of getting anywhere near the truth is if it's just me and you."

"All right. Then you should know, I might have made a plan with Tristram, but the one thing I didn't expect happened. I really did fall in love with Peter."

"Oh," Judith said, disappointed. "Please don't start lying again, we were doing so well."

"Let me tell you what happened. That was the plan. That I'd seduce Peter, we'd kill him together, and then I'd marry Tristram. But I really did fall in love with Peter and so didn't want to go ahead with my part of the plan. But Tristram wouldn't have any of it. And went ahead anyway. First, he thought he'd kill his father with cyanide, and then, when that was discovered, he came up with this other plan that he then carried out."

"You're saying he's the killer?"

"I tried to stop him, I begged him, but he wouldn't listen to me."

"Why didn't you go to the police?"

"Because, I'll be honest, I didn't think he'd actually go through with it. Not until it was too late. But it was Tristram. He killed his father."

"Very well. If that's true, how did he do it?"

"How do you mean?"

"It's the only question that matters. In this version of events you're now trying to sell me, how did Tristram kill his father?"

"It's like I told you. I don't think Peter was quite dead when I took his pulse."

"Yes, it was very clever of you to suggest that possibility to us all those days ago. That was when you decided you had to save yourself by throwing Tristram under the bus, wasn't it?"

"It's the only thing that makes sense," Jenny said, ignoring Judith. "Peter was still alive after the cabinet fell on him. And then, after we cleared the room, Tristram came back into the room and killed him."

"A wonderful theory, I agree. Except for three things. First, if Peter was in the study on his own, how did the cabinet fall onto him? Big pieces of furniture don't throw themselves to the floor for no reason. Second, the post-mortem said Sir Peter died from his injuries almost immediately. He wasn't lying there bleeding out for minutes while we tried to find him in the house, broke the door down, lifted the cabinet from him, and then cleared the room of people, only for Tristram to sneak in afterward to finish him off. And we all saw him. His arm was bent under his body, his hand was quite mangled. He really wasn't alive."

Judith was pleased with herself as she looked at Jenny.

"You said there were three things?" Jenny asked.

"Oh—of course! And your story doesn't explain the gavel in the ash."

"Stop going on about the gavel."

"I'm afraid I can't. But you raise an interesting point, because you've been so very clever throughout the investigation. Seemingly helping us at all times, but in reality, you were just trying to stay as close to us as you could. Making sure you knew what was going on. Trying to steer us away from certain conclusions and toward others. For example, having taken the will from the safe, it was you who tore it up and hid it in the compost heap. I should have noticed this at the time, but it was you who first suggested that we go outside to look for it. I'd already come to the same conclusion, so I couldn't wait to agree, but I should have been more suspicious. Was it entirely a coincidence that it was you who suggested we look outside, and then it was also you who led us to the compost heap where—once again—it was you who noticed that the mulch had recently been disturbed?

"And the missing envelope puzzled me at the time, but I didn't think through its absence to its logical conclusion. The fact that it wasn't torn up at the same time as the will suggested that it was incriminating—of course it was, it had your fingerprints all over it—but I should have realized the fact that it wasn't there implied that the scene had been staged somehow. After all, how plausible was it that Tristram would be so angry that he'd tear up the will and stuff it in a compost heap, but also be so very careful that he'd remove the envelope and separately dispose of it?

"But your real stroke of genius was when you made us consider whether Sir Peter was killed *after* the time we'd considered. Just like you're doing again now. It's such a plausible idea. So tempting as a theory. But it sowed the seeds of your downfall, I'm afraid. Because I have a rather logical mind, and your talk of Sir Peter maybe being killed *after* we'd thought inevitably made me wonder if he'd perhaps been killed *before* we'd thought. After all, the cabinet falling over was such a loud and dramatic event, who'd ever consider that that wasn't exactly when Sir Peter died?"

"But you just said he died instantly from his injuries."

"Oh yes, and he did. But the word 'dramatic' is very important to understanding what happened that day. The whole thing was a play put on by you and Tristram. And like all good plays, the stage first had to be set. Which is why Lady Bailey saw Tristram leave the house just before the murder. You see, while we were all outside at the party, Tristram was in the study, behind closed curtains so no one could see. The door was also locked, but then, as Chris Shepherd told us, Sir Peter had been keeping his study locked ever since his argument with Tristram. Tristram also made sure that the squeaky doors to the study had been oiled so that the various comings and goings in the study wouldn't be heard by anyone who might have been nearby. His choice was rather extravagant—olive oil—but it got the job done, and he was sure to wipe his fingerprints from the can before he put it back in the kitchen.

"While he was ensconced in the study, he took all of the lab equipment from the cabinet as swiftly as possible and very carefully laid it on the carpet in front of it so that, later on, when the cabinet fell over, all the glass would smash very loudly. Unfortunately for him, although he'd lined up nearly all of the glass lab equipment so it would be hit by the falling cabinet, there was one glass jar that must have fitted the gap between the shelves of the cabinet so perfectly that it survived having it fall on it. It was Becks who spotted how odd that was—that a glass jar would fall off a cabinet a good six feet or so and not smash. Especially when Suzie so very quickly proved how fragile the jar actually was when she knocked it onto the floor. But once Tristram was finished, the scene was set for murder.

"Following your very public—and also very staged—argument with Tristram at the party, you said you were going into the house to your bedroom, but you didn't go to your bedroom. You went into the study. I imagine Tristram left the key somewhere in the house for you so you could let yourself in. Then, when Sir Peter followed you into the house, you called him into the study. I'm sure he was surprised to find all of the glass lab equipment laid out on the floor in front of the cabinet. As he went to look at it, you took one of the heavier bits of science equipment—there was an old-fashioned metal oscilloscope, for example—and, with all the rage you could muster, you smashed Sir Peter over the head with it. He died within seconds, as the postmortem later confirmed, just as it also confirmed that he'd died from blunt force trauma. But would forensics ever know if that blunt force had come from an object falling onto him from the height of a tall cabinet, or from the strength of someone wielding it?

"You then wiped the murder weapon of prints and dropped it by Sir Peter's dead body. That was part one of the plan achieved. Sir Peter was dead, and no one had heard it happen. As far as everyone else was concerned, he was still alive. After that, you left the study as fast as you could, locking it behind you and racing up the stairs to your bedroom. As it happens, Rosanna was already there, which should really have scuppered your plans, but she'd hidden in the wardrobe which, very fortunately for you, later on made your alibi seem even more watertight."

"Are you serious?" Jenny said, shocked. "Rosanna was in the wardrobe?"

"She was. Don't worry, she didn't see anything."

"But that means there's a witness who'll say I was in my room when the cabinet fell over."

"There is, she has, and—to be clear—you were."

"So how are you suggesting I managed to push the cabinet over from my bedroom—a whole floor above the study—and with a witness in the same room as me?"

"You're quite right, I'm not going to suggest that."

"Then your whole story falls apart."

"That's because you didn't push the cabinet over," Judith said, interrupting the younger woman. "You let it fall onto him. And that's why I mention the mistake of you holding a winter wedding."

"Will you stop saying that!"

Judith was thrilled to see how much she was needling Jenny. This was exactly what she'd hoped would happen.

"Let me present Exhibit A, which is Lady Bailey's testimony. She said that, at three p.m., she was in the bushes at the edge of the garden, looking at the study window when she heard the cabinet fall over with a terrible crash. But she also said she couldn't see into the study properly because, although the curtains were by now open again, there was a flash of sunlight on the windows. I thought she was just being evasive at the time, but let's take her word at face value: the sun came out at three p.m. and caught the glass in the windows of the study. Very well. It was a cold but sunny day, it's hardly of interest. But then I offer Exhibit B, the glass jar we later discovered in the study that had survived the cabinet's fall. When I put it on the desk of Sir Peter's study, I made sure to put it in a sunbeam so I could look at it more carefully. It's how we discovered you'd cleaned it of fingerprints."

"And here's the anomaly. I put it on the table at about 10:30 a.m. But if the sun was shining through the window in the morning—as I knew it was, because I'd seen it with my own eyes—*how could it also have been shining on the same window in the afternoon?* The sun should have moved to the other side of the house after midday, and the sun is so low in the sky during winter that it really should have been very noticeable. As I say, if you'd had the patience to wait for a summer wedding, the sun would have been so high in the sky that I'm not sure I'd have noticed the difference between the angle of the sun at 10:30 in the morning and three in the afternoon.

"It was such an incredible realization! I knew I had to check. So my friends and I came to White Lodge just before three p.m. and stood by the laurel hedge where Lady Bailey had said she'd seen the flash of sunlight on the study window. And, just as I'd suspected, when we got there, the sun was on the further side of the house. It would have been impossible for there to have been a flash of sunlight on the study window. She was lying—at least, that was my initial reaction. But why would she lie about such an incidental detail? It set me thinking, what if she'd been telling the truth? But what could that flash of light have been if not sunlight on the windows? And that's when it came to me! I remembered that the glass jar that hadn't smashed in the study had once contained magnesium tape."

Judith saw Jenny go very still.

"Ah, I see you finally understand the danger you're in. Good. Yes, the jar had the words 'Magnesium Tape' written on the side, but, as it wasn't smashed, I perhaps should have found it surprising that it contained no magnesium tape. Because it's something of a wonder material, isn't it? I remember it from science experiments in school. It's a metal tape that you get in rolls, a lot like Sellotape, and while you can unravel it easily enough, it's really very strong. It's a metal after all. But here's the amazing thing about it: when you set fire to it, it burns incandescently bright—doesn't it?—the flame very quickly moving along the tape and turning it into a fine ash."

"So, although it's true that you were on a different floor to Sir Peter when the cabinet fell over, your bedroom is directly above the study—as I saw the first time I went into it. I looked out of the side window and saw the bushes outside Sir Peter's study right below.

"And there's something else that links the two rooms, isn't there? *They both have fireplaces.* Suzie even checked the flue of the fireplace in your bedroom when we were looking for Sir Peter's will. If only she'd realized the flue was a passage that led down to the study below just as much as it led up to the roof above, perhaps we'd have solved all of this much sooner.

"But that's how you managed to reach from your bedroom to the study on the floor below. When Tristram had set the scene in the study earlier, he'd not just laid out the glass equipment on the floor, he'd also tied magnesium tape onto the ornamental carvings on the top of the cabinet and then run the tape to the old hook that's screwed into the wall—with just enough slack on the tape so that, when he oh-so-carefully pushed the cabinet, it tipped over, but it was held from falling by the metal tape that was tied to the wall hook.

"At that point, leaning forward just enough for it to topple over if someone cut the tape—but only just enough—the heavy cabinet wouldn't have taken anywhere near as much strength to hold it in place. There was no momentum when it was pushed forward, Tristram would have made sure of that, and the full force of its weight wouldn't have been felt until the tape was released and it started to topple, gathering speed as it crashed to the floor with a bang that was made all the more impressive by the presence of all of the glass objects on the floor that it smashed into."

"And how are you saying the tape got cut?" Jenny asked, but it was clear she already knew that Judith had guessed the answer.

"That was quite simple, really. And it's where the gavel comes in. You see, once Tristram had the cabinet leaning forward a bit, all he had to do was run some more magnesium tape across the room from the hook to the fireplace. But how to connect that tape to the room above? Well, you'd already thought of that, hadn't you? Before the party, you'd lowered some magnesium tape down the flue from the bedroom above—although you'd have needed a heavy object to make sure it fell down to the fireplace below. And seeing as this object would later fall into the ash of the fireplace, it had to be something that would look innocuous if it were found. So you took the bronze gavel from the mantelpiece in Sir Peter's study up to your bedroom. You then tied it to the end of some magnesium tape and lowered it down the flue.

"And that was Tristram's last piece of scene setting that afternoon. He reached into the study fireplace and found the gavel hanging there. All he had to do was wrap the end of tape in the study to the end of tape attached to the gavel, and—voilà!—you now had a makeshift fuse that ran from the upstairs bedroom, down the chimney, across the study, and then connected to the restraining tape that was holding the cabinet back from toppling over.

"That's why Rosanna thought you had a cigarette when you came into your bedroom. She was wrong. From her position inside the wardrobe, Rosanna heard you strike the lighter, but it's lucky for you she couldn't see anything, as she'd have seen you leaning into the fireplace and the brightest of lights as the magnesium caught.

"Once alight, the tape became a terrifying fuse, consuming itself as it burned down through the flue, the gavel being released into the ash of the fireplace below as it then burned onto the next section of tape that crossed the room—which was the bright flash that Lady Bailey saw from the other side of the garden. Not sunlight on windows, but magnesium tape burning brightly inside the room. And as soon as the flame burned the tape holding the cabinet to the hook, you got the effect you'd been hoping for: the cabinet was finally free to fall onto the dead body of Sir Peter with an almighty crash of wood, metal, and glass—the remainder of the tape attached to the cabinet burning innocently to ash after the cabinet had landed. And in a room as dusty as Sir Peter's, and with a cabinet that old, who'd even notice the thin residue of white ash the burnt tape left behind?

"So that's how you did it, Jenny. Since you asked. And you were so clever, really. Because the cabinet was so very heavy, its fall would set in everyone's minds a time of death of that would be impossible to refute. Even though Sir Peter was already dead when the cabinet fell onto him. Which, incidentally, also fitted the postmortem. Tanika was adamant that Sir Peter was killed almost instantaneously. Well, we know that, because it was you who killed him almost instantaneously. And if you'd left too long between Sir Peter's murder and the cabinet falling onto him, I'm sure the postmortem would have been able to see that the cabinet had fallen onto a body that was already cold. But Sir Peter had been dead a minute when that cabinet fell onto him, his flesh and blood still warm. All of his injuries from being crushed would have only presented during the postmortem as being what they were, nonfatal injuries. Nonfatal bruises. Nonfatal broken bones. There was only one blow—to the head—that killed him. And it would be impossible for all of the witnesses, the police, and the coroner to believe that that blow *hadn't* been administered at the exact same time as the enormous cabinet fell onto him."

"You're so very sure of yourself," Jenny said, her voice acid. "I almost want to confess."

"Then you should. Because now they know where to look, the police will be able to find magnesium ash going across this room to the cabinet and going up the flue."

"You think you've been so clever, don't you?"

"As it happens, I do."

"Then how about the locked door?"

"That's easy. As I said, when you left the room that first time, having killed Sir Peter, you locked the door behind yourself and pocketed the key. Then, after the crash brought us all into the house, and Tristram had broken through the door, it was only natural that you, a trained nurse and fiancée of Sir Peter, would go to the body first. In all the confusion, it would have been a simple matter for you to slip the key back into his pocket.

"In fact, the whole plan was quite simple, really. A pre-set room, a fuse that ran to the floor above, and a locked door that would make all suggestions of murder seem impossible. But it was how you put them all together that was so impressive. The sheer theatricality of it all. But then, Tristram was part of the brain trust. If anyone knew about creating theatrical effects, it would be him."

"You can't prove any of this!"

"I won't need to, will I? Because it's your partner in crime who'll prove it. And you know it, don't you?"

"What are you talking about?"

"Because there was one thing you hadn't counted on. The fact that Tristram is impressionable cuts more than one way. Yes, you'd been able to groom him into helping you kill his father, but you weren't the only influence on him. It was only after you'd put your plan into action and come to Marlow that you discovered the existence of Sarah Fitzherbert, a woman with a historical hold over Tristram. A woman who'd waited all these years purely to marry him. As it happens, we know you eventually got Tristram back on your side, because Tristram told Sarah that it was over between them. Of course he did. He'd already risked so much with you, why would he allow his head to be turned by an old flame? So the pair of you carried out your murder, and everything played out as you'd hoped. You kept up your very public arguments with Tristram—even staging that splendid row when you rang me to come and help pull him off you. I fell for the trick hook, line, and sinker.

"But that was also when everything started to unravel. Because Tristram got that mystery phone call, which must have terrified you. Who was out there, other than you, who could get him wound up like that? I imagine you feared the worst, and when we later told you we'd lost sight of Tristram on Alison Road, I think we inadvertently confirmed your suspicions that Sarah had somehow got her claws back into your partner in crime. The man who you'd committed murder for. The man who *had* to marry you in order for your plan to work. From feeling you were totally in charge, you realized how little control you actually had. Tristram could in fact marry who he liked.

"And you lashed out. Having committed murder once, you didn't hesitate to do so again. You knew all about the cyanide Tristram had argued with his father about. So you went to Sarah's house under some pretext and made sure she drank a glass of water that had Tristram's fingerprints on, and Tristram's cyanide in it. It wouldn't be enough to convict him for murder. Sarah was his girlfriend, of course his fingerprints were on objects in his house, but it was a shot across the bows from you to him. He had to do as you said or else there'd be consequences. Fatal consequences.

"Of course Tristram attacked you when the police released him on bail. Killing Sarah, an old family friend and innocent victim in all this, had never been part of the plan. Finally, he must have realized he'd done a deal with the devil when he allowed you into his life."

"I'm not the devil."

"You once told me how hard you'd had to fight to get anywhere in life. To get an education. To escape your past. And I admire you for it. You've shown more resilience and pluck than the people you've worked for these last few years. But it must have grated to see how your clients took their wealth for granted. How entitled they were. I can well imagine how you came to realize that they didn't deserve to live. Admit it, because they don't, do they?"

"The rich are hateful."

"And why should you have so little, when you're so deserving, and they have so much when they're so worthless?"

"That's *exactly* it."

"And Sir Peter never felt the consequences of anything he did, did he? His whole life. He could betray his daughter, or his gardener—or throw his son out of his house, or pay his ex-wife a pittance—and he just didn't care. Nothing could touch him. He was rich, he was titled, he was insulated. I bet you couldn't wait to burst his bubble."

Jenny smirked, her eyes gleaming with private triumph.

"I bet there was a moment," Judith continued, "just before he died, when he realized you'd tricked him. You were going to end his life. How did he look? In that moment?"

"Scared," Jenny whispered, losing herself in the memory. "It was like he was stripped of everything. His wealth, his status. He was finally like the rest of us. Mortal."

"Did he call out?"

"He did."

"What did he say?"

"It was a question. One word. 'Jenny?' It was pathetic, almost funny."

"You found that funny?"

"You didn't have to live with him, or put up with his arrogance. Pretend to be the weaker sex. Pretend to love him."

"And nor did you. You brought all of this on yourself."

"I've brought nothing on myself."

"Oh no, you're going to prison for a long time."

"Nothing I've said in here will stand up in court. It's like you said. It's just between you and me."

"But it's like I said, Tristram will confess to his part in all this."

"He won't."

"He will when he realizes you're now saying it was him who killed his father. And he'll know because I'll tell him."

"Then I'll have to make sure you don't leave this room."

Judith looked at Jenny and saw that she was ready to pounce, her whole body quivering with rage.

"Yes, I suppose we were always going to get to this point," Judith said. "But before you try and dispatch me, I just wanted to say that your plan to kill Sir Peter at the party in front of a reliable witness—that witness being me—gave me an idea. In fact, I decided to take a leaf out of your book. Didn't I, Tanika?"

Jenny was confused—who was Judith speaking to?—and then Tanika stepped out from behind the cabinet, her smartphone in her hand.

"Hello, Jenny," she said.

Before Jenny could react, Tanika strode over and handcuffed her wrists together.

"I saw you leave!" Jenny spluttered.

"You're not the only one who can use theatre to create false narratives," Judith said. "Tanika, Becks, Suzie, and I all agreed on the plan this afternoon. Assuming Tristram came here and attacked you, Becks and Suzie would pretend to argue with me and storm off. But, in reality, it was only Suzie who drove off in her van. Becks waited behind. Then, when DI Hoskins arrived, Tanika knew she'd be able to irritate him enough that she'd be sent away as well. When we saw her squad car leave, it wasn't Tanika in the driver's seat. It was Becks. Which allowed Tanika to scoot around to the back of White Lodge, enter through the boot room, and hide herself in the gap between the cabinet and the wall. Then all I had to do was get you into this room and trick any kind of confession out of you. But here's the key point. Your confession wasn't just in front of me, it was in front of a detective sergeant and her audio recorder."

Tanika held up her smartphone to show that it was recording the audio of the conversation.

"When Tanika plays that recording to Tristram, you and I both know his defenses will collapse. He'll tell the police the truth, the whole truth, and nothing but the truth. And while he'll go to prison as your accomplice to one murder, you'll go to prison for considerably longer, as a double murderer."

"Jenny Page," Tanika said, "I'm arresting you for the murder of Sir Peter Bailey and Sarah Fitzherbert. You do not have to say anything. But, it may harm your defense if you do not mention when questioned something which you later rely on in court. Anything you do say may be given in evidence."

Jenny looked as though her world had just collapsed, which, in all respects, it just had.

Chapter 41

DETECTIVE INSPECTOR HOSKINS COULD BARELY contain his irritation when he returned to White Lodge to process the arrest of Jenny Page. He snapped at his team, and he was particularly grumpy when Judith explained how she and Tanika had trapped Jenny into talking about Sir Peter's last few moments alive before she killed him.

"It won't be admissible," he said, once she'd finished telling her story.

"I never imagined it would be. But Tristram's a very impressionable young man, I'm sure you'll be able to use Tanika's recording to get a confession out of him. That plus the evidence you'll be able to collect now you know where to look will be what convicts Jenny."

DI Hoskins could see the logic of what Judith was saying, but it didn't make him any happier.

When Tanika joined them, DI Hoskins's mood deteriorated further. He knew that Tanika would use her triumph to undermine his authority back at the station.

"Congratulations, sir," she said. "You played your part to perfection."

"What's that?" he said, confused.

"The way you went along with my argument with you just before you left with Tristram. It was only because you so publicly sent me away that I was able to slip back into the house to act as a witness to Jenny's confession."

It slowly dawned on DI Hoskins that Tanika was offering him a deal.

If he pretended their argument had been prearranged, then she wouldn't be in any trouble, and he'd be able to save face. It was an arrangement that benefited him far more than her, but it didn't make him happy. However, he realized he had no choice.

"I knew there had to be a reason why you were being so insolent," he said, testing the words out loud.

"Oh there was, sir," Tanika said with a smile. "There was."

DI Hoskins didn't quite know what to say to that, so he looked from Tanika to Judith, realized they were absolutely the last people in the world he wanted to be near, and headed off.

"I know what you're going to say," Tanika said, once DI Hoskins was out of earshot.

"This was your triumph," Judith said. "Why on earth are you sharing it with him?"

"It wasn't my triumph. It was yours. And my life will be significantly easier if the detective inspector is allowed to take some of the credit."

"That's not even remotely fair."

"I know. But it doesn't stop it being true."

A police car drove up to the house at speed, crunched to a halt on the gravel, and Becks and Suzie spilled out before dashing over to Judith.

"You're okay!" Suzie said, embracing Judith in a hug. "You're okay!"

"Of course I'm okay," Judith said, uncomfortable with Suzie's gushing. "I'm always okay."

"I'm so sorry about what I said in the house," Becks said. "I felt so terrible arguing with you."

"But it worked?" Suzie asked.

"It really did," Tanika said. "Even better than we planned. Judith was amazing."

"That's nonsense," Judith said. "I just gave her enough rope, that's all. And anyway, it was a team effort. If the three of you hadn't made it look as though you'd all left, there's no way Jenny would have felt comfortable confessing anything. But I'll tell you what I want to know," Judith said, looking at Becks. "What was driving a police car like?"

"It was amazing! So much fun!"

"Did you put the siren on?" Suzie asked with a chuckle.

"Oh no, that would have been wrong."

"Then what about the lights? Bet you had a quick whizz with the lights flashing?"

"Absolutely not."

Suzie realized the true depth of Becks's betrayal.

"You didn't even break the speed limit, did you?"

"Of course not. The speed limit's there for a reason."

"Why did I agree to let you drive the police car?"

"It made sense you drive your van," Becks said, not quite understanding the point Suzie was making.

"You know what?" Judith said with a smile. "I think this calls for a little celebration, don't you?"

"I reckon so," Suzie said.

"Agreed," Becks said.

"Tanika, would you like to join us for a quick drink back at my house?"

"I'd love to," Tanika said. "But I'll be needed at the station. To process the new evidence. Though, can I ask? My daughter, Shanti, loves the river. Do you think you might take us out on your punt one of these days?"

"I'd be delighted to. And I'd love to meet your husband as well."

"You'd take us all out?"

"Of course. We can pack a picnic and make a day of it. And your father as well, if he likes? There's plenty of room."

"I'm not sure you'd want my father in the same boat as you. Not unless you wanted to discover that the boat's the wrong shape, the river's not as good as the rivers we have back in India—"

"I can't think of anything I'd rather do," Judith said.

"Thank you," Tanika said. "And thank you, all of you. Without the three of you, Jenny wouldn't have been caught."

"Without the four of us," Judith corrected.

Tanika smiled, and her friends could see how proud she was.

"Yes," she said. "That's right, isn't it?"

As Tanika left, Rosanna cycled up to the house. Judith and her friends went over to meet her.

"Is it true?" Rosanna asked. "Jenny's been arrested?"

Judith explained that it was indeed true. She also explained Tristram's part in the murder of her father, although she tried as much as possible to paint him as the victim of Jenny.

"I'm so sorry," Becks said, once Judith had finished her story.

Rosanna looked utterly lost.

"He killed Father?"

"No," Judith said. "Because he was a greedy and craven young man, but he was no killer. It's like you always said. He was weak. That was his flaw. And it was his great misfortune that he met someone as manipulative and nasty as Jenny. If he'd never met her, your father would still be alive. Sarah Fitzherbert would still be alive."

"I don't know what to say," Rosanna said. "Or think. I just…"

"Go home to Kat," Becks said. "She'll look after you."

"And there's something she'll be able to confirm for you," Judith said. "You see, it's against English law to profit from a crime. So, seeing as Tristram was an accomplice in your father's death, he won't be allowed to inherit. No money. No business. No house. It will all go to your father's next nearest relative—which, I don't have to explain, is the person who should have inherited all along. His firstborn child. You."

"That can't be true?"

"It is. Which means, the firstborn male won't be inheriting the family fortune for the first time in four hundred years," Judith said with relish. "And it gets better than that. Because, once you get hold of the family estate and money, you'll be able to change the tradition and leave it to whoever you like, male or female."

"There's no more living in a canal boat for you and Kat," Suzie said, stepping back to admire White Lodge. "You've just got yourself a Georgian mansion."

"Although, one piece of advice," Becks said. "Sack Chris Shepherd."

"God yes!" Suzie exclaimed. "He blackmailed your father, he's not to be trusted. I mean, he's *seriously* not to be trusted."

"Are you really sure?" Rosanna asked. "I inherit everything?"

"Speak to Kat," Judith said. "She'll confirm that Tristram can't inherit, and that means—de facto—that you have."

Despite all of the shock of the day, the women saw a look that they'd not seen before in Rosanna's eyes.

It was anticipation.

Once she'd returned home with her friends, Judith poured a generous glug of whisky into three cut-glass tumblers.

"I'd really rather have a cup of tea," Becks said.

"Nonsense!" Judith said. "We're celebrating."

Suzie held out her glass for a quick refill, having knocked her drink back in one.

"Don't mind if I do," she said.

Once her glass was recharged, Suzie went over and sat in Judith's favorite wingback armchair. Judith smiled, telling herself that she didn't mind at all.

"Well, you were right," Suzie said. "Sir Peter was killed inside a room that was locked from the inside, the only key to the room in his pocket."

"*We* were right," Judith corrected.

"I never really thought it was murder," Becks offered, wanting to be honest.

"What are you talking about?" Judith said, holding up a glass in a toast for her friend. "You kept saying that no one could have been in the study when Sir Peter was killed. And there wasn't. You were more right than any of us."

Becks blushed.

"Well, you'll have plenty to talk about on the radio show tomorrow," Judith said to Suzie, going over to the padded seat that filled the bay window.

Suzie looked into her glass of whisky.

"What is it?" Becks asked.

"I'm sorry," she said. "For what I said back at Jenny's house."

"Of course," Judith said, realizing what Suzie was referring to. Their plan had always been that Suzie and Becks should pretend to lose their temper with Judith, but while Becks's fake row had been entirely generic, they'd all heard Suzie make some very specific accusations. "Don't worry, I deserved that. You're right. I do always think I know best. And I don't. I'm sorry."

"But the thing is," Suzie said with a sigh, "I agree with you. You *are* always right. I'm not doing my radio show tomorrow."

"Whyever not?"

"It was getting in the way of my work. In the way of me earning money. I mean, what dog-sitter would hire a dog-sitter to cover their dog-sitting? I've kind of got myself into a really bad mess."

"But you can't give up doing radio," Judith said. "You're so good at it."

"Judith's right," Becks said.

"You think so?" Suzie said, delighted by the compliment.

"Very much so."

"Then you'll be pleased to hear I'm still going to do one show a week. But on Sunday evenings. It's going to be called 'Pets' Corner'—for people to ring in with their news and advice about their pets. That way I can have any number of dogs with me in the studio, and it won't matter if they start barking. They'll be my crew."

"That sounds wonderful," Judith said, pleased that her friend had come to such a practical solution. It would also make Suzie slightly less famous in Marlow if she only did a Sunday evening show, Judith knew. It was a triple win as far as she was concerned. Suzie got to keep doing what she loved, she'd be able to earn money again, and the lower-profile show would mean that she wouldn't have her head turned by thoughts of becoming more famous.

"There was one thing," Becks said. "You know, when you were accusing Judith of all of those things? You mentioned that the building work at your home still isn't finished."

"Ha!" Suzie said. "That much is true. It isn't."

"Seriously?"

"You know what it's like. You try and set aside enough money to get a new builder in, and then, when you get a chunk of cash, you blow it all on a nice holiday and then you're back to square one."

"I'd like to help," Becks said.

This got her friends' attention.

"Because I took your advice, Judith. I spoke to Colin and told him everything. About how I'd earned all of this money. And guess what? You were right, he was happy for me. In fact, when I said I should give all the money away to charity, he got all cross and said I'd earned that money fair and square, it was mine, and I should keep it. In fact, he got really excited about the idea of me building a proper nest egg for our pension, seeing as the church pension is hardly worth much these days."

"How exciting!" Judith said. "You're going to be the family stockbroker."

"I think that's exactly what I'm going to be."

Judith and Suzie were thrilled for their friend.

"And no need to buy myself fancy clothes or sapphire rings," Becks said. "I'm saving for our old age. Maybe I'll be able to help the kids with university fees, or getting a deposit on their first house. But I had no idea you still hadn't finished your building work, Suzie. I'd love to help pay for it. It would at least put some of my money to good use."

"Are you serious?" Suzie asked.

"Oh yes. I'll be honest, it would make me feel better."

"You're one in a million."

"I really don't think I am."

"No, seriously. How many people do you know who'd be so stressed about making too much money? And then, when they'd worked out they could keep their cash, immediately try and give it away again."

Becks blushed, uncomfortable, as ever, with receiving any kind of a compliment.

"But I'm going to have to say no," Suzie continued. "You see, I've sorted out my extension."

"You've tracked down the original builder?" Judith asked eagerly.

"No, he's still not answering my calls."

"Oh. Then you've got in another builder?"

"Not exactly."

"Then how have you 'sorted' it?"

"You remember how I took the page from the *Marlow Free Press* that day we were all in the library?"

"Of course," Becks said, realizing she'd forgotten.

"Well, the page I ripped out was an advert asking for applicants for a new reality TV show. To do with people who've been let down by builders.

The TV company tries to find them. But the main thing is, they also finish the building work for you."

"You're going to be on TV?"

"I am!" Suzie said, with a level of excitement that significantly eclipsed the joy she'd shown when a listener had asked for her autograph. "And the show has nearly three million viewers, can you even imagine that! It's mind blowing. I'm going to be seen by three million people."

Judith took a moment to absorb what Suzie had just said, and found herself smiling—just as she saw Becks was. Of course Suzie had decided to solve her problems by going on TV. Despite Judith's hopes, Suzie loved the limelight too much. She wasn't ever going to change her ways, was she? Any more than any of them were.

They all heard a marimba chime. Suzie got her phone out and turned it off.

"Sorry," she said, "that's my alarm. I've got to get the train to London this afternoon. I'm meeting with the production team to discuss publicity for the show."

With Suzie leaving, Becks said she should be off as well, as she was taking Colin out for dinner that night to the Hand and Flowers restaurant—which, as the only two Michelin-starred restaurant in Marlow, was way out of Colin's budget, but well within Becks's. So she was getting her hair done that afternoon. At Divas and Dudes, she'd decided. She wanted to look her best.

Once Suzie and Becks left, Judith went into the next-door room to look at the homemade incident board she'd created. As she saw the spiderweb of red wool connecting all of the suspects to the clues—and to locations on the map of Marlow—she found herself remembering how, if it hadn't been for an encounter with a dead duck on her morning swim, she wouldn't have got into a fight with a swan and then been back home in time to receive the phone call from Sir Peter that had started her on the whole adventure. Not that it had been from Sir Peter, of course.

Judith found herself swelling with pride at what she and her friends had achieved. Buoyed by a surging feeling of self-confidence, she went to the far side of the room where the doorway led into the next room that was still waiting to be cleared of all of the oldest newspapers and other printed material she'd hoarded over the years. This was where all of the original reports of her husband's death were stored—the correspondence to her from the Greek and British police services, and from her local MP at the time—and the national newspapers, all of whom had wanted interviews with her.

She knew it was time to get rid of the final remnants of her archive of paper and dust, but she paused before crossing the threshold. No, she found herself thinking, she shouldn't get ahead of herself. One thing at a time.

She turned and headed back into her sitting room, stopping briefly by the sideboard to refresh her glass of whisky. So what was it to be? An evening swim? Or maybe she could settle down with some hot-buttered crumpets, a copy of the *Puzzler* magazine, and maybe a few glasses of the sloe gin she'd been promising herself for so long?

Judith smiled to herself as the rest of the day opened up with possibilities.

Don't miss the first adventure from the ladies of the Marlow Murder Club!

THESE LADIES TAKE DEATH SERIOUSLY

The Marlow Murder Club

A NOVEL

ROBERT THOROGOOD

Chapter 1

MRS. JUDITH POTTS WAS SEVENTY-SEVEN years old and entirely happy with her life. She lived in an Arts and Crafts mansion on the River Thames, she had a job she loved that took up just enough of her time and no more, and best of all, she didn't have to share her life with any man. This meant there was no one asking her what was for dinner that night, or wanting to know where she was going every time she left the house, or moaning that she was spending too much money on whisky, a small glass of which she'd have at about 6:00 p.m. each evening.

On the day Judith's life changed, it was the height of summer and England had been in the grip of a heat wave for weeks. She'd kept all of her windows open to capture whatever breezes blew down the valley, but it seemed to make no difference. The heat of the sun had gotten into the bricks and timbers of her home into the oak staircase and minstrels' gallery.

After taking her evening meal in front of the television news, she put her empty plate to one side and got out the latest copy of *Puzzler* magazine. She turned to a logic grid and started to work on it. Usually, she enjoyed reducing the language of the clues down to mathematical ones and zeros, but tonight her heart just wasn't in it. It was too hot to concentrate.

Judith's hand idly went to the key she kept on a chain around her neck, and her thoughts began to drift into the past, into a much darker time. She shot up from her chair. This wouldn't do, she told herself. Wouldn't do at all. There was always something else she could do to keep herself busy. She needed a change of scene, that was all, and she had the perfect solution.

Judith began to take off her clothes. With each garment she removed, she felt more and more released from the stifling constraints of the day. By the time she was naked, she was buzzing with an impish delight. She crossed the hallway, past the Blüthner grand piano she only ever played when she was really very drunk, and took up a dark-gray woolen cape she kept by the front door. Judith's cape was her most treasured possession. She'd tell anyone who asked, and many did, it kept her warm in winter, served as a picnic blanket in the summer, and she could pull it over her head if ever she was caught in a spring shower.

Best of all, Judith believed it was a cloak of invisibility. Every evening, come rain or shine, she'd take off her clothes, wrap the cape around herself, and step out of her house feeling a delicious frisson of naughtiness. She would plunge her feet into a pair of ancient rain boots and stride through the knee-high grass—swish, swish, swish!—to her boathouse. Like the rest of Judith's house, it was pink-bricked, timber-framed, and somewhat crumbling.

Judith entered the cobwebby darkness and kicked off her rain boots. She hung her cape on an old hook, and, still hidden from the outside world by a pair of ancient boathouse doors, stepped down the stone slipway and into the Thames.

It was almost a religious experience for her, accepting the cold water onto her skin, and she exhaled with a whoosh as she leaned forward into the embrace of the river. Suddenly she was weightless, supported by the soft water that felt like silk to her body.

She swam upstream, the evening sunshine flashing diamonds on the water all around. Judith smiled to herself. She always smiled to herself when she was out swimming. She couldn't help it. After all, there might be dog walkers on the Thames Path, and there were very definitely plenty of people in the near distance as she looked at the spire of a church and the span of the Victorian suspension bridge that linked the town to the neighboring village of Bisham. None of these people were aware there was a seventy-seven-year-old woman swimming nearby entirely in the nude.

It was just as Judith was thinking, *This is the life,* she heard a shout.

It came from the opposite riverbank, from somewhere near her neighbor Stefan Dunwoody's house. But from her position low in the water, it was hard for Judith to see exactly what was going on. Only the roof of Stefan's house was visible above the thick bank of bulrushes at the edge of the river.

Judith strained her ears, but all was quiet. She decided it must have been an animal. A dog or a fox maybe.

And then she heard a man's voice call out, "Hey, no!"

What on earth was that?

"Stefan, is that you?" Judith called from the river, but her words were cut short by the sharp retort of a gunshot.

"Stefan?" she shouted again, panic rising. "Are you all right?"

All was silence. But Judith knew what she'd heard. Someone had fired a gun, hadn't they? And Stefan's voice had called out immediately beforehand. What if he was now bleeding from a bullet wound and needed saving?

Judith swam toward Stefan's house as fast as she could, but as she reached his riverbank, she realized she had a problem. Beyond the bulrushes, Stefan had put corrugated metal across the span of his lawn to protect it from river erosion. Judith knew swimming through the rushes would cut her body to shreds, and even if she made it to land, she wouldn't be able to pull herself out. She wouldn't have the strength.

Ahead of her she could see a blue canoe wedged in among the reeds. Could she somehow use it to help lever her body out of the water? She tried to grab hold of the end, but she couldn't get a proper grip. It kept bobbing around like a cork, and she realized she didn't have the balance to climb up onto the canoe anyway. But she gave it one last go, and this time just about managed to pull herself up onto the back of it. And then, oh so slowly, she and the canoe barrel-rolled over, and she lost her hold and fell back into the water with an ungainly splash.

She came up for air and shook the water from her hair. The canoe was out of the question, so what else could she do?

Judith swam back to the center of the river, desperately looking for someone who could help. Where were the dog walkers or canoodling couples when you needed them? She couldn't see anyone. There was only one thing for it. She turned and swam for home as fast as she could.

Reaching her boathouse, Judith climbed out of the water, wheezing, but there was no time to lose. She threw on her cape and strode out onto the lawn, turning back to look at what she could see of Stefan's house. Only half of his garden was visible behind the weeping willow that grew unchecked on her side of the riverbank.

She ran into her house, grabbed up her phone, and dialed 999. As she waited for the call to connect, she moved over to the bay window to keep an eye on Stefan's property.

"I need the police!" Judith said as soon as the call was answered. "There's been a shooting at my neighbor's house! Hurry! Someone's been shot!"

The operator took down the details of Stefan's address, recorded what Judith had seen, informed her the emergency services would be on their way, and then ended the call. Judith felt deeply frustrated. Surely there was something else she could do, or someone else she could phone? What about the Coast Guard? It was a waterside catastrophe after all. Or the RNLI?

Judith peered out of her window at Stefan's property. It was still sitting there, apparently innocently, in the evening sunshine.

If anyone had been out on the river at that precise moment and had had occasion to look up at Judith's mansion, they'd have seen a very short and comfortably plump woman in her late seventies with wild gray hair standing entirely naked in her bay window, a cape over her shoulders as if she were some kind of a superhero. Which in many ways she was.

She just didn't know it yet.

Reading Group Guide

1. The book opens with an unconventional invitation to a drinks party. Why did you think Sir Peter Bailey made a point to invite Judith to his party? Would you have gone if you were her?

2. Tanika doesn't doubt Judith's instincts, but she does dread Judith's involvement in her case. Why is that?

3. Becks accuses Colin of being both controlling and jealous when he insists that she not get involved with Sir Peter's murder. Why is Becks so angry with him? Did you agree with Judith and Suzie's assumption that Becks was having an affair?

4. Tanika's father never asks her brothers for assistance, despite how demanding her career is, and she usually accommodates him as best she can. What does it cost her to stay in that role? What boundaries would she need to set to escape it?

5. Suzie struggles to balance her new radio gig with her existing dog-sitting business. Why is she so invested in the show when it endangers her livelihood?

6. Sir Peter's ex-wife mentions that he never felt guilt over any of his decisions. Did that help him throughout his life? What decisions would you make if you knew for sure you wouldn't regret them?

7. Chris Shepard's grandfather was cut out of the business he helped found just before it became successful, but Chris insists that he wasn't bitter about the way things turned out. Would you be satisfied, as he claimed he was, with being credited for your invention even if someone else was the only one profiting from it?

8. Jenny Page admits that Sir Peter's money was, indeed, a factor in her decision to marry him, though she frames it as a desire for security. Did her admission make her more or less suspicious?

9. What was your impression of Sarah Fitzherbert? What do you think Tristram thought of their relationship?

10. Tanika only says that her life will be "easier" if DI Hoskins receives some of the credit for solving the mystery. What does she mean? Would you have made the same sacrifice?

About the Author

ROBERT THOROGOOD IS THE CREATOR of the hit BBC One TV series *Death in Paradise*, and he has written a series of spin-off novels featuring detective DI Richard Poole.

He was born in Colchester, Essex. When he was ten years old, he read his first proper novel—Agatha Christie's *Peril at End House*—and he's been in love with the genre ever since.

He now lives in Marlow in Buckinghamshire with his wife, children, and two whippets called Wally and Evie.

Follow him on Twitter @robthor.